The Pleasure Garden

ALSO BY OAKLEY HALL

The Downhill Racers

Warlock

Corpus of Joe Bailey

So Many Doors

OAKLEY HALL   *THE*

PLEASURE

GARDEN

NEW YORK / *The Viking Press*

For Barbara, with love

Contents

PART ONE *The Pleasure Garden*

Timor mortis conturbat me.

—WILLIAM DUNBAR

It feels good to feel good.

—FRANK STRANAHAN

1: Captain Easy

THE FIRST SNOWFLAKES were blowing when he came down the mountain at four o'clock. Martha Schroeder was waiting for him in the bar, hair done up, eyelids blued, pearls on pink cashmere beneath her parka. She shaped a kiss of greeting with her lips; her eyes were bright. She was full of news.

"Darling!" she said in her husky voice. She took his arm and steered him outside again through the crowd of pre-Christmas skiers, clothes steaming, boots resounding, who had just come off the mountain wanting a beer—as he did. Outside under the porte-cochere, before the stainless-steel dancing figure on skis that had been Dick Macklin's creation and was the Dancer Peak symbol, in the sundown deep chill and the air aching with the snow coming, Martha said triumphantly, "Katey's just eloped with a graduate assistant!" Her breath steamed like a speech balloon in a comic strip. "Franklyn *thinks*," she added.

He made motor-revving sounds designed to have different meanings for her and for himself. He should have known this crisis would come. He should have been alerted by the distant vibration of the rails, the far-off hoots. He and Martha Schroeder had been conducting a relaxed affair for almost two years. The Schroeders had a cabin in the valley and Martha came up often alone, for her husband did not ski. Smooth, gray Dr. Franklyn Schroeder had his own affairs and all was modern and you-go-your-way-I'll-go-mine-but-we-won't-get-a-divorce-until-the-children-are-grown. But Peter, the older child, was established in pre-med at Cornell, and Katrin, the younger, had started this fall at the University of Arizona. He should have listened to that far-off, lonely whistle.

In the parking lot they separated, and she in her station wagon, he in his Jeep, drove up the subdivision road on the east side of the valley. As the road wound upward, Dancer Peak loomed above him to the south, a great, smooth, snowy, somnolent head, chin tucked in shoulder and bare rock outcrops like eccentric features. The mountain was obscured when another squall blew snow against the windshield. He made growling sounds as he followed the big-buttocked, chrome and glass and red-taillighted rear of the station wagon up the asphalt road. He supposed Martha's thoughts were as bright and Future-Perfect as her face had been, and the crisis was coming round the curve, a-whistlin' and a-screamin' and a-strainin' every nerve.

The Schroeder cabin was small and decorator-furnished. A framed photograph of son Peter on one end of the mantel, and of pig-tailed daughter Katrin on the other, faced a water color, badly done by Franklyn Schroeder, that hung over the couch.

He made drinks while Martha disappeared to repair the ravages to her face caused by driving down to the lodge and back.

"I don't even know what a graduate assistant is!" she called from the bathroom. She came out, smiling, apparently filled with confidence. "Is it like an intern?"

He handed her her gin. "Like that in a way," he said, whose one-time best friend had been a graduate assistant at Stanford. Now that graduate assistant was a professor of philosophy at the University of California, last seen running to fat and wearing a sweat-shirt with a Ban-the-Bomb symbol on it.

And now Martha's eyes avoided his as the confidence she had tried to repair in the bathroom buckled. They faced each other uncomfortably. If he said, "What's the matter, Pussy?" she would flush, smile, laugh, be relieved. He didn't say it.

He sat down on the couch beneath the big water color. She remained erect in her pink-colored cashmere sweater with the band of pearls at her throat, slim and long-legged in expensive, rose-colored stretchpants, her fine, tanned, over-forty face on the strain, gazing past his left ear.

"But what do you suppose a graduate assistant looks like, Easy? A beard? I'll bet no money at *all!* Of course she's pregnant. You really are supposed to see that they're taking the pills before they go off to college—my *God!* Well, I don't care!" she said in a rapid voice. "Let Franklyn care. Whatever *I* did or said it would just be wrong just because *I* did it. Franklyn and Katey have their nice

Freudy thing. But if she has run off and married somebody—I mean—it's finished. Isn't it? I mean, Peter's just fine and I'm *finished*! I mean—I've been so damn *patient*."

She stopped, and it was his turn. He had been blowing an inward raspberry that had a strong center of scorn melting to pity around the edges; he didn't know what to say. Her eyes, hot, brown, and damp, shifted slightly to gaze past his right ear. Little man, what now? Long ago he had said, said loudly and repetitively, that he had chosen a way of life which was Present-Perfect rather than Future-Perfect, and he would face the Future-Imperfect when it came. Or, happiness can't buy money. Now, with the Future-Imperfect looming always closer, he could thumb his nose at it by marrying a divorcee a number of years older than he and with an income comically greater, who admired him, loved him, was good and eager in bed, and claimed to want to spend the rest of her days living life up, playing, being beautiful, being free. Hadn't he been thinking for a long time that he must switch sometime from the First Personal Principle to the Second Personal, which was all of one's self applied, Peace-Corps-wise, to something or to someone else of sufficient worth to give a diminishing Meaning-in-Life new strength—the First Personal Principle, in fact, still fulfilled but through an exterior dedication? Was Martha of sufficient worth for the Second Personal? He would never be able to fool himself for a minute that she was.

Did he love this beautiful, sexy, expensive, nervous-about-life-getting-away, aging girl? He turned the raspberry on himself. But once he had loved the Golden Girl who had married the graduate assistant at Stanford. And once he had loved Maeve Olsen, the legend, for a little while and a little ahead of everyone else. Since then, though, he had loved either no one or a great number of women very casually, the same thing really, and maybe there had been a withering away of that function of the heart due to an excessive concern with the self. It was a special risk of his philosophy. And now, brushing a hand over the back of his head in the reproachful silence, he wondered if there was any real reason why he shouldn't do this. He did what he wanted to, didn't he?

"I promised Franklyn I'd get a California divorce when the time came," Martha said. "But it takes a year. Why should I wait a *year*?"

He could nod to that without committing himself. He sipped Jack Daniels. Was he already bought, being used to her good bourbon? He had always prided himself in keeping free of the Crock of middle-class attitudes, middle-class ease, middle-class slavery. "Fat-assed, uxorious, and grateful," someone had said—warned. Of course it had been Dick Macklin, nine years ago.

A strider, Martha managed to stride the two steps it took to span the Navajo rug before the fireplace. She turned, strode back, placed her gin glass on the mantel, clasped hands at the small of her back, and stood with her legs straddled, presenting her very stylish self complete with breasts thrown into prominence and the tight crotch of the rose-colored pants indicating heaven's gate. Certainly she was attractive: lean, athletic, and well coordinated, or slim, sweet, and abandoned—whichever she chose or needed to be. But the stiffness of her face, the hectic color in her cheeks, must be fear that he would reject her now that she was free, and perhaps it was not even the unadmitted and inadmissible fear of the Future-Imperfect that moved him, but a growing awareness of those frail antennae, like snails' horns, that people extended in their loneliness and their fear. More and more he flinched to see those tender horns recoiling in hurt.

"Hello, Pussy," he said.

She flushed. She smiled gratefully. "You're so quiet," she said.

He nodded, wondering if she would like her way if she got it. She would simply strive to turn the stud into a lapdog, be hurt if she failed and contemptuous if she succeeded. I've been so damn patient, she had said, who had never had to be patient at all. Daughter of a doctor, wife of a doctor, mother of a medical student, she was of the new aristocracy. It was not her fault that everyone all her life had spoiled her, that she had never been made accountable for anything, deprived of or crossed in anything. How was he any different, he asked himself, except in awareness?

"Easy darling," she said huskily. She sat beside him and leaned against his shoulder, expensive-smelling, crisp hair tickling his cheek.

"We can do anything we want!" she said. "We can go to Europe and ski Davos and St. Moritz and Zermatt, and—oh, and St. Anton and Lech. We'll buy a Mercedes and go *every*where. We'll have an apartment in Paris and discothèque every night and—"

"Wait!" he said, for all the *things* of Future-Perfectism were beginning to slip in. "I teach skiing here at Dancer."

She said in triumph, "Well, I want private lessons *all* this year.
And from now *on!*"

Everything is easy for you, the Golden Girl in his past had said,
the one who had married the sold-out Guru. And so it had been,
he knew; but less and less easy, more and more complex and slippery, always now the dangers of rationalization lurking in ambush.

He tried to say lightly, "Nope. If teaching skiing's a job it's all
right. But if it's a position it won't work. *I* won't work." He had
said all this so many times before, hadn't he? He felt an edge of
panic. "No, I can't go on your payroll, Martha," he said.

Out of the corners of his eyes he saw her make a face. She
tucked her long legs under her, sighed, and bent her head so a dark
wing of hair swung along her cheek like a curtain drawn. "Oh, it
sounds bad when you say it coldly," she said. "But it doesn't have
to be. If we just don't have silly attitudes about it. It's only
Daddy's money, and money's only the things you can buy with it."

He sipped her bourbon. He had wavered for a moment, but the
weakness was leaving him. After all, he was a monument, wasn't
he? He made scornful calling sounds down the avenues of his
mind, thinking of the people he wouldn't be able to face if he
married rich to escape the Future-Imperfect.

Martha said in a strained voice, "Easy—" The telephone rang.
"Oh, *damn*," she said and went to answer it.

"Hello?" she said, and the telephone cried shrilly, audible to
him across the room, "*Mother!*"

Martha made a furious face, holding the receiver away from her
ear. Once she had tried to tell him what he had missed by never
having married, by having no children. Now she said harshly,
"Don't *scream* at me, Katey, my *God!*"

He didn't have to listen to this conversation. He rose, took up
his black ski school parka, and said, "I'll be down at the Loup
Garou."

As he went out Martha was saying, "You mean it's not true?
But your father told me—"

He closed the door. Standing on the deck, zipping his parka, he
raised his face to the slow-falling feathers of snow, mocking, home-
free laughter in his throat. His luck had continued to hold. With

delight he looked at the delicate covering of snow that had fallen on the deck, the railing, the steps, on the Jeep and the big Crock station wagon and the roofs of the neighboring cabins. He scraped a handful from the rail and squeezed it to nothing in his hand. Dry powder skiing tomorrow. Everything is easy for you, the Golden Girl, Elizabeth Wagers, had said. Everything was easy when you were lucky, but luck was the benison of the gods on the righteous and the faithful. He jumped off the porch, clicking his heels together three times before he came down, with a cock crow of relief. In the Jeep he made his usual great business of adjusting the choke and poising his foot over the gas pedal. The engine caught on the first turnover, to his satisfaction.

He headed back down the hill, reflecting on the great things in life. He had always suspected that the truly great things had no semblance of greatness but were very small and ordinary-seeming. Knowing how to start the balky old Jeep with its weak battery at ten above gave him pleasure. The snow drifting softly down, burning when he raised his face to it, gave him pure and uncomplicated pleasure. Skiing a fresh fall of powder snow gave very great pleasure, perhaps less intense but rarer and fulfilling more senses than sex, God's Greatest Gift. Cold white wine on a picnic in the hot sun while spring-skiing was a marvelous thing and easy to undervalue. So was drinking beer in the Loup Garou, watching the World Series on TV. So was rereading Raymond Chandler or Hammett or Tolstoi, or listening to rock-and-roll music, or dancing, or a summer morning on a new carpentry job when crew and job looked pleasant, or the opening day of trout season when he went back to the wars on the river where the big, scarred trout lurking in familiar holes were old friends. These were all little things, seeming so unimportant and easily replaceable that anyone might let them slip out of his life. Always the mistake was to think the flashy would be more satisfying than the familiar—for instance, that skiing amid the glamour and romance of Davos, St. Moritz, or Zermatt could be better than cutting up the powder on the slopes of Dancer, or that dancing in the most select discothèque in Paris had anything over dancing to the combo at the lodge or the jukebox at the Loup Garou. He laughed delightedly and thumped the steering wheel, feeling close to ancient, hieratic secrets. For if you did not know the things that were the stone and mortar of the whole structure of pleasure in life, then not merely the pleasure but life itself could easily slip away from you unused, could be sold out for the pottage of a prospect of Future-Perfect-ism that had by its own nature to be always out of reach. He knew well by now his birds-in-the-hand, and he reminded himself again of their worth and irreplaceability.

In the Loup Garou, J.D. Daugherty, the proprietor, presided over an empty bar, his deep-eyed, long-upper-lipped face like that of a handsome, slightly effeminate monkey. Over in front of the fireplace three couples in ski clothes sat at a table spiky with beer bottles, breathing smoke and laughing.

"Evening, Ease," J.D. said.

"Evening, J.D."

J.D. wore a white tennis shirt with a red-and-black bird embroidered on the left breast. His cottony hair looked as though a damp comb had been run through it only moments ago. He made a bourbon highball with an expertise that showed this to be one of the small things of life that gave *him* pleasure. Bartending was something J.D. was good at and enjoyed; his other, more recent, and more prestigious role as a subdivider and venture-capitalist only gave him an irritable expression and seemed to be turning him into a right-wing extremist.

"Cold out?" J.D. asked.

"Feathers are falling from the great chicken."

J.D.'s front teeth appeared in a grin that was surprisingly sweet in his cold face. He produced a drink for himself, suspended the glass between his thumb and forefinger and sipped from it. "The great chicken!" he said in toast. "Well, it's a shame," he said. "All those Christmas schmucks coming in tomorrow just in time to ski hell out of the feathers. I hate to see the powder wasted on people from downbelow."

"Oh, we can share the wealth once in a while."

"Hell with share the wealth!" J.D. said with vehemence. Then he said, "Mrs. Schro coming up?"

"Came up last night."

J.D. squinted at the beer-drinking couples, who were laughing again. Among all of them who had labored to give birth to Dancer nine years ago there existed an old-companionship of great strength. So although he and J.D. Daugherty disagreed on a number of issues, distrusted each other, and would have traded shots over many different barricades, stronger than the disagreements was the bond of being an old-timer at Dancer, one of Macklin's Men, along with Badbody and Timbal Khan, John Henry and Rody Bliss; and even Isobel and Dickie Macklin. And of course Maeve, who, having received her elementary education from him and her baccalaureate from Macklin, had set out to conquer the world of men.

"Going up early to ski the powder, Ease?" J.D. asked.

That was another bond, the fraternity of the powderburners.

"Try and stop me."

"Yeah, well, I hope Tim doesn't remember I threw him out of here last night," J.D. said.

Tim's favor was necessary for the powderburners to be allowed on the lift before it officially opened. Timbal Khan controlled the virgin powder.

"What'd he do?"

"Nothing but bring everybody down. You know, you've got in a few fights in here, Ease, and busted things up, but at least you kind of make it fun." J.D. brought his glass out again, slowly, as though drawing it out of a deep hole. "But that fucking Tim," he said when he had drunk and replaced his glass. "It's like he gets some kind of monthly. Comes in here and just sits in the goddam corner spooking everybody. He gets all kind of hunched down and black-looking. He just sits there looking at people and bringing them down. They think he's some kind of goddam kook or something."

He shook his head over Timbal Khan, the Mountain Man, who was one of the lonely ones.

"I used to think he was mooning about Maeve," J.D. went on, "or Macklin getting killed. But now I don't know what the hell's eating him. Christ, I get fed up! He'll sit there looking blacker and blacker—like he's growing a beard while you watch him or something. So last night I told him to get his ass out of here."

"Did he go?"

"Yeah, he went. He didn't like it much though." J.D. made a sour face. "Poor mixed-up bastard, I'll bet he hasn't got laid since Maeve went away."

It was a statement of colossal bad taste and stupidity. He was on the point of challenging it when J.D. said, "Pardon me," took a tray, and ducked out under the bar.

Angrier than it seemed to him he should be, he considered the possibility of getting into a bar fight in order to cloud the issues when Martha Schroeder reappeared. He tried to recall fights he had had in the Loup Garou. He could remember few of the faces, except for that of one scoffing ski instructor he had known well. He could only remember the drunkenness and the wild excitement —excitement, of course, more than anger. Maybe being in a place where you could get into a fight as a pressure release, or whatever it was, was one of the important things. He didn't think it would be possible in St. Moritz, for example. It amused him to think of starting a bar fight in St. Moritz.

On the jukebox guitar chords sounded, country-and-western at first, then complicated and stylized. A very loud, joltingly familiar voice cried out: "*Hey! Going to build me a castle, forty feet high!*"

He swung around to see J.D. in front of the jukebox. J.D. brought a load of empty beer bottles back, placed the tray on the bar, and ducked under the bar to turn a knob, reducing the volume of the too loud voice of John Henry Collins.

"*So's I can watch Willie, when she goes by,*" John Henry sang.

"How about that folk singer?" J.D. asked, wooden-faced. "This one just came in. It's what gave Tim the hump last night." J.D. cleared the tray and loaded it with new bottles beaded with cold. "I don't like it much," he said, ducking out under the counter again.

He sat listening to the song John Henry had once sung for pleasure in the old T & O Social and now had recorded for profit in Hollywood. The deceptively crude style had become enormously polished. He liked the singer and the song.

But J.D. Daugherty, who had spent so many years waiting for the fortune his aunt was going to leave him—had finally left him —must of course be jealous of the folk singer, a celebrity, self-made, with his newest recording on the jukebox. That was a simple enough attitude to understand, though why J.D. must maintain that Maeve had been a whore was not. Timbal Khan, for his part, had chosen to make the root and sorrow of his life a great lost and doomed love for Maeve. So did the attitudes of each of them toward Maeve reveal each one's inadequacies, or rationalizations, or dreams?

He grinned, leaning forward on his bar stool, assuring himself that he was firmly planted neither in the past nor the future but the present. After all, God's total gift was the Present, wasn't it?

He made excited hoots of congratulation to himself, as he did when profound puns popped into his head, when his mind began to stretch out over meanings and parallels, over resolutions and principles. He was a monument, wasn't he? He sat on the bar stool of the Present-Perfect, listening to the voice of the Past on the jukebox and only slightly worried about facing the demands and recriminations of the Future when these caught up with him again.

2: John Henry

HEADING NORTH from Southern California, Highway 93 climbed in long swoops and inclined planes through pine forests. Late in the afternoon he had to turn the wipers on, when raindrops began to smear the windshield. The raindrops had little cores to them; all at once it was snow driving against the glass! He, John Henry Collins, was happy! Going back to Dancer Peak in his six-G Porsche, pleasantly alone and driving too fast, he was trembling with excitement in the swirling-toward-him snow, in the growing dusk and the smeary Christmas-tree colors of the lighted mountain burgs he rocketed through. Even the one traffic signal he hung up on, in the one town big enough to have one, showed him the Christmas range of orange, red, and green.

The snowcloud was thin at first. Sometimes he could see stars through it, and once he thought it was going to clear. But the Fresno radio said snow flurries in the mountains, and as he continued to gain altitude the cloud thickened and he knew it was no fly-by-night snowcloud.

"Snow! Yay!" he said aloud and lit one of his tan, sweet cheroots to celebrate. In the next café he came to he stopped for coffee but didn't, in his be-there impatience, even take time to finish it, going outside again almost immediately to stand for a moment admiring the swift shape of the Porsche and the fine, hard-on way his skis slanted off the rear bumper. Dancer-bound again, he patted the dashboard of the car that had been his dream-car all those lean, keen, skibum years. He put a hand back to pat the black case protecting his great, sweet-voiced, pale-faced Martin and in happiness twisted his face into a grinning grimace at the boundless horn-of-plenty of the weather, which was driving the snow in spirals against the windshield. When you lived in L.A. you forgot how great Weather was. He sang:

"Goin' home to Dancer feelin' glad,
Goin' home to Dancer feelin' gla-ad,
I'm goin' home to Dancer feelin' glad, Lord, Lord,
Good buddies, I—"

He broke off as his headlights fled palely over a billboard with the dancing skier on it: SKI DANCER PEAK.

The Porsche swerved as he braked, reminding him that the highway was slick, and he missed the number of minutes to Dancer the sign had announced. Less than an hour though, now, he thought; unless it socked in more or he had to put on chains. "Those pretty, pretty lights!" he said as he passed another cluster of homes with Christmas-tree windows. Damp came in his eyes because the lights were so homely-pretty, because for the first time in a long time he was free to think of *color* as orange and green and red, because he was going home to his soul-home, the ski re-sort where he'd spent six years lift-building, skibumming, instruct-ing, guitar-playing-in-the-bar; from which he'd taken off one day without even knowing it was the take-off, thinking he was only going down to Bakersfield to guest-play on a jerk TV program on a jerk channel with a jerk, country-and-western, dreadnaught-playing M.C. who'd heard him sing at Dancer Lodge. It had been the launching pad to the land of bread and honey, where he'd been ever since, black and blue from pinching himself to make sure it was for real.

" 'Hey! *Goin' to build me a castle!* ' " he sang and broke off. He had just finished recording his newest LP—"Goin' to Build Me a Castle, with John Henry Collins"—and the title song was already out on 45 and moving. He was a success! He'd made a swinging, bread success out of his *thing* that he loved. He'd given away no pieces of his soul for that bread either, the way Captain Easy had said you had to. What he had given away was himself, free, to al-most any charity that asked for him, till Sid-the-agent had said he'd given away twice what he'd made, which sounded so great and impossible he kept saying it over and over to himself. And now he didn't have to chew on himself about the Liberty Singers because he was headed for where white was the color of snow and black was nothing, seven thousand feet above all the things that brought him down.

He goosed the Porsche to make it jump. Wasn't he happy? Wasn't he proud? Was there even any *question?* Making it big as a folk singer, people *wanting* to hear *you, paying* to hear *you!* Making a success not just as a singer—he'd always been an easy singer —but as a guitar player too; that was what really made him flip, that had been pure guts and no talent—how many times had he thought he'd never master those ten fingers and six strings? But he had mastered them in the same stubborn way he had mastered skiing well enough to instruct in the Dancer Ski School along with Easy Clary and J.D. Daugherty, and had mastered the womanizing, the honey, the same way—who had once been a tongue-tied bush kid from Oregon. Now in the land of bread and honey there was so much bread that he could give away twice what he made, and so much honey—he laughed out loud to remember Sid-the-agent solemnly cautioning him to slow down.

Still, there was that black spot on the horizon, and the constipated feeling of a tremendous bill coming due—but he wasn't going to think about any of that for this coming great week.

He was as proud of being one of the old bunch at Dancer as he was of anything; one of those who had built Dancer from the ground up, from scratch and before scratch, who had seen nothing turned into something by their brains and muscle and hard work and love and maybe hate, too, that other Christmas nine years ago. For the first time in his life he had felt a man among men. In those eight months, working for Dick Macklin, working with Easy and J.D. and Badbody and Tim Soderburg, he, the Oregon boy, had become a man, had earned the big Block-M nobody could ever take away, and had seen a long, hard piece of work finished. And seen Dick Macklin finished, he thought all-at-once-soberly, when the Superchute cornice killed him.

And soberly, too, he remembered making it with Maeve Olsen for his Block-A. He had taken her down to L.A. on her flight from Dancer, and he had made it. But there had been no triumph; he had only been ashamed, because of his pretense that he was comforting her when she was so shook. In the morning they had had milkshakes and hamburgers for breakfast, and then he had let her off at the apartment house in Beverly Hills, where someone she knew lived, and watched her, still in her stretchpants and ski sweater and carrying her Valpack, run up the steps. She turned unsmiling to raise a hand and call good-by and thanks—and was gone, gone from his life and from Dancer, into a world of gossip columns and jet-set reportage, changed from Maeve Olsen to Maeve Herron, a starlet briefly seen as a switchboard operator in a tight sweater and harlequin glasses, and from there directly into the international league of fun and games, her name coupled with this or that actor or producer, bullfighter, racing driver, or playboy. Then finally she was out of the columns and into the raucous and contemptuous attention of the news itself as "The Mariachi Girl," when the Mexican bastard with his Charley Chaplin mustache had hired a mariachi band to follow Maeve wherever she went in Acapulco and bug her out of town. The papers had eaten it up. "Mariachi Girl," he said aloud, unhappily, because he loved Maeve and wished her well.

All the old misery of Maeve and Macklin and the avalanche came on him. He tried to will back the fine, shaky excitement of being alone in the Porsche, driving to Dancer in a storm. Snow was sticking to the asphalt now and spun more thickly against the windshield. He began to sing softly, not show biz, but one of the songs he had sung those nights in the old T & O Social at Dancer and had loved, loved and revered still, had once thought of pretentiously as his theme song, which was why Dick Macklin had started calling him John Henry, and Sid-the-agent had made it permanent.

> "Goin' to be the death of me,
> Goin' to be the death of me . . ."

Some songs were so deep, spacious, and precious, and some were so worthless he was sick of them before he'd even got through an arrangement one time. At least he sang more of the former than of the latter. Didn't he? This song was so true it brought tears to his eyes. Just hearing it running in his head could almost make him do what he feared so very much to do, could not do, because always the tune in his head faded before the silent movie running behind his eyes, of himself going down under the clubs and the freckled, fleshy, drawling men clubbing him down and kicking him in the balls.

Quit it! He almost shouted it aloud. That was enough of that! It was all right for Frisco Daley, who thought he was the new Woody Guthrie, to join the Liberty Singers; all right for the rest of them too. But he, John Henry Collins, was going back to Dancer where the only thing that mattered was skiing the Spoon and the Big Top with old friends and cutting up the powder in the Superchute.

Macklin had given all of them names but J.D. Daugherty. Such was the force of Macklin's character that those names, without exception, had stuck. It occurred to him, came phrased into his mind that way for the first time, that Macklin had been a great man. What a mark Macklin had made on them in those few months, spring, summer, and fall! They had loved him and hated him and worked their tails off for him, or maybe, at the end, for Dancer. But it was Dick Macklin who had grabbed the Forest Service leases on Dancer Peak; had beat his partner out of control of the land; run his contractor bankrupt putting in the lodge, swimming pool, and the Big Red One lift; cadged credit where credit had long run out; cajoled the last exhausted grunt of work from an inexperienced and unpaid bunch of skibums who, almost until the bitter end, had been hypnotized into a fanatic loyalty. Macklin had done it, seen it finished, and the lodge and lifts had opened for that Christmas season nine years back.

He would never forget the moment when the first skiers had arrived, two cars full of society types from San Francisco, asking for Macklin. He had gone running down to the basement where Macklin was helping Easy Clary put in the heating ducts. He saw right away that Macklin and Easy had been mixing it. Macklin came limping up the steps, brushing dirt off himself, and he had a dirty eye. But as soon as he got with the men from the city, Macklin said just the right things, as only he could do so well, to make them all laugh and at the same time think he was The Stuff. He took them up to ski off the top of Big Red One and had a party for them in the bar that night. Easy Clary had not come to the party.

At the moment when Macklin had come limping out of the basement they were out of the woods. All the fantastic, hopeless mess they were in had, just then, fallen right. He didn't know how it could have, but it did. Macklin's wife, Isobel, had been able to get hold of the money she'd gone to Hawaii for, everything that had been so balky and half-assed had begun suddenly to function, even the central heating, even the Platterlift, which had been his and J.D.'s particular nightmare. And in the week of triumph before that Christmas, as though the last screw-turn needed for the success of Dancer Peak Ski Area was a spectacular piece of publicity, Macklin had died in an avalanche.

For years after Macklin died they had spent long, drunken evenings arguing about why he had died, as though there had to be a reason. There was a theory that Macklin had died because he had finished Dancer and there was nothing more for him to do. There was somebody's simple-minded reason that Macklin had died for his sins—because he had shacked up with Maeve while Isobel was in Hawaii getting the money to save him from bankruptcy; and because he had been so rotten mean giving Maeve the moldy fig when Isobel came back. There had been many reasons offered, but now he, John Henry Collins, secretly, awfully, had come to know what the real reason must have been. Macklin had had all the luck in the world; everyone acknowledged that. Everything had gone his way; he had gained his heart's desire doing just what he wanted and made a success at it, and then the bill had come in. What the bill was exactly there was no way of knowing, but the bill for all the luck had come in and Macklin couldn't or wouldn't pay it. So he had been killed, not by the mountain as Tim Soderburg was apt to say, not because he had finished living as Easy said, not for his sins exactly, but for default. Maybe it was stupid, but it grabbed him.

His headlights illuminated another sign: COPE 11. Erskine was nine miles beyond Cope, and at Erskine you turned off Highway 93 into Dancer Valley, where a mile and a half of serpentine asphalt brought you to Dancer Lodge.

His mind's eye was filled now with Macklin's death in the avalanche, the only real avalanche he had ever seen, and the only death; the sudden, shocked apprehension on Macklin's face looking back up the Superchute at the first sliding rapids of the snowslip starting, and then the face jerking back to look up at the cornice; and, later, the cold, almost beautiful calm of his dead face when they had dug him out. He had thought then it was a terrible price to pay for the pleasure of skiing the powder.

No one could have known that the cornice would build up so big so early in the season, and, if anyone had, who was going to tell Macklin he couldn't go up and ski the powder on his own mountain? The only one who could have stopped him was Timbal Khan Soderburg, head of the ski patrol, in charge of snow safety, and Tim had passed out drunk somewhere, or anyway no one had been able to find him. Because of the tailfins! His spirits revived as he remembered Tim in the big orange rotary, wild as a bear, crunching the tailfins in the parking lot. That was a year of cars with monster, stupid tailfins, and Tim, who had finally flipped, had gone down the line savaging the fins with the rotary snowplow. So Tim hadn't been around to stop them from skiing the Superchute when the cornice was ready to let go, though he could remember Tim later on, probing the hard-packed, ugly washboarding of the avalanche track for Macklin's body.

He recalled with pleasure those mashed and twisted rear ends, the shards of red plastic taillights on the packed snow of the parking lot. But did he really remember—or had he been told about it so many times he only thought he remembered—Badbody running after the rotary, waving his arms as though trying to catch a bus, until finally Tim ran the plow into the side of Macklin's old Cadillac, jumped down from the cab, and walked away?

It was one of the great memories of that great time, The Time Tim Plowed the Tailfins. Like The Time Somebody Turned On the Swimming Pool Lights—that had happened before it had started to snow, in the blessed, endless Indian summer that year, when they had had a picnic on the mountain one Sunday, and, coming down after dark in the unseasonable heat, someone had suggested a skinny-dip in the brand-new swimming pool. Someone had sneaked into the lodge and turned on the pool lights, and— *Hello, Maeve!* And there was The Time J.D. Pissed on the Lamp Post in Cope, and The Time J.D. Schussed the Spoon and ran over Macklin's skis at the bottom. So many times he enjoyed counting over and was looking forward to reminiscing about back at Dancer this year again, all those times so memorable that he bubbled with pleasure just saying their names to himself.

Those eight months of the building of Dancer had been the greatest time of his life, the greatest time, he suspected, of all their lives. No other time had had such drama, such vivid colors. He recalled it now as a completely joyful time, and yet he knew his memory lied to him, for those months had been as tense, resentful, and miserable as they had been exciting.

COPE

POP. 653

ELEV. 6750

SLOW

Happy-melancholy colors of Christmas-tree lights in windows again; blasting through Cope he felt a little lonely. Nine miles to Erskine, and a mile and a half more. The Grundig in the dash buzzed where he had turned it on and forgotten it. He tuned in a crappy, commercial Christmas song and sang, mocking, along with it. Another sign loomed:

STAY DANCER LODGE

SKI DANCER PEAK

CERTIFIED SKI SCHOOL

Beyond this sign was a smaller one:

DANCER CHALETS

VIEW HOMESITES

J.D. DAUGHERTY

VALLEY CENTER

He remembered Captain Easy on the subject of the inheritance J.D. had spent those years expecting any day. He himself had thought it would be fine to know you were coming into all that bread. Easy had said J.D. was in slavery waiting for his aunt to kick off, and when J.D. finally got the money he would still be in slavery. If you had a great hunk of money in the bank or stocks and bonds, Easy would say, then you had to spend a lot of time being afraid you were going to lose it. Why would anybody with common sense want to spend most of his life being afraid? If you were always afraid you were going to lose your property, then you spent more and more time worrying about the Communists hiding in the bushes, and the next thing you had a shotgun and blasted away, defoliating the bushes, whenever the wind blew them— didn't you? What kind of a way to live, spend the one life you had, was that? Sure it was too easy, Easy would say, and laugh it off if you pressed him—except that if the wrong person pressed him in the wrong way Easy was apt to punch him in the eye.

He believed in Easy's philosophy because he believed in Easy. How many skibums and instructors had been preached to by Easy Clary as they passed through Dancer? Easy would make believers of them for a while, but always in the end they went back to the world downbelow and sold pieces off their souls. Your soul was the most precious thing you had, Easy would say, the root of yourself, the essence, the what-you-were of yourself, and when you broke it up for sale you did the unforgivable thing.

But John Henry Collins hadn't! So why did something in him have to keep pretending that he had? He sang some commercial, to keep the disks turning, and some true, for himself, and he gave away twice what he made. So what was he guilty of? Only that he knew he gave away not himself but time, so there would be no time left; and though he had kept his soul intact it was rotten with the corruption of cowardice and with his default on the bill that was due. He almost cried out that it was unfair. How could you help it if you had been born a coward?

Through Erskine, then the left turn into the valley. It was snowing harder; there was more snow on the road. The engine behind him echoed hollowly, and there was a queasy feeling in the rear end as he took the first turn too fast. But he was in a great hurry now. Pure, pale snowbanks rose along the sides of the road, and beyond them, faintly visible, rose snow-draped pines. Headlights approached and glared past. He began to sing, trying to regain his great mood, head cocked back to open his throat. Wasn't he happy? The recording session was over with an A-O.K. from Sid and the Discodisque people; no more dates till after the first of the year, nothing he had to do at all except maybe tonight call his shut-ins, his wheel-chair kids, to sing them a song over the phone, describe Dancer, talk a little about skiing—not so much that they would feel bad though. What was the *matter*? What was he afraid of tonight?

DANCER PEAK SKI AREA

"Home! Yay!" he cried. The road now was a sheet of white with two fading-gray wheel tracks running along the other side, curving between the snowbanks, through the white pagodas of trees, beneath invisible mountains. He skidded as he took the curves too fast, exulting in the adrenalin-thrill, as though fear could bring courage like pushups building muscle. Lights appeared through the falling snow, the first cabins. A little further on, at the Valley Center, was the Loup Garou, J.D. Daugherty's bar.

Parked before the Loup Garou were a Jeep and two other cars frosted with new snow. He turned in and stopped. Inside the amber-lighted bar anonymous figures moved. He slid out of the Porsche and deep-knee-bent to stretch cramped legs. Above him on the wooden sign, carved letters were underlined with snow. The carved wolf, erect, held up boxing gloves in an old-time prize-fighter pose.

When he went inside the first person he saw was Easy Clary, half standing, half sitting, at the bar, tall and thin in his black ski-school sweater with the narrow red band across back and sleeves and narrow-legged black ski pants. He noticed with a shock that Easy's rumpled black hair was thinning in the back.

3: Captain Easy

HE FELT a cold draft on the back of his neck and turned to see John Henry coming into the Loup Garou, grinning all over his face. For your dime you got not only the song but the singer.

"Easy!"

He leaped to embrace John Henry, slapping the quilted parkaback while John Henry thumped his. They separated and pumped hands, John Henry grinning ferociously beneath a scalloped tangle of long, light brown hair.

"Snowing powder for *me!* Yay!"

"It's the famous TV and recording star, John Henry Collins!" J.D. said, and John Henry swung around to shake hands with him. The two of them helped the star out of his parka, commenting extravagantly on its richness and beauty and exclaiming over the quality of the stretchpants and sweater beneath. They helped him, laughing and protesting, onto a bar stool. J.D. ducked under the counter and reappeared, brushing the palms of his hands along the sides of his head to refresh his hairdo.

"Build you a highball forty feet high?"

John Henry's eyebrows rose in his long, smooth, bland face. "Yay! You heard it yet?"

"Lives in that box over there," J.D. said.

"How do you like that break on it?"

J.D. made a complicated face.

"Powerful," the monument said.

John Henry looked touchingly pleased, and it was clear that John Henry, who by pluck and luck, by righteousness and faithfulness, sat squarely in command of his life, still regarded him, Captain Easy, as the super-skibum, the high priest of the sponsibles, the Guru of the powderburners, the monument. Mocking laughter rang in his ears.

"We've just been listening to you," he said.

"Yay! Plug in those dimes!"

"We'd be glad to see you back even if you hadn't brought snow with you. But of course it's better this way."

"Hey, I'm glad to be back, goodbuddies," John Henry said, grinning as though it hurt.

He wore a magnificent royal blue ski sweater. His tangled long hair was very clean. He looked prosperous, well tended, and humble. Now he began to make the stylized and violent gestures of poling down a steep slope in deep powder. "Yay!" he cried. "I'm tuned up and ready. How's the skiing been?"

"Been icy," J.D. said. "Say, your hair's getting pretty long there, isn't it, Hollywood?"

"My image," John Henry said. "Bucking for longhair. Up from Folk and Pops."

"What about these folk types going down to Mississippi to sing with the niggers, for Christ sake?" J.D. said. There was a little silence. "Buy you a drink, John Henry?" J.D. asked.

"Thanks, man. Scotch." John Henry grinned at him and said, "Hey, Captain Easy!"

He grinned back, but he was thinking of his last meeting with his own Guru, whose First Personal Principle was reduced to Ban the Bomb, End Capital Punishment in California, and the other prefab Second Personal dedications. Now, uneasy in the pose that John Henry somehow forced him into, he realized how self-conscious and uneasy Shelley Steinberg must have been with him.

As he mixed the drink J.D. asked, "Say, are you getting much down there, John Henry?"

John Henry slumped dramatically. "Burned out," he whispered hoarsely. "It's a real supermarket thing down there. I mean, you pick them over and throw back the ones with the spots on them. How's it been up here?" He did a doubletake. "Oh, Christ, you're married," he said to J.D. "How's it been?" John Henry demanded, turning to him.

Not bad, he thought, who had only tonight escaped, by great insight, fortitude, and luck, a deadly ambush of Future-Perfectism. But not too good, he thought, who was feeling a great melancholy

from the past blowing over him, with too many thoughts of the
Guru and the Golden Girl, of Macklin and Maeve. He made twin
machine guns of his forefingers and shot down John Henry Collins.

"Up here," he said, "we don't pick up the ones with spots in the
first place."

John Henry giggled. Sobering, frowning, he asked, "Hey, anybody heard anything about Maeve? I've been thinking about that
Mexican bastard giving Maeve a hard time."

"Jesus, another one," J.D. muttered and winked solemnly as he
drew his glass up to his lips.

"What's the matter?" John Henry offered a case of cheroots,
drew one out himself.

"We were just talking about kind of the same thing," J.D. said.

"No kidding?" John Henry said eagerly. "Well, the thing about
Maeve—"

Another cold breath of air on the back of his neck, and he
didn't get to hear what the thing about Maeve was, as Martha
Schroeder came in. When he helped her off with her coat her
hand clutched his with a hint of sharp fingernails.

"Katrin all right?" he asked from his position of safety.

She nodded. Her cheeks were pink with cold, there were jewels
of melting snow in her hair, she looked very angry. "Yes. *Damn,*"
she said through her teeth.

He was thinking about Maeve as he moved Martha to a bar
stool. He introduced her to John Henry, who had lit his cheroot.
She sat down between them, a square, unsteady set to her rose-
pink mouth. She asked for a Gibson, her shoulder touching his, leg
pressed against his, hand lying on his leg. But he was a hundred
miles away from her, ten years away from her, because all afternoon it had been coming on him, coming over him, and the thing
about Maeve was . . .

He had known Maeve before Dancer existed. They had both
been at Craven, an old resort north and east of Dancer, the winter
before Dancer had got started. He had been teaching part time in
the ski school, bartending part time, and skiing as much as he
could. He could not remember when Maeve had first appeared, no
electricity having struck at their first meeting. He remembered her

as a bunny in the ski school who had come on, who had got a job as assistant to the social director, helping to arrange races and parties for the guests and working up an Easter Hat competition in the spring. She still had bands on her teeth then, and though she was young she was not that young. It was assumed that her teeth had been damaged in an accident.

Though he couldn't remember meeting her, he could remember when he had first noticed her. It had been a very warm Easter, with skiers on the slopes in shorts or lederhosen and shirt sleeves. He was opening the Craven Lodge bar one noon when Maeve came in, wearing shorts and carrying creations in colored paper with which to adorn the deer, elk, and moose heads of the Craven decor. The porter brought a ladder for her. It lurched beneath her weight, and she made sounds of dismay.

He went to hold the ladder while she decorated the first of the stuffed heads. He made a joke. She laughed at it. She was standing turned toward him on the ladder, one moccasined foot a rung higher than the other, her right knee on the level of his eyes. He realized that he was looking at a beautiful leg, rosy, rounded, narrow, and perfectly articulated at the knee but with skiing muscles in her calf and thigh. His eyes traveled, with innocent lust, to the hem of her shorts, which were loose enough to reveal sweet secret flesh and the pale sheen of panties over shadows. With pleasure and surmise his eyes ran up over her hips and the wide belt cinching her waist, the swell of ribcage and the softer swell of breasts above it as she stretched an arm up, her still-smiling-at-his-joke pink mouth visible above her raised arm, fine glint of gold wire across her teeth. He made wolf-sounds of happy discovery to himself.

Thus it was that he came to notice her; much as, he realized, Macklin was later to notice her, and down the years since then many different men must have, dramatically, noticed her.

Craven had been established as a summer resort staffed by out-of-school young people, and a medieval policy still obtained regarding relationships between employees. Trysts at Craven were difficult and dangerous, he was not in a hurry, so he had made a game of seducing her by the Future-Perfect idea of the 24-Hour Love-making Derby the day Craven closed in the spring. He would drive

her home to Visalia in the San Joaquin Valley, and twenty-four
hours would drop out of their lives in a motel.

They made love through a long, dim, air-conditioned afternoon.
They swam in the motel pool. They showered together. She had a
beautiful body.

He made drinks from the supplies he had brought, and, with
the venetian blind adjusted to let a little more light in, they sat
facing each other, naked, in yellow wicker chairs. Maeve smiled at
him with pale lips, warm color in her tan cheeks, embarrassed still
by his eyes on her. He raised a foot to caress her thighs with his
toes. "Lovely legs," he said.

"No, they're—"

"Hush! Stop knocking yourself. They're lovely legs attached to a
lovely body."

More color came into her lips. Her smile was strained and
happy. "Flattery will get you anything you want," she said.

"How about a cigarette?"

She rose to get the pack from the table beside the bed, and he
grinned at the wicker design decorating her bottom. He watched
her scouting for matches, liking the way she moved, pleased that
she seemed less self-conscious, more natural, than she had been at
first.

She found the matches on the dresser and lit two cigarettes,
squinting through the smoke at her reflection in the mirror. She
brought him his cigarette. When she saw him looking at her
breasts her hands fluttered to cover them, then dropped away.

"Not worried about God watching any more?"

She shook her head, her nostrils trailing smoke. She said in an
uneven voice, "Do you think I'm pretty?"

He started to make a joke of it, but he saw she was very serious,
so he said, seriously, "I think you're beautiful."

She touched the gold wire across her front teeth with the tip of
her tongue. "This comes off this summer," she lisped.

"I'll miss it."

Her nose wrinkled when she smiled, the slitted gleam of her
eyes showed through thick lashes. Her face was glowing.

"Didn't you know you had a beautiful body?" he asked. "It's
the color of old pearls. Your face is the color of old mud from

spring skiing and it's better when you blush. Do you mind if I keep you blushing?"

"Yes," Maeve said. "No," she said, replenishing the smoke-screen between them. "I used to be ashamed of—myself. I used to go around all—hunched over." She illustrated. "Like I was carrying a bunch of books against my—against me."

"Well, I straightened you out," he said. He raised a foot and propped it on the edge of her chair. "You've enchanted me heart and sole."

"Heel!" she said, and they both laughed, she shakily, he with the excitement of finding her tuned to the melodies he enjoyed.

She began to talk about her childhood in Visalia, her parents who were dead, her grandmother and her aunts, her escape from the Companions of Jesus College in Visalia to secretarial school in San Francisco after her grandmother died, leaving her a small inheritance. He gathered that she had had extensive orthodontia.

"My grandmother and my Aunt Ellen were good," she said. "Have you known any really good people? Good people are awfully strong. Auntie Pett isn't quite so good. I can go home and see her now that Aunt Ellen is dead too. I loved my grandmother though. It was just that they—thought you were better being ugly and poor. Because then Jesus loved you more."

"Jesus should sue for slander."

"But I'm all right now," Maeve said. "Aren't I?"

"After the Twenty-four-Hour Lovemaking Derby you'll be perfect."

She rose and stood before him, blushing again as she assumed enticing poses. He kissed a small, hard, pink nipple when it came within range. "Plain or fancy this time?"

"Fancy," Maeve said. She was laughing when he took her on his lap. She pressed her face into his neck. "Show me I'm not a plain girl."

"Tell you what I'm going to do, my sister, my spouse, my Shulamite, my Rose of Sharon. I will show you your breasts are two leaping harts, your belly a heap of wheat, and all the rest of the Song of Solomon in all its glory. I will show you how you are perfect in every part so there will be no more talk of Jesus wanting anyone to be ugly."

"Yes," Maeve whispered, her breath warm on his neck.

So he showed her she was perfect, beautiful, and fancy, and pleased her and himself in many ways. Then he lay beside her on the bed, gazing sleepily at the slant of late sun through the blind and dust motes slowly spinning in the sunrays. Maeve moved to light a cigarette. He traced a delicate blue vein in her thigh and smoothed her ruffled feathers.

"What are you going to do this summer, Chuck?" she asked.

"Told you. I'm going to work over at Dancer Peak. New lift going in there."

"And what are you going to be doing next winter?"

"Teach skiing."

"And next summer?" Maeve asked.

He had thought, because they had seemed in tune, that the questionnaire would not be produced. But of course the summer of youth could not morally be spent in enjoyment of itself; it must be spent gathering the nuts that would make old age comfortable.

"Nuts," he said.

"What?"

"Nothing."

"I heard Mr. Murray talking about you. They offered you a good job."

"I don't want to be assistant manager of Craven, sitting in the office watching the happy people skiing the mountain out the window."

"But when Mr. Murray—"

"Don't want to be manager when Murray moves on."

"But what do you want to be?"

She wasn't pushing it, she was only puzzled. The dialogue was so familiar he could have wept. "Me?" he said. "Me. Just to be me." That was too smart-aleck. "I want to pursue the beautiful, Beautiful," he said. "A life of pleasure, Treasure. That's happiness now, not at age sixty-five." He raised himself on an elbow to grin at her.

But she was Future-Perfect-minded and not in tune with this song. Ain't it a shame? he said to himself, looking down at her closed eyes, her tight, full lips. Her cigarette raised a banner of smoke from the hand lying on her breast. He said, "I don't want to be the manager of a ski resort, sitting inside watching the good times roll by outside. I'm a really dedicated skibum, Maeve."

"You've been to Stanford. You're so—smart. You could do any-thing. You could be anything in the world you wanted to be."

He might have laughed if it had not sounded like such a cry from her heart. He was already the thing in the world he wanted to be. "Even president of U.S. Steel?" he asked gently, for it had been an example he, Elizabeth, and the Guru had often employed.

"Even president of U.S. Steel," Maeve said, "if you wanted to be."

"He's a slave and I'm free."

"He can do more things than you can do." Her voice was muffled as she covered her face with the crook of her elbow.

"I don't think he can."

"Put this out for me, please," she said.

He took the cigarette from her fingers and squashed it out in the ashtray. "He can only do things that will pay him a hundred and thirty-five thousand dollars a year," he went on. "He's a slave to that. He really is, Maeve."

"Well, he can have anything he wants."

"Oh, well, that's different."

"Yes, that's different," Maeve said as though she thought she had won the argument.

"Just a minute! I don't want what he has. Houses and cars and pools and boats. I don't want those things. And poverty's not what you don't have, it's what you want."

"Oh, hell," Maeve said, her arm still covering her face. "Okay. Let's not talk about it any more, okay?"

"Okay," he said angrily, but he felt the tenseness of her body beside him, and his anger dissolved in tenderness. Gently he pried her arm away from her face. "Are you really this way, Maeve? It's so bad to be this way."

"What's wrong with wanting nice things if you've never had anything nice?" She sounded as though she were fighting to keep from crying. "I don't believe it's bad to want things nice!" she said.

He stared down at her helplessly. He was afraid the Twenty-four Hour Lovemaking Derby was over, which was too bad, because lovemaking was one of the worthwhiles of life, and this argument was meaningless. No, not meaningless, for he cared about Maeve Olsen.

"Listen, Maeve," he said. "Listen. You have to try to understand that we are all hanging, strung up, right in the middle between wanting to squeeze everything we can out of every moment, get all the living there is to get out of the just one life we have, and wanting to be dead and at rest because everything is just too tough. Happiness or nothingness. Things are just the way you fool yourself, thinking they are happiness. But they're really nothing. Wait! And with Americans it's even more complicated because we are all supposed to be climbing the ladder of success or we are un-American. We are supposed to want to be president of U.S. Steel, and if we don't get there, which hardly anybody does, then we all have to feel we are failures. I mean being manager of Craven too. Then the next thing up, and the next, grunting and straining up and up and all the juice squeezed out of your life. Working as hard as you can all your life so you can be a failure, and be dead. I don't want to be a failure. I—"

"But I don't see what's wrong with wanting a nice life!" Maeve broke in. She hadn't listened. "And you can't do it on nothing!"

"You don't have any idea what I'm talking about."

"You're talking as though nobody but you wants to be happy. Do you think I don't want to be happy?"

"But we were happy just now and you want to change it! You think because we are happy together we ought to get married and settle down and start climbing ladders. I mean, you're willing to pass up present happiness—the real thing—for a phony raincheck on the future. Pie in the sky by and by is worth any amount of pie on the table, in other words. Why can't we just enjoy what's on the table now? I don't know what you mean by living a nice life, but I know living life isn't anything to do with nice houses and cars and better jobs. It's skiing down a place a little too steep that scares you, and making it. It isn't even as big a thing as skiing, or a Lovemaking Derby. It's having a cigarette while you're making love, or laughing, or—"

"A really dedicated skibum," Maeve whispered to herself.

"Why won't you *listen?*"

"Because you're just trying to make the way you are sound—"

"I'd think coming from that kind of religious background you'd understand," he interrupted. "Revolting against it, I mean. Because, can't you see, it's the same dirty trick? *Don't* live now so you can have a happy life with Jesus after you die. *Want* to die so you can be with sweet Jesus. Like wanting to be ugly so He'll love you more. And work like hell, all your life, up the ladder, so you can accumulate the money and the things that will make you happy at the end of all the working and climbing and accumulating. Only by then you've used up your life and you're dead."

Suddenly he was tired. Always, when he got on his horse, it ran away with him. "I'll tell you some more of the worthwhiles of life," he said. "Steak. And a baked potato with sour cream dressing and chives in the dressing. And wine—maybe a Cabernet Sauvignon."

"And salad?" Maeve said, making the effort too. "Is salad one of the nice things?"

"Certainly. Salad. Plain or fancy dressing?"

"Oh, I think plain oil and vinegar, don't you?" Maeve said, and they laughed, and almost it was all right again.

He lounged in one of the wicker chairs, watching her dress for dinner, make up her face, brush her hair. She wore a suit that resembled mattress ticking, and as she ran the brush through her short, bronze-streaked blond hair he admired the lift of her breast with the motion of her arm, the rich curve of her buttock beneath the striped material of her skirt, the sudden loose knot of muscle in her calf, the fine narrowness of ankle. Her high forehead, very tan from the spring sun, was marred by a small, circular scar, which she told him came from a fall on a tin toy when she was a baby. Her eyes were dark brown in her brown face, her nose short; her mouth, especially when she spoke, looked as though she were very conscious of the thin gold wire across her front teeth, or even as though it hurt her, as it must often have hurt. She had a lightness and a softness and a grace about her, but she no longer looked happy.

"You got class, baby," he said. It was a joke he and Elizabeth had had from reading Hemingway together, and he was pleased to see Maeve flush.

At dinner, with the steady frantic flow of headlights past the window on the freeway, she urged him into talking about his youth in Los Angeles, his mother and father, Stanford and Korea. Responding to her, to the steak and the wine, the coffee and the brandy, absorbed in her vivid-colored, soft-focus face, he began to wonder if, as he was convinced, happiness was the accumulation of the worthwhiles of life, might love also be? Was love a gazing into a face you thought beautiful through cigarette smoke, over brandy, with headlights fleeing past? Love, a sudden resolve to please more and more and more? Love, his knee touching Maeve's not even meaningfully? Perhaps, he thought, there was no actual boundary where, on one side, you were not in love and on the other you were, no gate you passed through, bridge crossed, intersection; only, finally, an awareness of being in a neighborhood where there were more trees and flowers and green lawns. He knew he was close to venturing further along this flowery street than he had ever done before.

"You must be very good to be this strong," he said, his knee pressed against hers.

"Can we go back to our room and talk about how beautiful I am?" Maeve asked.

"Right now?"

"Right now," she said, rising.

Inside the room, with the door closed and the one russet lamp burning over the bed beneath a colored photograph of the Golden Gate Bridge, he put his hands on her shoulders, pushing her back against the door. He braced his hands on the door, on either side of her head, and gazed into her eyes. He was breathing with difficulty and he was aware of her shaky breath. The tip of her tongue appeared, to touch her lower lip. There was a glint of golden wire. She closed her eyes when he kissed her soft, hurt mouth. She laid a hand without weight, formally, on his shoulder.

"Come and skibum with me, Maeve," he said.

"Yes," she said without opening her eyes.

"Do you mean it?"

"Yes," she said.

Excitedly he said, "And summers we'll go to Hawaii and surf and live on the beach."

"Yes," Maeve said gravely.

"And winters skiing the powder, and skiing the pack, and making love, and—"

"Yes," Maeve said, nodding.

He went on, talking fast and wildly, full of excitement and hope as he stared into the dark disks of her eyes, turned on him now while she listened and nodded almost absently to what he was proposing. He was aware that he was drunk with love and wine and tragically fooling himself, because the Crock could never be this easily defeated. And all at once he was aware that the hand on his shoulder had weight.

Maeve said, "If you wanted to be ski school director, how—"

"Oh, hell," he said, stepping back away from her.

"What's the matter?"

"Thought you loved me," he said with an effort to make a joke, with sickness running through his veins. "Thought you loved *me*, not what kind of job I could get."

"I do!" she cried. "Oh, damn it, you can't just—"

"Yeah, I can." He made a face, squeezing his eyes tight shut for a moment. Then he jerked loose the knot of his tie. "Come on, let's get back to bed. Talking's the bad part."

But they had not stopped talking, as each of them tried still to reach what was unreachable in the other. There were recriminations, raised voices, and tears, and hope leaked away. Once she tried to tell him in more detail what her life had been. She made it sound very like the months of gray, chill, horrified misery he had spent in Korea, when he had learned the absolute, ruthless senselessness of the Crock, the Reality-Principle, which, at war with life, made wars, which ruled the society of men through a deadly establishment of the old, the never-had-lived, wanting-to-die-but-afraid-to-die-alone old men, the youth-killers.

It seemed to him that Maeve, brought up in Visalia by the three old women who probably had been more stingy than actually poor, trapped in a religion even more joyless than the run-of-mill Protestant-Christian life-aborter, had learned a lesson that was both similar to the one he had learned in Korea and just the opposite.

"The eligible men are supposed to be found in ski resorts," Maeve said. "And I found you." She made an attempt at a laugh.

"I'm sorry you didn't find the person you wanted."

She said nothing, and he went on, "Maybe you'd've done better in a place like Sun Valley. If you're on the make." It sounded colder than he had intended.

"Maybe I would've," Maeve said, coldly too.

"This Macklin sounds like he's rolling in the true, the authentic, the only real source of joy."

"Who's Macklin?"

"Man I'm going to work for this summer. He's got heaps of the *stuff*. He's got a wife and kid though; too bad."

She didn't answer, and he didn't like what he had said. In the darkness he felt for her hand and pressed it, but there was no response. "What's your hurry?" he asked. "You've got a few years yet before you lose your looks."

"I can't waste time, can I?" Maeve said. "I have to get started living life, don't I?"

He made one last attempt at salvage. "Tell you what I'll do. When you've married Mr. Right, the dull, rich bastard, I'll sneak in your window sometimes and show you you're still beautiful."

She giggled almost hysterically. "Will you? That's romantic."

"Promise," he said. He lay holding her unresponsive hand that he did not want to let go yet. He could feel the weight of the column of darkness above him that extended to the limits of the atmosphere.

After a long time Maeve said, "It's been fun, but—do you know what I thought? I know it's silly now."

"What?"

"Oh, when you kept talking about our doing this, I thought we would fall in love this way. And we'd get married and you'd take the job working for Mr. Murray and then he'd go away next year and you'd be in charge at Craven. And you'd do a wonderful job because you are so much more intelligent than Mr. Murray and because you really want people to be happy and having a good time. And because I'd be helping you. Then you'd go on to a wonderful job somewhere like Sun Valley or Aspen, or a new place like Dancer. And we'd have—"

"I'm sorry," he interrupted. He didn't want to hear what they would have had.

"But you don't love me enough."

"I love myself too much. If you don't love yourself you can't love anybody else."

"You've got a theory about everything," Maeve said, "haven't you?"

He supposed that he had. He began to wonder if he were bound by easy rationalizations and juvenile pronouncements out of a college bull session. He tried to examine coldly his own dedication to himself, his life, his liberty, the pursuit of his own happiness, the First Personal Principle and the Present-Perfect tense. In his dedication to his own principles was he, as he had accused her, denying the true manifestation of happiness when it came? But he could not examine his principles coldly; they were himself.

He said, "Listen. When my father died he had spent his entire adult life doing exactly what he didn't want to do. Doggedly doing what made him miserable, was slowly killing him, what never had interested him. Probably most people spend at least a little time doing what they want to do. I think he spent almost none. Imagine going up before God or whatever It is that gave you this one life to lead, this *gift*, to tell him you hadn't enjoyed a minute of it. He'd feel the same way you would if you'd given a child a bicycle, a really beautiful red bike, say, the only bike he was ever going to have, and he wouldn't even learn to ride it. All he'd do was drag it around, scraping and banging, until it was ruined, and he was glad in the end to get rid of it because it was only trouble."

When he paused for breath Maeve said, "I don't believe in God."

"My father did."

Maeve said, "You're afraid to try to be a success at anything, so you have to say it's bad to be a success."

"I suppose that's possible."

She got up and went into the bathroom. When she came back neither of them spoke and there was no contact. He lay trying to sleep, but he was angry, bitter, and confused, questioning what he had long ago worked out to be the truth. He knew that Maeve was awake too, but there was nothing more to be said.

In the morning he drove her down to Visalia and let her off in front of a small, 1920-style shingled house with a brick wall around a garden in which stiff rows of rosebushes were visible through an iron gate. He watched her let herself in at the gate. A gray-haired woman in a gray cardigan came running to embrace her, and he crunched the gear lever into unsynchronized low and gunned the VW away from there.

Almost immediately he was on Highway 50 heading west. He

knew where he was going without making a conscious decision—
going to Berkeley to see Shelley Steinberg, the Guru, or maybe it
was to see Elizabeth Wagers, the Golden Girl. He had not seen
them since they had returned from the University of Chicago.

In a phone booth in a gas station in Berkeley he found the
number in the phonebook and dialed. Elizabeth's "Hello?"—a
voice he would have known anywhere, Southern-California-
drawled, Stanford-husky, Present-Perfect-pleased that someone
had phoned, rolled the years away. "Hello?" said Elizabeth
Wagers.

"Did you really kill Goliath?" he said. It was a line from a Bibli-
cal movie they had seen together.

"Clary!" Elizabeth cried. "Are you in town?"

"I'm here!"

"Come over! Shelley's got classes, but come right now!" She
gave him an address, directions, descriptions, admonitions to
hurry. But now he was feeling a curious reluctance to see her again
and he did not hurry.

"Wagers!" he said when she opened the door for him.

"Clary!" she said. She was all the warm shades of brown, rosy
olive-brown skin, reddish-brown slanting eyes, dark brown hair
drawn into a bun. Her face was so neatly, perfectly formed it
seemed made not of flesh and blood at all but of some new Southern California substance having all the good qualities of flesh but
none of the disadvantages. He had forgotten how short she was.
She wore a blue muumuu, and at first he thought she had let herself get fat, for she had always been a great lover of candy and
pastries. But when she threw her arms around him and he felt the
hard roundness of her belly, he realized with a shock of anger that
she was pregnant.

She kissed him and scratched his back and worried his ear lobe
between her teeth, growling. "Ah, Chuck Clary, you handsome,
skinny bastard!"

When she released him he patted her stomach. "How'd that
happen?"

"Well, it wasn't any goddam golden rain," Elizabeth said.
"Come in, come in!" She closed the door behind him and made a
sweeping gesture to indicate the room, which had grass matting on
the floor, a beat-up black sling chair, and a swirling abstract paint-

ing in the dining alcove, all violent reds, oranges, and yellows, like a solar explosion. There were books in stacks everywhere. On a round library table, which had been cut to coffee-table height and painted flat black, were a red ashtray, a sherry bottle, and two glasses.

"Sherry?" Elizabeth asked. "Shel won't let me have anything stiffer around." She looked at him over a round shoulder. "I'm a secret drinker."

"Drunk any good secrets lately?" he asked, feeling strain.

She grinned at a nice try. "As a matter of fact, I have. Being pregnant may be one of the worthwhiles. I may take it up."

"That's good!" he said. He sat in the sling chair, as she indicated he was to do. She picked up the cigarette that was raising a feather of smoke from the Chinese-red ashtray and stood, four-feet-ten-and-a-half-inches tall, squinting at him, cigarette raised not quite to her lips, left hand holding the elbow of the right as though the cigarette had great weight.

"Jesus, the beautiful life really agrees with you," she said. "Are you still playing?"

"The only real activity for the real man is play, if we're still quoting Sartre."

"We're not quoting him too much these days," Elizabeth said, seating herself on the windowseat opposite him. The sunlight through the window behind her gave a hazy golden outline to her head and shoulders. "Have you ever played with a pregnant woman?" she asked, pouring sherry into the two glasses.

"Not that I know of, no."

"Shelley says it's really good. Finish your sherry first, of course."

"I came down here for solace. I've just had an unhappy love affair. My second," he added and immediately wished he hadn't.

She gave him a long, unsmiling look. "Lucky you," she said. "I've just had the one." She took a deep breath. "You don't mean you want solace from Shelley? *That* goddam stuffed shirt."

He looked uneasily around at the stacks of books. Finally he said, "I guess the Guru went ahead and signed the loyalty oath. After—"

"Oh, the loyalty oath," Elizabeth said, gesturing with her cigarette, which dropped gray specks of ash on the rug. "Talk about snatching at gnats. Camels we've swallowed. We're middle-class! I go to tea with the faculty wives, buddy! We're married, did you know that? You didn't know it because we didn't send out any goddam announcements. As soon as he knew I was knocked up he couldn't get me downtown for a license fast enough, the bourgeois bastard. The Guru," she said with only half-humorous contempt.

She sipped sherry. "Ah, the good old days," she continued. "We all talked so good, didn't we? Even me. It was so lovely for me with you two philosophers who were going to be men of action and remake the dirty old world—in love with *me!* I loved it! Can we have it like that again? Why'd you have to go off to Korea and spoil it? And it wasn't silly either. The First Personal Principle. And the Schweitzer Second. We are in Third Personal, here, kind of. Shel wasn't ever in anything much else really, you know. Oh, but he was so great when he and you were working it all out. He was full of power. He's got a beard now, you know. It's as though everything that was inside him so powerful and clear—it really *was* clear—has come out on his face, and all it was was a lot of pubic-type hair. But he was great, wasn't he, Clary? Or was I just a stupid Stanford coed?"

"Certainly he was great. And you were great and so was I. Never been anybody like us. Those were the great days of our youth. You can't expect them to go on forever."

"Don't be a goddam hypocrite," Elizabeth said. "*You* do."

She raised her sherry glass before her left eye, squinting at him through it as though through a jeweler's monocle. "I see all things," she said. "I see you've hung in there and your soul's as big as a football field. You're still sticking to First Personal, aren't you?"

"More or less," he said. "Yes," he said, nodding.

"The beautiful life," Elizabeth said.

He nodded.

"Everything's always been so goddam easy for you," Elizabeth said.

There was a bad silence before she went on. "We're leading the life-ugly here," she said. She swallowed most of her sherry with one tilt of her head and changed the subject. "I remember how we used to jargon it up about infant sexuality and the mother's breast. Now I'm about to become a mother's breast."

"How do you feel?"

"All right most of the time. Sometimes I feel like an earth-mother and sometimes I just feel beat."

"A plaything of the Life Force."

"You know what? I may know more about the Life Force than you or Shel ever did, and I think it may not be so bad. It's been a good thing for me. I was getting pretty mixed up. Drinking. You know, it's all guano for Shelley, though he's tried, God knows. Are you in love with this girl, Clary?"

He shrugged, made a face, made a variety of gestures with his hands designed to get him out of answering directly.

"Did you ask her to come live the beautiful life as your mate, Tarzan?"

"She has a different definition of the beautiful life."

He could feel her antagonism and he wondered at it. Maybe it was because Elizabeth wished to be the one and only Golden Girl, or maybe it was because he had hung in there. She said in a dull voice, "Someday you're going to have to run up against the old Crock and get a nosebleed. Someday you have to, don't you?"

"I run up against it all the time. I have to make a living like anybody else."

"Someday," Elizabeth said. "My mother's dying," she added.

He remembered Mrs. Wagers, trim, tan, smiling, comically vague, standing in a tennis dress in front of the big white house in Pasadena. "I'm sorry," he said.

"She had a stroke," Elizabeth said. "Then she had a lot more strokes. She's lost her—faculties. She can't even talk any more. She's just going to die of a stroke any day, or month, or year. And she just lies there and knows it. Clary, I mean, that's the real solid iron *Reality-Principle*. You can say, sure, we've all got to die some-day, and go on saying it, and it doesn't mean a goddam thing. It just takes something like your silly old mother starting down the chute to make you realize it. I mean, not dodge it or fight it or anything but stand there and face it. We are so goddam shielded from death in this country."

"So you got pregnant," he said.

"Bright boy," Elizabeth said. "Pardon the somber notes," she said, widening her beautiful brown eyes at him. "Maybe I'm just a little jealous of the beautiful life, Clary. I guess the Crock must be

thinner up there in the mountain air. How does the Crock go?
The Judeo-Christian-Platonic-Finance Capital-Madison Avenue
Hammerlock?"

"You left out Life Force."

"I left it out on purpose," Elizabeth said. "Clary, why don't you
run down to the corner and get a fifth? I'll get sick if I go on
drinking sherry all afternoon."

He went out for a bottle of bourbon, and by the time Shelley
Steinberg came home they were both tight. Elizabeth had always
almost as a matter of principle drunk more than she could gracefully hold. The liquor acted as it was supposed to do, dissolving
stresses, strains, and old scar tissue. They complimented each
other's ironies, admired each other's wit, and trotted out private,
hilarious jokes from the time before Shelley Steinberg had come
into their lives, and before he had gone off to Korea for his lessons
from the Crock and she had begun her Life with Shelley for, it
appeared, hers.

Shelley came in wearing a stained gabardine topcoat and carrying an enormous brassbound leather briefcase. He stared unbeliev-
ingly at Clary; they leaped to embrace each other. Shelley had a
professorial smell of lint and pipe smoke.

"You welcome bastard!"

"Guru!"

There was more premature gray in Shelley's curly black hair,
none yet in his short black beard—a junior Assyrian beard. He
dropped his briefcase and kicked it under the table, grinning delightedly. "When did you come?"

"He's been playing with the baby's mother all afternoon," Elizabeth said.

"What's that, liquor?" Shelley said.

"I brought a fifth along. You'd better start saucing, we're way
ahead of you."

"I see you are," Shelley said, teeth white in his beard. He
rubbed his hands together. He had pale, lightly freckled cheeks
and an askew nose, like an old boxer, though the Guru had never
taken regular exercise of any kind, which was a paradox since the
physical figured so strongly in the philosophy the two of them had
hammered out that wonderful year before the Crock in the guise

of his draft board had flung him into Korea as though to prove to him forever that the principles he and Shelley had framed together were right and true.

They had resolved, almost as blood brothers, that as the very prologue of their explorations they would accept not one convention of society or civilization without a skeptical examination to make sure it was not a tentacle of the Life Force-Judeo-Christian-Platonic-Finance Capital-Madison Avenue Hammerlock, the Reality-Principle in disguise and sugared, which they had come to call the Crock; that marriage was such a convention, children such a convention, labor beyond that necessary for minimum subsistence such a convention; that the world was a pleasure garden or a sweatshop, whichever way you decided to have it, and to treat the world as your pleasure garden was the much more difficult course since it involved swimming upstream all the way; but it was only out of the pleasure garden that your own salvation could come, and so, ultimately, the world's salvation, since war was for the world of men what the death-wish was for individual men, and so the world was bound to kill itself unless saved by reclaimed individual men strong enough and pure enough. It was granted that the Reality-Principle had certain possible legitimate or anyway inescapable contentions in earning a living, in disease and death, and in certain more marginal but still impossible-to-dodge claims in the matters of the draft, drivers' licenses, and so forth that must be rendered unto Caesar; but anything more than the bare minimum offered the Crock was your own waste of your own life. The First Personal Principle was the life of your self—enjoying to the fullest the pleasures of the mind, the senses, and the body; the beautiful, simultaneously self-produced and self-consumed in pleasurable activity. There was a Second Personal Principle, which was a self-fulfilling service to humanity, the dedication of a self not whole or complete enough to sustain First Personal, to an outside agency, person, or persons, or even abstraction, though this principle was inherently suspect and must be engaged out of First Personal motivations and never from duty, guilt, flight-from-living-one's-own-life, etc. The Third Personal Principle was the beautiful life produced through contemplation and perfection of the whole system of defense against the Reality-Principle and Death-in-Life, and the dissemination of the Word. The Third Personal he, Clary, distrusted almost totally, smacking as it did of Platonic-Cartesian ascetics, but he had accepted it to please Shelley, who had an unfortunate tendency that way. Shelley celebrated the life of the body in lip service but, beyond being obsessed with going to bed with Elizabeth, had no real joy from skiing, tennis, swimming, surfing, or dancing, activities his disciple enjoyed much more than the mental or purely philosophical efforts—though that year, when he had been flunking out of Stanford and getting his education by exploring the Greeks, Schiller, Heidegger and Kierkegaard, Nietzsche, Sartre, and Freud, he had been a complete man as he knew he might never be again, filled with power as Elizabeth had said Shelley had been. He may not have had Shelley's power but he had been much more a complete man, for Shelley had never known how to enjoy the whole of the pleasure garden as he, Clary, somehow had known from the beginning. As Elizabeth had said, everything had always been easy for him.

Shelley had been his best friend and mentor, Elizabeth the girl he had loved off and on since junior high school, who had a facility for always reappearing in his life—until both of them had appeared in his life at once, and Shelley, the Jewish graduate assistant from Chicago, had fallen in love with the Golden Girl from Pasadena. Elizabeth had preferred them as rivals rather than friends, but he had never interfered in the affair that had developed between Elizabeth and Shelley. Stepping gracefully aside had been a debt paid to the Guru for the doors he had opened and the excitement he had brought, and to the anti-Semitism of the time, especially that of Elizabeth's parents. But he knew he had disappointed Elizabeth by refusing to be a rival for her favor.

"What was it today?" he said to Shelley. "The *Republic* to a section of freshmen? Idols of the cave?"

"Very close," Shelley said. He folded his coat over the back of a chair and sat down on the windowseat with Elizabeth. "How's the little old genito-urinary system?"

"Going like sixty," Elizabeth said.

Shelley patted her knee, grinning with teeth like white eggs nested in his beard. Shelley pointed his bent nose toward him, raising Elizabeth's glass. "To the beautiful!"

"To the Present-Perfect!" he replied more loudly than he had intended—with Shelley Steinberg he tended to wave his arms and overemphasize his natural exuberance. He felt that he was not welcome, that Shelley was not pleased he and Elizabeth had been drinking together and resented him. "To the new member of the group," he said, indicating Elizabeth.

For a moment Shelley looked as though he did not know what was meant. Then he grinned and patted Elizabeth's belly. "A little engagement with the Life Force," he said. "Trapped by the tyranny of the orgasm. Actually I believe in *coitus reservatus* as a principle, but just at quitting time I find nature at her most implacable."

Lighting a cigarette, Elizabeth watched the Guru as he continued, "There were many things in heaven and earth we didn't dream of in our philosophy, Chuck. For instance, what was once a minor footnote on children is going to have to be considerably expanded." He rubbed the back of his neck in a familiar mannerism, sighted along his nose, rested a hand possessively on Elizabeth's knee.

That was a familiar mannerism too; it was strange that during the intervening years he had recalled only what he had liked about the Guru.

He could give the Guru a good run on the subject of children, having argued the matter with a number of women who had tried to convince him a bachelor's life was unfulfilled and barren. But he had a premonition that the Guru was going to have to be superior and offensive because he was on the defensive, and it would be best to stay out of arguments.

"And how are you finding the view from the mountains?" Shelley asked.

"Fascinating sociologically," he said.

The two of them sat together on the windowseat watching him with similar, not-quite-hostile expressions.

"People have more money now," he went on. "More leisure. They don't have to spend all their time scrambling for subsistence. In a ski resort you can see the quandary they're in."

Shelley fished a cigarette from Elizabeth's pack on the table, frowning. "What quandary is that?" he asked.

"They feel they have to get out and enjoy themselves, the way they are supposed to be earning the money to do. Guilty if they're not living it up," he said and laughed. "But they don't know how. They have to be taught. They—"

"By you?" Shelley said, smiling. "What, into Second and Third Personal already? I thought you were the purist."

As always, when criticized, he first considered hitting the critic. Then he considered how necessary it must be for Shelley to catch him in error, Shelley who had fallen from the days of his greatness to signing the loyalty oath, to making a living for Elizabeth and her child and a career for himself teaching Plato, the enemy, to freshmen at the University of California.

"Got to keep preaching the Word," he said, managing to grin back at the two of them.

Shelley blew smoke, examining the cigarette between his fingers.

"Smoke 'em up, boy," Elizabeth said. "Whoops, you can quit again tomorrow." She rose and excused herself.

"Managing to keep all the skiing maidens happy?" Shelley asked when she had gone.

"Part of Second Personal, isn't it?"

"You really have it working for you, you lucky bastard," Shelley said.

A strain was gone. Maybe it had gone with Elizabeth. He grinned and said, "I don't think I ought to be discussing women with you, you're a married man. Anyway, sometimes I can teach people to enjoy themselves skiing. It's a satisfaction. Why don't you and Elizabeth come up and ski next winter?"

"We'd just break something, I'm afraid," Shelley said. "We are fragile city people."

They were silent for a time. He remembered that Elizabeth had been a fair skier in her college days. He said, "How's everything with you, Shel?"

"It's all right, I think," Shelley said quietly. "Liz hasn't been too happy. I don't blame her. For a while there the Crock jumped us every time we turned a corner. In Chicago, but out here too. It's better now. Everything is better since she got pregnant."

"You got married, she says."

Shelley looked ironically down his nose. "It didn't matter to us and it made her parents a lot happier." He laughed. "Though it was a terrible battle for her father. I pitied him, I really did. But he's happier with his daughter married to a Jew-boy than living in sin with one. Did she tell you about her mother?"

"Yes."

"Very tough," Shelley said, closing his eyes and shaking his head. "But Liz thinks it pleased her. And my mother is very much happier that her boy Sheldon is married. And I'm sure the Philosophy Department is happier. Everybody so happy about such a silly little ceremony! I signed the loyalty oath too, by the way."

"She told me."

"It was extremely amusing for a while there, the principles that were being trod upon. We were laughing? The oath doesn't matter any more, except that we'd made such an issue of it when it did matter."

He took a drink, nodding with pursed lips. He heard the tap of heels on bare floor, then muffled on carpeting. Elizabeth appeared, misshapen in the blue muumuu, shoulders back, belly out. "Shel, do you want to go out for chow mein or stay home and eat hamburgers?"

"Let's eat at home, Liz, shall we?"

"These are going to be Life Forceburgers actually," Elizabeth said.

When she had gone again he said to Shelley, "I came down to get my faith recharged, Dr. Frankenstein. Tell me I'm on the right track."

Shelley looked almost pitifully pleased. He blew smoke and plucked expansively at his beard. "Just remember never to look back," he said. "Something's sure to be following you, and you'll turn into a pillar of saltpeter. Problem?"

"Love."

"Remember the world is full of women," Shelley said with a false lightness. "As Elvis Presley once said, before the Crock got to him, why keep an apple tree when you can pick all the apples you want through the fence?"

He stared at the Guru and felt sick. Shelley looked on top of things now, nodding at his own wisdom and humor, holding up his cigarette and examining it with dramatic interest. His button-down collar was none too clean, his tie crookedly knotted.

"Oh, yes," Shelley said. "When I was young and full of juice I worked on the grand theories. Now I labor the small paradoxes

that trouble them. Take this common or so-called filter-tip cigarette. Let us try to grasp society's, the Life Force's, the Judeo-
Christian-Platonic-All American-AMA oriented-prescribed attitude
toward smoking, one of the most complex tiny problems to
confront us in many years. Is smoking death-wish or pleasure-
principle? Is guilt because we can't stop smoking the secret pleasure of the cigarette?"

So Shelley didn't want to be on a personal basis with him, and
maybe Shelley was right, maybe there was either too much to be
said or nothing. He felt as depressed and alone as he had ever felt.
He said, looking straight into Shelley's eyes, "Do you know what I
keep almost yelling at you?"

Shelley licked his lips. His fingers plucked nervously at his beard.
"What?"

"Why aren't you happy?"

The Guru fluttered his eyelids as though in recognition of a
serious charge. With dignity, with irony, he said, "Having won the
heroine is the hero responsible for her happiness forever after?"

He was shaken, as the Guru had always been able to shake him.
While he had been considering why Shelley resented him, Shelley
had been pondering the same thing about him.

"I'm afraid I made no such bargain," Shelley continued, smiling
like Rasputin. "Besides, maybe only the loser wins happiness."

In the silence Elizabeth's heels sounded again. From the
kitchen doorway she said, "One of you is going to have to go out
for a jug of red if any philosophers want to get stoned."

"I'll go," he said, quickly rising. "I need some fresh air."

"It's just around the corner," Shelley said easily. "At least the
Crock's not the only thing that's always just around the corner."

He went out and bought a gallon of red and came back. There
were jokes and laughter at dinner but nothing was said, and he left
early. He didn't see them again for several years, when they had a
house high on a hill behind Berkeley, with a barbecue in the back
yard, a pretty boy of almost four, and a fat-faced girl of eighteen
months. Elizabeth looked very well, but Shelley had put on
weight, lost his beard, and wore a sweatshirt with a Ban-the-Bomb
symbol on it. They watched the Forty-Niners play on TV, drank
beer, barbecued steaks, and talked about the campaign to end capital punishment in California, EPIC, with which Shelley was in-

volved, and civil rights, which was Elizabeth's particular interest. The old principles were never mentioned at all.

Maeve Olsen had come to work for Isobel Macklin at Dancer, and Macklin had noticed her in a remarkably similar situation to the one in which he, Chuck Clary, had come to notice her. When Macklin was killed she went off into the great world like a rocket. Her successes over the years were noted in the newspapers, as was her recent humiliation in Acapulco, which was so remarkably similar to her humiliation by Macklin. The lives of those he had known and loved seemed to him to have very short trajectories and did not end on the grace notes he would have projected for them.

4: Timbal Khan

TIM SODERBURG, CALLED Timbal Khan the Mountain Man, came down the mountain in the late afternoon on his scarred black skis. In his swift descent his heart was as close to singing as it ever came, with the speed, the smell of the air and the color of the sky, and the plumes of snow blowing from the cornices that told him a storm was coming in.

His skis rattled on ice, dragged on soft snow, the forward pitching damped in his knees by the unthinking, instant competence of his body. New snow was needed for Christmas; the old snow was turning to ice and wearing thin on the trails.

In his downward flight he watched for the crossed skis that marked an accident, checked on his mind's list the presence of his ski patrolmen, and kept a sharp eye to see if any fallen skiers were in trouble. He passed two ski school classes; one was making broad serpentine turns, the other half-mooned around an instructor. From a nearby knoll ski school director Hans Zimmerman, known as the Austrian Admiral, was monitoring the class.

Tim waved to Hansy in passing, a glove was flicked in reply— each of them checking on his skibums. Because the pay was low the patrolmen would quit and go bumming if they weren't permitted a certain amount of fun-skiing. The trick was to keep them on the ball just short of that quitting point. The Admiral's ski instructors had a little better stake than the patrolmen, but both he and Hansy had trouble finding responsible men. Sponsibles, Easy Clary called the skibums.

He flew down beneath the brown rock face of the Scarp. Here was the perfect position for the intermediate tower of the new gondola lift, but Badbody was against the idea of a gondola. Too much money, Badbody said.

He took the high traverse over to the Spoon, a long, fairly steep bowl that debouched in front of the lodge and was served by the Platterlift. The Spoon was badly moguled. Humps had been formed by the flow of skiers turning always at the same points, each day's traffic building the mounds higher and cutting the tracks between them deeper. A simple procedure with cat and blade would smooth out the moguls, but Badbody said no, it was unnecessary expense, it would snow soon, and anyway it was bad precedent for Dancer Peak Ski Area to assume responsibility for the trails.

He sideslipped fast along the top of the Spoon, surveying it. A girl in a blue parka and hood was bent over, round-bottomed, to latch a ski back on. Another girl followed a man down through the moguls, turning cautiously on top of each mound and slipping down the side. He swung with a lift out of his sideslip and started straight down the bowl, pulling up his knees to fly from bump to bump, hitting harder and harder, faster and faster, until the bounding was staccato and uncontrolled and he was speeding like a crazy man, schussbooming, All-Out Soderburg rocketing down the mountain with jackhammer legs. Blurred, startled faces peered at him as he shot past the man and the girl, and now there was the pleasant twisting of fear that came when he was out of control. The lodge and the flat at the bottom and the flagpoles and their flags hanging limp and the clustered planes and uprights of the bottom lift terminals and Big Red One bullwheel rushed at him, enlarging, and it was like coming down Exhibition on that Olympic-year downhill course at Sun Valley, the funnel at the bottom rushing at him just this way, he knowing he was hitting it much too fast, that he would never make that turn at the bottom where the lift tower was padded with bales of straw. "Goddam lucky you didn't break every bone in your body, boy," the doctor, who had seen him hit, had said. And so he was off the Olympic team with his splintered leg, when he had wanted so much to ski in the Winter Olympics and bring home a medal, hadn't he? Hadn't he? "A race that didn't even matter!" Rody had cried at him. "Of all the stupid things I've ever seen, Tim!" the coach,

Pete Schramm, had said, a little icicle of snot hanging from one nostril in the Sun Valley cold. "I ski all out, Pete," he had managed. "Well, you are all out now, for sure," Pete Schramm had said. All-Out Soderburg.

And his mind was on The Time J.D. Schussed the Spoon. Macklin had done what he had done to Maeve in front of all of them and walked away, and the only one of them not paralyzed, or maybe in the end not afraid of Macklin, was J.D. Daugherty. J.D. had come down the Spoon like a bowling ball toward Macklin, who was helpless and unmaneuverable on his skis at the bottom, J.D. yelling "*Track! Track!*" and people aware of what was going to happen and in horror of the meat-against-meat crash that seemed certain. J.D. had missed Macklin by inches, running over his skis; only J.D. had done something for Maeve. The real schussboomer, the real downmountain racer, had done nothing that mattered at all.

At the bottom of the Spoon his speed began to diminish, but he had enough momentum to carry him across the slow snow of the flat and up the Big Red One ramp, where a small knot of skiers waited to get on the lift. The bullwheel ground around, teeth slavering with grease, steel strands shining where the cable was worn. The new man, Digarmo, who was clipping tickets, gave him his wino's servile grin. Jack Bacon was helping skiers into the chairs that swung around the bullwheel.

"Just a minute," Jack said, arming back the couple next in line. "Ski patrol has priority." With a wink at him, Jack said, "Okay, Mr. Ski Patrol!" Disliking the fuss, Tim slid into position, Jack eased the next chair against the back of his legs, he sat. The chair bore him up and out, and he made a crossbar of his poles, leaning forward against them and drawing deep breaths of the lung-aching air as he looked, first, down at the dark trees and the bright colors of the skiers on their skis or sitting on the sundeck, and then up at the great white head of Dancer gazing down at the valley like a lover. He knew the features of that sheer face so well, the scalloping of snow on the dark vertical rocks, the long slanting fault like a scar. As he rose, the sun appeared for a moment in the clabbered sky, dazzling his eyes downward. Ascending, he felt himself relaxing, resting, felt peace, a kind of happiness.

The wildness of running at speed downhill, alternating with the rest of riding up again—was it all there was? Maybe it was enough, though he would like once more the importance and dedication of building a new lift, even bigger than Blue Two, even more difficult than Big Red One—a gondola or an aerial tram.

Up and up he rose in the shadowless, flat light, in the heavy chill of sundown, his chairhanger rattling over the sheaves at each tower; now he dipped down toward the Intermediate Station, where Hartman waved to him from inside the attendant's steamy shack, then steeply climbed once more.

Rody and her squad of junior racers were over on the Tasket, where colored bamboo poles were set up in a slalom course. One of the juniors, in a red sweater, was diving down through the gates. The smallest boy would be Stevie, Stevie Bliss, Rody's son by a downbelow schoolteacher he, Tim Soderburg, had never met. Rody with a son eight years old! Rody had been a junior racer herself such a little while ago, though when he counted the years they were not so few. He remembered her at the top, her top and the top of the Hahnenkamm downhill course, with fog on the lower part and ice all the way, Rody with her wax lips and her face working as though she were trying to keep it from freezing. He, still in his walking cast then, had kept kneading his fingers into her back, trying to get those knots, at least, untied, talking to her continually. Then she was stretched out in the starting gate, and the countdown, *"Drei, zwei, eins,* LOS!*"* and her muscular behind in sudden action as she poled and skated to get started, while he hung over the rope barrier to watch her down the steepest, slickest, roughest piece, yelling encouragement after her as she took the bad part at full bore, exactly the way he had told her she would have to take it. She had run the course just as they had worked it out, only Adele Franchet had done it a hair better. But a second to the best woman racer in the world in the Hahnenkamm was something, wasn't it? It was the best race Rody had ever run, but after that nothing had gone right for her, and now she was determined to see that Stevie made the Olympics when he was sixteen or twenty, see that he made it or kill him trying. She had always been the competitor he, Tim Soderburg, had never been.

Macklin humping her. "Now I know what it means to be ravished," Rody had said. And Macklin humping Maeve. Dancer Peak had punished Macklin totally. When he had found Macklin's body, the severe, handsome face had been crusted with packed powder snow.

He sat hunched in his chair, eyes closed, weakly hating, and waiting for the two faces of Dick Macklin to leave him, the goat face panting over Maeve and Rody, and the dead, cold face in the snow.

At the top he coasted off the ramp, zipping up his parka, forcing gloved hands through pole loops. He ran fast down the trail to the Tasket, knee-springing, loose, going to see Rody Bliss and Stevie. She stood at the bottom of the slalom course in her blue racing toque and black ski school parka, a little stockier than she had once been, skis braced apart as she watched Stevie weaving down through the gates in the well-worn rut, while four other boys sidestepped up again. Stevie came down very well, narrow-shouldering through a tightly set combination and driving low out of it more gracefully than he, the power skier, the gut skier, had ever managed. But Stevie drifted wide on the next gate and so hit the following one too low.

Rody yelled, "Stevie!"

Stevie zipped through the last gate and in a tuck shot down toward his mother, cutting to a stop just below where they stood. "Hi, Tim!" Stevie panted, his mouth sucking with his panting, his cheeks brilliant with color.

"You did the same thing *again!*" Rody said to Stevie. "You've got to get *down* on your skis so you can stay high there. You've got to stay *high!* Now go back up there and do it right!"

"Just lemme rest a minute, Mom!"

"Back up!"

Stevie looked at him with tears showing on his eyelashes but managed to grin and say, "Okay, Mom." He took two skipping sidesteps and started the long stump back up the slalom course.

Too tough, Rody! Pushing too hard, Rody! He remembered her bitter weeping over that second in the Hahnenkamm. He had tried to explain to her there was no way out of the fact that Adele Franchet on an ordinary day was half a second faster than Janet Rohde on her best day. Rody had never been able to understand that second meant she was better than everyone but the very best; she could only see that second meant someone was better than she was.

"Barometer's down," Rody said, turning her round, brown, poker face toward him. Once, long ago, Rody's face had always been in motion, always so responsive she had been kidded about it. Now, with him anyway, her face was composed, wooden, watchful; her after-Macklin face. Once All-Out Soderburg and Janet Rohde had been fellow racers on the circuit and had been at the same time best friends, companions, fellow-competitors, and two people in the cold cuddling together for warmth. Now they were only acquaintances with wooden faces when they spoke together.

"Stevie's looking really good," he said.

"He's all right. He's lazy though."

"We're all lazy, I guess."

"I don't want him to be lazy," Rody said, waving a pole to start the next junior down the course. "I think I can fix it for him to race a class up this year, so he won't be running away with everything." She megaphoned a hand to her mouth and yelled, "Tight! *Low* on your skis when you come out of there! Now step *up* if you're too low!"

He looked sideways at her intent pale eyes with the sun-wrinkles hatching out from the corners, remembering that summer when Rody had been at San Francisco State finishing work on her teaching credential, and he, working so hard at Dancer, had fallen totally in love with Maeve Olsen, all the brain and blood and bone of himself obsessed with Maeve. Rody had come to Dancer to take a job helping Badbody in the office just in time to see Macklin show him, Tim Soderburg, to be a tongue-tied, awkward coward. So Rody had been pleased to be ravished by Macklin.

After Macklin had died and Maeve had left, he and Rody had tried for a while to remake something where nothing could exist any more, and then, abruptly, Rody had left Dancer and gone downbelow, where she had married a schoolteacher named Bliss. A year or two later she had come back to the Sierra, divorced, with her hair cut short, her face turned to wood, and her baby. They had not tried again, but now she needed a man so she would not dry up as unmarried women were supposed to do, and, even more, needed a man to be father to Stevie, for she was bearing down on the boy too hard.

Rody finished talking to the junior who had just come down and gave him a swat on the bottom to start him up the hill again. She was no tougher on Stevie than on the others, but the others were all two, three, four years older.

"I guess you're glad to have Christmas vacation for a while," he said.

"Right!" Rody said. "A really bad third grade this year, mean little brats." Her lips bent into a grin. "And how's your ski patrol?"

"Not too bad this year."

She gestured for the next racer to start. Sometimes, as now, there would be the illusion that he and Rody were having a conversation, but how could they talk for even these few minutes without speaking of their Cope Joint Union High School days, or the Cope Ski Club Junior Ski Team, or of the Junior Nationals the year he and Rody had been the twin hopes of the Sierra, of the Roch Cup at Aspen, the Olympic tryouts, and that season in Europe? After he had broken his leg, money had been found for him to accompany the Olympic team, and he had gone to Europe as, instead of the star downhill man, Rody's private coach, waxer, repairman, errand boy, and emotional stabilizer, but none of those old times could be mentioned because that autumn at Dancer nine years ago, the time of Dick Macklin and Maeve Olsen, could not be mentioned, and they could not really talk together because always Dick Macklin and Maeve stood between them; and so all the past was concealed behind secret faces and short, unallusive sentences, and the present consisted of an uneasy relationship in which he was invited to dinner at her house every month or so, and once or twice a year he would take her and Stevie to the steak house in Cope. These were trying, cautious times when they made much over Stevie because they had little to say to each other, for they could have no reminiscences.

Stevie came down the course again, and it seemed to him the boy had done everything right. "That's a damn good run and you ought to tell him so," he blurted as Stevie, skis apart, bunched himself in a tuck for the last schuss.

Rody gave him a glance that glinted like lightning out of the pale circles of her eyes. He tried to turn it aside. "I was a coach too, remember!"

"You were too easy," Rody said as Stevie cut to a stop with a spray of snow.

"Hey! Pretty good run, huh, Mom?"

"That was a pretty good run," Rody said.

"You were really moving there, Stevie," he said.

"Pretty good!" Stevie said. "It was *really* good, Mom!"

"Back up on top and let's see you do it again."

"Just lemme rest a minute! I been going up and down like a yoyo!"

Rody made a quick movement of her head. Stevie didn't look back as he started the long climb again.

"I guess I shouldn't butt in," he said, clearing his throat. Rody's expressionless eyes gazed into his. What did they see, looking at Timbal Khan the Mountain Man? "Too tough on him, Rody," he said. "Sure you want him to be in the Olympics. But what good is it if you make it so tough he can't stand the sight of you by then?"

"He'll thank me," she said calmly. "He's a competitor, don't think for a minute he isn't."

"Sure he is. But—"

"You weren't a competitor so you wouldn't know," Rody said. "You were just a wild man. You just came down the mountain fast because you got a kick out of it, not because you loved winning."

"Yeah, but—"

"Beating everybody else," Rody said. "That's what you get your kicks from if you're a competitor."

He examined the quality of her contempt. He licked his lips. "There's this thing I've learned running the ski patrol, Rody. If you work them too hard they'll quit on you."

"He'll never quit on me!" Rody said. There was a splintering sound of pride in her voice. She raised her pole and brought it down. "Okay, Bobby, hit it!" she cried, and the biggest of the boys started down, all reversed shoulders, flung-out arms, and awkward eagerness.

Timbal Khan the Mountain Man said, "Well, I'll see you, Rody," and, stretching his arms to dig in his poles, started himself on the last run down the mountain to check on his domain. He was never through checking and watching and worrying—no sponsible, he—to make sure everything did not start going wrong the way it had all gone wrong the day Dick Macklin had died.

At the lodge for a cup of coffee before the scouring of the mountain after the lifts had closed, his parka unzipped, heavy-striding in his unbuckled boots, he brought his hot paper cup out on the sundeck to sit with Badbody and the Admiral.

The Admiral was sipping tea in the continental style, as though the rules called for one elbow on the table at all times. ". . . ski instructors, no good lazyheads," he was saying, looking like a bad-tempered bug in his curved yellow glasses. "Only want to ski, talk pretty girls, more money. In Arlberg—"

"I know what you Nazis did in the Arlberg," Badbody broke in, raising his beer glass. He had crisp, graying hair and amused eyes behind solemn black-rimmed glasses. "Well, I'm sorry, but you cannot shoot lazyhead instructors here. The State Division of Employment people would be on our necks in a minute." Badbody winked gravely at him.

"Nazis!" the Admiral said. He got to his feet, ponderous and bowlegged as a bulldog. Scowling ferociously, he pulled up his sweater, shirt, and undershirt to reveal a hairy white belly decorated with four deep-set navels. "I show you what Nazis have done!"

"I understand you've been telling young ladies those are American-made perforations and when they sympathize demand a reciprocal accommodation," Badbody said. "Pull down your shirt, you hairy kraut!"

The Admiral sat down again, reunited his elbow with the table, and sucked tea; his expression, after the bout with Badbody, was pleasanter.

"Everything trim with the ski patrol?" Badbody asked.

Tim nodded, swallowing a mouthful of hot, sweet coffee. Glancing sideways at the Admiral, he said, "No good ski patrol only want to ski, talk pretty girl, more money."

The Admiral smiled, purse-mouthed. Badbody snorted. "Where *are* all these pretty girls?" Badbody asked. "I see only the usual bad-posture secretaries and airline hostesses with pancake makeup and pancake busts. In the Great Past Time the girls were all lovely and nubile, and the ski instructors supermen who undertook to fulfill every one, never a lonely secretary known to leave Dancer without a romantic memory. Now it seems to me the instructors think only of more skiing and especially of more pay, giving insufficient weight to the fringe benefits. And the ski patrol too. I don't mean to slight your fine though more rough-cut fellows, Tim. Ah, the Great Past Time," Badbody said.

The Admiral, having finished his tea, groused unintelligibly and took his leave.

"The Admiral has taken to carrying his money in the seat of his pants," Badbody remarked, looking after him.

"What're you going to give for Christmas bonuses this year, Badbody?"

"Same as last year, I'm afraid."

"No more?" He started to argue it, pointing out that at least two of his men would quit, but Badbody said they would probably quit anyway, taking more Dancer Peak Ski Area money with them, and it was possible that Badbody was right.

After Macklin's death, Badbody had taken over the management of Dancer with a real grip, and all of them who had looked upon him as only a yes-man were surprised at how sure of himself and go-ahead he became. After those first seasons of shaking down and consolidating, Badbody had seen that a new lift was needed up the Big Top and had got Macklin's widow Isobel to put up the money for Blue Two and for the new wing on the lodge. For a long time, then, everything had gone well, but now it was time to get moving again, to put in a gondola or at least another double-chair lift, and another addition on the lodge, to buy another Snocat and a new rotary, and extend the parking areas. But more and more now it seemed that Badbody said no without even thinking a suggestion over; more and more he seemed afraid to take chances. He had become a terrible tightwad. The Area was making money, times were good, skiing was booming as a sport, but it was impossible to squeeze any better wages out of Badbody. So each year the seasonal people that could be hired were a poorer bunch than last year, and each year the skiers who put out the money for a lift ticket got a little less for it.

Badbody was watching him with an eyebrow raised, pale-faced and pink-cheeked in his black turtleneck sweater and sheepskin coat. His fingers tapped his glass. "I had a phone call late last night asking for accommodations over Christmas," he said. "I managed to make some space too. Can you imagine for whom?"

All the rooms at the lodge were reserved for the Christmas holidays at least two months ahead. He named illustrious names, but Badbody only shook his head.

"A Mrs. Herron," Badbody said finally.

For a moment it meant nothing. Then it was as though his face, catching fire, understood before he did. Herron was the producer Maeve had been married to for a while in Hollywood. His face burning, he leaned back in his chair, stretching his neck where his shirt felt too tight, while Badbody gazed at him with an interested smile.

"Oh, Maeve, huh," he said.

"Asked about you. I told her you were on top of the mountain in all senses of the word. She asked about all the Great Past Timers."

"You've got room for her, huh?"

"I found that a foolish Bay Area millionaire had not followed his reservation with a deposit, as per instructions. It is to be hoped he is not a dear friend of Mrs. Macklin's." Badbody rocked forward slightly and touched an extended forefinger to the bridge of his glasses. It was one of a number of Badbody mannerisms that he considered fruit but harmless.

"Said she would be staying indefinitely," Badbody continued. "In the end everyone comes back to Dancer. And if that is so, why leave in the first place? Though of course Maeve's departure was very dramatically motivated." In a different voice he said, "A little perturbation of the spirit, Tim?"

"Huh?" he said, pretending he had not understood what Badbody meant. He was searching for Maeve's face in his memory's eye, but he could find no more than a hazy, blond, featureless outline. Maeve was coming back. He said it to himself.

"She said she would be glad to stay in the dormitory if we couldn't fit her in anywhere else," Badbody went on. "But that wouldn't have done."

"I guess not," he said.

"A celebrity," Badbody said. "I remember seeing her referred to once as an ex-starlet. A nice distinction. Have you noticed how the term Mariachi Girl, which at first was a kind of snicker, is losing its original connotation and taking on an exotic quality? Our Maeve."

He nodded without understanding. All he understood was that the careful balances and compensations that held his life together were in danger.

"It's time she came back to Dancer," Badbody went on. "After all, Dick Macklin gave her her start."

"What?" he said. "How do you mean?"

"I'm not sure how I do mean, now that you mention it," Badbody said. Fingers spanning his glasses, he drew them away from his eyes, squinting foolishly in the failing light. He replaced them. "Did Dick provide her impetus by embracing her or by relinquishing her?" Badbody said.

"By dying," he said.

Badbody looked shocked.

"See you, Badbody," he said and, crumpling his paper cup, rose. It was time he went back up the mountain for the sweep, but instead he headed inside toward the bar. The ski patrol could make the end-of-day check to see that all the skiers were off the mountain without him this once.

Pushing his way through the crowd talking and laughing around the bar, he saw Easy Clary with Martha Schroeder hanging on his arm and looking up at him the way women always looked up at Easy. He managed to squeeze up to the counter between the window and a man in a red sweater who was talking to a tall girl with an aerated hairdo. He ordered a draft beer.

Smitty the bartender brought his beer and the chit. "Going to snow, Tim?" Smitty asked.

"Feels like it."

"Sure need some snow," Smitty said, wagging his head.

He grunted. Maeve would be bringing the snow with her. Perturbation of the spirit, Badbody had said. "Well, take it easy," he said to Smitty, hoping he would go away.

"Hah!" Smitty said, leaning on the counter. "We'd better all be taking it easy because tomorrow they start packing in for Christmas and there'll be no rest for the wicked for a while." He turned, did a doubletake. "Hey! Who's making the sweep?"

"Frank," he said, and Smitty went to attend to other customers.

He drank his beer too fast, and it was as though some stricture in his throat kept the liquid suspended there. He wiped foam from his lips and glanced around at the faces hanging like balloons over the bar. Some he knew by name, others he recognized from the mountain. Near the grand piano stood a Christmas tree sprayed with silver so that it looked made of plastic. But it was a real tree. He had cut it over in the Badlands, dragged it up to the shoulder of Dancer, and schussed the Superchute and the Chute, dragging it behind him.

Outside the window the Big Red One bullwheel turned, chairs sailing empty down the line, swinging around, ascending. There was no reason Frank Dow couldn't make the sweep as well as he could. It was only a matter of knowing where to look, like an Easter Egg hunt. They didn't find a person a year—last year the girl behind the tree with a concussion. Dick Macklin, hard-mouthed, talking to him about how he had to learn to delegate authority and not try to do everything all by himself—well, he was delegating the sweep tonight, and he was going to sit on his bar stool drinking beer and thinking about Maeve, or else trying not to think about Maeve. It had been bad enough last night with that song of John Henry's on the jukebox in the Loup Garou. How was he supposed to act when Maeve came back? He had always acted with Maeve, always pretended to be the person she thought he was. But now maybe he didn't have to pretend any more, because he had actually become Maeve's rough-cut old bear, Timbal Khan the Mountain Man.

"Hi," Rody said, appearing beside him. She had her parka slung over her shoulder. "You're here in the bar gone to hell, are you?"

"I was just going up for the sweep," he said.

"Want to come for dinner?"

"Well, sure! When?"

"Seven or seven-thirty. We won't eat till I get Stevie in bed."

"I'll be there." He gulped the last of his beer. "Well, I'd better be moving," he said, sliding off his bar stool.

He left the bar. Perturbation of the spirit meant pure terror at having to face all the things in himself that would come untied when Maeve came back. Maeve's particular demands on him were now confused in his mind with Janet Rohde Bliss cracking the whip over that small, lithe, tough, defenseless boy, and Rody asking him for dinner with the knowing, not-quite-contemptuous look in her pale blue eyes.

Loading into a chair on Big Red One, waving a hand at Jack Bacon inside the shack, he told himself he wasn't going back up the mountain because he couldn't delegate authority. He could count on Frank to make the sweep before dark if he had to. What was it then? It was that he felt safer on the mountain, at home on the mountain—on top of the mountain in all senses of the word, Badbody had said. Tense in his chair beneath the solidified sky, he tried to recapture the almost-happiness, the almost-peace, but this time it would not come, and his mind skittered like grease in a pan. He leaned back in his chair, stretching, relaxing tight muscles, feeling the coming snow heavy in his sinuses. He gazed up at the head of Dancer above him, taking great breaths of the freezing, fragrant air, and he began to think about the old Maeve, the make-believe Maeve, not the one who was coming back to Dancer.

When he thought about the Old Bunch, those Badbody called the Great Past Timers, it seemed to him that they were a larger race than those same people, Badbody and Easy Clary and J.D. and even himself, grown nine years older.

He had come to the Dancer Peak Ski Area through his job with Barney Skinner, the contractor who had gone bankrupt putting in the Big Red One lift, the swimming pool, and the lodge. Along with Joe Cunningham, Barney had early in the game been enchanted by Dick Macklin's plans, enthusiasm, charm, and money, and early, too, had been disenchanted and ruined.

Barney Skinner had been quite a man himself. It was funny to think that Barney had viewed Macklin as a greenhorn and an easy mark, and how shocked Barney must have been to realize that Macklin had outsmarted him. Easy Clary and John Henry had also worked for Barney that summer. Badbody was part of the Macklin operation, as was Maeve, whom Isobel Macklin had hired away from Craven. Isobel Macklin, they had all found out later, besides being the general secretary-treasurer, the commissary department, interior decorator, mother and wife, was the financier. Even Badbody was her cousin. Macklin, who had seemed so completely in control, was only the plans, enthusiasm, and charm who had married Isobel's money. All this was not realized until after Macklin's death.

Everything at Dancer that summer and frantic fall had been connected. Everyone had worked for and with everyone else; they had all lived in one another's laps and in the middle of one another's lives, moving physically closer for warmth as cold weather came and the Social Hall of the old Northern California Thermal and Outing Club was partitioned into rooms. The T & O Club had flourished at the time of the First World War as the lavish camp of a group of San Francisco tycoons who came to Dancer Valley on a special spur track laid for them by the railroad, to bathe in the hot springs, fish, hunt, play cards, and enjoy girls sent over from Nevadaville. Joe Cunningham had bought up the T & O holdings at a tax auction, Joe and Dick Macklin had formed a partnership that somehow was later dissolved, with Joe Cunningham squeezed out, and the Dancer Peak Ski Area, Inc., had ended up with everything.

A number of the T & O buildings had still been standing, eight log cabins and board-and-batt houses, all roofless and broken down in varying degrees. The cabins were roofed with corrugated iron to house carpenters, laborers, and others. The two largest structures, the Social Hall and the Big House, had survived almost intact. The Social served as dining room and kitchen. The Macklins— Dick, Isobel, and Dickie, who was fourteen then—took up residence in the two-story Big House. While the major phase of the construction was going on, a number of house trailers were brought in for Barney Skinner's equipment operators, complete with wives and a few children, but gradually these disappeared, and in September, when Macklin and Barney Skinner had their blowup, only the Great Past Timers remained.

A payment on Barney Skinner's contract had come due, and Macklin refused to make it on the grounds that the lift towers had not been put in according to specifications. Everyone knew this was true, but everyone thought Macklin was going along with Barney's corner-cutting. Obviously Barney had thought so too. Macklin also claimed that although Barney had completed the nonessential swimming pool, he was far behind schedule on the essential first unit of the lodge. There had been a great deal of drunken shouting on Barney's part, and gunning of his Jeep with its broken muffler up and down the valley road; then abruptly he departed and was never seen again. It was rumored that he had run out on a bond and fled to Mexico, that he was in jail, that he had gone bankrupt and was working for a house-moving outfit in Lincoln, Nebraska.

With the departure of Barney's crew, and the nights growing colder, they had all moved into the Social, which was heated, a rectangular building of pine boards weathered as delicately gray as spiderwebs, with rusty tin-can-lids tacked over the knotholes and "Social Hall" in faded but still handsome curlicues over the front door. Inside, part of the dining hall was converted into a common room, with couches, captain's chairs, and a ping-pong table. There was a large kitchen with blue-and-white linoleum on the floor where deaf, drunken Al Finney held sway. The sleeping quarters were squares made of eight-foot-high sheets of plywood that furnished only visual privacy.

Those months of building Big Red One were the most important of his life. When the finishing of the lift became his job, the lift towers were up, but the sheaves had not been installed or the cable hung. The top, bottom, and intermediate stations had not been built, and four of the towers were on a bad slope where the first avalanche would knock them out, even though Barney had bulldozed mounds of earth which he thought he had convinced Macklin would serve as avalanche deflectors just as well as the concrete abutments the contract called for.

Macklin did not want to spend the money to put in those concrete deflectors after Barney was gone. Tim argued and fought with Macklin, insisting that they had to be there, and he prevailed. His crew consisted of Easy Clary, John Henry, and a tobacco-chewing Southerner named Rufus Billings who quit somewhere along the line to be replaced by J.D. Daugherty. The four of them poured concrete, built the top and bottom stations, installed sheaves and hung the cable, and then John Henry and J.D. went to work on the Platter while he and Easy hung chairs and started work on the Intermediate Station. The lodge, though far from finished, was fortunately roofed and closed, and Macklin, Isobel, Badbody, and Maeve worked in the lodge with a couple of non-union carpenters who came in from Erskine every day.

Maeve was Isobel Macklin's Girl Friday. She helped Isobel

paint, drove Dickie to school in Cope every morning and bought the groceries, made a second trip in the afternoon to the lumber yard and hardware store and to pick up Dickie, ambulanced the carpenter who skilsawed his finger to the doctor in Erskine, made the trips to the air freight office at the airport for vital lift parts. Isobel called her Maevie.

"Maevie I'm in love with you!" to the tune of "Maybe I'm in Love with You": he did not remember if he had made it up in his own mind or if it had been one of the funny songs Easy and John Henry sang evenings in the Social. The "I" wasn't specific, for they had all been in love with Maeve, even the drunken cook Finney, even J.D. in his sullen way. Everyone loved Maeve, with her freshness and her eagerness, and her bright hair and face— except, at the end, Macklin.

Maeve's room was next to his in the Social, and at night they whispered together through the plywood partition. "Bear?" she would call softly in the darkness in which he had been waiting. "Are you asleep, Bear?"

"No." He would have been lying on his cot, aching with exhaustion but fighting sleep and listening to Maeve undressing and for the final creak as she got into her cot. Perhaps in the common room Easy, J.D., and John Henry would still be talking, or John Henry strumming his guitar and singing. In his memory the sounds of Maeve undressing and getting into bed and finally her longed-for query, "Bear?" were always set to the background chording of "Birmingham Jail," or "John Henry," or "Careless Love," or "On Top of Old Smoky"—and no fancied-up versions that John Henry Collins made in Hollywood would ever compare to those songs sung in the common room of the T & O Social.

"Did you have a good day, Bear?"

"Pretty good. Pretty tired."

"You work twice as hard as anybody else."

"Pouring concrete's the hardest kind of work. Just when you think you have a minute to rest there comes the ready-mix truck with another load. And then you have to fight Macklin for every dime!"

"I know something," Maeve whispered. "I don't think there are many dimes left. Don't say a *word!*"

"I won't."

"I heard them talking about it today. They can't borrow any more where they've been borrowing it."

"Well, we can make it if the snow will just hold off. If there's early snow this year we're sunk."

Hers was the corner room, and next to him slept Al Finney, who drank himself into a stupor every night and slept without his hearing-aid anyway. He could hear Maeve's covers rustling. They were alone with only a quarter-inch of plywood between them, and he played Omar the Tentmaker whenever he heard her moving in her bed.

"If they can't meet the payroll again this week people're going to start quitting, aren't they?" she said. "Why do you suppose somebody like—oh, say, Easy Clary—why doesn't he quit? Someone like Easy can't like working twelve hours a day and not even getting paid."

"Oh, nobody's in it for the money. We want to see the lift built. The operation go," he added, for he was embarrassed to try to tell her how important it seemed to him that the lift be finished.

Maeve said, "Everybody's so loyal to Dick Macklin. It must be something great generals have—kings, I mean. Something that makes everybody loyal even when—like Napoleon."

"He's a little Napoleon, all right," he said. "I'm not loyal to him. I'm just loyal to—just to getting it all *built*. In a way that lift has got to be just as much mine as Dick Macklin's."

Again he was confronted by the impossibility of putting what he felt into words. He knew what Clary would say. Easy Clary would say he got his kicks out of working for something that was going to give a great many people a lot of pleasure. Clary thought skiing was one of the best things life had to offer; God's Second Greatest Gift, Easy would call it, when tight.

But skiing did not seem that important, nor was he that unselfish about wanting to provide for the pleasure of others. He thought that, in a way, the building of Big Red One meant to him what the U.S. Marine Corps had always meant to his father— something outside of and bigger than himself—like religion. And there was the mountain itself. From the beginning he had felt the pull of Dancer Peak; from the beginning he had had an ease and

competence in everything to do with the mountain that he had
never had anywhere else.

"No, you're loyal to Dick Macklin too," Maeve said. "I've heard
you arguing with outsiders on his side. And Isobel's so loyal to him
even though he"—her voice dropped—"says terrible things to her
sometimes."

"What kind of things?"

"*Terrible* things. Once I was going in the door and I heard
them fighting. First I thought Isobel was *singing*. But she was crying, and then I heard him saying these things. I tried to sneak out
again without their knowing. Dickie was sneaking away too, poor
kid. Did your parents fight, Bear?"

"They sure did! They threw things at each other. Once my father threw a pair of pliers and hit my mother in the stomach."

"Oh! That's terrible!"

"I threw up," he said. "When they'd fight like that—I mean,
hitting each other—I'd always throw up. So they'd stop."

He heard her moving, and Omar roused again.

"My parents never fought," Maeve said. Then she said, "You
pass my door, you pass my gate."

"Pardon?" he said, then realized that down in the common
room John Henry was playing "Careless Love," and Maeve was
singing. She sang:

> "Pass my door, you pass my gate,
> But you won't get past my thirty-eight."

Abruptly she said, "Are you ambitious, Bear?"

He shook his head at himself. "I guess not," he said. From time
to time he had daydreams that he supposed had to do with ambition, but as he had never enjoyed beating other competitors racing,
so he could never picture himself in the even more personal competition of trying to be somebody. He had had a job downbelow
for six months as assistant dispatcher for the Harrigan Trucking
Company. He had been no good and knew it, and then that little
bastard Johnson, hands on hips and red-faced, yelled at him about
something that hadn't even mattered. So he had quit, for he had
realized that the world of ambition, like the world of competition,
was dominated by little men like Don Johnson, like Pete

Schramm, and like Macklin too, who could talk faster, say what they meant, cut and slash with words, unafraid because they knew big men were too cautious of their own strength to hit them.

In the end it had been a terrific relief to return to the mountains to work on construction projects and with heavy machinery, which he understood and did not fear, and finally to go to work as a bulldozer operator for Barney Skinner at Dancer.

"It's just that there are so many wonderful things to do in life," Maeve said. "Oh, I don't mean *things*, but all the places there are to go, Europe and the Riviera, and parties and cafés and the theater. I'm ambitious to do all those things, not just ski. I suppose because I want to so much I can't understand that other people might not want to, too."

"Well, Maeve, you're smart and you can do anything, and everybody likes you. And you're so—good-looking. But some others of us can only do a few things well, and we're not going to get by on our looks. Haha!"

"Oh, haha to you! You're a handsome old Bear and you know it."

She was silent for a long time after that, and he lay straining to keep his heavy eyelids open, trying to think of some topic that would interest her so she would not go to sleep just yet. John Henry's guitar still chorded softly.

"Maeve?" he whispered.

"Yes, Bear?"

"What are you thinking about?"

"Oh, I was thinking about Dick Macklin. He's going to make millions out of Dancer, isn't he? He and Isobel. And nobody else is going to make anything at all, but we are all working so hard for him."

This was true, but it didn't matter much. Macklin wanted the money and the power or whatever he was going after, and probably he would get it. But he, Tim Soderburg, did not want money, he only wanted to scratch a hole in the hard, shiny surface of the world that he could occupy, and he had found it here. He started, jerking awake after dozing off.

"Good night, Bear," Maeve whispered.

"Good night, Maeve," he said and let his eyelids close.

All those nights he and Maeve had talked together through the plywood wall, and he couldn't really remember much of what had been said; just as, the years passing, he could no longer recall her features. What he remembered most about those nights was the mood, a campfire and sweetly, languorously erotic mood, with the guitar in the background. A few times Maeve had come into his cubicle, but they had not been able to talk so freely then as they could through the plywood partition.

Rody had come to work for Badbody in October, but she lived with her mother in Cope and drove her old Chevvie back and forth every day. She came to the Social only once in a while, when there was a party.

By Thanksgiving it had still not snowed and most of the work on the mountain was completed. The stations and ramps on Big Red One were almost ready, the Platterlift far enough along so they could finish it with snow on the ground. A few days after Thanksgiving came the first snow, a foot on top and a few inches around the lodge, where it melted off in a day. Then came a very late Indian summer with hot sun and the barometer high. The swimming pool, which could be made warm by pumping in water from the hot springs, was allowed to cool off again. They began to worry that there would not be snow for Christmas.

On a hot Sunday afternoon a beerbust was organized on the mountain. Some of them walked up to get ski legs in shape; others rode in the Jeep pickup with the beer, hotdogs, and buns. Isobel Macklin had not come along, being a little too stiff-necked to mix with the troops. They drank the half keg of beer and had a fine time with singing, horseplay, and jokes, and Macklin relaxed and was his old quick-witted, charming self. It was after dark and turning cold when they started to leave, only to find that the pickup had a flat tire and no spare. So they trooped down the mountain together, and that had been the best part of the picnic, the stumbling, laughing descent in the dark, with Macklin's jokes and Maeve's clear laughter, and Clary and John Henry making up verses to a song about everybody walking down the mountain in the dark, breaking their legs one by one, and two by two, and three by three.

It was very chilly coming down the mountain, and at the bottom someone had a bright idea and they all began to run, heavy-footed and shouting with excitement, for a swim in the warm water of the pool. He could remember everything with pleasure still, to this point. The day had been full of the special magic of those building-of-Dancer days, so many of which were the pearls of effort and satisfaction and even of joy that Easy Clary said you had to capture and crystallize by realization so as to make them yours forever, until you had a string of such pearls, which was the aim and purpose of your life. The beerbust had been such a pearl, and the hike down the mountain after dark a great pearl; then the inky gleam of water, the stripping of dusty clothes, the pale, shivering bodies dimly visible, the splashing and the laughter.

When they began coming out of the water to get dressed, someone had turned on the underwater lights.

The pool glowed with the blue-green phosphorescent magic of sudden color. Alone in the steaming water was Maeve, swimming on her back with foam caught like jewels in her hair and along her gracefully moving arms and legs. Bubbles spread in a wake behind her.

She swam a moment longer, then turned and dove, and finally huddled against the side of the pool, laughing. In that moment of seeing her he had flung out his arms as though to protect her from all the other eyes.

But of course Macklin, who had been standing not far from him, shirtless and shivering, with his pants pulled half on, had seen her. They had all seen her. But it was Macklin, of course it was Macklin, who had made the long, slow, sucking sound of indrawn breath. Did Macklin, as someone had joked later on, look at her with the expression of Balboa first viewing the Pacific Ocean? He hadn't noticed how Macklin had looked at her.

But within two weeks Isobel Macklin had left for Hawaii to get money, and the night Isobel left, Macklin summoned Maeve into his bed.

5: Badbody

HE DID NOT SKI any more, and in the failing day he sat in his office watching through the window those who did. He watched them with contempt, the contempt still softened with amusement because the season was young and they had not yet begun to threaten him. By the end of the Christmas holidays, strongly with him would be the obsession of how peaceful, good, and secure a kingdom Dancer would be without these hordes of invaders.

He shook his head to see a skier totter and ungracefully, dangerously, fall on the runout of the Bunny Hill, and another, grotesquely crouched, schussing out of control through the end-of-day skiers, miraculously not ramming anyone. Two others had stopped, chatting, at a point where they most incommoded traffic. Amid the moguls on the Spoon were crossed skis marking an accident, and a patrolman with a toboggan was picking his way down through the shadowed bumps.

Even to appear here these people had spent many hundreds of dollars for skis, bindings, and poles, for stretchpants, sweaters, parkas, and boots, and for a formidable list of extras such as afterskiboots, caps or earbands, goggles or colored glasses, waxes and clamps and racks and laminated long underwear and foam-rubber-lined gloves. In addition there were outrageous daily charges, for room and board, for lift passes and ski lessons, all for a few joyless runs on treacherous snow. How infinite was the human capacity to believe that joy or love or light could be encountered upon the darkling plain, if only one went where the action was with the right equipment.

Surely at any moment they must all realize their own asininity, whereupon the ski resorts would immediately become empty ruins.

Instead, more madmen constantly arrived, equipped and hopeful. Even in the beginning he had been disbelieving. He had been the office manager of the Benning Foundation in New York, and Dick Macklin had been a vice-president. One weekend Dick had gone skiing in Vermont with some of the young Bennings. He had come back and announced that here was a way a fortune could be made in quick-time. As usual, Dick had not been wrong. The road to Cibola had indeed lain in catering to idiots who could buy many expensive accouterments and transport them, with a maximum of difficulty in the way of miserable driving conditions, to a remote and frigid area, there to engage in a pastime whose concomitants were cold hands and feet, frostbitten noses, aching muscles, and a constant statistic of so many broken bones per so many skier-hours. He would never believe the sport was not overdeveloped.

Now in the late afternoon the lifts were stopping, skiers were making a last run and would soon be gathering in the bar, where they would try to convince one another that they were having a marvelous time.

He was an observer who never ceased marveling at the insanity around him. By temperament and conviction divorced from the life these fools were trying to live, he knew he should possess a serenity of resignation. Instead and increasingly he was prey to every odd guilt, fret, and anxiety that came knocking at his mind for attention, and to long, aching might-have-beens as eroding as a low-grade fever. Almost as objective an observer of himself as of those around him, he recognized the dis-ease. There was a certain point in life, some divide or watershed, where all at once the end appeared in the defilade in which it had been previously hidden. From then on it was never out of sight, never out of mind, the true shape of the worry hole, which had to be filled by inventing minor, inessential, substitute worries, the shape-at-the-end-of-the-path from which the eyes must always shift right, switch left, but never gaze straight at.

Outside his office Annie was cutting a stencil, her head cocked to one side as she batted the typewriter keys in her pugnacious way. Through the arched window facing on the lobby, he could see Betsy-the-barmaid of the spectacular shape come down to the cashier for change. Betsy was having an encounter with Burning

Sappho, his name for the very rich Mrs. Donna McIntyre with
whom Betsy lived and loved off and on. Off now, for Betsy had
moved into the employees' dormitory a week ago. He frowned at
himself: calling Mrs. McIntyre "Burning Sappho" was a Macklin-
ism.

On the wall beside the door into the inner office was a calendar,
December marked with a heavy red box around the two weeks of
the Christmas holidays. On his desk was a brass prism bearing the
Observer's name, Bradley Peabody. Leather-covered In and Out
boxes were empty, but before him was a stack of reservations.
Stapled to the top one was the telephone memo of the call from
Mrs. Maeve Herron.

Memories of Maeve: he remembered her young, high-breasted
body, her particolored short blond hair, soft mouth, brown eyes,
her eagerness. Once, so briefly, a fool too, he had thought he had
found in her his own joy and love and light. He had felt an almost
savage satisfaction at her humiliation in Acapulco, an emotion out
of proportion and out of character, for he was not a puritan nor
had her life been that scandalous. Finally he had realized the reason: because once he had almost committed his emotions to her,
and his hopes, and it had come to nothing, as of course it had to
come to nothing. But he had loved her as he had loved Dick
Macklin, for the life bursting from her.

Memories of Maeve: his mind, as it had always been able to do,
began to push them out, encysting, as it had always done, the unpleasant, the shameful, the guilt-filled. He lit his pipe as though
the little ceremony was a kind of exorcism.

Shaking out the match, he watched the cook approaching
through the lobby, fork in hand, on the warpath. Out of sight for
a moment, the cook reappeared, easing his great belly past the
stencil curling out of Annie's typewriter, which ceased its clacking.

Clad in his chef's cap and double-breasted white jacket, the
cook brandished his trident like a Neptune. "You tell that son-of-a-
bitch to stay out of my kitchen, hear?"

"Who, Cook?"

"That goddam nosy Dickie. You tell that kid to stay out of my
kitchen or I'm through, hear!" He made a slashing gesture of
severance.

The manager of Dancer relit his pipe, unnecessarily. He

squinted through the smoke at the cook, who was a natural hysteric like all cooks, and said gravely, "I'll tell him."

"You tell him," the cook said, sounding instantly mollified though maintaining his furious expression. "When are you getting a new dishwasher?" he demanded.

"Maybe next month, Cook," he said, and the cook grunted and left, pushing out past Annie's stencil again.

"Fire in the hole," Annie observed.

He bit down on the hard rubber nipple of his pipe. Was he merely irritated? Worried about the possibility of the cook's quitting inconveniently? No; it was the sound of distant, threatening drums. He was the possessor of a philosopher's stone that could translate any base substance into golden fear. Young Dickie Macklin, out of graduate business school less than a year, was assistant manager of the lodge, and how could the son and heir fail to better himself? And looking at the present manager through Dickie's eyes, observing the Observer, he had to recognize that during his nine-year reign he had grown spoiled, grown indolent and crotchety, grown so much older. The thought of having to seek another job at his age filled him with a terror so profound that he could neither face it squarely nor free himself from it.

He felt the familiar slow pumping in his chest as he tried to reassure himself. He knew his managership was not entirely satisfactory to the minority stockholders, some of whom wished larger returns on their investment while others racketed for a completely unwarranted expansion of the Area. But in the most delicate and important of relationships, that with Isobel Macklin, he had been secure until her son Dickie had come to work at Dancer.

He could picture himself in no other position than the one he occupied. It seemed to him that if ever his stewardship at Dancer was lost, then he himself was lost. The pay was not great, but his expenses were almost nonexistent and his savings by now so large that he had been considering the establishment of a small scholarship at the University of California, where he had been an undergraduate, for needy boys from Hawaii. He knew now that he would never have any children, and such a scholarship would provide a little immortality for his name, save something from the final anonymity.

He could picture no other position in which the fringe benefits could fit him so exactly, the jurisdiction over others, the niceties of housing, food, and drink, the service and the freedom. All these he had never appreciated so much as now when they were threatened.

"Where do you suppose I could locate Dickie?" he called to Annie.

"Try the lounge," Annie said.

"Ah, yes, Betsy's on duty," he said.

Annie smiled at him, mother-hen anxious, for she liked Dickie. He also liked Dickie, was Dickie's godfather and cousin, had once been Dickie's "Uncle Brad." He had known Dickie for the twenty-three years of his young life, had known Dickie's mother almost all her life, had been Dickie's father's best friend in college and thereafter his associate and employee—and possibly his pimp, yes-man, sycophant. For the second time the usually ironclad protection of his memory buckled and creaked.

He rose and, as he moved around the desk, met the eye of Richard Everett Macklin, Sr., that in memoriam, or pretense to Isobel, or simple masochism, gazed down always over his left shoulder. The aging Beautiful Youth, crew cut and cleft-chinned, with his aristocratic narrow nose and hooded ironic eyes, wearing the brown-and-white Cowichan sweater that had been his luck piece through the heroic labors of the building of Dancer, gripped a pair of gloves in his right hand, so that his pose strongly resembled that of Rouault's Old King. Richard Macklin made no sign when saluted with his pipe.

"Mr. Peabody," Annie said, "what shall I tell Mr. Best if he calls back?"

"When in doubt always say no," he said and proceeded to the lounge in search of the son of Richard Macklin.

Dickie sat in a corner beneath one of the gleaming brass sconces, ring notebook laid open before him on the marble-topped cocktail table. He was talking to Betsy-the-barmaid, who towered over him with one hip cocked so that her neat, independently suspended buttocks in tight blue stretchpants were arrayed on a slant. Her hair was done up on top of her head, revealing sweetly jugged pink ears and a tender and defenseless nape-of-neck. With Burning Sappho, these two formed a triangle the Observer loved to speculate upon. Soon the triangle would be richly augmented by the arrival of Isobel Macklin and the Proper Girl, chosen by the mother for her only son.

"Oh, hello, Brad," Dickie said, red of face, and indicated the chair beside him.

Betsy turned, managing to look instantly on-the-job. "Scotch high, Mr. Peabody?"

"Yes, please, Betsy-dear," he said, and she went off with her hippy walk. He sat down. Dickie was frowning at his notebook; in his business courses he had been taught to make many notes and lists.

"Cooks are a strange and enigmatic breed," he began, and Dickie flushed more darkly. "I've found that if you have a good one it's best to leave him alone as much as possible. Tolerate almost anything, let him humiliate you as his malignant ego seems to require, or else he will choose to quit with the third order of filet well done on a Saturday night in the middle of the season."

Dickie grinned, embarrassed but grateful, when he stopped. Betsy arrived with the wheat-yellow potion and departed again.

"I apologize for riling him," Dickie said.

"The only real difficulty is that now he thinks he can extort a new dishwashing machine from me."

"Why don't we buy him a new dishwasher?" Dickie said. "That machine's enough to turn anyone paranoid."

"There's never been any trouble with it before. It's just a personality clash."

Dickie shrugged, gave a shuddering, disarming shake of his head and torso, and drank deep from his Pilsener glass. He was an uneasy combination of righteous prig and pleasantly open boy—who looked at him with increasingly perceptible criticism, he reminded himself.

"Mother's flying in tonight," Dickie said. "I'll go pick her up unless you're going anyway."

"Not I. Miss Hamilton's accompanying her, is she?"

"Evvy's not coming out," Dickie said. He assumed his constipated bulldog expression of self-consciousness, and perhaps of guilt. Was guilt so easily discernible? The Observer watched Dickie's eyes range toward Betsy, who was bent attractively over a nearby table; when the eyes turned back to him they were antagonistic, and Dickie raised his glass in what was for him a reckless gesture. "Here's to old Dancer Peak Ski Area and a prosperous Christmas season!"

"Hear! Hear!"

Dickie made a number of exaggerated gestures and expressions, as though he had decided to feign drunken boisterousness. He closed his notebook with a slap, inserted the pencil through the rings, and took another drink of beer, squinting one eye at the Observer as though sighting along a rifle barrel. In face and body he was a clumsily made copy of his father, not pulled together yet, loutish and puppylike compared with the exquisite original. His dark blond rebellious hair was combed in an old-fashioned manner, from a low, dandruff-flecked parting. "Going to write a book," he announced, patting his notebook.

"Oh?"

"Textbook on the Dancer operation. A classic case of everything done incorrectly."

He struck a match and applied the flame to his pipe, noting the steadiness of his hand. "Ouch!" he said.

"No criticism of you!" Dickie said too quickly. "As I see it, you are only carrying out the revealed policy of my father as maintained by my mother. As somebody said about something—it's not remarkable that it goes badly, it's only remarkable that it goes at all." His face creased, his eyes squeezed shut, and he laughed with an unpleasant, affected, popping sound. "Too many cooks!"

He felt fury foam over an ocean of panic, the fury dissolving into helplessness and defeat.

Dickie went on, pompously now, "I mean, it's a shock learning how different things can be from the textbook examples. For instance, what you said just now about the cook ought to be a lot of nonsense. If your cook is inefficient and probably crooked, you fire him and hire an honest, efficient cook on the labor market." He laughed the nervous laugh again. "But what can be done in a situation where the cook doesn't mind being fired because he can always get another job and likes a change anyway? And most likely he's saved enough so that with his unemployment insurance he can stay on as a paying guest. And as far as cooks are concerned, the labor market—oh, and so on and so on," Dickie said.

To maintain a tension on Dickie's nerves, he sucked on his pipe for a while before saying, "These are things we grow gray learning, yes."

"But, Brad—" Dickie screwed his pomposity up tightly again. "But, Brad, there are certain things we ought to be talking about. Impossible situations. Soderburg in charge of snow safety and ski patrol—one good man holding two relatively unimportant jobs. And Keckley in charge of the lifts, a half a man for a big job, though everyone knows Tim really runs the lifts. And then there is the assistant manager, me, supposedly in charge of the whole operation of the mountain with Keckley and Tim under me. Three men in positions that have no relation to reality, Brad."

Not much of a battle could be joined on this issue, and the Observer sighed with relief. The patchwork quilt that disturbed Dickie had been put together years ago, and, although difficult to explain, it covered the subject. If Dickie had learned how difficult a cook could be, he still had to see Timbal Khan in a black rage or Bob Keckley on a self-pitying, paranoiac drunk. He said, "Tim doesn't want to be in charge of the mountain, Dickie."

"I know he *says* that. But you really ought to fire Keckley—"

"No."

"You always say no," Dickie said.

"Listen to me. Tim will take on work entailing responsibility in incredible quantity, but you cannot *give* him responsibility. In your textbook cases nobody is abnormal or sick, or maybe even human."

Dickie looked at him blankly. Did Dickie consider himself normal, non-sick, in whose voice quivers of ashamed hate still sounded when he spoke of his father, nine years dead?

"I just can't believe if you told Tim he had to take on the whole mountain or else we'd bring in someone—"

"I'll forgive you if the cook decides to quit," he interrupted. "But neither I nor your mother would forgive you if you badgered Tim too far." He stopped to sip scotch and draw on his pipe, feeling on firm ground. All this would be relayed by Dickie to his mother, but Isobel knew Timbal Khan. He said, "Tim is responsible for everything on the mountain, only not on paper. He does the work of three good men, and if he is happy with everything just the way it is, then it behooves us to be happy too."

"Well, it's wrong," Dickie said stubbornly.

"It works."

"I don't think it works as well as it should."

"Nothing is going to run perfectly until people are perfect. Unfortunately many people at Dancer are imperfect, including the cook, Timbal Khan, and me."

Dickie pursed his mouth disagreeably and flipped the cover of his notebook back and forth.

"What do you have down there about the Admiral?"

"Not much," Dickie said. "I guess I'm prejudiced against him. I suppose he runs a competent ski school."

"But don't you think Captain Easy could run a brilliant one?"

He had meant to embroider the charms and imperfections of Easy Clary into his thesis, but Dickie said, "I'm tired of everybody raving about what a wonderful fellow Clary is. What a wonderful instructor. What a ladykiller. What a whata. I guess he could run a brilliant ski school if he wanted to, but he doesn't want to because all he is, really, is a wonderful bum."

"Perhaps we are all bums here."

"Everybody's sick and everybody's a bum," Dickie said. "A bunch of sick, abnormal bums trying to run a place where people come to have a good time."

Definition of a bum: someone who had made a separate peace with life's demands? Perhaps not with life's demands, for those were met as they appeared, but with the demands of the world, or of society. A normal, healthy bum, then, would try to make the sun run if he could not make it stand still, while the sick bum, his separate peace shaky, guilty, and terrified, would himself try to run and hide. And that was a caricature of himself. Where now were all those hopes, confidences, and certainties he had had at Dickie's age? He had had intelligence once, goals and the means to achieve them, and yet his life had been spent in mediocrity and futility.

Dickie was scowling and leafing through his notebook as though it could contain answers or even real questions. Of course there was pressure on him. A woman who was both his mother and majority stockholder in the corporation for which he worked was arriving tonight, and Dickie would be required to make some kind of personal report, produce words of wisdom on the operation of Dancer, on the lifts, the lodge, the management. For his own part he could and would make a good report on Dickie, who had settled well into a difficult situation and over the past few months had earned much respect, and enmity only from the cook.

The Observer returned to the con as Dickie stiffened and glowered at Donna McIntyre, who had just come in, shapely in her beige stretchsuit and fur-topped boots. "Hello, Betsy-dear!" she called. She waved a gay hand toward them. Her hair was done in two girlish pigtails tied with pink ribbons, her face made up in an even tan with pink mouth and green-underlined eyes like startling holes in a fabric.

"I can't stand that woman!" Dickie said in a low voice. They watched her talking to Betsy, one hand flipped inward to her breast, the other outward as though indicating the world. Finally she sat at the bar while Betsy, with her eye-collecting walk, went about her round of taking orders, delivering drinks, and arranging change on her tray so as to snare the maximum tips.

"Her account runs a thousand to fifteen hundred dollars a year," the Observer said. "Mainly bar."

"I know that," Dickie said. Dickie seemed relieved now that Burning Sappho had left Betsy alone, but he said in the low voice, "Betsy says she's going to move back in with her."

"The employees' dorm has its bleak aspects," he said. But he felt a twinge of compassion. "That's too bad," he said.

"I don't understand a thing like that," Dickie said, breathing heavily. "Sure. Everybody's sick. Everybody's a bum. You grow gray learning that, all right." He made a helpless gesture.

The Observer knew the meaning of the gesture. It was a big world which opened out and out, full of good and evil and wonder. What Dickie didn't realize yet was that after a point, which wasn't even noticed in passing, the world began closing in. It was the Bradley Peabody Theory of Relativity, the Diamond Shape of Time and Life.

"Can you understand a thing like that?" Dickie said.

At first he felt like Uncle Brad again. Then he saw further into the question. He might, after all, be a pervert himself, all bachelors over a certain age being suspect. "Possibly I can't completely understand it," he said. "I accept it. Betsy is a very decorative young lady. Mrs. McIntyre finds her attractive and good company. And Mrs. McIntyre is used to having what she wants," he said cruelly and signaled for another drink.

"Rotten old queer," Dickie said. "You can't even see her behind all that makeup. I just don't understand Betsy. I asked her *why*, and she said she just wanted to be taken care of, that's all. She just had to have somebody take care of her."

The decorative one was bringing him his second highball on her tray, pearls of teeth showing in her small, smiling mouth, curls springing prettily from the band of her topknot. Her eyes were crudely black-framed in the current fashion, but this only increased an effect of fragility and innocence that was, on the slightest reflection, ridiculous. She was six feet tall, obviously very strong—she was reputed to have been a championship softball pitcher—and she was a grossly sexual creature. Strange images came to mind of the father, nine years dead, and the son in competition for her. He traced this surprising thought to Maeve's return, mixing memory and desire. Betsy waited while he signed the chit. Dickie sat stiff and silent and shook his head when asked if he wanted another beer. The Observer noted that Burning Sappho occupied the stool next to the service bar, where she could chat with Betsy while the barmaid waited for an order to be filled.

"Fond of her, are you?" he said to Dickie.

"Yes, I am. I suppose it shows."

"Yes, it does."

Dickie made a gesture of acceptance. "She's a—damn sweet girl," he said. "She really is. It's just"—he paused to finish the beer in his glass—"it's just that I feel like the prince trying to save the princess from the dragon. My magic sword and all that," he said, flushing, wiping the foam from his upper lip with a paper napkin. "Except that the princess doesn't mind a bit being held captive by the dragon. She just wants—'someone to take care of me!'" He mimicked the phrase angrily. He got to his feet. "So I don't know what to do!" he said and abruptly departed, moving with his forward-leaning, tending-to-important-business walk between the marble-topped tables, slapping his notebook against his thigh. He left the Observer heavily remembering another time Dickie had confided in him, about another relationship Dickie had been unable to bear or understand.

He had been sitting in his room in the lodge with a blanket wrapped around him and the electric heater buzzing, reading over the letters Janet Rohde had typed that day. She was an adequate typist but her shorthand was only bluff, and he had to read the letters with close attention for howlers. They had a very good letter worked up pleading for time from pressing creditors, but the heating contractor, who felt especially ill treated, could not be swayed without money and so there was no heat in the lodge although it was well into December and snowing. Isobel had gone to Hawaii to borrow money on her Bradley-Beeson stock.

There was a timid knock, he called a come-in, and Dickie entered, aged fourteen. His hair was awkwardly combed from an uneven part even then, his eyes were dark, round, and self-consciously tragic.

"Pretty cold in here," Dickie said, pushing back with his behind to close the door.

"I can't stand an overheated room."

Dickie moved over in front of the electric heater to absorb its inadequate rays, waiting to be asked what was wrong. There was no need to ask—what was wrong was Dick and Maeve. As Uncle Brad he supposed he should have tried to shield Dickie from the sordid realities of that, but he had known no way. He had been hard put to shield his own abraded emotions.

Dickie abruptly sat down on the bed, legs apart, hands jammed into his parka pockets, feet in black sneakers tipped on edge. "Dad wants me to move into the Social," he said. "I can't get any studying done in the Social, Uncle Brad."

He cleared his throat. "I'm sure it would be difficult." Rage and wonder at what Dick Macklin thought he could get away with flowed and ebbed in familiar channels.

"I don't know what to do," Dickie said. Leaving one foot on edge, he carefully planted the other on top of it, his turned-down face studying the operation.

"I don't know what to tell you, I'm afraid."

"Called me a damn eavesdropper," Dickie said, rubbing the back of his wrist across his nose. "Well, I don't know how I was supposed to keep from it. I don't know how they can make so much noise anyway, chasing each other around and—" Dickie stopped.

He checked a place where Rody had gotten off track, put

the sheaf of letters to one side, drew off his clouded glasses, and rubbed the palms of his hands over tired eyes. The weary fury surged and receded. "Hard to study," he commented.

"Yeah."

"The fact is that men are not monogamous creatures. Society tries to make them that way, and often fails."

"I know all that," Dickie said, revealing for a moment a tear-stained, scowling face. "There've been other—you know, women, too. I've heard Mother and Dad fighting about that."

"Everyone is a collection of faults and virtues," he tried again. "Women are one of his—faults. He has great virtues, however."

Dickie didn't say anything.

"I've been upset when I've felt he was treating your mother unfairly," Uncle Brad continued. "But I think she knew his faults and virtues when she married him."

Dickie raised his face again to fasten a knowing eye upon him. Of course Dickie would be aware that he and Dick Macklin had been friends and fraternity brothers at Berkeley, and that he and Isobel had once had an Understanding. In the senseless movements of war he had been sent from Hawaii to Texas to train in dull mediocrity in the army, while Marine Lieutenant Richard Macklin, the Beautiful Youth, had burst upon Honolulu like a shooting star, en route to Guadalcanal, from whence he had reappeared, first in newspaper reports, then in a quick cheap book about heroics in the Solomons, finally in person, wounded and a hero, to sweep the cool Isobel Bradley literally off her feet and relieve her of that long-preserved virginity. How quickly they had married, and how quickly a son had been born to them. He, Bradley Peabody, friend, cousin, disappointed lover, had been sucked into their orbit, or maybe it was only their wake, and remained there still.

"I don't know what I can do, Dickie," he said.

"Well—I thought—you're his best friend. If you could talk to him. If—" Dickie stopped. They were both shaking their heads. "No, what the heck would you say?" Dickie said. "But—it's bad, Uncle Brad."

It seemed a strange understatement. "Is it?" he said.

"Well—sure, I've been listening! I mean, I don't want to know all the—dirty stuff. I'm not trying to watch or anything. But I have to listen so I can find out if he's going to do something to my mother, don't I?"

"Of course," he said. The old weary fury had taste. It tasted like the dust beneath the bed.

"He talks like my mother isn't ever coming back from Hawaii," Dickie said. "I mean, about what *they*'re going to do as though she wasn't coming back. About being free and— She is coming back, isn't she, Uncle Brad? She wouldn't just go over there and leave me here with him and not come back because she couldn't get all that money, would she?"

"She's coming back," he said. "I suppose they're not looking forward to it, so they try to ignore it. That's a thing grownups do." He remembered when he, at Dickie's age, had filled out a self-help test in a magazine. One of the questions requested a statement of philosophy-of-life. He wrote in the space allowed: "Always have something to look forward to." His mother, who was in one of her difficult phases, had found this. "What's going to happen when you get to my age and you don't have a single damned thing to look forward to?" she had asked him, fixing him with a manic eye. "Then you're going to need more than this to hold you, buddy-boy." He realized that as he had been Dickie's age then, so must he now have reached that age of his mother.

"I don't hate *her*," Dickie said, bending his head down again. He went through the complicated procedure of re-sorting his feet, the other sneaker down, the first on top. "I mean, maybe you think I hate her but I don't. She's always been okay to me. But— it's so bad of him, Uncle Brad! I get kind of sick, hating him so much. God, I hate him when I hear him talking. Talking and talking."

The room smelled of fresh plaster and sweat and human emotion. He was being called upon for help as he had been called upon rarely in his life. He was ashamed that he, an intelligent man, could think of no way to help, and he was ashamed that this human contact, like how many others, would pass, would vanish, because of his futility. His glasses had fogged again, and he polished them on a piece of Kleenex and squinted through them at the opal-glass lighting fixture.

Having been offered so little comfort or advice, Dickie got to his feet. "Well, I guess I've got to do something," he said and left.

But apparently Dickie had found that although it was easy enough to resolve to act, it was even easier to rationalize away the need for action. Perhaps the paralysis of Elsinore could only be broken when Hamlet happened to be where the action was, with the right equipment.

6: *Richard E. Macklin, Jr.*

IN THE SMALL apartment that had been built for him attached to the Big House, Richard Everett Macklin, Jr., constructed a knot in his tie, slid the knot up to meet his Adam's apple, and engaged the buttons of his buttondown collar. The tie was a gesture of respect to his mother, whom he was going to meet at the airport at seven-forty. It was good for him to be dressing in a jacket and tie; possibly he should consider putting on a suit. There was a tendency at Dancer to lounge around in ski clothes, a sloppiness he should correct more often. He doused his scalp with Vitalis and kneaded with determined fingers. Parting and combing his hair, he regarded himself in the mirror. "You'll never be as handsome as your father" rang through his mind down the years; and Betsy saying, "How come you comb your hair in that funny, old-manny way? Why don't you just really let it grow long or something?"

He took from the dresser the stainless steel box that had been his father's, made in a Pacific island machine shop by an enlisted man who had worshiped his father, as everyone, it seemed, had worshiped his father, thinking with a kind of blank and weary resentment of the little box he had bought in Fez to replace this one, Moroccan leather of a tasteful design, with bright-colored panels. It had fallen apart almost as soon as he was home after that graduation summer abroad. He took a roll of breath mints from the box and immediately grunted and replaced it, not so much in rebellion against his mother as against the part of himself that would want to conceal from her the fact that he had had a couple of beers. His mother was no puritan. Why was he this way? he wondered as he closed the lid of the well-made little box with a click.

The room was small, with a high ceiling that made it seem even smaller. His books were in the wrought-iron and pine-board bookcase beneath the window, art books laid flat on the bottom shelf. The narrow bed was covered with a spread of white silk-and-wool caftan material. On the wall above it, like a museum display, was his collection of Berber weapons—two silver-chased rifles, a brace of pistols, a copper and silver powder horn. He did not approve of the display on the wall, which seemed ostentatious in so small a room, too much tourist-back-from-abroad with slides and souvenirs, but they were mementos of the month he had spent in Fez with Topher Brooks, and it seemed a pity, and possibly an admission of guilt, merely to store away the handsome, metallically glowing weapons.

He shrugged into his jacket. Twisting his neck in his collar and flexing his shoulders to settle the coat, he looked at the image in the mirror again. He had old-manny hair and he was never going to be as handsome as his father, and that was just fine, he accepted it; he was the way he was.

The face in the mirror scowled back at him as he thought of Betsy saying in her childish voice, "But I just want someone to take care of me!" She was a complete child; the whole thing was incomprehensible. She made very good money from tips as a barmaid—she made more than he did!—she had the privilege of living in the employees' dormitory for next to nothing, and she skied free every morning and on her day off. She had no responsibilities, no problems; she had a Karmann Ghia convertible he both envied and disapproved of—what did she mean, she just wanted to be taken care of? A fist of fury formed in the pit of his stomach as he thought of that rotten perverted old woman making a Lesbian out of Betsy Kimball. Lately the dreadful picture in his mind's eye of the girl and the woman writhing naked together had become sickly confused with Fez, with that pinkish-pearly, down-in-a-hole city where the women's kohl-rimmed eyes looked haunted and there was an appalling, palpable climate of homosexuality pervading the whole of the down-sloping city: the boys and young men holding hands and flirting, and Colonel Bosinée with the lipstick-and-rouged boy who couldn't have been more than twelve. The whole experience had had the terrible, too-much quality of the last books of *Remembrance of Things Past*—that time in the garage when he'd been waiting to have the spark plugs replaced in his car and the boy apprentice-mechanic, speaking to him in French, asked if he liked Maroq, if he thought it was beautiful, and so forth, until finally—eyelashes flickering sunnily at him, nose wrinkled girlish and gay, gum-showing smile—even with his insecure French he recognized what was an unmistakable pass. And to top it all, Phillippa McAndrews actually had accused him and Topher Brook of being pansies, in the café where they had gone to drink mint tea and listen to the muezzins' mechanically amplified voices calling all over that slimy city. That afternoon he had left for Tangier.

Yet he didn't think he had ever met anyone who seemed to him less sick than Betsy Kimball. "I hate that terrible women's dorm," she said. "Everybody snores and smells bad." Someday he was going to have to face having a talk with her about why she really wanted to go back to Donna McIntyre. But he knew that if he brought up the subject of Lesbianism she would look at him with her violet eyes in their Rouault dark frames, almost like the Moroccan women's eyes, and ask him what was wrong with it. Then everything would go to pieces, because if they didn't both believe it was wrong, how could they talk about it? He had terrible failures of communication with Betsy, as though it was a delusion that even their language was the same, for not each word but often key words would have subtle differences of meaning. He had never known anyone like her.

He had better leave now in case he had a flat tire on the way to the airport. As he turned from the mirror his eyes caught the spiral notebook with the blue cover, on the right-hand corner of which was inscribed, in mechanical-drawing-class lettering, RICHARD E. MACKLIN, JR. He blushed to recall his talk with Brad, blushed on blush to remember his earlier disastrous encounter with the cook. The whole thing had clearly given Brad an ascendency over him, made him appear to be a time-and-motion-study, textbook-worshiping schoolboy. How Brad, who laughed in easy contempt at everyone, must laugh especially at him.

Yet it was a fact that Bradley Peabody was a bad manager who should have a fire lit under him. Better still, he should cold-bloodedly be replaced. And the president of Dancer Peak Ski Area, Inc., his mother—so the chain of logic followed—was a bad president who kept on a bad manager not even out of nepotism but because Brad had been hopelessly in love with her all down the years, and because she had married Brad's best friend and turned Brad into a kind of parasite. "Your father and I are responsible for what Brad has become," she had told him. "Therefore I feel responsible for what becomes of him." When he had tried to argue with her she had said, "You will collect this kind of responsibility too, as you go through life."

She owned eighty-two per cent of the stock—what was to keep her from doing as she pleased? She did not want total efficiency, she said. She was interested in Dancer having a heart, in Dancer being what his father would have wanted it to be. Looking at him with her deep-set, sharp eyes, she had said, "One of the last things Dick said to me was that we had built a pleasure garden here, a place for people to come and take pleasure. I insist that it be that."

His mother had become interested in Dancer again when he had come to work here. Before that she had been content to let Brad run the resort without interference. She hadn't been to Dancer more than three or four times a year since his father had died. It was all very well for her to speak of Dancer as a pleasure garden, but a pleasure garden wasn't what Brad, with his contempt for skiers and skiing, was running. And although the pleasure garden concept might be an attractive one, Dancer would never be anything at all until it was first an expanding, efficiently operated business enterprise.

Because of Brad it was certainly not efficiently run or expanding, though the sport of skiing was growing by leaps and bounds and the nearby resorts of Craven and Bojangle Peak, under alert, modern management, were taking advantage of the boom, building new facilities and taking skiers away from Dancer. Brad seemed prepared only for a bust.

Upon finishing graduate school he had decided that he would rather go to work at Dancer than join the Bradley-Beeson Company in Hawaii, for which career he had always considered himself preparing. His mother had assigned him the specific duty of finding out how a ski resort operated, what was right about the way Dancer was being operated and what was wrong, for her own information and for his own education and future. But now, he knew, if he told her that what was right about Dancer was very little and what was wrong almost everything, specifically the manager, her cousin Bradley Peabody, she would be disappointed in him, would only shrug and smile and say that nothing could be done about that.

Now he had to pick her up at the airport, and she was going to be angry because he and Evaline Hamilton had quarreled on the telephone and Evvy had changed her mind about coming to Dancer for Christmas.

It was snowing when he went outside and walked toward the lights of the lodge. The swimming pool, gleaming acid blue in its lighted glass enclosure, looked like some kind of steaming gypsy caldron. In the darkness he could hear the long soughing of the wind up on the mountain. When he glanced into the lounge Betsy was bent over a table placing glasses before three men. More curls had come loose from her topknot and a scimitar of hair had fallen across her forehead. He watched her joking with the men when she had finished serving them and was relieved to see that Donna McIntyre was not present.

Under the porte-cochere he watched the snowflakes drifting densely down in the light. The black of the asphalt was beginning to disappear. He felt the excitement of snow coming, of the mountain replenished, the trees stacked with new snow, and fresh powder to ski on, as well as the challenge of the Christmas season, which could mean a profit or a loss for the year's operation. He paused to turn up his coat collar before stepping out into the snow again, thinking of all the people downbelow packing and readying their equipment preparatory to charging up into the mountains tomorrow.

A car with blazing, close-set headlights came speeding into the parking area and slid to a stop under the porte-cochere, a Jaguar frosted with snow, two wiper-cleared half-moons on the windshield. It occurred to him that he might have to put on chains coming back from the airport.

Bobby-the-bellhop appeared, in his blue jacket with brass buttons, to open the door of the Jaguar. A woman got out, the car's only occupant. There was a pair of skis on the top rack, tips knowledgeably to the rear.

"Bring everything in and park it for me, will you, please?" the woman said in a familiar voice. All at once he found himself almost hiding behind the post nearest him, staring.

She had long, pale blond hair that caught the cold lights. Her face remained in darkness. The Jaguar had a Texas plate, partially obscured by snow. She came slowly out in front of the car, where its lights struck her glossy fur jacket, blue jeans, sealskin boots. She stood looking at the dancing skier on the side of the lodge, standing with her boots set apart, shoulders straight, hands in jacket pockets. He sighed as she turned slightly and light flooded her face.

Her face seemed to him much more delicate, finer, more beautiful than the one he remembered or had seen, blurred, in the newspapers since. He felt, rather than saw, her eyes pass over him. She wouldn't recognize him, who was a grown man now, and he was grateful not to be recognized, for, taken by surprise like this, he did not feel himself a grown man but still a sneaking boy. She was looking up at the porte-cochere, new since her time, like a student returning to the old school. Bobby said, "Pardon me, ma'am," as he passed her, carrying her matched airplane bags and a big suitcase bound with black straps.

In his nightmares of guilt after his father's death and her flight, she had assumed a kind of frozen, stylized attitude like Joan of Arc upon a pile of faggots, El Greco eyes raised to heaven. In the old Jeep pickup she had driven him to and from school in Cope, and they had talked of many things. She had been his friend.

He was startled to hear her speak as she moved forward, a sentence he couldn't make out, that ended in his name. ". . . Dick Macklin." But of course it was his father's name. She passed him and went on into the lodge. The door closed behind her with its cushioned clop.

He leaned against his post. The lights of the Jaguar burned into the falling snow; the driver's door stood open. He saw that the car was not new, was splattered with mud beneath its frosting, the right front fender deeply creased. Bobby came hurrying out to reach inside the car again, while he, Richard Macklin, Jr., walked on over to his own car and eased himself inside its thick blind chill. He started the motor and let it warm up for the advisable length of time before backing out and driving slowly out along the valley road, wipers laboring.

At the Valley Center a number of cars were parked before the Loup Garou, and on an impulse he swung into the parking area and stopped. If he had to change a tire or put on chains on his way to the airport his mother would just have to wait. He was thinking about that terrible payday in the lobby of the lodge; he felt very shaky and wanted another beer.

During that time it had been necessary that he eavesdrop whenever he could. There were so many things it was vital that he know. He had appropriated a number of coigns of vantage to his purpose—one was the balcony overlooking the living room of the Big House. He could easily pass from his own room to the balcony without being seen from below, and from the balcony he could see most of the living room and hear what was happening in the dining room and kitchen. In the basement, if he stood with an ear close to the sheet-metal box that surmounted the furnace, he could hear the sounds from his parents' bedroom. His father was clearly audible, but Maeve's lighter voice did not come through as well.

In the lodge his post, used only once, was a corner of the lobby, which had been partitioned with some concrete-stained sheets of plywood into a storage closet for tools, cartons of nails, and caulking. Most of the lobby was visible through the cracks between the plywood sheets.

When his mother sent back from Hawaii the money to pay the overdue wages, before she herself returned, there was a ceremony in the lobby, as there had been on a previous occasion when his father had been unable to write paychecks for a time. He watched the ceremony from the toolshed.

His father was very drunk, and there was a heaviness and a grimness about him, even though he was being very witty in the slight British accent he would put on sometimes when he was drunk and it was necessary that he be witty. It was an accent Uncle Brad assumed sometimes too, as though one had copied it from the other, or both from someone else they had known when they were fraternity brothers in college.

Shivering a little, his hands crammed in his parka pockets, he watched through the widest crack. His father, wearing the Indian sweater, was sitting on a stool at the chest-high counter, handing Finney his check. Finney giggled at something said to him, holding the slip of paper in one hand and the other cupped to his ear, then walked out in that queer way he had, with his legs flapping out at angles rather than straight ahead. Easy Clary, J.D. Daugherty, John Henry, Janet Rohde, Tim Soderburg, and Maeve all sat around the half-completed lobby on cartons or sawhorses or lounged on the burlap-covered rolls of carpet and pad. They all had drinks. Uncle Brad wasn't present.

His father would take a swallow of liquor, hold a check before his eyes with a mechanical motion and study it for a long time before calling the recipient. He called J.D. and didn't say much; called John Henry and made some jokes. Everyone laughed. Another drink, another check; his father looked gravely around the lobby as though he were nearsighted.

"Mr. Soderburg?"

Tim rose and went up to the counter.

"Now, Mr. Soderburg, we have here a little token of our esteem. A trifle really. You must realize it would have to be many, many times larger to convey any true, er, recompense of our gratitude to you. Mr. Soderburg, you have labored long and hard for the sodality, for the cause, for country, king, and God, home and motherhood, hearth and hamburger. And for all the good things of our way of life not covered in the preceding paragraph. It is, indeed, unfitting—not to speak of occasionally painful—for the management here to reward your services merely with money. But there it is. May we have a handclap for this splendid fellow, please?"

Everyone clapped. He watched his father and wondered how he could be so clever, and so funny, and make all these people who didn't really like him, like him now.

Blushing and awkward, Tim took his check and went to sit down next to John Henry on a roll of carpeting. His father brought the next check up before his eyes, tucked it back last among the checks, and chose another one. "Ah. Mr. Clary, please."

Easy Clary came forward, arms folded; he didn't seem to be enjoying this as much as the others.

"Captain Easy. In this, the winter of our discontent, it has been your—" his father belched and muttered, "Pardon—your, er, smile, your merry quips that have kept the table in the road and the show on a roar—I seem to have that mixed up. But we all know you, Captain Easy, as no mere jester. A more profound spirit moves you. Sweet are the uses of philosophy! Though there's nothing to compare with a straight left. How impossible for mere groundlings to devise a fitting emolument for these vasty *recherches* of the spirit, conducted under the auspices of our local foundation. So we can only offer this inadequate mite, Mr. Charles Clary! Please!"

Clapping. Someone cried, "Hear! Hear!"

His father took another long drink, selected another check, and called for Miss Janet Rohde. As he handed her her check he said, very seriously and confidentially, "Friends, we live in a paper world. The moon, as King Cole has proven, is paper. The sun is paper, at least in Chicago. What is the womb but a paper bag, and we poor mortals, bound for the grave, as disposable as Kleenex. Miss Rohde, this check is—paper. And so it shouldn't bounce this time. Unless my wife has played me false." He wiped a hand across his mouth and added, as though to himself, as Rody turned away, "And no such luck."

In the dark toolroom, peering through the crack into the light, he felt his face prickle at the mention of his mother. He didn't understand what his father had meant, but he dug his hands deeper in his parka pockets, hating. His father almost finished the liquor in his glass before picking up the last check.

He looked at this one even longer than usual, and at first there was silence, then a couple of nervous laughs. "Ah, Miss Olsen," his father said.

Maeve went forward and stood before the counter, round-hipped in faded, paint-stained blue jeans.

His father didn't look at her. This time there was no affected British accent when he spoke, and no humor. "I suppose there are a certain number of good women in the world, and I suppose there are a number of natural whores, but why I have to be afflicted with both at once I don't know. Here's your gold, baby, with time and a half for overtime."

He saw his father's wolf-jawed brutal face through a pink mist, his father's hand holding out the check to Maeve. She didn't take it. He said something in a low, harsh voice and thrust it at her; her hand came up uncertainly to accept it. He drained the last of the liquor in his glass, got to his feet, and walked away, deliberately, almost strutting, and with no sign of his limp. Maeve turned slowly to watch him go and turned still more when he had gone.

Through the crack in the plywood her face swam in his gaze as she seemed to look straight at him—although she could not have known he was inside the toolroom—at him who had done this to her. And as though speaking to him she said, "I don't—I don't know—I don't know what I did to deserve *that*."

Someone—he couldn't make out who—cursed.

Easy Clary put his arm around Maeve. Tim joined them, his heavy face pale. John Henry and J.D. still sat on the carpet roll, looking paralyzed, Rody on a sawhorse with arms hugged to her chest as though she were cold. They all hung there in a tableau as he moved back from the crack so he could see them no longer, took another step back until the crack was only an innocent line of light in the darkness.

"The son-of-a-bitch!" someone said hoarsely.

"I don't know what I did to—" Maeve's light voice started, stopped.

"Somebody ought to kill the son-of-a-bitch," the hoarse voice said.

He thought he was going to faint. He shut his eyes against the lurching darkness and the hypnotic line of light; he leaned for support against the wall. All the hate he felt was now turned upon himself, all the contempt and the disgust. Somewhere he had read that eavesdroppers always heard what they did not want to hear. "Mother," he whispered to himself as though it were an excuse. At least his father seemed to have realized that she was a good woman. In the lobby confused voices were talking.

He heard Maeve say, "I'll have to go, I guess. I can't stay here now."

"You'll have to go." Janet Rohde's voice.

"Back to Visalia," Maeve said.

"Touch home and start again." Easy Clary.

"Let's all quit on the son-of-a-bitch." That was J.D.

"No, I'll have to quit," Maeve said. "It's only—me."

"Don't give him the satisfaction of quitting," Timbal Khan rumbled. "Stay here and we'll all help you spit in his eye."

"Come on back to the Social, Maevie," John Henry said in his high, nervous voice. "It'll all blow over. He's just—"

"It's just—I'd just like to stay till Dancer's going," Maeve said. "I don't want to run out on everybody."

Rody said, "I don't see how you can stay with Isobel coming back."

He began feeling his way past the stacks of cartons toward the door and away from what his father had done, what he himself had done, to Maeve Olsen who had been his friend. Outside the lodge he drew deep, shuddering breaths of the cold air, trying to overcome the sickness that coiled in his stomach. It was snowing. He bent and balled together a great double-handful of snow and pressed it to his hot face, and then he flung the snowball as hard as he could at the stainless steel dancer on skis on the side of Dancer Lodge.

7: J.D. Daugherty

A BARTENDER was used to listening, and a good listener heard all sorts of tunes going on behind the one being whistled up front. So, though it appeared to be just a happy threesome at the bar with the big folk singer coming on funny about his musical director and his agent and this guy and that chick in Hollywood, still it was clear that John Henry had something on about the Commie folk singers who were going down to Mississippi to stir things up; maybe he was talking so much and so fast so nobody would be able to bring up the subject again. And Martha Schroeder was throwing down the Gibsons faster than she usually did, so something was wrong there too. Easy seemed easy enough—why wouldn't he be, with John Henry buying the drinks and Martha keeping a hand on it? He didn't have much use for Easy, a bleedingheart, blowhard fuckoff who was happy enough to see everybody else's money given away, not having any himself to bother with. Clary traveled with a whoop-up pack of ski instructors and skibums and sleep-around babes where he was king stud, or else; though a good lot of the time now he was servicing Martha Schroeder. With Martha and John Henry both on hand he was in fine shape, but it was just the kind of situation where Clary would start sounding off about his principles and how stupid everybody else was until somebody called him on it, and then there'd be a brawl. A brawl in the Loup Garou didn't bother him too much, if there weren't many people around, since a brawl livened things up and, on succeeding nights, brought in a lot of customers hoping to see another fight or to talk about the last one. He had noticed that Easy Clary was always careful not to choose anyone who could put him on his ass.

John Henry, Easy, and Martha were on one side of the draft-
beer lever. On the other were Stoney Stone and a friend. Three
of the tables were occupied, and a girl was feeding the jukebox
and waving a fat butt for someone to come dance with her. Rock-
and-roll was booming away just at the point where at one more
scratch of volume he would have to turn it down. Whatever hol-
lows and voids there were in the music were filled with talking
and laughing, and there was a good smog of cigarette smoke and
liquor smell. It was just the way he liked it. He felt host at a
really good party.

Sometimes he would enter into conversations, or he would just
listen, really listen. But sometimes, and coming on more and
more, it would all go bad, and instead of being happy at his party
his mind would get away from him and hang up on crappy
things, filling and spilling over with worries, resentments, and
rage and fear about money and the planning commission and the
State Board of Equalization and Internal Revenue. He would be
unable to get his thoughts off an article on the U.N. in *American
Opinion* that had made him mad, or off the money being wasted
on the space program or civil rights.

Now it was swelling up in him like that, and, to stop it, he
leaned against the back of the bar beside the cash register, hung
the telephone receiver against his neck, and dialed home.

"'Lo, hon," he said when Peggy answered, conversation secret
behind the music and the bar talk. He and Peggy had their happiest times on the telephone.

"Oh, hi, Jimmy!"

"I don't know when I can get home, hon. This barman the union's sending out called up and he can't make it before nine or
ten, his battery's dead or something. You can't depend on these
fuckoffs—they'd rather be on unemployment anyway."

"Gee, that's too bad, Jimmy," Peggy said, but she sounded as
though she wasn't paying attention. Probably she was nursing the
baby, which was what she spent a lot of time doing. A year ago
when he had married her she had been the cutest trick on the
mountain, with her red-gold hair and a sweet little behind he
could almost hold in one hand.

"You feeding Honey-boy?" he asked.

She giggled. "How'd you know?"

"I can hear the little bastard getting his gun off. You tell him to save some for Daddy, hear?"

"Jimmy! *Shhhh!*"

"Well, you tell him not to hog it all."

"The Internal Revenue man was here this afternoon," Peggy said. "I told him you were working."

"Fuck him!" he said.

"Jimmy! You curse too much!"

His voice didn't sound like his own. "Bastards just want to get the money away from the people that work and give it to the fuckoffs."

Now the conversation was spoiled. "Well, maybe I'll call you later, hon," he said and hung up. He was shaking with fury and dread. They were going to get him, there was no doubt about it, and he was really going to have to pay. He busied himself making Stoney a bourbon high and checking the other glasses along the bar. He ducked out through the stoop hole to play table waiter. When he returned, Dickie Macklin had come in, all decked out in a coat and tie, and was standing behind John Henry. He drew a beer for Dickie.

"I just saw Maeve," Dickie announced.

"You *what?*"

"*Maeve?*" John Henry said.

"Where?" asked Easy, who had switched around on his stool.

"At the lodge."

"Maeve?" John Henry said as though he hadn't got hold of it yet.

"Did you talk to her?"

"No. She drove in just as I was leaving. It was Maeve." Dickie took a long pull on his beer, looking important.

"May I have another, please, J.D.?" Martha said. There were some who didn't have to say please, but she was one of the ones who didn't mean it when they said it. He ignored her glass, reached for the telephone, and placed it in front of Easy Clary.

"How about calling Badbody?"

He made Martha's drink while Clary dialed, asked for Mr. Peabody, waited, and finally said, "Is she really there?" Clary listened, nodding once or twice, his narrow dark face with the gull-wing eyebrows intense and frowning. Martha, beside him, picked a grain of tobacco from her lower lip. John Henry wore an exaggerated expression of surprise. Dickie drank his beer, keeping his mouth pursed between sips.

Maeve was really there, and everybody was supposed to go over to the lodge for a party for her.

Before he found out whether he was asked or not, he announced that he couldn't get away, and Dickie said he had to leave for the airport to pick up his mother. Then Maeve was on the wire, and Clary turned tied-up and phony. He remembered that Clary and Maeve had both worked at Craven before Dancer got started; a friend of his, who had worked there too, said that Clary had declassified all the cute new girls at Craven, including Maeve, and he and Maeve had had a real letch thing going. If you were one of the old settlers at Dancer you were supposed to be out of your mind with the hots for Maeve, like the frontier-days shepherds who had carved the whoreboots in the trees you could still see. He supposed part of the tradition Maeve had become was due to the home-town girl having got to be one of the all-time great pieces of ass, jet-set tail. He himself had never been half so mad for Maeve as he had been mad at Macklin.

Now it was John Henry's turn to yell into the phone. In a pause in the music a small, mechanical voice was saying, "I'm here! And I've brought the powder with me! Isn't it heavenly?"

"Thought I brought it!" John Henry cried. "You mean *you* did?"

So that he wouldn't be passed the telephone and have to say stupid things to Maeve, he moved on down the bar. Stoney's friend needed a refill, and he made it. Clary, Martha, and John Henry got up and began milling around, putting their coats on, Martha pretending she wasn't griped to hell, and John Henry full of yays and hip talk, and Easy not as easy as he'd been. Dickie had already left.

When they were gone he dropped their glasses into the sink and mopped all sign of them from the shiny dark wood counter. He had no intention of joining them at the lodge, but he would meet them at the bottom of Big Red One in the morning and, unless Tim cut him off, go up to ski the powder with them. One of the things he still loved, one of the things that had not been spoiled for him yet, was skiing the deep powder.

It was the deep powder that had got Macklin, he remembered, leaning beside the cash register. He was trying to remember if he had hated Macklin from the beginning. He had hated him for what Macklin had done to Dickie, hadn't he? He had hated him for what he had done to Maeve, hadn't he? Calmly he faced the possibility that he had only hated Macklin for what he himself, J.D. Daugherty, had done.

He and John Henry had put the Platterlift up the Spoon. It had been the hardest work he had ever done. Neither of them had been in charge, they had just worked together, jealous of their independence. Tim had not bothered them much, and Macklin not at all, since what they were doing was visible from the bottom and Macklin did not do any unnecessary stumping on his gimp leg. They had lived with the Platterlift all day and slept with it on their minds at night, and finally the six towers were up, sheaves hung and cable strung, just like a giant erector set with no instructions a maniac Santa Claus had left under the Christmas tree. They had hooked in the power and it had worked, just like that, no problems.

That night at the bar in Cope he had got so drunk all he could remember was falling off his bar stool and, outside, John Henry trying to stop him from pissing on a lamp post. John Henry loved to remember that night and had talked about it so much he, J.D., had got to be proud of having pissed on the lamp post in Cope, though not so proud as he was of the other famous time, the morning after Macklin had given Maeve the shaft. Standing near the top of the Spoon, he had waited for Macklin to show up below, feeling hate like a cleansing flame. When Macklin had appeared at the bottom he had started down, yelling *"Track!"* just for the record, because he knew of a schussboomer out of control at Mount Marie who had killed a guy and hadn't even been prosecuted, since skiing was a dangerous sport and you always had to watch out for yourself anyway. He was going to kill Macklin for what he had done to Maeve, to his wife, and to his son.

In the end he had veered off just enough to miss him; he had never really meant to hit him, just to scare the crap out of him, and he had done that, all right, running over the backs of Macklin's skis. Missed him by a hair, cut to a stop, and skipped back up to tell Macklin, white as skim milk, what he thought of him; he had called him every name he knew, and he knew a few from having spent four years in the U.S. Navy. Over the years, because it had been talked about a lot, he had been very proud of what he had done; but now no more.

Because you might kid somebody as simple as John Henry, but you couldn't kid yourself. Because your ear could not help hearing the tunes behind the tune of pride and revenge being whistled up front. Between those two times, when he had pissed on the lamp post in Cope and when he had schussed the Spoon, there had been another time nobody talked about. After which he and John Henry had never again been the friends they had been during the building of the Platterlift; after which he and Dickie Macklin had hardly been able to look at each other; after which he had had to hate Macklin so much. It was the day he had learned to keep his mouth shut. When you were stupid you yacked away and listened only to yourself talk. When you got smart you shut up and listened to others crucify themselves. He had learned to keep his mouth shut by hurting Dickie so badly it still hurt to think about it.

Dickie often came up on the Spoon, after school and weekends, to talk to him and John Henry while they worked. Dickie was so grateful when they allowed him to help that they always tried to think of something for him to do, even if it was only to run down for bolts or a wrench they didn't particularly need. When Isobel Macklin went to Hawaii for money and Macklin started banging Maeve in the Big House, it was awkward with Dickie because they had to be careful not to mention the situation, or even Macklin.

They were almost finished then, and it had already snowed, but snow on the ground couldn't stop them now. This day they had the cat up at Tower Four with a load of sheaves, and they were sitting behind the tractor taking ten for a smoke. He remembered the stink of gas—the tractor's tank leaked when it was parked on a slant—and worrying a little about smoking with that gasoline stink. And did he remember what he and John Henry had been talking about while they took a break and smoked a cigarette in the middle of the afternoon?

He did, in detail. They had been talking about Macklin and

about Maeve. But he couldn't even let himself off that easily. He had been doing the talking and John Henry the listening, because in those days he had been the authority on ass; because he was a little older, because he had been four years in the Navy, he had thought it was expected of him.

He had spoken on the old question of little men versus big men in the matter of satisfying women. He had had a lot to say about the more-than-slightly-queer setup of Macklin, Badbody, and Isobel. He had lectured on men getting sick of their wives, inventing, to bolster his thesis, the rotten lie that his father had said he couldn't get a hard-on with his mother except in a motel. He had gossiped about Maeve and Clary at Craven, embroidering on what he knew of that; he had speculated, as though the speculation were truth, on what went on back in Maeve's and Tim's corner of the Social; and he had lied, filthily, stupidly, that he had made it with Maeve himself.

He could not understand why he had needed to try to snow John Henry Collins that way, and when he tried to examine himself it was like looking inside at all sorts of nasty pieces-of-gut and black-slug sorts of things that he didn't even want to understand.

When they had finished their cigarettes and got up to go back to work, he heard John Henry suck in his breath as though he'd remembered something important that had been forgotten. Standing beside John Henry, looking down the Spoon where John Henry was looking, he saw Dickie Macklin in his red sweater walking down the lower part of the hill. Dickie picked up a rock and tossed it at one of the Platter towers when he passed it. His footsteps in the snow showed where he'd been.

And now it was like a joke on him, or something worse, that John Henry had got to be the king stud in Hollywood, where sex was a supermarket thing and you threw back the ones with spots —John Henry screwing some different glamorous babe every night while he dragged home to Peggy, who stank of milk and claimed she still had a sore twat from the stitches. Maybe it was the hell he had damned himself into that day, and maybe it was fair enough.

8: Captain Easy

WAITING IN THE LOUNGE at the party, which was still shy its guest of honor, he carried on an only slightly preoccupied conversation with Badbody, John Henry, and Martha, and, if not with, at least in front of, a silent Tim Soderburg.

He grinned at Badbody, who was looking thoughtful, and said, "Well, here we are waiting for Maeve."

Badbody smiled back with amused understanding. Tiny clusters of lights from the sconces danced in the lenses of his glasses. John Henry was gesticulating as he explained something to Tim, who sat with his neck hunched into his barrel of a body, his cropped hair with its deep widow's peak like a sketch of hair on his dark head. Martha, irritated, pretended to be listening to their conversation, smoking cigarettes and snubbing them out in a stack of butts.

To Badbody he made deep-breathing sounds dramatizing nervousness. "What's she like?" he asked. "Does it show?"

Badbody always seemed to know on what level he was speaking. "Not in the way you might think," he said. "Not hard."

"That's good."

"She wears her hair long now."

Badbody watched him gravely as he nodded. "Of course a great courtesan must have to be a great lady," Badbody said.

"Is she a great lady?"

"Is who a great lady?" Martha demanded, butting in.

"Yay! Maeve!" John Henry said. "Is she great, Bads?"

"Yes, she may be great," Badbody said, nodding seriously. "I don't think you'll find her quite what you expect," Badbody said, looking from John Henry, to him, to his wristwatch.

He made catcalling sounds at the back of his mouth, thinking of Maeve waiting in the wings and putting this pressure on the old boy friends.

"I really don't know why I'm here," Martha said, finishing her Gibson and adding another bent-double butt to the ashtray. "I should be at home calling Franklyn. She pouted at him; he wasn't being a good guy tonight. She was in a poor position here, with the ex-suitors of the great courtesan. "I think I really will go home and call Franklyn," she said.

He recognized it as a test. He should offer to take her home. "Take my Jeep," he offered.

She went. He felt very much part of a group, sitting with the other waiting-for-Maevers, watching Martha stride out of the lounge. Betsy, alerted by the departure, came over to see if more drinks were wanted. It was a tribute to Maeve that no one watched Betsy returning to the bar.

Tim was biting his lip. John Henry lighted a cheroot. Badbody's face was lined, thoughtful, a little sad. Over the last few years Badbody had lost much of his old humor—his mockery had taken on a bitter edge—and this was not the first time he had seen the sadness in Badbody's face-in-repose. Although he might have talked a problem of his own over with Badbody, their relationship was not such that he could ask the other what was wrong.

Okay, Maeve, it's time.

They rose as one man when she appeared. He was surprised at how slight she was.

She came toward them through the tables, wearing an ankle-length skirt of some heavy blue-green material, a cream-colored blouse with full sleeves and a high collar, a wide leather belt. Around her neck hung a number of gold chains of varying lengths. White-gold hair lay in a fringe on her forehead and fell in a long hank in front of one shoulder. Her thin face was very brown, her eyes dark in it, her mouth light and smiling as now, closer to them, she came on with her torso slanted back like a bullfighter's and her arms stretched out, palms down, in a posturing he found unbearably trite.

Unfortunately she encountered Badbody first, who had already seen her; but Badbody helped her carry it off. His arms came out in imitation of her, to meet hers. Their hands gripped. They stood for a moment slanting away from each other, and then Maeve leaned forward for a kiss.

He found himself grinning like a madman, in mockery. He stopped grinning when Maeve faced him. He gazed into the blue-shadowed eyes that seemed to absorb his. He felt the great unfocused magnetism of her and, feeling it, recalled it totally. After a moment the power seemed to switch off, not purposefully but as though it had peaked out, or the inner coordination necessary to maintain it had failed. Her smiling face enlarged as it came toward his, and he kissed her mouth and smelled her perfume, but did not, any more, feel the power of her presence, although he saw what Badbody had meant about her greatness. She was very light in his arms. "Hey, hey, hey, hey, *hey!*" she whispered in his ear in some jet-set incantation before moving along.

He almost cheered aloud, as she kissed John Henry, at the poignancy of the moment she was creating. She moved from John Henry to Tim, whose face was red as a wound, kicking a foot back as she raised her face to be kissed. John Henry made a face of awed approval, winking an eye, twisting his mouth and clapping hands, once, silently, like a parody of an English lord. Badbody was Kleenexing emotion from his glasses.

Then they were all standing in a row, having been kissed by the Mariachi Girl, and Maeve, holding on to Tim's arm, was smiling brilliantly at them, having run the gantlet.

"Well done, Maeve!" he said, and he was pleased to see he could still make her blush with a compliment.

Badbody arranged a chair for her, and she sat down, holding her hands together in her lap. She appeared tired beneath her warm tan. She turned toward Tim with an emphatic, stylized swing of her head that put her long hair into motion. "Bear," she said. Then, smiling at each of them in turn, she said, "John Henry. And Easy. And Brad." And now she engaged the machinery of gallantry: Badbody leaned forward to offer her a cigarette, he himself patted his pockets in search of matches, John Henry produced lighter and flame. He watched her and admired everything he saw, but something was missing.

A stop-start conversation began, keeping to commonplace and safe subjects. He did not participate, trying to get the feel of what Maeve was now, great courtesan or great lady, or only great. He saw that although she was very much in control she was tense with the effort. A solitaire diamond on her finger threw cold sparks when she moved her hand, the gold chains of many sizes and patterns around her neck were as though she wore her wealth like a primitive. She was very polished, very accomplished and confident, and, as Badbody had said, she was not hard.

They talked about John Henry's success and about mutual friends she and John Henry had. There was discussion of how Dancer had and had not changed; Isobel Macklin and Dickie were mentioned, and the ski school, the lifts, and the mountain. She had not heard that old Finney had died in the fire that had destroyed the Social. For the first time he found her phony, her eyes rounding and mouth turned down with the tragedy of death by fire, and suddenly the monument felt called upon to issue a statement.

"What's so bad?" he said. "He was seventy years old. We all heard him telling about all the things he'd done. He'd lived it all the way and he was ready to go. He couldn't even see any more, you know—they think that's what happened. He tried to get his fire going with gas instead of kerosene. What's tragic?"

It was a pat Easy Clary speech right out of the catalogue, and he was surprised at the reaction. Maeve and Badbody looked at him as though he were a pup who'd dragged in something smelly. Tim started to add something but stopped himself.

"Well, how long're you going to stay, Maeve?" John Henry said quickly, always sensitive to friction.

"Oh, I thought I might stay for a while," Maeve said.

"Yay!"

She laughed with an attractive wrinkling of her nose. "Maybe I'll stay till the powder's gone."

The impression came to him that she meant to stay longer than merely over the Christmas holidays; it seemed as if she had been addressing him in particular, though she had not looked at him since his faux pas.

Tim stirred in his chair to herald a speech. "There'll be good powder tomorrow all right, Maeve."

"I want to go up in the Superchute," Maeve said intensely.

"Can we, Bear? A powder party? I've been thinking of it for so long, though I'm terrified I won't be able to make that first turn. How's the cornice?"

He started to say the wind hadn't been blowing enough to build the cornice, but it was not his place, it was Tim's mountain.

Tim rumbled, "You don't have to worry about any cornice tomorrow. I keep them knocked down pretty good, Maeve."

He saw Badbody's hand nervously spanning his glasses, slipping them off, then on again. The trail of association was clear enough: powder-Superchute-cornice-avalanche-Macklin.

"It's settled then," Maeve said. "We're all going up to ski the powder in the Superchute tomorrow morning."

"Just-for-us-powder! Yay!"

"It's all I've been able to think about for so long," Maeve said.

"Here comes Mrs. Macklin," Tim said.

They rose as though called to attention. Isobel Macklin was approaching, a step ahead of Dickie, her pale, soft, stern face and shining gray hair ensconced in the high collar of her mink coat. Maeve turned her head with the affected-effective hair-swinging motion. Each cried out the other's name, they surged toward each other and embraced.

He chortled delightedly and exchanged glances with Badbody, whose face had taken on its familiar mocking expression, as the two women kissed and exclaimed as though they were genuinely fond of each other, had genuinely missed each other—the two women who had shared Dick Macklin in his last days.

And maybe, he thought, they were glad to see each other, maybe enough years had passed for time to heal all those old wounds. And so maybe now he himself could look rationally at that day in the basement of the lodge when he had thought that Macklin, the old bull of the woods, was trying to cut him down. Maybe the young bull had been mistaken, maybe it was not that at all, and so maybe in his fear, in his rage, in his jealousy, it was Captain Easy who had crucified Dick Macklin.

Macklin had been a small man with a limp—one of his legs was slightly shorter than the other from a war wound—and a heavily lined, handsome face. He was tyrannical, sarcastic, mean, and charming, though his charm had decreased and his meanness increased in direct proportion to how much back pay he owed his employees. And no doubt Macklin's irritability had been due to the situation in which he was trying to juggle several dozen balls at once, kicking the ones he dropped under the table so no one would notice.

Everyone had been too busy to notice his failures. It had been impossible not to notice his last success. Isobel had departed for Honolulu, and Macklin had exercised his rights as lord of the manor, or more probably hadn't had to, and Maeve had taken a giant step along the road she had chosen for herself. But Macklin's appropriation of Maeve had been intolerable to all of them. There had been mutinous talk, and righteous talk about poor Isobel and poor Dickie. He supposed everyone else had been, each in his way, as jealous as he was. But he was the one who had thought he was joking when he had suggested Macklin as a prospect to Maeve.

The exact sequence of those days escaped him now, Time being lost in time. The frantic effort had been to get ready for the Christmas holidays, for it was clear that if the Christmas business was lost, Macklin, in deep trouble already, was himself lost. He remembered Badbody, Maeve, and Macklin painting in the lodge; Rody typing, running the mimeograph machine, and answering the telephone; Dickie and Maeve staggering with huge cardboard boxes through the lobby; John Henry and J.D. up on the Spoon installing the sheaves on the Platter. Luckily the snow held off that year.

He and Tim were building the off-ramp at the Intermediate Station. When the snow did begin it came in a series of small storms, and many mornings they all went up on the lift early and skied the powder in the Superchute and the Chute for an hour before starting work. Fortunately for them, Macklin had been a powderhound too; unfortunately for him.

So they skied hard and worked hard, and Macklin had Maeve to warm his bed and was hated for it. Each day there was a new crisis, and each new crisis was either solved somehow or made to get in line with the old crises. One day the crisis was that the heating contractor walked off the job without hooking up the lodge furnace to the registers, demanding money first. That was the weekend before the lifts were scheduled to open to the public.

Macklin disappeared all day and returned at dark with the pickup stacked with lengths of asbestos-coated duct, like white cordwood, and announced to Tim that he was borrowing him, Easy Clary, the next day, to help install the ductwork. By then each of them was a prima donna, considering his own project the most important one. Tim swore hysterically, but Macklin replied mildly that skiers could fall off the lift at the Intermediate Station if necessary, but there must be heat in the lodge or the pipes would burst. He did not look forward to working alone with Macklin.

Early next morning they began moving the lengths of duct down into the basement and making the connections to the plenum. They worked silently around the great black furnace, its mouth open to reveal pale peach-colored flames. It was uncomfortably hot near it, and they worked fast to get away, more slowly as the first duct line lengthened. Finally Macklin said, "Break, Captain Easy?"

"Right."

They sat on the concrete step furthest from the furnace; he produced cigarettes and Macklin lit them. He felt the need to seize some advantage in this cigarette-break intimacy. "Well, do you think you'll make it?" he said.

Macklin drew on his cigarette, frowning as though considering the question carefully. "Oh, I think so," he said. "Yes, I think it will be made."

"You have faith."

"Yes. Well, faith is better than hope." Macklin laughed and added, "And anything's better than charity."

He laughed too, gazing at the open mouth of the furnace. Above it was a curved chrome mustache bearing the embossed inscription B-T-U-ERATOR, MUNCIE, IND. He was feeling the famous Macklin charm. It irritated him to realize it.

And Macklin said, to show him his place, he thought, or perhaps only because he wanted some light, "Somewhere we've got a fifty-foot extension with a lamp on the end. Do you suppose you could find it, Captain Easy?"

When he returned with the light, Macklin had almost finished the shortest duct line. The last section had to be cut, Macklin seemed hesitant, so while his employer watched, he did the measuring and, hacksaw shrieking, made the cut. The moment was unpleasantly freighted with importance, and he was relieved when the piece fit.

They started on the next line, forcing the duct together and nailing slings of steel-strap to the joists. The portable light gleamed on Macklin's cropped hair, on his sweaty, dusty face, and made harsh oblongs of shadow under his eyes. Macklin dragged armloads of duct through the dirt to hand them to him.

"How is it you know how to do things like this?" Macklin asked. "I thought Southern Californians spent their youth lolling in the sun."

"I've had a lot of odd jobs to keep from having any other kind," he said. Another cut had to be made, and he said, "Hand me the handsaw, not the hawk."

Macklin chuckled and again watched him measure and cut, and again there was the unpleasant feeling that Macklin was willing him to make an error. The antagonism between them seemed to be nourished by every exchange.

The next time they took a break Macklin said, "I think the name Captain Easy was one of my better efforts, don't you? A handsome, indomitable character out of the funny papers. Implications of the easy rider, the easy way, lotus-eating."

He stared back into Macklin's shadowy, dirty, deeply lined face, with the cigarette fork-fingered to the corner of the mouth. He felt trapped.

"I understand your purpose in life is merely skiing?" Macklin said.

"That's right."

Macklin was silent, as though considering whether he needed taking down and, if so, how to do it.

Macklin didn't return to the subject until they were back at work. Then he said, "Your snow's too limited. You're just cutting up one little slope when there's a whole world of powder to exploit."

He didn't answer, almost abstractedly watching the chemical reaction in himself. He had never been able to bear criticism. He slid a length of duct forward, but not far enough, so that Macklin had to strain to reach it. Macklin hunkered back a yard, fitted the piece of duct to the last piece, slapped a block of two-by-four across, and tapped the wood with the hammer.

"You don't feel the need to make anything?" Macklin asked. "Build anything? Change anything? Leave anything behind you that wouldn't have existed if you hadn't existed?"

"Only thing I have to make is my own life," he answered. Having said it, he examined the statement almost in panic, as though Macklin, by some evil power, was endangering his Principles. *You've got a theory about everything, haven't you?* Maeve had said to him. And of course Maeve was in a way the subject here.

"Just make your life the way you want it," Macklin said, grunting as he worked in an awkward position.

"Right."

"Just skiing the powder as pure pleasure of the senses?"

"That's it."

"You're not skiing the powder at the moment. You're down in this dirty basement sweating like a horse. You haven't been paid for six weeks and may never be. I'd like to feel it's out of loyalty to me, but I hardly think so."

"To what you're doing here. I'm not only interested in skiing the powder myself. I'd like to see everybody doing it."

Macklin dropped his hands into his lap and sat with his shoulders slumped. "Change jobs," he said. "I'm beginning to have the Jesus cramps. Has it ever occurred to you that in the crucifixion Our Savior's arms were nailed into the position of benediction?"

Sliding past each other in the dirt, they changed places. Now Macklin could watch his illuminated face from the shadows, as he had been watching Macklin's.

"So you think I'm doing a good thing here?" Macklin said.

He nodded. "A pleasure garden," he said.

"Pleasure garden!" Macklin sounded pleased. "What do you think I'm doing it for, Captain Easy?" he said.

"Make something, build something, leave something." He felt as though he had won a point in a losing game.

"Maybe," Macklin said, chuckling. Then he said, "I do know I'd like to do it all over again. Maybe the best thing would be for the Indians to close in right now and throw me out. Anybody could run Dancer from here on, and I'd be free to make and build, and maybe to leave it, too, all over again. The worth-while part. And free—you don't know what free means until you face slavery." In a tightening voice he said, "Fat-assed, uxorious, and grateful, sitting down running a successful operation."

In his own self-consciousness he was unable to digest all that Macklin had said. It seemed to him that Macklin meant that Dancer was finished as far as he was concerned, that Macklin would like to cut out now, leaving his wife; and so Macklin must want to go with Maeve.

"Do it all over again?" he said, just to be saying something.

"Because it was really living," Macklin said, and then, as though he felt he had talked too much, given himself away, he returned to the attack. "You're just a chip dancing along on the bubbly surface of life, Captain Easy. What about the profound depths? What about living life to the hilt?"

Macklin went on, increasingly sarcastic, increasingly obnoxious. Of course Macklin would have perceived that he must be attacked from the left since all of his defenses faced right. He felt the poison of adrenalin in his body, and there was a metallic taste to the roof of his mouth. Almost coolly he told himself he was going to hit Macklin the next time Macklin called him "Captain Easy."

"You're living on whipped cream instead of red meat, Captain Easy," Macklin said.

In instant, almost relieved reaction his hand shot out straight-arm fashion. The heel of his hand struck flesh, not particularly hard, an introductory blow. Macklin grunted and fell back, then scrambled to his feet. They faced each other. Macklin looked shaken and tired, his mouth tightly closed and bent down at the corners.

He realized with a shock that Macklin was afraid of him.

"What the hell did you do that for?" Macklin whispered.

He did not have to try to answer that question because just then John Henry came running down the stairs; friends of Macklin's had arrived from San Francisco. Macklin followed John Henry back up the steps, limping more than usual, brushing the dirt from his clothes. He didn't look back.

That was the last he saw of Macklin that day. He finished installing the ducts by himself, working furiously to get the job done. Macklin had taken his friends skiing off the top of Big Red One, and that night there was a party for them, men only, in the almost completed bar, with J.D. mixing drinks and John Henry playing the guitar. Lights were reflected like spilled luminous paint on the snow outside, and he could hear the sound of the guitar and the heavy laughter of men almost to the Big House.

It was possible to look into the lighted bedroom window of the Big House by scrambling up on the narrow, snow-covered shed roof that adjoined the kitchen, standing on the eave of the shed, leaning out at approximately a seventy-five-degree angle and supported by a hand on the window frame.

The walls of the room were studded with framed art prints. There was a king-sized bed with a red-and-black coverlet thrown back to reveal white sheets. A table beside the bed held a marble clock and a book turned face down. His body on the strain, arm cramping, toes hanging in space, he gazed into the room until Maeve appeared, like a character opening a play. She was wearing a pair of men's black-and-white pin-striped pajamas. Her short hair gleamed. He watched her looking at herself in the mirror, touching her face in a peculiar way and leaning forward as though she were nearsighted. After a time she took off the pajama bottoms and, kicking them ahead of her across the floor, went over toward the turned-down corner of the bed. Without the pajama bottoms she looked like a sexy photograph from a men's magazine.

He tapped on the window.

Her face jerked toward him, but she didn't look frightened. She came to the window, obviously unable to see him until her nose touched the glass, its tip turning white. He mouthed the words "Open up!" He had to push himself back onto the shed roof so she could open the window. Overhead the moon was fat and white as a pillow. Maeve squatted down behind the sill so he couldn't see her bare thighs.

"What are you doing?" she whispered. He could hear the guitar strumming behind him in the lodge like an audible pulse beating.

"Told you I'd come, didn't I?"

She made an apprehensive face. "Shhhhhh! Dickie—"

He leaped through the window opening like a Hollywood pirate, banging a knee as he slipped. Maeve rose and backed away, holding down the hem of her pajama top.

"I just didn't think I'd have to come so soon," he said and took her in his arms as masterfully as he had ever seen it done on the screen.

The moment of leaping through the window and sweeping Maeve into his arms had had its humorous aspects. After that there were none. In Macklin's bed, in the darkness, there had been the wildest excitement he had ever known, the fiercely burning, bitter-sweet joy of tragic love and renunciation. They had sworn, welded together, that although their demons drove them apart, they would love forever.

Over the years he found himself able to laugh at the scene. It had been so very, very corny, and of course Maeve must have forgotten what for her was merely another incident in a life crowded with assignations, lovers, and declarations of love undying. Yet still, over the years, ridiculed and dishonored, that night had retained a certain power in his memory, the night a jet-set sexbox and Mariachi Girl to-be and a gigolo of a skibum had wept in each other's arms and vowed eternity.

He had always been afraid, from what developed at the paycheck ceremony, that Macklin had found out what had happened, and he had been guilty and furious, a little smug, but terribly sorry, that Maeve had been so hurt because he had come tapping at her window.

But now he wondered if Macklin had really threatened him as he had thought himself threatened, and now he was beginning to wonder if he shouldn't feel sorry for the way Macklin, not Maeve, had been hurt.

9: *Timbal Khan*

SHE WORE GOLD CHAINS that looked so heavy his neck ached in sympathy. She was much thinner than she had been, and she had lost her girlish pink-and-whiteness. He thought she was very beautiful.

Talking to Isobel Macklin, who was sitting on the other side of her, Maeve must have felt his eyes, for she turned toward him with a heart-pulling swing of her long hair. She smiled her old smile at him. "Bear," her lips said, without any sound.

Everyone else was talking, and there was a loud squall and beat of music from the combo.

"How are you skiing, Maeve?" he asked her.

"I'm very good! I've had lessons from all kinds of instructors—French, Austrian, everything."

"What'd *you* need lessons for?"

She laughed. "I'm afraid I'm going to need some lessons in the powder. It's been so long!"

"You'll remember how to do it. It's just sitting back and rotating. Clary always says it's mostly faith." He looked down past John Henry to where Easy Clary was illustrating something for Isobel Macklin, using his hands. Probably Easy was making his airplane noises too, but these were inaudible.

Maeve said, "I want a powder party with everybody up on the Superchute just the way we used to do it, Bear." There was anxiety in her voice. Skiers who had been away from the powder for a while, with a broken leg or off somewhere on business, were always afraid they wouldn't be able to ski it again.

"Well, we'll sure do it," he said. Mrs. Macklin glanced down at him and smiled in her stiff way and out of his Maeve-inspired confidence he said, "Are you coming skiing the powder with us in the morning, Mrs. Macklin?"

"Oh, no." She frowned. "Oh, I'm afraid not, Tim, thank you," she said. She turned away to rub her cigarette out in an ashtray.

"I want it just the way it was the last time I skied the powder at Dancer," Maeve said softly.

She must not realize what she's saying, he thought. The last time she had skied the powder at Dancer, Dick Macklin had been killed. Her eyes burned brightly into his, as though to convey something she was not ready or able yet to put into words. She wore a high-necked blouse that had a sheen to it, and beneath the weight of the gold chains her breasts made points and shadows in the shiny material. But she was not the old Maeve, the make-believe Maeve, not the voice from behind the plywood partition. Although it was a disappointment, even more it was a relief. He remembered that he was due at Rody's.

Easy Clary, with his close-set eyes beneath cantilevered brows, was saying to Isobel Macklin, "Sure it's fun skiing packed slopes, but the super-pleasure is the powder. Because it's sensation all mixed up with adventure and a little fear—taking chances. It's when you're out early after the powder that the avalanche gets you."

He was shocked that Clary would say this to Isobel Macklin, and Maeve turned to stare.

Betsy came up just then to see who wanted another drink. Dickie Macklin was sitting in an awkward, juvenile position with his legs spread, scowling as he talked to Badbody, and, standing behind him, Betsy looked down at him protectively.

"Can you cut an avalanche with your skis, Bear?" Maeve said in the private voice. She was holding her martini, moving her hand slightly to swing the flat plane of liquid in the glass. It seemed to him she should know that much about avalanches, having worked at Craven and Dancer and skied a lot.

"Sure you can. I do it all the time."

"How do you do it?"

"Well, if you pick the right place you can ski right across and cut it loose, like cutting a piece of cloth with a knife. Above you it stays—it better! And it peels loose below you while you traverse across. You've got to know what you're doing, but it's not too dangerous. If you miscue, at least you're falling down the mountain on top of it, not it on top of you."

"You don't just—ski across to a place and stamp?"

"Sure. I do that too. Stamp to see if it'll hold. Lots of places you want to cut a slide loose at a point, not a line going across."

She smiled. She nodded and turned to listen to what others were saying. He supposed this was how she played her game, flattering him by pretending to be interested in the mountain and snow safety. He was flattered that she would take the trouble. Watching her face, he remembered the color that had always come and gone in it so readily. There had been a brightness in her face that he missed. He wondered if she was really beautiful or only beautiful to him, only tan, blond, slim, cleverly made up, and clever about making men want her.

Suddenly she said, "Bear, why do you suppose the cornice came down that day?"

"It could've been anything," he said. "A change of temperature could've done it, or—"

"I always thought somebody knocked it down."

"Well, sure, they probably cut it loose skiing out in the bowl. I don't know what happened up there except what everybody told me when I was trying to find out where you'd seen him last. He'd skied out ahead of the rest of you. I remember how he liked to cut up the powder first."

"Then what happened?" Maeve asked, staring into his eyes.

He became aware that Isobel Macklin was watching him too, little muscles pulling along the edges of her jaw like piecrust crimping. Avoiding her eyes, he said to Maeve, "Well, he started a snowslip, I guess. It carried him down a way—that's not too dangerous, that'll happen sometimes. Except the cornice was pretty big. No one could've known it would build up so big so early in the season. It can build up really big just overnight if the wind's blowing the right way, but we didn't know it yet. Anyway, the snowslip knocked the cornice loose. And that was a hell of a lot of snow coming down."

He felt that she didn't remember he hadn't been there that day. "I wasn't up there," he said. "Remember?"

"Because of the cars," Maeve said. "But then you were, later on, when they were—looking for him."

He felt as though he had been accused of something. At least Isobel Macklin wasn't listening any more. He took a deep breath and said, "I didn't know they were going up." Wasn't that a lie, the first lie? "Anyway," he went on quickly, "he'd canned me, so there wasn't anything—" That was clearly a lie. The point was that it was the last time he had let personal considerations cause him to fail the mountain, but there was no way he could tell Maeve this. Looking down at his hands spread on his knees, he said, "I was so damn busy then, just before we opened. I didn't have time to think. I just didn't have time to check on the cornices. Trying to keep the road plowed and Big Red running, and a bunch of college kids—" He stopped, his heart beating painfully as he said these things; and he remembered his heart beating just this way when he was lying on the cot in the concrete cube of a room beneath the Big Red One terminal, listening to the bullwheel creaking and grating as it turned above him.

"I've never thought it was your fault, Bear," Maeve said and rested a hand on his hand.

When he looked up she was smiling affectionately at him, her head cocked, a tan rim of ear showing through the blond hair. He thought he understood now. She was not so afraid of skiing the powder as she made out: she was only thinking of Dick Macklin in the avalanche. She was not trying to flatter him with her attention: she was only thinking about Dick Macklin. Through her marriage and all her affairs, and all those parties and flying around Europe doing the wonderful things she had told him she wanted to do, she had only been thinking about Dick Macklin.

He rose. "Got to go. I'm supposed to go to Rody's for dinner."

"Rody's still here! She'll come skiing with us tomorrow, won't she, Bear?"

"I'll ask her. Sure she will." Probably, he thought, Rody was obsessed just the same way, who had found out from Macklin what it meant to be ravished.

"You and Rody didn't get married after all," Maeve said, looking up at him. "I always thought you would."

He managed to laugh. He shook his head. "I'm married to the mountain, I guess, Maeve."

Her eyes dropped away from him, and he felt as though he had

been released. He said good night to everyone, thanking Badbody
for the invitation to dinner. He hurried out of the lounge with
self-conscious strides, though most likely no one bothered to look
after him. He was heavy with the memory of the bullwheel
creaking above him and, before that, of the fight with Macklin.
What was important about the fight with Macklin was that it had
not been a fight at all.

Those days when Maeve was living with Macklin in the Big
House had been, for him, a time of corroding resentment and
savage daydreams of revenge, a time of overwork and anxiety
and his nerves sticking out all over him like boils to the touch. He
had been so tired. He had worked so hard so long, spread himself
so thin—trying to see that Big Red One kept moving; watching
out for J.D. and John Henry on the Platterlift without letting
them think he didn't trust them, seeing that the trails were
marked and that "Avalanche Danger" and "Not Patrolled" signs
were painted and ready, when he hadn't known a quarter enough
about snow safety; and trying to get some discipline or at least
routine into the bunch of bums and college boys Badbody had
hired for ski patrol and lift attendants. There was no way of
knowing from one day to the next whether anybody would come
to work or not, because Macklin had been as tightwad then as
Badbody was to become later. And to top everything, a blizzard
had come roaring in, luckily not as big as many they had had
since, but big enough and tough to cope with, especially trying
to keep the road and parking lot cleared. The rotary was supposed to be John Henry's job, with Badbody helping him, but
Badbody was always being called to the lodge for some crisis
there, and John Henry dreamed along, singing, and let the
blower clog and got the machine stuck. And when the rotary was
in the ditch, call Tim Soderburg to get it out.

It had seemed to him that he was trying to run everything
alone. He was always on the edge of blowing up, he never had
time to shave, his eyes felt as though people had snubbed their
cigarettes out in them. Whenever he tried to grab a couple of
hours sleep in the concrete cell beneath the Big Red One bullwheel, someone always waked him up to come fix whatever had
gone haywire now. It seemed to him the others spent most of

their time drinking coffee, though they always got up on the mountain early when there was fresh powder to ski. They always had time for that. He would see them doing things, but in his angry fatigue he suspected they spent most of their time taking coffee breaks and talking about the powder and about what they would have him do next. Not getting paid hadn't mattered.

Then the paychecks were given out, and Macklin had called Maeve a whore. Later, lying awake, waiting for Maeve to return to her cubicle in the Social, he heard her come quietly in, heard her undressing and that final creak as she got into her own bed. Neither of them spoke.

At first he had blustered to himself that he would kill Dick Macklin, but it was a passion of the mind, thought instead of felt. Much more powerful was his relief that Maeve was all right after all. From the moment Macklin had seen her naked in the swimming pool, it was as though he had watched, in horror, someone taking a terrible fall, an eggbeater, say, down the Scarp toward the brown rocks at the bottom, helpless as she spun faster and faster down toward the rocks. But when she hit she had only a bloody nose. He felt that kind of relief when Maeve came back to the Social.

That was the weekend the lodge opened. Somehow the roads and the parking lot were kept clear, somehow Big Red One and the Platter did not immediately break down, and luckily no real test came for the scrubbiest of ski patrols. But even though Maeve was safely back in the Social his rage at Macklin continued to fester. He had worked so hard, they had all worked so hard, and Macklin sneered at them and would rake in the profits, and when he was done with them would throw them out as he had thrown Maeve out. He did not know until later that Rody had filled Maeve's place in Macklin's bed.

He didn't see Macklin until the next day, when he had to consult with him about problems on the mountain. In the lobby, among Dancer's first paying skiers, he was aware that he looked like a tramp, unshaven, long-haired, red-eyed, in his filthy parka and jeans. Rody was typing behind the arches over the counter, and Badbody, wearing a jacket and tie, was busy at his desk. Macklin, in a new ski outfit instead of his lucky sweater, came out of the inner office just as he leaned on the counter. He did not yet know that a little while before J.D. had schussed the Spoon and almost wiped Macklin out.

"Well," Macklin said, "it's Timbal Khan the Mountain Man!"

Rody stopped typing and looked up, smiling briefly, and then her eyes slid embarrassed between the two of them.

"More weather coming in," Macklin said.

"I guess so."

"And what else is new in the hall of the mountain king?" Macklin's face was a sneer, and he spoke with the fake British accent he put on sometimes. Macklin sneer-grinned at Rody, who laughed in an ass-kissing way.

Before he could reply, Macklin, ignoring him, looked at his watch and said to Rody, "Didn't Miss Olsen go to pick up my wife at the airport? They should've been back by now, shouldn't they, Miss Rohde?"

"They ought to be back any minute, Mr. Macklin," Rody said, looking at her watch too.

And with an ugly, suggestive grin, Macklin had sneered that the two women were probably weeping in each other's arms.

Leaning heavily against the counter beneath one of the arches, he felt whatever reserve he had left suddenly go. Macklin had as much as said Maeve and Isobel Macklin were queer for each other, talking filth the way J.D. Daugherty talked filth. His voice sounded rusty when he spoke. "You shouldn't talk that way in front of decent people."

Macklin's eyes jerked toward him, his mouth falling open a quarter of an inch. "What did you say?"

You rotten horny bastard—he couldn't call Macklin that in front of Rody. He was conscious of her anxious eyes as he said, "I said you ought to be careful how you talked in front of decent people."

Macklin's face turned pale. Then it turned so bruise-dark that he thought Macklin must be having some kind of attack. Macklin began to shout at him but quickly got control of himself and cut him to pieces with the clever razor of his tongue, pierced him and flayed him, Macklin standing on the other side of the counter with his hands at his sides and fingers working nervously in the palms of his hands, the continuation and the ultimate of all the sharp-and-sure-tongued, sharp-eyed little men who knew his in-

adequacy and broadcast it for all to hear; Macklin calling him
names whose meanings he could only guess at, describing
him with adjectives he had never heard before, but each of
which fit him like a finger slipped into a glove finger; Macklin,
whose body he could have broken over his knee like a piece of
lath—how could Macklin have known that Timbal Khan the
Mountain Man was afraid of him?

He listened, paralyzed, and Rody listened, and Badbody, and
some of the skiers passing through the lobby stopped to listen.
When Macklin finished, there was a hot, head-pounding, echoing
silence. It was either go around the counter and kill him or take it
just as Maeve had taken it.

Rody wouldn't even look at him now that she had seen at last
what he had hidden so well all those fast-skiing, plunging, downhill years. He turned away and went on out of the lobby past the
skiers stamping the snow off their boots as they came in. Outside
the sudden cold air cooled his cheeks.

Confronting him there were Maeve and Isobel Macklin in her
fur coat with the collar turned up, both of them wearing dark
glasses although it was snowing. "Hello, Bear," Maeve said in a
strained voice. "Good morning, Tim," Mrs. Macklin said, unsmiling. He managed a good morning in reply and hurried on past
them. Still he might have swallowed it, got it down, if Badbody
hadn't come out after him.

"Tim," Badbody said, catching his arm, "try to understand.
He—"

He snatched his arm away.

"Isobel coming home," Badbody said. "The music to face. I'm
trying to tell you he's not himself. He—"

To keep from facing Badbody he turned aside and saw before
him the crazy steel dancing figure that was Macklin's trademark.
"God damn him to hell!" he said. "Leave me alone!" He began to
run.

The first thing he passed was Macklin's Cadillac arrogantly
parked in the loading zone where only yesterday he had stuck a
"No Parking" sign, and without even reflecting that it was not
Macklin who had put the car there but Maeve come back from
the airport with Mrs. Macklin, he found direction for his pounding feet. Panting, his nose beginning to run, he lumbered down to

the end of the lot where he had left the rotary. He cranked the engine to life in a stink of exhaust fumes and headed the plow down the lot past the ranked tailfins of the diagonally parked cars. He could see Badbody running toward him. As he passed Badbody he swung the wheel a hair, and there was the stomach-loosening, knee-weakening crunch as he clipped the first car, a sound like a load of sheet metal dumped when he hit the second. His spirits came surging back. Almost he could picture himself as All-Out Soderburg again, the old downmountain racer, the wild man running wild down Exhibition as he was running wild now, taking off the tailfins with the snowplow unafraid of the consequences or of small men yelling at him. The rotary bucked and crunched down the line of cars heading for Macklin's Cadillac in the "No Parking" zone, with Badbody running and shouting after him. The snowplow stalled when he hit the side of Macklin's car.

He jumped down. "You can tell the deputy where he can find me," he called to Badbody's white face. He strode away, not to his room in the Social, for he did not want to encounter Maeve, but to the concrete cell beneath the Big Red One bullwheel where there was a cot and a sleeping bag. He waited there all day for the deputy, who didn't come. He slept there that night, full of misery and hate, with the wind whining like an animal outside.

And in the morning early he heard the creaking turning of the bullwheel and assumed it was the ski patrol going up on snow safety before the lifts opened; of course he had assumed that. It was the natural assumption, as it was also natural to assume he was fired and that a warrant had been sworn and the deputy would come and arrest him.

It was Clary who found him and told him Macklin had been buried by an avalanche.

10: Miss Bliss

SHE HEARD Tim's Scout backing and filling down the snowy bank below her house and saw the lights pale on her window for a moment before they were shut off. Forty-five minutes late! She supposed she should be surprised he had shown up at all. Now he would be coming up the snow path Stevie had widened and restepped, especially for him, and past the colored lights in the juniper that grew through the deck.

Stevie came out of his room, saying, "Is that him, Mom?" And she said, "Yes, it should be," shuffling together the spelling papers she had been correcting and replacing them in their manila folder. She went into the kitchen to see if the roast was shriveling in the oven. Stevie had opened the front door and was calling to Tim.

"Hi, boy," Tim said in his deep voice. Through the kitchen doorway and the open front door she had a glimpse of him scraping the snow from his boots, snowflakes falling in the light on the porch.

When she returned to the living room he was hanging his red ski-patrol parka on a hook in the entry, the man for whom the word burly could have been invented, with his heavy body on heavy legs, his bullet head with close-cropped dark hair, and his mild, weathered-dark face and eyes like semicircles of blue sky.

"Say, I'm sorry to be late, Rody," he said.

"Sit down and let me fix you a drink."

Stevie was squatting at the base of the Christmas tree, plugging in the lights. His behind in his jeans looked six inches across. He was narrow-boned, and he was going to be tall, not stubby as she was, not the fire hydrant he would have been if he had been Tim's and hers. He was going to have a perfect slalom body, in fact, and her heart turned over gently as she thought of him coming down through the gates today. He was so good. He was so damned good already, and not only from the coaching she had been giving him. He was just good from having her genes and having sucked her milk when he was a baby.

Tim sat on the flowered chintz couch cover with his knees together and his surprisingly small snowboots pointing toward the Christmas tree. "Say, that's really pretty, Stevie," he said as the lights came on. "Got a lot of presents stacked under there, haven't you? That's a fine tree, Rody."

"This one's for you, Tim," Stevie said, fishing out the manzanita pipe rack, which was lovingly wrapped in yards of white tissue paper and red ribbon, Tim's name emblazoned on it with a felt-nib pen. The pipe rack had originally been her answer to what Stevie should give his father for Christmas. Having finished it, and it was a good job, he had decided to give it to Tim, who did not smoke a pipe, rather than to his father, who did.

"Well, now, what do you suppose this is?" Tim said, holding the package up.

"Probably something for your feet," she said. "Everything we give for Christmas around here seems to be footgear. Do you want a highball?"

"Yeah, please, Rody," he said, glancing up at her. He'd already had a highball or two, she knew. Did he need them for courage to come here, or was it only long-sufferance? She supposed he tanked up every night at the Loup Garou. What else was there for him to do after work? He had never read anything but the sports pages. So he drank and dreamed of Maeve Olsen.

She went out to the kitchen to make highballs. When she returned Stevie was curled up on the couch beside Tim, looking up into Tim's face with those candid, admiring eyes, his hair catching a halo of gold in the lamplight. Tim was telling him about bringing somebody down in the toboggan.

". . . he was up there on the north side of the Scarp. You haven't been up there. It's—"

"Sure I've been up there," Stevie said. "Me'n Billy went up there last weekend."

"Don't you go up there any more," Tim said with steel in his voice. "This fellow shouldn't've been up there either. He'd busted himself up pretty good, a compound. I couldn't get the toboggan to him alone so I had to get Pete Barrett to help me. We dug in a place to set the toboggan and got him in the basket, and then Pete was supposed to hang on to the drag rope and let it down easy while I snowplowed down holding on to the handles. I don't know what happened, something gave way or Pete just lost his balance, but all at once we took off down that face, me in front and the fellow with the compound on the toboggan gaining on me, and Pete banging along on the end of the rope. I yelled at him to get that rope loose from himself before he hung up on something and we all got killed. He got it loose some way, and I really went flying down there with that toboggan on my tail. When I'd look back I'd see that poor fellow's head sticking straight up like some kind of turtle. I thought he'd probably have a heart attack on top of everything else. Well, you know what he said when we finally got stopped? He said, 'Well, that's one ride they don't have at Disneyland.'"

Tim guffawed, and Stevie, who had been on an expensive trip to Disneyland last summer with his father, laughed delightedly at being told this man-to-man, inside-ski-patrol story, and he would tell it himself, as part of the half-mythological Timbal Khan he believed in, over and over.

Handing Tim his drink, she frowned at Stevie, who had lied to her about going up on the north side of the Scarp. She hated to catch him lying. Don't lie, buddy. Don't lie, because sometime, with some lie, you may get stuck and have to live the rest of your life hanging from that lie. Once she had realized that "lie" was "life" with the "f" left out, and she had wept because it was so funny, and so apt, and because there was absolutely no one in the world she could tell it to. Miss Bliss, her third-graders called her.

She sat down on the piano bench with her drink, watching the two boys together. She didn't know whether she was jealous or gratified that they were so fond of each other. Tim treated Stevie as an equal, Stevie loved him for it, and of course Tim was a natural hero, an adventure-story character, schussing the mountain with a casualty on the toboggan, tossing hand charges around to knock avalanches down, an old-time, all-out downhill racer, renowned not so much for his victories as for being a wild man; and now he was chief mountain man in his red parka, faded jeans, and girl-size, aristocrat's boots, all muscle and ready-for-anything self-sufficiency. This in comparison to Norman Bliss, Stevie's father, with his no-hair head and his jiggle-belly, and feet that turned out slip-slop when he walked. And his big, embarrassing, inappropriate presents. Norman and his second wife, Marie, had three girls and obviously weren't going to go on trying for a boy. So Norman was courting Stevie, and Stevie couldn't stand him. When she was carrying Stevie, not knowing whether the unwanted thing in her belly was boy-Bliss or girl-Bliss, only knowing that she and Norman were never going to make it together, she and Norman had agreed to separate as soon as the baby was born; she would keep the child until it was five; then, if it was a boy, Norman was to take him. She considered this now a completely foolish and juvenile agreement, and she had reneged on it with a good conscience. Norman regularly reminded her of it, begging, reasoning, and threatening.

She knew it was not ideal for Stevie to live alone with his mother, a mother who had a full-time job and moonlighted teaching skiing on weekends in the winter. Still, how much worse it would be for him to live with his stepmother and stepsisters, and his father, who was a miserable, half alive, uncoordinated, hollow, money-making phony. Norman had quit teaching school to become a salesman after they had separated, and now he made a fantastic income selling some kind of investment stock. He and Marie had a beautiful home in Walnut Creek, with acreage and horses. He wanted Stevie to come live with them so he could learn to ride, so he could attend an expensive boys' school nearby and prepare to enter a good university. In sophisticated Walnut Creek, Norman pointed out, there were Little League, Junior Football, Junior Cotillion, and, of course, swimming and horseback riding. In Cope there were only winter sports, and Norman thought he was offering a life for Stevie she could not reject. She had not even considered it. Because in ten years Stevie would be an Olympic competitor, there was no doubt of it. And unlike his mother, Janet Rohde, who had also been an Olympic competitor, he was going to bring home a medal or two.

"Okay, buddy," she said to Stevie. "Go do that page of combinations I set up for you."

"Aw, Mom! Can I come back after?"

"You can come back after if you get them all right, and no fooling around."

" 'Kay," Stevie said and rushed off. He stopped in the hallway to make slalom motions with his hands and arms, flexing his knees and grinning back at her and Tim. Then he disappeared, to begin calling immediately, "Mom! I can't find a pencil!"

She went in to settle him with a pencil, focus the mini-lamp on the sheet of addition and subtraction combinations. She kissed him on his crown of short blond hair and went back to sit on the couch with Tim.

He said, "I'm supposed to ask you to come up and ski the powder in the Superchute tomorrow morning. About nine o'clock."

"Well! Just like old times."

He seemed even more embarrassed with her than usual.

"Yeah, like old times," he agreed and added, "Guess who's here."

"Who?"

"John Henry."

"Is he going to be singing at the lodge?"

"I think he's just up skiing."

She thought without much pleasure of the parties in the old T & O Social, John Henry playing guitar and singing and all the men attentive to Maeve Olsen like dogs around a bitch in heat, sniff, sniff.

"And Maeve's here," Tim said in a throat-clearing, rough voice.

The jolt of adrenalin hit her very much the way it had with the starter's "Go!" at the top of a downhill course, but nowhere to go, nothing violent to do to relieve the queasy tension. Maeve must have felt the emanations along the airways to wherever she had been—Hollywood, New York, Rome, Paris, or Acapulco—Rody's making a play for Tim Soderburg again, better get back and break it up. Surely a hand-adzed mountain man like Tim wasn't worth the trouble of the jet-set doll. Still, he was a man, and it wouldn't do for Miss Bliss to get one, would it?

"Are you kidding?" she said.

Tim shook his head, nodded, shrugged, all in one comprehensive gesture. "She's back all right," he said. "She wants to get all the old powderhounds up skiing in the Superchute in the morning. The way we used to do. We ought to go up early though."

"Trouble with civilization creeping up here is that you have to keep getting up earlier to hit the powder first," she said.

"That's all right. We run a resort so people from downbelow can come up and ski. But they have to give us first crack at the powder." Tim seemed relieved that she had not said anything more about Maeve.

"How's Maeve?" she asked.

"She's all right. She's thinner."

It came to her that without even realizing it she had won a round in the long, losing battle with Maeve. Because for all the Playboy breasts and long, showoff legs, the marriage and the lovers, there had been no child. She was suddenly fanatically proud of herself for conceiving, bearing, suckling, and raising the thin, graceful, intense boy-Bliss with his halo of crew-cut blond hair, who one day would ski for the United States in the Winter Olympics.

"She looked worried about something," Tim said.

"Oh?"

"Worried," Tim said and looked worried himself.

Stevie came trotting out of his room, holding the paper. "Finished," he said, and he was so jolly she couldn't send him off to bed right away even though he had missed three of the subtractions. At least he had tried.

In the kitchen, putting the meal together, from time to time she glanced into the other room at Stevie curled up on the couch by Tim again. She was finding a certain humor in the possibility that Stevie might be more important to Tim than Maeve was now. Wouldn't that be funny? And if that funny possibility was true, what of herself and Tim?

She had always felt herself superior to him, knowing her wit to be much quicker than his, and she had been a top student in school while he had always had grade trouble. Her mother, who had run the gift shop in Cope, had been a college graduate and a poetess often published in the weekly newspaper, while Tim's father worked at menial jobs. Yet she had always assumed that she and Tim would marry in the end. Infatuated with immortality, she had taken her fling with the Olympics and had come home, whipped, to find him infatuated with Maeve, and in her jealousy of Maeve she had told the ultimate lie, pretended to a passion stronger than death because of the strength of his passion, and on the hook of that lie all the errors of her life hung. Yet out of that, lie on lie and error on error, had finally come Stevie, her son. What a cosmic irony it seemed that Tim now should love the boy.

She had planned that they would sit down to dinner after Stevie had gone to bed, but she relented and let Stevie sit on a stool with them. And so they were able to talk only of things that included Stevie and interested Stevie.

She had planned a candlelit dinner with her wedding silver, but her courage had failed her. Still, it was pleasant eating at a card table before the fire in her pleasant living room, with the ivory-colored piano and the chintz curtains drawn. They talked about school, the children in her class, and about Stevie's class; about the senior races scheduled, and the junior races—she was hoping to arrange for Stevie to forerun the Christmas Day Giant Slalom. They talked about the ski patrol, and the lodge, and snow, and about nothing previous to day-before-yesterday.

When Stevie had to be sent to bed, he went aggrieved, tired, and weeping, and she had to go into his room, first to try to comfort, then to threaten him. Coming back, she found Tim standing in the center of the living room, of course to go, for what would they find to talk about now with Stevie in bed? But he said he'd have a try at fixing her sink, which she had mentioned leaked.

He lay on the kitchen linoleum with his head under the sink, grunting as he tried to tighten the trap with the pliers which were the only appropriate tool she could offer. In the end he took the trap apart and packed cotton string into the joint.

When he had finished and was wiping the grease from his hands with a paper towel, he seemed embarrassed by her gratitude and her flattery.

"Rody—" He stopped, quickly said, "Well, thanks a lot for the fine dinner." It was not what he had started to say. "I guess I'd better be running along," he said. "I'll have to be getting up pretty early in the morning."

She walked out to the entry with him and watched him get into his parka and check pockets for cap and gloves. At the door, half turned away from her, his face flushed a painfully dark red.

"Listen, Rody."

She was listening. "Yes?" she said.

"Listen, Rody, maybe we ought to be thinking about getting together."

She had been thinking about it. "Getting together?" she said.

"You know what I mean."

She supposed in some way she had Maeve to thank for this.

"You be thinking about it, huh?" Tim said and fled out the door.

She heard the starter of the Scout; the headlights illuminated the window palely again, then vanished. She turned off the outside tree lights and went into the kitchen to stack the dishes.

Because it was early still, she tried to go back to work on the spelling papers. Her mind would not stay on it. In bed, having drunk too many cups of coffee, she could not sleep. She heard the pad of bare feet.

"Mom?" Stevie whispered. He crept into bed beside her. It was something he had not done for a long time now. She disapproved of it. Once he had had an erection, which had shocked her with images of horrid perversities. But tonight she hadn't the heart to send him away.

"Mom?"

"Yes."

"Are you awake?"

"Yes."

"Mom, did you and Tim used to go around together?"

He knew they had. He loved to hear her tell of her youth, the racing years, the Olympic years, and Tim Soderburg.

"Yes, dear," she said.

"Tell me about it, Mom."

"Well, we went around together in high school and we went to all the races together. Like Barbara Giesel and Jack Davis."

"Did you hold hands like that, and twist together?"

"Nobody twisted then. We held hands sometimes."

Stevie was silent, contemplating that.

"Then we were both selected for the Olympic team, but Tim broke his leg. He came along to Europe anyway to help me—"

But this time it wasn't the Olympics Stevie wanted to hear about. "Why didn't you and Tim get married, Mom?"

"Because I married your daddy instead."

He was silent again, breathing heavily, and finally he said, "Well, why don't you marry Tim now, Mom?"

She stared up into the darkness. Why, now that everything at last, at long last, seemed to be going the way she wanted, did she feel so leadenly reluctant? "Oh, because a lot of reasons," she said aloud. "Maybe I don't love him. Maybe he likes being a bachelor, and maybe I like not having a big smelly man around the house. Anyway, I don't need a man. I have you. You're my man." That was really bad, she told herself.

"I'm just a little boy, for geez sakes," Stevie said disgustedly. "Well, I love Tim. Can't you marry somebody if you don't love him?"

"You have to swear you love him."

"Can't you just say you love him and—"

"That's not honest. I did that once and I won't do it again." Now she was in trouble.

"Didn't you love Daddy?"

"Maybe I thought I did. I can't remember now."

"Well, what happens if you never get in love at all? Do you just go along and never get married to anybody?"

"I guess so."

"I guess Tim's never been in love with anybody then."

"He was in love with me once."

"He was? Was he? Did he say so?"

"Said so all the time. That was a long time ago though. Okay, hush now, buddy. You'd better get back to—"

"Well, I'm never going to get married," Stevie said, seeing he would have to switch to a different subject or get booted.

"Sure you will, handsome brute like you."

"No, I'm not. I'm never going to be in love with any old girl. Except you though. I'll always love you, Mom."

"Thanks," she said, grinning savagely in the dark.

"I wish you'd married Tim though, Mom."

"Then you wouldn't be you. What about that? Okay, you go get in your own bed now and go to sleep. It's late, late, late."

"Wait a minute, Mom. I—"

"Off with you!"

"Oh, okay," Stevie said and got out of her bed and padded off into the darkness to his own room.

She turned face down, trying to click the switch of her mind off, and then not trying. She had promised Tim she would think over their "getting together." Instead she was thinking over how they had come apart.

She had always been amused at Easy Clary who, because he didn't want to settle down and go to work, had elaborately rationalized that skibumming was good and settling down to work bad. But work, making a living, was what in the end you had to settle down and do. She made a living teaching third grade at Cope School. She didn't get much satisfaction from teaching, though she thought she might if she went down to Cal and took her master's in testing methods, as she had often considered doing. Tim got both a living and satisfaction from his job on the mountain, vocation and avocation rolled into one, and he was lucky. The main run of people, like herself, just gritted teeth and stumped.

She was a divorcee schoolteacher with a son eight years old, and she was responsible to Stevie, and to her own integrity. She was to consider getting together with a hardshell bachelor who had no interest in anything that interested her other than skiing and Stevie, and no responsibilities other than to Dancer Peak and Dancer Peak Ski Area, Inc. Maybe now she was only hurt because Tim had no interest in her, only in his mountain and Stevie.

Though she had known him almost all her life there was the old incongruity in his character that had always puzzled her. As a person he was mild, steady, and dependable, but as a downhill racer he had been just the opposite. At Sun Valley, after they had been chosen for the Olympic team and were almost due to leave for Europe, in a silly downhill race that meant nothing at all, he had come down over the bumps on Exhibition at sixty miles an hour and hit the bales of hay around the lift tower so hard people had screamed to see it. They had had to wire his leg together with pounds of platinum, and he was finished with racing.

He hadn't seemed to care much, and, his own chances gone, he had pitched in to help her. Had she appreciated it, snotshot racer that she had been then, thinking everybody owed her everything? She would never let Stevie get that way.

She had needed Tim during those six weeks in Europe, and yet she had been contemptuous of him, because he could seem to pick up no French or German, because he was so clumsy and apologetically clownish in his walking cast, because he would not fight for her advantage with Pete Schramm, the coach; and contemptuous of him because, in the end, she was in the top seed of world-class ski-racing and he was her flunky.

The next autumn she started college at Davis, while Tim went to JC. He did not compete any more, while she was skiing better than ever. The next year she made the FIS team. Tim dropped out of JC to work downbelow for a while, and then he drifted back up to the mountains. She did not see him very often. She kept studying and skiing, gritting teeth and stumping, and her senior year she made her second Olympic team.

Pete Schramm used her only in the downhill, and she fell on the fallaway turn, that rotten airplane turn. It was the end of her chance for immortality or whatever it had been she was after, it was the end of her racing, and from then on, she knew, there was nothing but to live out the rest of her life in the shallows.

Even as her skis went out from under her in the speeding, flailing, spinning moment of her fall, when she knew her all-or-nothing gamble had failed, panting for breath, with both skis Markered off, trying to drag herself off the course with her helmet slipped over her eyes, she was planning her future: go home, finish teacher training, and, all in good time, resume her old relationship with Tim, finally marrying Tim and having a family, all that; almost pleased that she was free now to plan these normal, human, poopy things, and pleased at the thought of giving herself to Tim like a princess making a gift to a slave.

She had not written him of her decision, considering it settled. She got her certificate after summer session, came home to Cope, and took a job at Dancer, planning to start up with Tim again. Crazy in love with Maeve, he had hardly realized she was there. She had been hurt as she had never been hurt in losing any other race. So it was then, in her mind, that she had begun to enter Macklin in the competition too. She had been flattered when Macklin paid her attentions, made sexy jokes in her presence, patted her not quite on the behind, and she had been sure of a more serious pass when Isobel Macklin left for Hawaii to dig up more money. But of course Maeve had won Dick Macklin too.

He had told Maeve off the day before his wife was due home, and Maeve hadn't had enough pride to make herself scarce, humbly moving back into the Social again. All that day the office had been filled with tension, for Dick Macklin had been drinking and drunk, with heavy-lidded glances and slow movements. She was sure that this night he was going to take her and, this time, she was ready in her mind. But he had made no move, and at the end of the day she had driven home to her mother's in Cope as she did every night after work.

The next day Macklin had the scrape with J.D. on the Spoon and he was in such a savage mood because of it that he jumped Tim. She thought Tim was going to lose control of himself and kill Macklin, come across the counter and tear him to pieces; she had been poised to leap on Tim to try to stop him. And it was then that she was so grateful and relieved that nothing had ever happened between her and Macklin, because she was seeing him for what he was, a small, dirty-mouthed man squalling at Tim, who stood calm and silent before the disgusting things Macklin was saying, realizing that Macklin was terrified of him, and of J.D. Daugherty, and of his wife who had the money and was coming home to find out about Maeve. Macklin had been as far beneath contempt as Tim had been above it.

And then Tim had run wild in one of those incongruous, senseless actions like the downhill in Sun Valley, smashing fifteen cars in the parking lot, including Macklin's, with the rotary snowplow. Though over the years The Time Tim Plowed the Tailfins had taken on a hilarious, Paul-Bunyanish aspect, at the time she had only been horrified.

The next day Macklin died, Maeve fled the valley, and Isobel Macklin went back to Hawaii, leaving Badbody in charge. Things settled down. Life, which had been so exciting, became routine, a little dull. She assumed that now, finally, she and Tim would dully, duly get together. She hadn't realized the full power of Maeve Olsen.

One night she and Tim were at a party in the Sportsman's Club in Erskine, sitting together at a table in the smoky, beer-stinking semidarkness, watching everyone else dancing. She had had too much to drink.

"You hear from Maeve, Tim?" she asked.

He shook his head. "Haven't heard from her," he said. They watched the people jigging around the jukebox, which glowed with nasty pinks and yellows. Tim didn't dance.

"She doesn't write you every day?"

"No," Tim said, sprawled out in his chair, his dimly visible face embarrassed and unhappy, eyes glancing nervously toward her.

Leaning her elbows on the table and pretending to be sympathetic and understanding, she said, "Things pretty dull around here without her, huh?"

He looked even more unhappy. She remembered him scouting the Hahnenkamm course on one ski, for her. Her eyes were smarting from the smoke in the Sportsman's Club.

The music roared with rhythm and brass, and Easy Clary and a cheap girl in bright red stretchpants shook their middles at each other. "Tell me something," she said. "Did you and Maeve use to have orgies back in that corner of the Social?"

"No," Tim said.

"I always thought you did."

"No," Tim said sullenly. After a pause he said, "You shouldn't talk like that." Nobody was to say dirty things about his Maevie, not Macklin and not Janet Rohde, either.

"I'm sorry," she said, and all at once she felt very solemn.

"It's okay."

"You love her a lot, don't you?" she said. She was crying, but in the darkness no one would be able to tell. Through her tears she could see Tim's jaw tragically set. She patted his hand, grieving for him for loving Maeve, who was a bitch, but feeling a nobility in that doomed love. "You poor guy," she said.

And then without even thinking what she was doing she had hung herself on the hook. Because she was a competitor, because she could not bear to lose, she had said, "I know how you feel. In a way I do. It's such hell to know that—"

"What?" Tim said.

She had a chance to stop then, but she had not stopped. What was so queer was that she had almost believed it herself, weeping as she told Tim of her affair with Macklin. She had talked and talked, trying to beat Tim's truth with her lie, embedding the hook deeper and deeper. On the table their hands were gripped tightly together.

Silently they had risen, gone out of the Sportsman's Club, got into Tim's Jeep, and made desperate love. But afterward Tim had acted as though he were ashamed of having been unfaithful to Maeve. After that wild encounter, as wild as her fictional encounter with Macklin, they had reverted to a relationship of hardly speaking, hardly noticing each other, until one day she had had enough.

She quit without notice and went downbelow to stay with her mother's sister in Sacramento, where she began her teaching career as a substitute. There she met Norman Bliss, who seemed to think her attractive or anyway desirable. She married Norman and immediately found herself pregnant and at the same time aware that she could not stand this approximately three-eighths of a man that she had married. But she stuck it out until Stevie was born, stuck it out a year longer, left Norman for three months while she lived with her mother in Cope and didn't see Tim once, then went back to Norman for another try, gritting teeth and stumping. But finally she had to give up.

She filed for a divorce and came back to the mountains, not to Dancer, but to work in her mother's shop and substitute at the school. The next fall she began teaching full time. When her mother died the sale of the gift shop made a down payment on her house, which was a nice house. She now had tenure at the school, which was a nice school. What was the matter with her life the way it was? It was like the lives of ten million other people, and they managed to stump on through.

She thought if she did not have Stevie, and the Olympics eight years away to look forward to, she could not have endured the days as they passed.

11: Badbody

AFTER TIM left the party for Maeve Herron in the lounge, the Observer listened to Maeve, Easy Clary, John Henry, Isobel, and Dickie conversing on the subjects of skiing and ski resorts, snow and powder snow. No one had yet mentioned the name of Dick Macklin, who was nonetheless present. They were planning an early morning expedition to the Superchute to ski the deep powder, and certainly Dick would be there too. It was strange to find himself in good spirits in the face of the tension that always accompanied Isobel to Dancer, of the attempt to suppress all the old memories that had come back with Maeve, of Dick's ghost grinning delightedly in the midst of each conversation, and of the not-quite-confronted-yet déjà vu of this expedition to the Superchute beneath the cornice.

According to the weather forecast, the storm would not put down snow in quantities that would create a removal problem, but enough to please the skiers. The powderburners were filled with anticipation and would all be on hand in the morning, tearing through the fresh light white blanket as though both possessed by it and trying to possess it all, because there were few things more transitory than fresh powder. The powderhounds would ski it into furrows, the hordes of ordinary skiers into pack, and if the sun came out too brilliantly it would turn into Sierra cement, difficult to turn in and dangerous. Then the ski-patrol toboggans would begin to come off the mountains carrying the wounded and the broken.

The powderhounds considered themselves the elite of skiing. Deep powder skiing, because the necessary conditions were not common, was to a certain extent limited to expert skiers able to get up the mountain on short notice, and was also limited to the western part of the country where precipitation was sufficiently heavy to produce six inches to six feet of the subject of the mystique. Dick Macklin had died of his devotion to the deep powder, and so for the Observer the White Goddess presided over death and he no longer partook of any intimacies with her. The general run of powder-worshipers thought of their deity in sexual terms. They were usually uncomplicated people, and their minds ran to sex as the most apt comparison to the pleasures of their sport.

He would always remember one time when, riding up in the chairlift, he had watched a skier swooping down the mountain, skis invisible in a fall of powder, carving long, smooth, linked commas, the snow that plumed behind him in a roostertail of speed slowly settling, the graceful, swift rhythm of those suave turns, the deftly planted poles, the springy bounding from side to side. The skier had been Easy Clary, and as the chair had passed over the ski instructor, he had been keenly, sharply aware of his own failure, for he had seen in Easy's face the incandescence of all delight caught in a moment.

In his chosen role as ironic and detached Observer, he could not feel the same contempt for the powderburners that he felt for the ordinary weekend skiers who worked so hard, endured so much misery, and spent so much money in what could only be a futile effort. Now Easy was telling about last year's great powder days during the January storms, and Maeve's face was bright with anticipation.

"I can't wait!" she cried. Her face turned toward him. "Are you going to come up to the Superchute with us in the morning, Brad?"

"Oh, I don't ski, Maeve," he said. Gazing back into her thin, brown, thoughtful face, he reflected again that the life she had led, which might have coarsened her, had refined her instead. Her sexiness, which had once been almost as brash as Betsy's, was now a much more complex and subtle emanation. He could remember the power of her appeal when, as someone had said, Maeve had been responsible for more erections than the FHA. Now the appeal was not so blunt, not so troubling, almost aesthetic.

"The pusher stays off the needle," he said.

She smiled as though her mind were elsewhere, and he looked from her to Isobel, who was listening attentively to Easy. Isobel's pink and pale, soft face was handsome, youthful, and interested tonight, beneath a cloud of pale-tinted hair.

He said to Clary, "I have the final definition of powder skiing, Easy. Powder skiing is the objective correlative of the pleasure principle."

Easy whistled with admiration. When he was at a loss for words his sound-effects department was immediately engaged.

"That sounds good, Bads!" John Henry said.

"What's an objective correlative?" Maeve asked.

"Something that's abstract made concrete, isn't it?" Dickie said.

"This stuff's too light for concrete, man!" John Henry said, to general laughter.

The Observer was amused to see Isobel amused. These nine years she had chosen not to mingle with the Great Past Timers.

"Of course the pleasure-principle must rule the pleasure garden," she said. "That's what Dick said he was building here—a pleasure garden."

Clary clapped a hand to his chest. "He stole that from me!" He rose, banging himself on the chest again. "*I* told him that! I told him he was building a pleasure garden!"

So at last Dick had been mentioned and seconded. He had seen no one flinch. Isobel was laughing at Easy's protests, Easy was talking in his old exuberant way, and John Henry was clowning as he had used to clown. Was it some magic of Maeve's or only everyone performing for Maeve?

Sitting down again, Clary said to Isobel, "I mean, I'm flattered he liked it, but that's *my* thing. He made up people's names, remember? I work on these slogans in my M.R. department so as to spread the gospel."

Isobel looked pleased. The Observer could tell that Clary was nervous by the degree of winsomeness he was tuned to.

Clary said, "I mean, here are these downbelow types dragging themselves up to the mountains to ski, like grubs crawling toward the light. *Do* grubs do that? Anyway, some ancient instinct toward self-preservation. I get them in ski-school classes, and they're in such terrible shape they can't raise a leg high enough to make a kick turn. They've never kicked at anything in their lives. Fall down, they can't get up. They get cold. They wonder if it's worth while being all that miserable just to have fun."

"That's subversive thinking," Dickie said. Betsy, standing behind him, made a slight face at the self-conscious joke. She was posed in a drooping-lily position, waiting for orders for drinks or merely listening, occasionally brushing at a nonconforming lock of her hair.

"Then I give it to them," Easy Clary said. He rose again, shaking a fist to illustrate intensity. Almost religiously he raised his eyes toward the mountain, pointed with a slow, ceremonial motion, as though heavily robed, and said, mimicking himself but impressive all the same: "Class! People climb mountains because they are there!" All eyes were riveted on him. He paused, then continued in a solemn voice. "Class! We ski down them to prove we are *here!*" He burst out laughing.

John Henry leaped up to clap him on the back. "Lead us, Moses! Let my people a-go-go!"

The Observer had not heard Clary in his pulpit for a long time. The sermon was charming as always. He wondered if Easy believed in it still, if it sustained him still. All at once what Clary had said seemed to be a finger pointed at him.

"Easy is himself again," he said to Maeve.

"It's what I came back to hear," Maeve said. She called out, "Is there more, Easy?"

"I'm communicating!" Clary said. "Do you know why?"

"Tell us, man!"

"It's because I'm here!" Clary said, triumphant. He added, "Not many can make that statement."

He watched Clary raise his hand again. The finger pointed not at him but at heaven. Clary said in a pompous-ski-instructor tone, "Now, class. Why do we ski? Anyone? Ah, well, to ski, class, is to be alive! To ski is to realize that the human body is a mechanism competent to engage in actions and movements more interesting, more complex—more *thrilling*, class!—than signing checks, watching TV, or driving the automatic-shift down to the supermarket. Skiing, class, is proof that life is *living!* Am I still communicating?" he asked and he grinned down at Maeve.

The Observer realized with a shock that Clary was courting Maeve. He was further shocked to realize that it bothered him; he was reluctant to look and see how the courting was being received. He saw that Isobel, whom Easy Clary had been courting too, was fascinated.

"I like it!" Maeve said.

"Powerful, man!" John Henry said delightedly.

Dickie's face wore an expression of disapproval; seeing it, he realized his own disapproval of Clary's clowning and exuberance, and realized, too, that much of his disapproval was envy. He was always the sober man shrinking away from the drunken party. Dick Macklin, very much here, had had even more strongly than Clary this facility for holding everyone's attention, gaining everyone's admiration. But Dick had been well aware if anyone was disaffected, as Dickie was now, as he was; and Dick would have set out either to charm, or to humiliate, the unappreciative.

"Another thing, class," Clary continued. "Skiing—*skiing*, class —is the way you can find out if your five senses work or not. This"—he waved a hand to indicate the surrounding mountains —"this is the country of the senses. We live through our senses. We experience pleasure through our senses. *Open up your senses, gang!*"

Clary bowed to the applause and reseated himself. Flushed and grinning, Clary said to him in an aside, "Actually, powder skiing is the complete life of the senses."

"The last time I heard you on the subject it was connected with virgins."

"No more, no more. Deflowering virgins is out of style."

Betsy-the-barmaid said suddenly, "What you say is, something else that's really good, you say it's almost as good as skiing the powder."

Everybody looked at her. The Observer noted that Isobel was frowning as though a screw slot at the bridge of her nose had been given an eighth of a turn. A Great Past Timer was one thing, a bar employee another.

Betsy held up her tray and said, "Refills, anybody?" She took orders and retreated. John Henry watched her go with interest.

"There's a little old powderhound, I bet," he said. "She'll be up there in the middle of it tomorrow morning."

"She's a good skier," Dickie said defensively as though Betsy had been criticized.

"I don't want her up in the middle of it tomorrow morning," Maeve said. "I just want all of us who were here—before."

Everyone looked embarrassed at the strain in her voice. He was thankful when John Henry leaned back in his chair and sang casually, " 'Two boards upon cold powder snow, yo-ho! The very best thing that I know.' I'm going to do a collection of ski songs sometime, Ease. You've got to help me put decent words together. I mean, like decent."

Her frown dissipating, Isobel caught his eye and smiled. It was a particular smile, and an acid of fear ran through him. She was a lady except under the influence of gin, and she had been steadily swallowing martinis. It had been years since he had last been summoned—and failed. Not very flattering, Brad, she had said. Failed and failed again, and third time out. But the years had passed, and he had almost come to think that danger over, that particular of the living of life, at least, no longer necessary. But this was an evening full of past time and old thoughts, excited by Maeve and intensified by Easy Clary.

Betsy appeared. "Mr. Peabody, there's a long-distance phone call for you. Do you want to take it up here or down in your office?"

"In my office," he said thankfully and excused himself. His good spirits had vanished; everything looked aqueous through his misted glasses. The phone call was from a man full of self-important bluster demanding Christmas reservations for a family of four. He refused even to take down the name. The call hardly touched the grim array of his thoughts.

When he had hung up he sat in his enclosure, lighting his pipe. He found it almost comforting to consider the possibility that the cook, badgered by Dickie and refused a new dishwashing machine, might quit tonight when too many people demanded dinner after dinner hours were past. He tried to fill with small, safe worries, the chasms that had opened in his mind. But in the shadows there loomed the specter of Isobel summoning him to another failure tonight, Isobel, insulted and furious because of his failure, casting him out, and behind and beyond increasingly dim, increasingly dread shapes crowding.

Sanity was represented by Betsy sauntering across the empty lobby toward him, tray in hand, a glass on the tray. She came into his office. "Mrs. Macklin said to bring you down your drink in case you'd got tied up. Are you tied up?"

He nodded, surprised that he was able to smile. "Thanks, Betsy-dear," he said, mimicking Donna McIntyre.

She grinned back, leaning a hip against his desk. "Just don't say it when Dickie's around. It makes smoke come out of his ears."

"I'll be careful."

"Why don't you go back to your party? You don't look tied up to me."

"A few phone calls to make."

She smoothed at the errant curls escaping the confinement of her topknot. If Dickie's ears, flaming with anger or embarrassment, did appear to smoke, so her own ears, pink with health, looked edible as cake frosting. Her breasts in her tight sweater swelled independently. Her shadowed eyes had a quality half tragic, half comic. She lit a cigarette. "First time I've seen Dickie with his muthuh," she said in a superior voice. "That's why he parts his hair that way, huh?"

He raised his eyebrows questioningly.

"Yes, Muthuh, no, Muthuh," Betsy said. She drew deeply, her nostrils whitening, and blew smoke. "I've never known any people like that. She's really rich, huh?"

"Very. So is Dickie, by extension."

"You're kidding," Betsy said. "No, I know he is. I just don't believe *he* knows it."

"He's a very conscientious boy."

"Is that what you call it? I call it hung-up. Christ, he's tight!" Smacked with her balled fist, the tray rang sourly. "What's the use of having money if you don't do anything with it?" she said. "Enjoy it or anything? Well, I'm going back up and learn some more."

"Beware of Muthuh," he said beneath his breath. "By, Betsy-dear," he said aloud. She gave him an affectionate, cocked look over her shoulder as she free-wheeled off.

Pleasurably, good spirits restored, he watched her go past the arches over the long counter. He reflected that Dick Macklin would have had her installed in his bed long ago, as once Maeve had been installed there. Was Maeve in bed as satisfying, as complete a life of the senses, as deep powder snow? Many men must have found her so. Or was she incapable of fulfilling the anticipation she aroused? Once— He relit his pipe, sipped his scotch, and by a conscious act of will set about sealing off that particular room in his memory.

When he saw Isobel coming across the lobby his first impulse was to pick up the telephone and pretend to be finishing a conversation. He resisted it as though all honor were at stake.

She was carrying a martini glass. In her dark blue knit suit she looked quite slim, but it was only a triumph of corseting, for every year her flesh grew slightly more abundant. Yet she was a handsome woman, his employer. He rose as she came in.

She sat down beside his desk and adjusted the position of the brass name prism which she had given him. "I told everyone I'd try to get you back," she said with a coyness that was abrasive to his sensibilities. "We're going to eat soon. Can you come now?"

"Certainly." He started to rise again, but she held out a hand indicating that there was to be some conversation first.

"Brad, is Dickie having an affair with that bar-girl?"

Various loyalties presented their credentials. "I don't think it's reached that point yet," he said.

"I doubt that," Isobel said. Grimly she essayed a light laugh. "I suppose he has to be his father's son in *some* respect."

He remembered her in her last days as a girl, in those terrible, exalted days after Pearl Harbor in Honolulu, with fair hair long to her shoulders and heaped in curls on her forehead; dancing with her at some patriotic function at the Elk's Club, where he had blundered around the edges of the dancefloor until she had said, dark red lips smiling, not so shy as they had once been, newly impatient with him, "Let's get out on the dancefloor, Brad." Obediently he had steered that way. But he had never been able to venture out onto the dancefloor of the greater ballroom, and so the time was ripe for the Beautiful Youth, for the young Lochinvar out of the Southwest Pacific. His mother had told him, having learned it from Isobel's mother, that the night before their engagement had been announced, coming home from a dance to an empty house, the great Bradley house in Nuuanu Valley, Dick and Isobel had celebrated their engagement in every bed in the house.

"My God!" his mother had said in awe. "What a man!" Had she been sorry for her son, contemptuous of him, or merely unthinking? "Was she a virgin, Buddy?" his mother had asked. He had replied that he didn't, of course, know; probably she was. "My God!" his mother had said. "What a woman! It just shows that a blueblood Bradley could make the grade in an Iwilei house if she ever had to."

Isobel had always been a virgin as far as he was concerned until at last, Dick dead, there had been that sweet moment when he had understood what she wanted of him, sitting at Dick Macklin's desk in Dick Macklin's office with Dick Macklin's widow come to him for solace. He had thought that the meek had finally inherited the earth, only to find that the earth was no longer coveted. It was too late. The inheritance had turned into merely a casual, cousinly accommodation during Isobel's three or four visits a year to Dancer, nothing more. And then, finally, even in that cousinly arrangement he had failed, and terrified by the failure, failed the more. "Not very flattering, Brad," Isobel had said, hurt of course, icy-eyed, business-voiced. But no ax had fallen, and that had been that.

"Isobel," he said now lightsomely. "I believe you have dyed your hair."

"Do you like it?"

"Very much."

She sipped her martini, touched her hair, regarded him with her deep-set eyes that were a little sad but very sharp. It was a full face with soft, sensual pads of flesh covering the cheekbones and a prominent, soft chin. He realized that he had never had the slightest idea of what went on behind the face of his employer, his cousin, his lost love. She put a hand across the desk to touch his hand and said in a husky voice, "Brad, I may marry."

"Oh?" he said. He cleared his thickened throat. "Who?" he asked.

"Bart."

Bart Weaver. Her face misted, her eyes seemed to swim at him. There was, at first, only relief that nothing more would be demanded of him now, no more unflattering command nonperformances could be held against him. Barton Weaver was a New Yorker, a lawyer for the corporation and a small stockholder, a dyspeptic man with a small mustache, a skier with grown children, recently divorced from Irene Weaver.

"I say I *may*," Isobel said, patting his hand once more. "It's not settled yet."

"That sounds wonderful, Isobel!" he said, trying to say it genuinely but not effusively, trying cravenly to act as she would want him to act, his relief already fading. Bart Weaver.

Isobel's cool hand was drawn back. "Thank you, Brad," she whispered with a drunken little kissing moue.

He felt he had passed a preliminary test. But in his brain great ice blocks were beginning to shift, combinations of meaning forming and re-forming, each new possibility more deadly dangerous to him than the last. All at once he thought he must be going mad. Out of terror it came clearly to him that death must first begin as mental disease, the gods made mad whom they would destroy. Death stalked those who had lost their reason for living.

Carefully he placed his pipe in the ashtray on the desk blotter, drew his handkerchief from his pocket, removed his glasses, and, squinting, began to polish the lenses. Isobel's now-distorted face gazed back upon him with sympathy—the essential and totally mistaken sympathy for the twice-disappointed lover.

"Bart's very lucky," he said. "He's a fine fellow, Isobel."

"There's no reason for me to go on living as half a woman."

"Of course not," he said and put his glasses back on.

"I'm afraid I simply haven't the temperament for irregular arrangements," she said meaningfully.

"Maybe it's simple morality, Belle. I think there is always a basic awe of the Commandments. I know I've found it in myself." He hoped she understood that he was speaking not merely of adultery but of incest. They were first cousins. It had been an excuse.

"You and Bart do get along," Isobel said, and he nodded. He and Bart Weaver did get along, but they would not get along once Bart married Isobel. He could not even think about a future in which both Bart Weaver and Dickie were ranged against him. "Nothing will be changed, my dear," Isobel whispered as though she knew what he had been thinking.

"Thank you." He tried to smile.

Isobel rose and said briskly, "Now come along. We're going up to dinner." She took his hand and drew him along with her as though they were children again.

Isobel thought it would be fun to eat in the lounge instead of the dining room, and dinner was a confused affair of bar tables pushed together and Isobel calling to familiar faces to come join them, each new arrival causing a general rising and chair shuffling. Martha Schroeder appeared, overdressed in a long shiny-black gown, and sat between him and Easy Clary. The band had begun to play on the adjacent side of the small, yellow-shining dance-floor, drums and bass pulsating like jungle signals, the rosy-throated trumpet turned toward the ceiling and yowling. The pianist held the microphone by the throat like an enemy and shouted tuneless lyrics at it. Clary talked to Maeve, danced with Maeve, made jokes with John Henry, and paid no attention at all to Martha Schroeder.

"He's in love with her, isn't he?" Martha said to him, making no effort to lower her voice. She clicked a scarlet fingernail against her wineglass, her handsome, mannish, expensively groomed head tipped forward so he could see little of her face. Her nail tapping on the glass was an unpleasant sound.

He was in no condition tonight to reassure anyone. He likened his spirits to a dead storage battery to which a few revs of the engine could give a spurious charge. But with the slightest discharge, down, down, he went, like glistering Phaeton. He found, though, that Martha's misery took some edge off his own.

"They're old friends," he said.

"Friends," she said bitterly. "Everybody's talked about her as one of the old bunch here, but I hadn't realized she and Easy were such *very* old friends."

He said nothing, not wanting to encourage her to unburden on him. She needed no encouragement.

"We'd actually been talking about getting married. Isn't *that* ridiculous!"

The possibility that Clary had been considering an end to the good life, the living life, the free and sponsible life—just for a handful of security he left us—amused him, and almost he felt the Observer again. "Ridiculous," he said undiplomatically.

Her eyes flashed at him. "You don't like him! He may be only a ski instructor but he's a fine, fine person. Some people just happen to be less strongly motivated than—"

"But I like him!" he protested. Detached again, pulling the screen of irony and pity between himself and the action, he could feel sympathy for Martha Schroeder. "It's nothing at all but old time's sake," he said. "Everyone here was in love with Maeve once. Even I. And she's been a magnificently notorious figure in the meantime. Of course she's fascinating."

She was shaking her head. "No. No, he's showing me I've had it." She stared boldly at Maeve for a moment, then at Clary, before turning back to him. "Why did you say it was ridiculous?" she demanded.

There was no use in pointing out that it was her word. He was too familiar with feminine logic. He said, "Oh, I suppose because of what Wendy would have found out if she'd married Peter Pan."

"What?"

"That she hadn't married Peter Pan."

She looked at him blankly. Then she asked, "What am I supposed to do, just cool my heels till he gets tired of her?"

The question hung there as the band finished a number and, as one man, reached for their highballs. Clary turned from Maeve and smiled blankly as Martha spoke to him. Martha pushed her chair back, rose, and went off toward the ladies' room with a stiff, offended back.

The band's next number was a slow one, and he asked Isobel to dance, his dancing a sedate promenade around the floor, a pretense of dancing. Perhaps, he thought, it was even pretense that he was on the dancefloor at all, a merely dutiful performance and going-through-the-motions, like his life, in which, dutifully and with a pretense of meaningful motion, he dully moved around the edges. From the vantage point of the moment, as he danced with Isobel Macklin, Isobel Barton to be, he surveyed the life that had been his, was, and was still to come. Easy Clary's finger in evangelistic accusation pointed toward him; did Easy have the answer? He thought that there was no answer, that this was all, and that this all was not enough to warrant the horror of the end.

The slow foxtrot over, that one for the old folks, the band

shifted into high gear once more. He and Isobel drifted over to sit at the bar not far from John Henry. They watched the younger people dancing, watching in particular Maeve and Clary. He could not stop thinking of Clary's easy attitude toward life. Gobble it down like candy. How was it that to Easy Clary life seemed so wonderful, while to him, the Observer, it seemed preferable only to not-life? But he had had no choice, begotten by the Anglican minister who had married his mother and run off with her to the coast to live on her capital while he tried to write—verse, plays, novels, anything—and shot himself when it was clear not merely that he had failed but that the money was used up. Was it possible to claim foreordination? Were there any acceptable excuses? Who would listen when he tried to explain that he came from the shabby, genteel line of a blueblood Island family, his father a failure and a suicide, his mother a bitter neurotic; that he had had a terrible inferiority complex as a boy and that that inferiority had been continued and confirmed by his relationship with Dick Macklin. With whom did you register excuses?

Seated beside Isobel, he watched Clary and Maeve violently, totally, engaged in what must be the wildest of the current dances. It was as though a spotlight shone just on the two of them where they shimmered, separate from the other dancers by reason of their violence, as though they must make of the dance itself a dangerous adventure like skiing at the edge of control down a treacherous slope. Clary resembled a duelist in some old motion picture, in his white turtleneck shirt and tight black ski pants, white teeth gleaming in his dark face. Maeve's skirt swung with motion like a bell, her legs in blue leotards flashing, the gold necklaces thumping on her breast, her tan face set in a fixed smile, long blond hair bouncing with the rhythm of her hips. Clary prowled around her golden figure like a great cat, crouched, slipping forward and darting back while she faced him in her wild, skirt-belling motion, in the huge beat of the music.

The dance was a ceremony of mating, generating lust. Yet it seemed a competition too, the king of the skibums testing himself against the Mariachi Girl. He reminded himself that this dashing duelist was a no-longer-young ski instructor, this glittering, spinning girl a publicly humiliated demimondaine. But there were innocence and desperation in her that touched him, a masculine mastery in Clary he envied to the bottom of his soul.

Isobel's hand fell on his arm, her fingers clutching. When he glanced at her he saw tears on her cheeks.

"Why, what's the matter, Belle?"

"Oh, God!" she whispered. "Oh, Brad, life's so unfair! She's got cancer."

"*Cancer!*" It was the ultimate nightmare punishment for his own sins, of omission, not commission, a name for the coiling monster in the black pool of his mind. He almost retched. "Did she tell you that just now?"

"No," Isobel said. "I heard it from Ellen Shippey. No, Maeve didn't tell me."

The music ended on a long groan of the horn. Couples halted in flight. In bursting horror he watched Maeve standing before a motionless Clary, with all the dance gone out of her, no longer a wild, searching flame of a girl but a tired and sweaty woman. As she came off the floor with Easy, the defenses of his mind were crumbling; out of the past the black dog came surging at him, monstrous in its portent of death. Through the years he had come to accept that dog as the death of his abortive clutch at fleeing life, as only the objective correlative of his own failure to accept his own fate.

That day long ago when Isobel returned from Honolulu, having pawned her Bradley-Beeson stock for the money to save Dancer, was the day Tim ran wild with the snowplow in the parking lot and then disappeared. He and Maeve went out to look for Tim that evening in the pickup, he and Maeve in the short, intense mountain dusk with the snow gently falling and the silence-filling radio turned on, he leaning over the steering wheel to peer out the windshield, she sitting in the corner of the seat with her coat collar turned up and gloved hands clasped in her lap, sometimes humming the song on the radio. They had finished talking about Tim, and now the air in the metal cab was heavy with what needed to be said.

Driving slowly with one hand on the vibrating gear lever, staring straight ahead at the falling snow, he said, "Was it very painful with Isobel?"

"Yes," Maeve said in a small voice. "No. Not as bad as—" She hesitated before she said, "Maybe I won't have to go."

Action and reaction: Dick's cruel action resulting in J.D.'s furious reaction; in the violent testimony of the rotary piled against the smashed Cadillac; in what other reactions he could not know. If humanity's purpose in life was the collection of acknowledgments to its own existence, then tremendous acknowledgments had been made here, in the actions and reactions. Why shouldn't Maeve want to stay in Dancer, who was its spirit, heart, chief focus, and concern? Her humiliations and injuries were only a part of her deification. But now it was his turn, out of love, to make her see that she must go.

Perhaps she had been reading his silence. She said in the small voice, "I've always been so lonely. It's just that I've really belonged here."

He nodded. His head felt very heavy. Before he could speak she began again.

"Once I thought I wanted something else. I knew I was attractive to men—*could* be. I was sure I could get what I wanted out of life. Do all the things—" She was speaking in quick bursts as though she were very short of breath. "All the *things*," she said and laughed. "The high life. I thought I wanted—that." She made a gesture as of throwing something into the air with her gloved hands. "But maybe I don't want that any more. I thought I could be ruthless to get what I wanted. But maybe I don't want that kind of life enough to be so ruthless, to be so lonely—get hurt so when someone else is ruthless. Maybe I'm afraid to go out into that kind of world now. It's—it's—" She laughed breathlessly. "It's so warm and safe in here."

He had already begun to shake his head. "Go out and get what you want. Don't stay in here where it's—where it seems so safe."

As he stared ahead at the broken white line down the center of the highway and the snowflakes falling, disappearing, it seemed, inches above the black paving, he could feel the intensity of her eyes. "You don't want—" she started. "Everybody else—" She stopped.

"Everybody else wants you to stay because they love you," he said. "I want you to go because I do. Don't be afraid. Go out and get what you want. Otherwise—" In his turn he also broke off.

Otherwise what? Thinking of her future, he was forced to contemplate his past. He didn't want to sound like a Jamesian character admonishing another to live, but it was what he must do.

"I'm speaking with the authority of failure," he said. "Because I've stayed in one of those safe warm places. But you have to live your own life. You have to take chances—hurt and get hurt. Go out in the cold, in the main stream, in—" He did not know how to say it except in clichés or overemotionally; where was his irony now? "I want you to get what you want out of life," he said. "The high life. All the *things*, if that's what's important. Everything there is to be gotten. Otherwise—" He stopped again.

They came into the lights of Erskine, and he turned in to stop, nosed against the old hitching rail before the Sportsman's Club. He helped Maeve out, and they went inside. Tim was not there and had not been there. They sat down at a table, and the bartender with the wen on his cheek brought them drinks. A little light caught in Maeve's hair as she sipped her gin. He was shivering although it was warm in here and safe enough.

"But I can stay, you see," Maeve said as though explaining something to a child; maybe as though she were explaining it to herself. She said, "I think Isobel will—forgive me." She frowned down at the glass in her hand. "You see, I could marry somebody and stay here in Dancer and just be—*that* kind of happy. I guess I mean content."

He was struck by the implications of what she was saying. He had never been slow to understand, only slow to believe in himself, and anyway his effort here was to be honest for Maeve's sake not clever for his own. Because honesty was what was important now. He said roughly, "You're going away if I have to take you myself."

Her face was luminously pale in the beery gloom. Always he had been afraid to commit himself for fear of failure, but now he was very close to commitment, and he was only ashamed that he must grin at her with the pretense that his proposal was partly in jest, in case she refused it.

She said nothing. He gathered a little more courage. "Maybe I could help you get a start in the high life. I know a good many people in New York." He continued to grin at her, desperately.

Maeve gazed back at him with liquid gleams of light showing in the whites of her eyes. He couldn't make out her expression. Quickly he finished his drink and said, "Maybe we'd better get on with our search for Timbal Khan. We can eat in Cope."

"All right," Maeve said.

Outside snow was beginning to stick on the streets, and the wind had come up. In the cab Maeve sat closer to him. His mind was electric with the realization that he had not been refused, with optimism, almost with certainty—he who had never known any certainties except negative ones. They would eat in Cope and talk about the future, and maybe, urging her to go, making her realize why she must get out into the great moving river of life, he could himself break loose. He felt frightened but very brave even to contemplate it—out into the great uncaring world where, after a little while, the beginning pain of the acknowledgment of his existence would come through pandering for her to have the life she wanted, into which he, of course, would not be able to accompany her very far. But the pain and the pleasure were inseparable in the totality, weren't they? And his own life depended on getting out of this neither-pleasure-nor-pain, safe, warm, protected, deadly, vicariously-through-Dick-and-Isobel-living non-life. Freeing Maeve, he could free himself. He kept shivering to the compulsive beat of the music on the radio.

He must have been in the process of putting his arm around her when the dog was killed. It was a completely ordinary, medium-sized black dog, portentous dog, that died to show him he could not escape himself. It appeared just outside Erskine, half seen, seen-too-late, running into the glare of the headlights. Thump and yelp. His knees turned to water, and he almost ran off the road at the glimpse of the black body flung into the air, red mouth open. When he got control of the pickup again there was nothing visible in the rearview mirror but darkness and the watery red glow of his own taillights. He did not stop. The dog was dead, certainly dying. There was nothing to be done except drive on and try to forget the tragedy and the horror of mortality.

And of course that had been the end. They had not found Tim in either of the bars in Cope. At dinner they had spoken only of Tim and of trivialities. He had said no more about taking her away from Dancer himself. The death of the dog had finished all that, for death had shown him the hopelessness of any attempt to escape, and now, it seemed to him, the dog had forewarned him of Maeve's cancer and Maeve's death.

What had finally freed Maeve and sent her off to the high life was Dick's death the next morning.

12: John Henry

PARTLY BECAUSE Easy and Maeve were so preoccupied with each other, his great yay mood had got away from him. He thought he would call his shut-ins. It was nine-thirty, but Teddy Applegate would still be up, sitting in his wheel chair in that dark, narrow room, putting together plastic airplane models or just waiting for a phone call.

He went outside, where the snow was floating down like butter-flies, and got the big Martin in its case out of the Porsche. When he came back into the lounge, with snowflakes melting in his hair, he found an empty stool at a corner of the bar, took the guitar out of its case and tuned it close to his ear under the big beat of the combo, a little disappointed that no one came around to see what he was up to. Everybody was dancing or watching the dancing. He asked the bartender for a brandy and the phone. He gave the switchboard the Burbank number. Out on the dancefloor Maeve and Easy were really swinging. The barmaid was scouting among the tables for business; a lot of chick, that one. Dickie Macklin came toward him frowning, not-too-happy, the way Dickie had al-ways looked, and he had to remember Dickie walking down the Spoon, tossing rocks at the towers, after J.D. had been saying all those crappy things.

"Are you going to play something?" Dickie asked him, not very interested.

Gripping the phone between his ear and his shoulder, he said, "There's this shut-in kid. You know, crippled, so he can't ever get out of the house much—"

The phone began to ring thinly in his ear, once, twice—twice was par—and then Teddy's voice, thin as the distant ringing of the phone bell, "Hello? Hello, John Henry?"

"It's snowin' up here, man. What's it doin' down there?"

"It's not doing anything down here, John Henry." Teddy sounded pretty restrained, as though something bad had happened —the doctor had just been there or Dobber had been at him. Dickie had moved away slightly, toward where Badbody and his mother were sitting.

"Did you ski yet?" Teddy asked.

"Not yet, man. We're goin' up and ski the deep powder way up on the mountain tomorrow though. That's the real light kind of snow. Like the foam on the waves out at Malibu—you know, the spindrift. You kind of float on it like surfing, only better."

"Gee, that sounds wonderful," the small teary voice said.

"What's the matter, Teddy, man? Who brought you down, Teddy? That brother of yours?"

Teddy sobbed.

He hung on to the phone with the crotch of his shoulder, tuning the Martin all over again with rage hurting at the backs of his eyes. "What'd Dobber say this time?" he asked.

No answer.

"Play you a little song, Teddy?"

"John Henry?"

"Yay?"

"I said you was going to phone and he said you wasn't either."

"Well, I phoned, man! I'm *on* it!"

"I tried not to cry, John Henry. But he said a lot of mean things. He said did I know why you played a guitar instead of a banjo, and I said you said a guitar was a really beautiful thing and it sat on your knee so good—I forget what you said. But Dobber said it was because a guitar was so beautiful and sat your knee so good, all right, but mostly it was because a guitar had a great big hole right in the middle of it. He's a really dirty guy, John Henry! He said all kinds of dirty old things about you and a whole lot of old starlet girls." Teddy began to sob again. "I'm sorry I let him make me cry after I went and promised I wasn't going to any more."

He swore that this time he was going to wring Dobber Applegate's neck. *Kill* him, he thought suddenly, viciously. There were people you went to hire, some Cosa-Nostra-type gun, to kill someone who would do a son-of-a-bitching thing like that to a crippled, dying kid. Have him beaten up anyway, he thought, softening a little. *Just leave your brother alone from now on, you hear?* Pure, suffocating, killing rage filled him when he remembered Frisco telling him *Life* had promised to send a writer and photographer along to do an article on the Liberty Singers, and it was as though the article was already printed in *Life* and Dobber already taking it in to Teddy, asking how come John Henry Collins wasn't there?

"That durn ol' Dobber," he said gently. "He really is a bad guy sometimes."

"He sure is, John Henry," Teddy said, sniffing.

"He's just jealous, Teddy. I told you that."

"It's not so though, is it, John Henry?"

"Nothin' anybody tells you when they are spun out like that is so, man. Don't you know?"

"I guess so," the wisp of a voice said.

"Say, I got a pretty nice break worked up on 'Railroad Bill'— you want to hear that?" He strummed minor chords.

"That'd be good," Teddy said.

The combo was between numbers, and people came around to hear him as he began to pick and strum, which soaked some of the rage out. He watched his thumb and fingers at work and then tipped his head back.

"Hey, Baby! You think I'm a fool?
You think I would leave you when the weather is cool?"

He heard somebody whisper, "He's singing to a little crippled boy." The telephone receiver listened, lying on the edge of the bar, as he played the long break. He was feeling better, feeling happier, feeling the bill-coming-due not so much on top of him now as he grinned around at the people he could make happier with his playing and singing. He leaned down toward the receiver and said, "How'd you like that, Teddy, man?" He finished the song and said a few more things to Teddy, very show biz now because of the people listening, and hung up.

He played a couple of south-of-the-border songs, made a joke about the band coming back to get everybody turned toward the dancefloor again, settled the guitar back in its case and gave it to the bartender to stow behind the bar where it would be safe.

"How about a drink?" he said to Dickie, who looked as though he didn't know what to do with himself.

They went over to an empty table, and the bar-girl showed up right away. It was clear from the complicated way Dickie had of not looking at her that he had a thing going there.

Dickie said, "You were playing for a crippled boy?"

"Well, it's a thing somebody like me can do for these shut-in kids. It cheers them up."

"That's nice," Dickie said.

"How're you liking it back at Dancer, man?"

"Well, fine," Dickie said. "Fine, John Henry."

"So it's fine now, huh, man?" he said.

Dickie licked his lips, grinned flickeringly. "Yes, it's fine now."

Here was one little bill that could be settled. He took a deep breath and said, "This kid I was just talking to. He's never going to get out of his wheel chair again. He's probably not going to live more than a couple years. He's a brave little kid. When he cries—" He stopped, took another deep breath, and said, "Anyway, he's got this real shit of a big brother that's jealous because Teddy gets a lot of attention from his mother and dad, and from me. He's always putting me down to Teddy. Telling him bad things. So I was just thinking," he said, looking straight into Dickie's not-too-happy face and feeling pretty good that he was finally getting around to doing this, "so I was just thinking about some pretty bad things that you happened to hear once when you were a young kid. That J.D. and me wouldn't've wanted you to hear for anything, because we liked you a lot."

Dickie didn't look as though he had got it.

"Remember when you used to come help us work on the Platter sometimes?"

Dickie licked his lips and nodded. "Yes."

"Well, there was that time we were talking about your dad. We'd been taking a smoke break, and when we got up to go back to work you were going down the hill again. Remember that?"

Dickie's cheeks were hollowed as though he were sucking on

something. He looked a lot like his mother when he frowned, but you could see Dick Macklin there too. Dickie nodded slightly.

"Well, I wanted to tell you I'm goddam sorry."

Dickie muttered something that sounded like "Okay." The bargirl came back with the brandy and the beer. He produced cheroots and offered one to Dickie, who thanked him, no. The girl lit his cheroot for him, showing off her buffet when she bent over, then left them.

Filled with the righteous humility of apologizing for something he had not, in fact, been responsible for, he blew smoke and said expansively, "Anyway, it was bullshit, man."

"Pardon?" Dickie said.

"About your old man. What J.D. was saying."

Dickie squinted at him grotesquely. "I don't understand you," he said, his formal voice lost as the combo began to whoop it up.

"All that bullshit about your old man," he said, impatient with Dickie's obtuseness. "J.D. was always full of that kind of snowjob. He—"

"It wasn't true?" Dickie said suddenly and cleared his throat as though it hurt him.

Feeling very much older, wiser, more experienced, the bearer of gifts of revelation, he made a scornful sound. "Whenever J.D. got on *that* subject you just kind of closed up your believing valves."

Dickie turned aside, clearing his throat again. "You mean the subject of Maeve?"

"I mean sex. You know how people are."

Dickie didn't look as though he did.

"I mean, you know how people get spun out on their mother or the first-grade teacher's cans and all that stuff. That's the way J.D. is. You just didn't ever believe him when he got started on that. I don't know if he's still that way now he's married."

Dickie nodded as though all were clear now, looking out at the dancefloor. He must be watching Maeve.

Still feeling expansive, he continued. "I always liked your old man. He was the most *Reader's Digest* Most Unforgettable Character I ever knew. A lot of people hated his guts, but I liked him." As he talked he became aware that a part of him was standing off to one side, frowning and shaking its head. Probably he shouldn't have said anything about people being down on Dickie's father.

"I mean, in a way your dad had to be an S.O.B. to get this done," he went on hurriedly, swinging an arm to indicate what Macklin had got done. That said, it also seemed very square. "But mostly it was Maeve," he said. "Mostly everybody got mad at him because they were all so hot for Maeve." Now he was really in deep water.

"But then what J.D. said was true," Dickie said.

"Well, man! It was true everybody liked Maeve a lot, but—"

Like a lawyer, Dickie pinned him down. "What about Maeve and Easy Clary at—"

"Do you know what a blivvy is?" he interrupted. He blew expensive, sweet smoke, trying to get his cool back. He grinned at Dickie, who was shaking his head. "It's a five-pound sack with ten pounds of bullshit in it," he said. "And that's what J.D. was when he got on *that* subject." It occurred to him that he was talking to Dickie the way Sid-the-agent often talked to him; why didn't he just stop? "Anyway, your dad was a hell of a guy," he said to end the conversation.

"He was a rotten bastard!" Dickie said.

His first instinct was to agree, his second was to be ashamed of himself for wanting to agree. He had always shrunk from fighting for an opinion, partly because he could immediately see so much to be said on the other side, partly because he didn't want to displease, be disliked. This time that part of himself which had been off to one side watching saw the chicken inclination to give ground and sneered, and sneered too at his phony expressions of affection for Dick Macklin. His whole relationship with Dickie's father had been soiled with this same chickenness.

So it was out of self-disgust that he leaned back in his chair and said coldly, "Putting your old man down doesn't swing any more, man." He blew smoke and was cool, pretending to be what he was not, and Dickie glared at him.

Isobel Macklin was coming toward them, and she didn't look too happy either. "Here comes your Mom," he said, and they both rose.

"Take me home, please," Isobel said to Dickie. "I'm suddenly very tired."

"All right, Mother."

"I've asked Maeve to come and stay in the Big House," Isobel said. "There's been a mixup about some reservations."

"All right, Mother," Dickie said. They all said good night.

He sat down again, watching Dickie follow his mother out of the lounge, walking three feet behind her like a chauffeur. He thought it should seem pretty funny that Maeve was going to be sleeping in the Big House again, but nothing seemed funny.

Why was it that something went wrong whenever he tried to do a good thing? He had only wanted to apologize to Dickie for that time up on the Spoon, but it had turned ugly, just as the thing with Teddy had been turned ugly by Dobber's jealousy. Maybe at the bottom it was his own fault that these things always seemed to go wrong. Maybe it was because his motives were wrong. Maybe it was part of the bill-coming-due that ruined anything decent he tried to do. Maybe it was simply that he himself was all wrong inside. He was tired of himself tonight, tired of being the way he was and of always trying to hide it instead of trying to change it.

He got up from the table to try to find Easy Clary, or someone, to have fun with, on the chance that this first night back at his soul-home could still be saved.

13: Isobel Bradley Macklin

SEEING HER SON again after they had been apart for some time, seeing him freshly, she was apt to feel that she had been cheated by her own contrivance; he was not what she had wanted. Yet she knew she must accept the responsibility—heredity and environment and traumas—for what he was. She and Dick. There were layers of gloss, of prep school, of Cornell, of his summer alone in Europe, the young-businessman finish-coat of graduate school, but underneath, clearly visible, was the hurt child, the not-very-manly, not-very-brave, unfinished, not-loved-enough son she had had by Dick. How could she blame the boy because he was not that rare Dick Macklin who had come into her life one day and, for that so-little while, made her life Life, showed her joy and sorrow, love and hate, pain and pleasure? When he had gone she had stored away in mothballs all those throbbing responses to life.

Sometimes, in her dissatisfaction with her son, she would realize that, loving Dick as she had loved him, disapproving of him as she had disapproved of him, she had determined from the beginning that Dickie would not grow up to be like him.

Now, walking along the shoveled brick path with the delicate snow falling slowly against the lights of the lodge and the magically, palely glowing glass walls around the swimming pool, she was filled with the beauty of the world and with its ruthlessness; Maeve with cancer of the uterus—Ellen Shippey, a mutual friend from Dallas had told her—Maeve who once had had the pure animal power of sex the bar waitress with the obscene caricature of a feminine body had used tonight to capture the eyes and the lust of all the men, and especially of her son.

In the misty, snowy, glowing beauty of the night she was aware, too, of the dreadful responsibility of parents, who could, in their stupidity, dig such a hole for their children that the children would spend a lifetime trying to struggle out of it. How was it, she wondered, that men like Easy Clary and John Henry could be so free of strictures? She had been interested that Clary had claimed Dick's phrase "pleasure garden" as his own. With Dick's death the pleasure garden had become her responsibility, and she had preferred to be an absentee owner, delegating her responsibility and devoting herself to Good Works. If Dancer was to be regarded as a pleasure garden, she could think of no one less qualified to operate it than Brad, who had spent his life fleeing pleasure; no one less qualified to assist him than Dickie, down in his hole. Dick should have lived to run it. Oh, Dick! She felt strong emotions here in Dancer, where she had always felt them. Had she shunned Dancer and her responsibilities to the pleasure garden all those years, relieved that those passions and responses were safely in mothballs, plastic wrapped, locked in a chest? Certainly Bart Weaver had no key to the chest, nor did she want him to have one. When she married Bart the chest would remain locked forever, and she would slide placidly, securely, unfeelingly, down the remainder of her years.

"I'm thinking of marrying Bart Weaver, dear," she said.

Dickie replied calmly, "That's wonderful, Mother."

It was inadequate. She felt cheated again. Yet what had she wanted? A jealous fury? Sullen shock? Ill-concealed contempt for two middle-aged people creakily treading the marriage dance? Just *some* response. The father had always responded—pro or con, prejudiced, opinionated, often violent, but always a response. The son calmly said the conventional thing and apparently reacted in no way at all. She missed Dick so suddenly and so sharply that she almost gasped with pain, like a pain in her side from violent exercise. Holding her son's inert arm, she walked toward the Big House, her residence in Dancer.

So much concentrated life had taken place in the Big House that when she stayed away from Dancer for a long time it seemed to her that she was letting the house lie fallow. On occasion she lent it to friends who were coming out skiing, to a few of the other stockholders, to Bart and his former wife and their two girls, but usually it remained empty except for her dutiful, seasonal visits to Dancer, a week at a time, four times a year.

Three years after Dick's death she had had the house redecorated. The master bedroom was now the guest room, furnished with Danish Modern. The old guest room, with a stone fireplace added, became her room. The partition separating the second floor into two small bedrooms had been removed, turning the balcony into one large bunkroom. Last spring an apartment had been added, communicating at the stair landing and with an outside entrance, for Dickie. No doubt it was where he brought the waitress. Dick had always considered the use of the female help as one of the perquisites of management, hadn't he? Brad obviously did not, and she felt both approval and contempt.

When she had told Brad that Maeve had cancer she had thought he was going to faint. From what? From the shock of hearing that Maeve was dying or merely from the fear of death? Pity and contempt. Fear had never touched Dick, but then, as Yeats said it, Dick had not lived to comb gray hair. Had he felt fear when he looked up at the Superchute cornice and saw that it was going to fall and bury him?

Dickie opened the door for her. The slate-floored entry was gleaming clean, the heat had been turned up, in the living room the lamps on either side of the couch glowed in homecoming; Brad would have seen to it that the housekeeper attended to all this. Brad was always considerate of her comfort.

"Let's have a fire," she said to Dickie as he helped her off with her coat. While he knelt before the fireplace arranging back log, paper, and kindling, she put classical guitar music on the stereo. The music came on as Dickie lit a match. Flames began to spiral, smoke leaked from the corners of the fireplace. Dickie sighed and got to his feet; she saw that he was thinner. She knew she didn't know him. She didn't even know how to try to know him. As she watched him her mind, always past-absorbed here, moved even farther back in time, and she realized how much her son resembled her father in an old brown photograph of a football team lounging in various poses of studied casualness around a central football that had CORNELL inscribed upon it.

Dickie turned toward her and, smiling meaninglessly, asked, "When's it going to be, Mother?"

"What?"

"When are you and Bart—"

"No date yet," she interrupted. "No final decision even."

"I suppose you'll quit working for the library fund when—"

"My part's finished," she said. "The money's all in and construction's started." She waved her hands. She didn't want to discuss the prospect of her second marriage any more. "Would you see if you can locate any Grand Marnier, dear?"

Squeaky-shoed, he went to the liquor cabinet and brought out the proper bottle. He poured the proper amount into the proper glass and gave it to her. Why wasn't he the son she had wanted?

Dickie sat down on the couch, rubbing his hands slowly together. It irritated her that he had not poured a drink for himself. To shake him up she said, "Are you sleeping with that bar waitress, Dickie?"

His tanned, inward face turned muddy red, responding at last; but he managed to look dignified, not caught out.

He didn't answer promptly, and she said, "Yes. I see. Evvy Hamilton was reluctant to tell me why she had changed her mind about coming for Christmas. I imagine she was not urged to come."

Dickie licked his lips.

"Was she?"

"I'm afraid not, Mother."

"Certainly you're not under the impression that you're in love with this B-girl?"

"I'm very fond of her, Mother."

It was so unlike him to speak up in this way that she felt a respect for him mingled with a desire to take a switch to the backs of his legs as she had done when he was a boy. She sat down in the teak chair opposite him. "I'm sure she must be very satisfactory in bed," she said.

She was leading them into a fight, or as close to one as it was possible to get with Dickie, on the subject of the bar waitress. But the subject was really Dick, and maybe Maeve as well, who was coming over tonight to sleep in the Big House. To sleep, as it happened, in the guest room where each of them had slept with Dick. This hadn't occurred to her when she issued the invitation. Curiously, it pleased her.

Dickie was chuckling. It was a nervous sound, and she noticed that his chest continued to shake after the sound had stopped, as though he were shivering in the warm room.

"Very accomplished," she said. *You'd be able to find the needle in any haystack,* Dick had said to her once.

"As a matter of fact—" Dickie blurted, caught himself.

She was amused that he had almost revealed some temper. Then she began to regard herself with revulsion. She was being the kind of mother that, in fiction at least, she would despise, a wealthy widow trying to force her son to marry a society girl when he was in love with a simple and honest proletarian. Soon she would be warning him that the waitress was after his money, position, prospects, and so on. She had said those things to Dick about Maeve, hadn't she? And Dick had replied in the four-letter words she had possibly deserved. In fiction the poor girl would be sweet, honest, and shy, the rich girl depraved and smug. In actuality no one was more sweet, honest, and shy than Evaline Hamilton, while the bar-girl was blatantly on-the-make and was overconfident besides. If your son was ensnared by a whore it was necessary to interfere.

"As a matter of fact, what?" she persisted.

"As a matter of fact she's not satisfactory at all," Dickie said. He rose to stand hulking with his toes turned in and hands in his hip pockets. He said, "I don't think you should talk over your love affairs with your mother. Topher Brooks' mother was always—" He stopped. Topher Brooks was his best friend at college, who had gone into the Peace Corps.

He moved to the liquor cabinet and bent over to see what there was, still with his hands in his hip pockets. Finally he poured a portion of Grand Marnier for himself. Always thoughtful, he came to refill her glass.

"Nonsense," she said. "Oh, I know mothers aren't supposed to have any sex life, but you don't want me to think you are a monk, do you?" Of course what Dickie meant was that *he* was not satisfactory but young, fumbling, and awkward. Of course that was it, and why pursue it to his shame? "What do you mean, she's not satisfactory?" she pursued nonetheless. "Do you mean she thinks you're not—"

"She doesn't believe in the orgasm," Dickie said, turning the unattractive, muddy red color again. Then he grinned.

He was grinning at her discomfiture. "Well!" she said. She could feel her own cheeks burning. "Well! How dainty of her!"

Dickie sipped his liqueur, turning half away from her. "You don't understand. She doesn't believe in *any*body's."

"Poor boy," she managed.

"As a matter of fact, I haven't been to bed with her," Dickie said.

"She sounds like a pervert," she said. She didn't believe for a moment that he hadn't been to bed with the waitress, and she was confronted by the possibility that, as she had known more about sex at this age than her mother, so Dickie knew more than she did. Certainly she had never heard of the orgasm being questioned before; could that be the new thing?

"What's a pervert?" Dickie said. "Like a sexual Communist?"

That brought back other conversations they had had, when his refusal to be baited had caused her to make more reactionary statements than she had intended. She said coolly, "Well, you must admit that there are normal sexual practices."

"What's normal?" Dickie said. "I read recently that there is a great deal of homosexuality among animals. For instance, a higher incidence among whales than among people."

Her son had gone far past her.

Looking at her boldly, he said, "I thought for a while she was a Lesbian. But maybe it's just the way she says it is, enjoying—uh—sensation is more fun than ending it."

She was afraid she was being mocked. "She must be some kind of beatnik," she said ineffectually.

"I don't know what a beatnik is," Dickie said. "Just something you don't approve of, like a Communist or a pervert?"

The trouble with the second person plural pronoun was that it was impossible to tell whether her son was being censurably rude or only making a silly generalization. He seemed more and more sure of himself, strutting across now to stand before the fireplace where flames were swarming over the pine logs.

"I mean, all this talk about homosexual and Lesbian," he said. "I'm not sure we even know what those words mean."

"Well, you've been talking about them, dear, not I." She had had enough of the whole subject, though she didn't see how she could say so, having initiated it. She wondered how much of Dickie's knowledge of life and sex had been accumulated because there had happened to be a balcony in this house when he had been a fourteen-year-old boy and the house had been full of dramatic moments. What if he had heard that climactic scene between her and Dick? Could this talk about Lesbianism be a sly allusion to that?

Coming home triumphant from Hawaii with the money that would finish Dancer, put them out of trouble, and save her husband, she had been confronted, first, with Maeve's abject confession; next, with the spectacle of Tim Soderburg in the snowplow trying to smash all the automobiles in the parking lot, and, finally, with Dick himself, drunken, hateful, and offensive. Before she had been able to demand an explanation, he had accused her of a Lesbian attachment for Maeve.

He had made an accurate case, correct—for he was very clever —in many insights and assumptions; but the whole was untrue, and he must have known it was, simply choosing to attack her rather than to defend himself. She had found Maeve Olsen bright, congenial, and full of youth, like a tonic. She had hired Maeve to help her just as Dick had hired his band of skibums. But Dick made it sound as though the two of them were rivals for Maeve, his victory a triumph of the normal over the perverse, as well as another triumph for Dick Macklin over his adversaries. In pain, seeking to hurt as she had been hurt, she accused him of exhibiting his lust before his son, like Noah in his drunkenness. He slapped her. And then he told her that she need never worry, he would not leave her. She had bought him, he had said, but what she had bought was nothing.

"Maybe you have to take people as being what they say they are," Dickie was saying in the infuriating superior tone, unaware of the grief that had seized her like a dog playing with a stick. It had been bred into her that emotions were not supposed to show, and she would not allow hers to show now.

"What does she claim she is?" she asked in what seemed to her a perfectly normal tone of voice.

"She says she's a powderburner."

This mystique of the skibums had been discussed ad nauseam earlier in the evening by Clary, John Henry, and Maeve, with the bar-girl butting in. She wondered why she should sneer at it, for hadn't Dick been a powderburner, literally as well as figuratively, and actually dying of it? Hadn't Dick considered life his deep powder snow to be tracked up, violently used, squandered, until he had died of the squandering and not of cancer nor the slowly paralyzing fear of death itself that was killing Brad?

"Oh, she has it all figured out," Dickie went on. He tipped his head back to finish the liqueur in his glass. His Adam's apple protruded jaggedly, as though he had swallowed a sharp-cornered object—it was not a handsome aspect of him. "She says she just wants to get all the kicks out of everything, the fun out of everything."

Life was full of parallels, and this one was too much like herself and Dick, student and tutor. "You're in love with her, Bunny," she said. She hadn't called him by that name since he was a little boy.

His lips fell into a slack smile, his jaw lengthened bulldoggishly, his eyebrows jerked in a semaphore of concurrence. And all at once, at this childish grimace, she felt close to him, and with the closeness came a certain humility.

"I don't like anything about her," she said, "being your mother. But she sounds a little like your father. He wanted the best out of everything too." She considered for a moment, with a hand raised to keep him from breaking into her thought. "No, that's not right. He wanted *every*thing out of everything."

She smiled at him, thinking that at last they could join, if not in admiration, at least in remembrance of Dick, but Dickie's face struggled to become polite and aloof.

"Oh, stop it!" she said, suddenly furious.

"Stop what?"

"Stop being a juvenile Oedipal priss."

He stared at her, the muscles straining in his neck. Then, stiffly erect, creaky-shoed, he moved back to the liquor cabinet for the bottle of Grand Marnier. He held it up toward her, tight-lipped.

"No more, thank you."

He refilled his own glass and replaced the bottle. As he sipped, his eyes slid past hers. "I can't help what I am," he said in a smugly martyred tone.

She groaned with dismay.

"Mother," he said, "if we're going to have a talk I'd much rather we discussed Brad and what's happening to Dancer. I've some ideas that might—"

"That's not the point," she said. "The point's your father."

"I'd rather not talk about him."

"Afraid?"

"Why should I be afraid?"

"You might have to thank him for something."

"*Thank* him—" Dickie took two steps back and sat down on the couch a little more precipitously than he had intended. He gazed at her with a hurt, sullen expression. But now that she had him in a posture to be lectured, she did not know how to express what filled her. She could not merely command him to love and honor his father. The whole responsibility of parenthood oppressed her again.

"I don't know how to say this," she began. "For a while, after he died, I couldn't bear it here. I thought I would have to sell. But I didn't, because it was his, because he had worked so hard. Maybe I was thinking of it as a tombstone. But I've been realizing tonight that it has to be—no, I've realized that I'd forgotten it was to be a pleasure garden. That was the point. That's the memorial. It has to be that." She took a deep breath and said, "And now you are working here. Maybe someday it will be yours. But you are never going to run it or have it unless you—unless you—" But she could not bring herself to say it, it seemed too sentimental, too emotional. "I had more to forgive than you," she said. "It's time you forgave."

He made a quick, almost secretive, negative motion of his head.

She told herself that this was ridiculous; it didn't matter whether he forgave Dick or not. Dick didn't care. But she cared, and she could feel the whole shape of her will flexing and pointing. "Why?" she said harshly.

"I don't want to talk about it," he said, turning his face aside, and she sighed, relenting. She felt very tired.

"I guess I'll go to bed now," Dickie said. He was asking permission.

"All right," she said. "Good night, dear."

Without another word he rose and vanished, squeaking. She heard his steps mount to the landing, the door of his apartment close. She sat with her hands in her lap waiting for Maeve, counting over what she had to forgive Dick for, like precious stones.

When she was a girl she wore shyness like a muumuu. She lived with her parents in the big old white house with its broad verandas in Nuuanu Valley, and the only person to play with was her cousin Bradley, who was a year older. They climbed from the roof of the porte-cochere into the mango tree, and in mango season their mouths were always irritated from eating the green fruit. Once from the top of the tree they watched President Roosevelt driving up Nuuanu Avenue in an open limousine toward the Pali; he was waving and smoking a cigarette in a holder, exactly as in the cartoons. He had a big pink face. She and Brad must have been in their teens then, but in her memory it seemed that they were always children.

Her mother and father hated Roosevelt. Brad's mother, who was her father's sister Milly, thought Roosevelt was wonderful and often said so at family gatherings, causing stony silences and embarrassing Brad horribly. Aunt Milly had eloped with a young Episcopalian minister to the mainland, where Brad had been born. They had lived in Marin County while the minister had tried to make a living writing poetry. He had committed suicide when Brad was seven. The family rumor was that he had killed himself when he learned he and Aunt Milly had been living, not on Milly's money, but on an allowance sent by Milly's brother, her own father.

Her father paid Brad's bills at the University of California, where he was supposed to take accounting so that he could work for Bradley-Beeson, Ltd. Brad took an English major instead and in the end didn't even finish the work for his degree. Her father was furious. She accepted the fact that Brad had always been in love with her the way she accepted the fact that her name was Isobel Bradley and that her father was president of Bradley-Beeson. Later on she was to realize that Aunt Milly had always been the kind of burden to her father that Brad came to be to her.

Dick Macklin arrived with the Marines en route to Guadalcanal early in the war. She had been hearing about him from Brad for years. He was Brad's best friend at the university, president of Brad's fraternity, a track star, actor in student productions, debater, and president of the student body his senior year. Brad had been his campaign manager in this. Of most of these things she disapproved, having been taught that public notice was notoriety, not fame. Three hours after Dick Macklin telephoned to ask her, as a friend of Brad's, to attend a dance with him at an officers' club at Pearl Harbor, they were parked in her car on top of Punchbowl and drinking a toast from Dick's bottle of Southern Comfort to her lost virginity.

She was his mistress and his slave for two weeks, until one day, without warning, he was gone. He was back in Tripler Hospital within three months, a wounded hero, and she gloried in the newspaper and magazine stories about him even if they were notoriety. Her father took them to lunch at the Pacifica Club, and her mother invited Dick home for dinner. Her father told her he thought Dick the finest, most promising young man he knew and hinted that there might be a very good position waiting for him with Bradley-Beeson if Dick was interested, though of course it would not do to broach the subject yet. Her mother told her she thought Dick one of the handsomest young men she had ever seen. It was a pity he was so short, but he held himself well. Her friends envied her. Brad was somewhere in Texas in the Army. She hadn't written him that she was in love with Dick Macklin. She couldn't bring herself to write him when she and Dick became engaged, though she knew by now that some friend, and certainly Aunt Milly, must have told him. What they were doing to Brad was a pity, she and Dick would say to each other, as though both were trying to feel the appropriate guilt. She was to feel guilt enough later on, but at the time she felt only a complete delight in the body and hands and mouth and eyes and wounds of Dick Macklin. They were married in the house in Nuuanu Valley, Dick in his blues and walking with a cane, her friends in bridesmaids' gowns of pink and white, and orchids everywhere. It was a lovely Island day with a delicate rain patting on the leaves of the mango tree and the sun shining through the rain.

They went to live in a honeymoon cottage on the Ala Wai Canal in Waikiki, two blocks from the beach, on Pau Street. The honeymoon went on and on, lapped with happiness, drenched with happiness, but of course it had to end. Dick had introduced her to life, and there was more to life than happiness.

The visit to old Dr. Quin, which she thought would result in happiness too, turned instead into horror. Dr. Quin said this sort of thing often happened in wartime. Dr. Quin said it had been discovered very early and he could clean it up in no time at all. She was so ashamed she thought she would have to kill herself; she even planned to walk out through the warm, calm water of Waikiki until it was deep enough to drown her in her shame. Then suddenly coldly furious, she thought she must kill her husband, who had done this to her. That brown, scarred, beautiful body was full of disease.

She left the car where she had parked it and took the open streetcar out Beretainia, with the trade wind cooling her burning face. The streetcar crossed the canal and turned onto Kalakaua Avenue, where she got off. She stood for a time looking at the name of the street on the lava curbing, because "Pau" means "finished" in Hawaiian. When she got home Dick was still at the beach. She sat in a wicker chair with her handbag in her lap and her feet in spectator pumps placed close together. Sitting still, she could feel her ragged breathing become more and more even and shallow, until she hardly seemed to be breathing at all.

She held on to herself very tightly when she heard Dick's bare feet coming in the back door, the slam of the screen, and then its softer closing as it eased past the black rubberball bumper. She heard the squeak of the icebox door, the thud as it closed, the rattle of the bottlecap dropping onto the drainboard. Dick came in through the bead curtain, surprised to see her, brown beer bottle raised to his mouth, tanned almost black but still painfully thin, with the pink-white marbling of the scar across his left breast and shoulder, and long and cruel down his left leg. Even his scars were beautiful. Her fingers knew them by heart.

"Where's the car?" he asked.

"I left it downtown."

He sucked the beer bottle, frowning. His deep-set eyes were quizzical, his nose narrow and sensual. Extending from the nostrils to the corners of his mouth were the sharply cut lines of old pain. "What said the kindly old medico, honey?"

Tears scraped at her eyes; no words would come. He moved toward her, limping. His hand was the same color as the brown bottle it held. As he stood over her his other hand rose to smooth the scar branching up from his breast.

"Bun in the oven or not, honey?"

"It's not a bun that's in the oven," she said. "You God-damned *haole!*"

He took a step back. She couldn't look into his face now. Outside, myna birds argued in the monkeypod tree. "God *damn* you!" she whispered.

"Touch of the clap?" Dick asked.

She didn't know the word, but she nodded.

"Are you pregnant, honey?"

She shook her head. He raised his bottle to drink. Every muscle in his belly was visible beneath the thin brown skin. "It's no worse than a bad cold, honey," he said.

"It's a venereal disease! It's a dirty, filthy disease from prostitutes! I got it from *you!*"

"Toilet seat," Dick said.

"He said people tried to tell doctors that sometimes, but it was nonsense. He said I might as well face up to it." And then, as though she had to try to excuse him somehow, she said, "He said it happens all the time in wartime. In the other war—"

"It happens all the time all the time," Dick said. He bent over and, before she realized what he was going to do, kissed her on the mouth. She thrust at him, jerking her head away. "Sorry, Izzy," he said in a thickened voice.

"I'm *dirty,*" she said. "You've got it too!" she cried at him.

He sat down opposite her, crossing his scarred leg so the ankle was supported on the right knee. Golden hairs gleamed on his tan legs. "I thought I'd been pretty careful all along with the Trojans, but things might've got away from me that big night at your house."

"Some prostitute infected you!"

"Toilet seat." He grinned a little.

"*Liar!*"

His grin dissolved. "If you want to know I'll tell you."

"Of course I want to know!"

"You don't really want to know."

"I have to know!"

"Honey, do you know what the FMF is doing when it's not fighting? Or working? Or eating?" He raised his hands all-inclusively. "It's trying to get a piece of tail. In Iwilei if we have to, but classier stuff if it's available. Do you know why? Because we love it. Men do. I'm pretty sure by now most women do too. It's the best thing there is. It scares the hell out of a man to think of getting killed with all those good shots left in the locker. That's what the kindly old doctor meant about it happening all the time in wartime. Do you understand, honey?"

She didn't understand anything except that Dick didn't even take it seriously that he had given her a venereal disease. "I want to know where you got it," she said.

"I'm trying to tell you I don't know where I got it."

"Oh!"

"You don't want a catalogue, do you?"

"*Oh!*" she whispered, for it had come to her that he had had it that night under the full moon on Punchbowl, that first night. She whispered, "You mean you did it with me, knowing you had it? You—"

"Honey, that's officially what a rubber's for. But I guess I must've—"

"Oh, God," she said, and he stopped. "You got it from some prostitute on the coast and came over here and gave it to *me*." She tried to picture in her mind the awful, diseased woman. This afternoon she had accepted the fact that men were beasts. So were women, then, beasts, who would do that to clean young men.

Smiling the one-sided, teeth-showing grin she didn't like, Dick said, "Well, I'm not so sure I picked it up back in the states. I might've got it over here."

"Don't you dare—"

"Honey, there wasn't any doubt about you being cherry. But I can't say as much for some of your girl friends."

"I don't believe it," she whispered.

"Believe what, now?"

"That you did it with anybody—with any— You liar!"

"Well, not since we've been married," Dick said easily. He finished his beer and hung an arm down to stand the bottle on the floor beside his chair. "You've been keeping me too busy."

"Who?" she whispered.

"Never mind it, Izzy. I'm sorry I brought it up." He rose and went through the bead curtain into the kitchen again. She stared at the bright window, a moan aching in her throat. The black-and-yellow myna birds were strafing the neighbor's cat, which scurried along the sidewalk like a furry centipede. Kitty Gardener.

Dick came back with another bottle of beer. "Do you want a brew, honey?" he asked solicitously.

"Kitty," she said.

"Right," Dick said.

"I don't believe you."

He grinned the dirty grin at her, and the moan came hurting in her throat again. She put a hand over her mouth to stop it, as though to keep from throwing up. And then she almost cried out to see what his hand had been doing, gross and bestial. She covered her eyes.

"Can't stand the sight of the villain of the piece?" Dick said in a coarse voice. "Come on and I'll give you a treatment right now. Come on, Izzy, let's share our sickness and health and everything. We'll go get our shots together."

"You gave me a disease!" she cried through her hands. Horrible as this was, it didn't matter enough for her to leave him. She loved him too much. Yet she couldn't let him get away with this, sleeping with prostitutes, with Kitty Gardener, with anyone, because—because— "What if I can't ever have a baby?" she cried.

"What'd he say about that?" Dick's voice said, nearer, worried.

She didn't uncover her eyes. "He said it was lucky I came in when I did."

"Sure. Everything'll be all right."

"How do you know that?"

"Because I'm lucky." His hand rested on her knee; he was kneeling beside her.

"How could you do it, Dick?" she said. She began to sob, twisting her hands together in her lap. She could smell the beer on his breath. "Now Kitty's got it," she said, sobbing, "and I have to go and tell her so she can go to the doctor, and she'll know I know you—and she'll—she's so damn—"

"Don't be silly," Dick said. "She hasn't got anything."

"But she was a friend of mine, she was a bridesmaid. How do I know you just won't go on doing it with—with whoever you want to?"

"Honey," his voice said, so close now she could feel the warmth of his breath on her cheek. "Honey, just ignore it."

She started to cry out again, but his hand tightened on her knee and the warm, beer-breath voice said, "Honey—honey, we'd better get all this straight now," and something in his voice made her pay attention.

"I almost got killed," he said. "It was very close. They got me out, but they might not have. It just happened they liked me enough to take some chances for me. They might have been a little slower, and that would have been too slow. Or there might not have been a corpsman there. And it just happened the corpsman knew what he was doing. Or they might not have been able to get me out to the destroyer that night. I was almost dead. I'm only alive because of one piece of luck after another."

He had told her all this before but not in this same way; or maybe she had not listened in this way. "That's called contingency," Dick went on. "And you get to understand that contingency is there all the time and goes along with you wherever you go and every minute. If you can luck in, you can luck out. I think a person doesn't really know how to live until he really realizes contingency. Maybe you have to almost die to realize it. Anyway, I'm alive on contingency, and so are you though I don't think you know it yet. So I'm going to have everything there is to get out of my life just because I realize how lucky I am to be alive.

"Now, what I love most of all—the person—is you. But what I love most of all—doing—is what we've been talking about. I want all I can get. Maybe there are other good things, and maybe as I get older and there's no war on so the contingency's not quite so tight, it won't be so important. Maybe I'm just oversexed, but I love it. For me right now it's the best thing the great big surprise package that life is has to offer. Nothing else even comes close. I think about it all the time. I think about you that way all the time."

In spite of herself she felt a fierce little thrill of joy. He paused, and she heard him draw a deep breath. He said, "I haven't thought much about anybody else that way since we've been married. But I'm not kidding myself that I'm not going to. And not just think about it. When I get to wanting it enough I know I'm going to do something about it. It doesn't matter just yet, but it will. So if you aren't going to stand for it, if it's going to hurt you too much, then we'd better know it now and quit. I'm trying to be honest with you, Izzy. I love you. I really love you. But knowing what I know about contingency, I'm going to squeeze everything there is out of that surprise package, everything I can—not just sex, though that's the most important thing right now. I'll try not to hurt you. I promise that. I'll—"

She cried, "Isn't *this* hurting me?"

"Not as much as you think you're hurt," he said. "I think you're mostly afraid Dr. Quin'll rat on you. I'm serious, honey, just as serious as I can be. I love you a lot more than I thought it was going to be possible for me to love anybody, but I've got my lusts. I'm not going to just swallow them and have gas."

"I'm not enough for you. That's what you're saying."

"You sure are, right now. After a while you won't be. It's not your fault. I don't think it's mine either; it's just men and women."

"Then I can have lovers too!"

But he wouldn't give her the satisfaction of that meaningless ultimatum. "No, honey. Never do that to me. That's a different kind of thing."

So all she had in the end was the sop that at least he would care if she was unfaithful to him. And so, honestly at least, as he had said, their life together had been built. There had been many women, and she had been hurt, but she had been able to appreciate that, until Maeve, he had tried to keep from hurting her. And, as he had also said, women had come to matter a little less as he grew older. When the concentrated work at Dancer began, that summer and fall, women, including herself, obviously mattered hardly at all. She had thought that the building of the lift and the lodge was using his vitality to the utmost.

Later she realized it was the lack of money, worries over money, the demeaning, debilitating fighting for money or credit that had drained his power. A master of men, little by little he had lost his command in the nagging and fretting and penny-foolish helplessness of being without money, even failing with her because his mind was obsessed with the lack of money instead of with what he had once called the most wonderful thing in the world. So she had flown to Hawaii to beg and threaten the Bradley-Beeson board of directors into loaning her a hundred and ten thousand dollars on her stock, to save Dick.

And while she was gone he found in Maeve someone to make him a man again. How could she blame him? Or blame Maeve, who might have tried, instinctively, to save him with her young body? And Dick had told her quite clearly, hadn't he, that he had chosen her money over Maeve's body?

For a year after Dick's death she was not able to come near Dancer. She spent the remainder of the winter in solitary and self-indulgent grief in the house on Kauai that had been left her by a distant relative, while Dickie stayed in Honolulu with her mother and attended Punahou. She took Dickie on a European trip the next summer, put him in a prep school in Connecticut in the fall. She purchased an apartment in New York, where she attended the theater and the opera and the art galleries and met many men, not one of whom she could consider marrying. She began to do social work in a small way.

She corresponded regularly with Brad, who had taken hold at Dancer with a surer grasp than she could possibly have hoped for. When she saw him again, having finally returned to Dancer to see about the financing of the second chairlift, he seemed more his own man than he had ever seemed before, mature, decisive, in charge, much more of a man, indeed, than any she had met in New York. She began sleeping with him during her quarterly visits to Dancer. She could not remember which of them had instigated it; she believed it to have been as nearly mutual as those arrangements ever could be.

It was not entirely satisfactory. There were clinical aspects, careful bathrobe-and-pajama routines, overemphasis on the music, lights, and wine, as though, because there was no real passion, there must be a very careful attention to detail. It lasted for six years, this relationship with Brad.

One of the first things she remembered about Brad, when he and Aunt Milly had returned to the Islands after his father's suicide, was the solemn, chubby boy of seven or eight advising her that it was all right for them to play together but that they must never marry because his mother had told him that would be incest. When Brad brought up the subject of incest again it was at the end of those six years of casual adultery. She was aware that men failed sexually earlier than women, and all at once Brad failed, with the pitiful talk of incest to excuse his impotence.

So her life seemed to her to have the structure of a human symphony. There was the quiet pastorale of her girlhood; the great appassionata of her marriage to Dick; the rather confused and slow-paced widowhood, with its attention to the arts and social work. Now the final, placid movement would begin; she would marry Barton Weaver, gently wrap herself and life's turmoil of emotions in cellophane, place the package in a chest and the chest in storage. *Pau.*

14: Richard E. Macklin, Jr.

TIRED AS HE WAS, he knew there was no use getting into bed, so he put his new Ornette Coleman on the turntable and sat in his pajamas, slippers, and robe, watching the spinning black disk with the blob of highlight reflected from the lamp. The horn, bright as the sun coming from behind clouds in this one place, could lift his soul right out of the despondency he was in, his anger at John Henry mixed with the out-of-the-past depression.

There was another passage a little farther on, very muted and minor, that acted on him exactly like Marcel Proust's madeleine-dipped-in-tea. Strangely it called tea to his mind too, the super-saturated sweetness of mint tea in the teahouse on the road above Fez that looked down on the pearly, diseased city, and the muezzins distantly calling, so like the muted horn's call; he and Topher Brooks, and Phillippa McAndrews. It was an afternoon that had started so pleasantly and had ended in shame. He and Topher had never even written.

Phillippa McAndrews had been older than most of the other Peace Corps people he had met in Fez. She had served in Algeria with the American Friends, had a little Arabic, and a self-confident, superior air; her project was going much better than any other. The hill women spent almost all their time gathering twigs and faggots to bake their bread; if she could persuade just one village to build a communal oven, others would copy, and she was making great progress in discussions with government officials and village headmen. Topher, whose water project was impossibly bogged down, said she had a Schweitzer complex, but he admired her. Obviously Topher had slept with her, obviously she was a hysterical old maid jealous of the time Topher spent with him, and of the basketball and swimming and ping-pong aspects of his and Topher's friendship; and obviously she was as sickened by the blatant homosexuality in that shimmering, stinking city as he had been. He knew all those things, had calmly and rationally considered the scene and the motivations within it from all aspects, but still the shame remained and still he had never been able to write his friend Topher, who was at Yale Law School now, he had heard.

He wondered if Maeve had come over to the Big House yet, if Maeve and his mother were sitting in the living room talking, if they were talking about his father. He reminded himself that if they were talking about his father it was not important, he was not concerned. But Maeve and his father talking about his mother had been very much his concern.

The record finished without his attention, the arm moved into the center, where it swung eccentrically for a moment before returning to its rest as the machine shut itself off. How convenient it would be, he thought, if your mind could shut itself off like that. Instead the click of the switch reminded him of the waited-for sound of the front door closing, his father coming home with Maeve. It was the sound that had often come while he was asleep, but it had always wakened him, and then he would hear the quiet voices, especially the timbre in his father's voice, which he seemed to feel along his nerves rather than hear.

And if he heard their voices in the living room he would slowly slip out of bed, slide onto the floor on his hands and knees, and push the door firmly outward so that the latch made no sound when he turned the knob; then he would crawl to the balcony railing where he could hear and, between the slats of the rail, see most of the back of the couch facing the fireplace. Once, by firelight, he had seen Maeve's white legs rising from the couch, waving like something growing on the bottom of the sea.

He turned the record over. This time by a major act of will he concentrated on the music all the way through. There were no memories on this side, but no glory either.

When the machine shut off again he got to his feet, forcing himself to yawn. Now he would go to bed and read *U.S. News and World Report*, then go to sleep. But he knew he would only keep turning his mind left and right like eyes watching a ping-pong match—to keep his eyes off the ball rather than on it. He had not been able to tell John Henry that the point was not that he hated his father so much, it was that his father had hated him. Maybe his father had cursed him or maybe it was only a prophecy that had come due in Fez years later.

This was all nonsense and fantasy, and he paced up and down, trying to talk sense to himself. Halting, he found himself facing the door that opened onto the stair landing of the Big House.

From the stair landing there were eight steps up to the second floor, which was a bunkroom now, an open balcony. When he opened the door he could hear the flamenco music on the stereo. Very sure of himself in the dark, he made his way up the eight stairs and across the balcony. He was breathing deeply when he stopped at the railing, looking down on them.

They sat on the couch facing the fire, two heads curiously complimentary in color, his mother's hair a silvery shade of blond, Maeve's pale gold. They were sitting at either end of the couch, and for a time, with the wild guitar pyrotechnics, they didn't speak.

Then his mother tossed her head slightly, turned her face toward Maeve and in profile to him, and smiled overbrightly. He was right, they had been talking about his father. His mother said, "I don't think I'd ever seen him so on the offensive before. One would have thought *I* was the guilty party."

He was watching Maeve's tan hand, with its pale, shiny fingernails, lying on the back of the couch. At first the fingers tapped nervously on the upholstery material; with the last words, like little animals sensing danger, they curled into a fist.

"As though *you* were guilty," Maeve echoed.

There was another pause. He was grateful that the subject was changed when Maeve said, "I'm so frightened about skiing in the Superchute tomorrow. What if I can't do it! I wish you'd come with us, Isobel."

"I haven't skied for nine years," his mother said.

"Since Dick died," Maeve said. "I was trying to remember"— her fingers, which seemed to have a life of their own, had reappeared in a spread-out, strained position on the back of the couch—"if you were skiing with us that day."

"I never skied well enough for the Superchute. I was never asked to come along on the deep powder expeditions."

Maeve's fingers doubled up as though in disappointment, then spread out again. "I always thought you would marry Brad," Maeve said. "After Dick died."

"Did you really?" his mother said, not pleasantly.

"Yes." Maeve's hand moved from the back of the couch and she slipped down in her seat until the back of her head rested on the cushion behind her. "Because he was in love with you once, wasn't he?"

His mother sat very stiffly upright. He thought she was not going to answer, but finally she said, "Yes, he was. Years ago."

"I hope you don't mind my asking about it, but I—did hear a rumor that you were having an affair."

This time his mother said nothing.

"You do mind," Maeve almost whispered.

"Yes, I do. I'm not the woman of the world you've become, Maeve."

"I'm sorry," Maeve said.

He could feel the muscles of his jaw aching, his mouth stretched into a painful grimace of protest. The world seemed full, not of evil, but of disgusting middle-aged accommodation.

"I'm sorry if I've offended you," Maeve said. "It's just that I've been thinking of so many things, coming back here. It's all a part of thinking about death, I suppose."

"What?" his mother said. She cleared her throat, but her voice was still thick when she said, "What, dear?"

"Thinking about Dick dying," Maeve said. "So many things keep coming to my mind." Again they were both silent for a time and there was only the nervous, jagged music. Then Maeve said, "He acted as though *you* were the guilty one."

"I'm sure he found attacking me more pleasant than defending himself. He said terrible things. Poor Dick, he was losing the charm with which he could once charm anyone. And his force. And now he was caught out in—" She didn't finish.

He could feel the tension between them. He had never heard his mother criticize his father before.

"What kind of terrible things?" Maeve said in her light voice.

"For one thing, he accused you and me of having a Lesbian relationship."

His breath came so hard he was afraid it would be heard. He

remembered what he and his mother had been talking about just before he had left her, too close to this, too close to Phillippa Mc-Andrews and the slime of Fez. And surely next on the agenda would be Maeve telling his mother what his father had said to *her*, surely Maeve must still wonder why his father had said what he had said when he had handed her her paycheck.

But before he fled he heard Maeve laugh and cry out in mock dismay, "Oh, dear!" Shock on shock; how could they speak of this thing to each other, much less laugh about it? Someday would he and Topher be able to laugh at what that silly old maid in Fez had called them?

Back in his room, he put the Ornette Coleman record on the turntable again. For a moment the needle tracked silently, then, slowly blossoming from the speaker, the horn began to sound. With stubborn concentration he tried to keep his mind on the music, waiting for the glory which was only glory as a part of what came before it. But his concentration slipped slowly, like a man hanging by his fingertips from a ledge, slipped until he was thinking of his mother saying his father had said terrible things to her, and John Henry saying that you didn't believe J.D. Daugherty when he got on that subject, and so finally, reluctantly, he had to re-examine the terrible things his father had said to him.

All those days when his mother was gone and Maeve was in the house he knew he was going to have to do something. It seemed to him that if he were a boy in a movie he would have known what to do. For one thing, there would have been a kindly old servant to help him, and there would have been a trick as simple as Hamlet's trick with the players to show his father that Maeve was bad and at the same time make him realize what a fine woman his mother was. But Brad was not a faithful servant and did not know what to do, and it was difficult to convince even himself that Maeve was bad. She had always been nice to him, she had been his friend when no one else paid any attention to him, and they had had good long talks when she was driving him to and from school.

But he knew he had to do something because, listening by the furnace in the basement, he had heard his father's voice saying in the bedroom, "You think it isn't war, but it is. You grab any club you can reach, sex or children or money, anything. Now she's got the great big iron-studded club and she's going to save me with her money. On her side of it, I don't think she's got any idea of what she's trying to do to me." Maeve said something inaudible, and then his father said, "I know how to win the battles. It's just the war I'm worried about."

So he had not understood except that if it was war he was on his mother's side. And when he had overheard John Henry and J.D. talking about the men Maeve Olsen had done it with, he had convinced himself, first, that he didn't owe Maeve any more allegiance, and, second, that now he knew how to help his mother, and, third, that he really owed it to his father to tell him what he had learned about Maeve.

A number of days passed before he had the courage to match his certitude. He phoned the lodge and asked for his father. Fortunately for his resolve, his father wasn't in his office, and he told Janet Rohde that he had to see his father at home, it was very important.

While he waited he paced the living room like a soldier. He strode to the refrigerator and poured himself a glass of milk, spiking it with vanilla extract. He carried his drink back into the living room, where he managed to sit still until he had finished it. Then he resumed his pacing. Sweat from his armpits tickled down his sides.

His father looked worried and irritated when he came in. "What's the matter?" he demanded.

"I heard something I have to tell you about," he said. "I mean, I think I better."

His father faced him, only an inch or two taller than he was, with his lined face and the gray showing in his cropped hair. His father looked as though he knew somehow that this was going to be bad news. It was the first time he had realized that his father was growing old. His father stared at him for a long time, while the sweat ran down his sides and his confidence began to drip away.

"It's about Maeve Olsen," he managed, and his father said in a mild voice, "What is it, son?"

He told his father what J.D. had said about Easy Clary and Maeve, Timbal Khan and Maeve, everybody and Maeve, tempering the four-letter words as much as he knew how but having to use them sometimes, while his father stood gazing at him out of the two rectangles of shadow that were his eyes. The lines that ran from his nose to the corners of his mouth were like knife slashes.

"I just thought I ought to tell you, Dad," he finished in a rush.

His father turned away, walked over to the bar and got a square whisky bottle from the liquor cabinet. Pouring liquor into his glass, watching the level mount, he said casually, "John Henry was concurring in this, was he?"

"Yes, sir."

His father nodded, sipping whisky, standing with his feet set apart and his head lowered. "Well, you've overheard a lot of things in your time, son," he said. "This last must have been a little painful." And then he said, "Probably someday you'll understand about it all. The trouble is, when you finally do it's too late."

He didn't know what that meant.

"Love your mother, don't you?" his father said.

"Yes, sir," he said.

His father was talking in a very disconnected manner. "Any proof?" he said. "Was it a handkerchief? Sex and money and children too." Then his father's face jerked toward him, violent red swelling up in his neck. He cried, like a whip snapping, "Don't smirk at me, you son-of-a-bitch!"

Before he had time to think he had cried back, "Dad, I only thought you ought to know!"

His father looked apologetic after his outburst. He drank and wiped his mouth with the back of his hand. His eyes seemed to have sunk into his head. "I'm becoming an authority on the Christ position," he said, mild once more, making a flapping motion with his free hand. "Did you know that crucifixion was the prescribed execution for slaves?"

"No, I—no, sir."

"Slowly the arms are bent into the essential position. Thorns grow around the brow. The feet are crossed, right on left, and nailed into position." He sounded drunk. "Oh, baby," he said drunkenly.

He was afraid his father would lash out at him again, but his father went limping around the room, looking at the paintings on the walls. One, which his mother hated, had been done by a

Marine Corps friend, a lush, careful-leafed jungle, a mechanical-drawing-class machine gun, and a helmet with three bullet holes in it that was incorrectly highlighted; no people. His father stood gazing at this for a long time. Without turning, he said, "Come on over here and sit down, son. I want to give you a lecture."

He went over and sat down, shivering as he stared at his father's back. His father's right knee was slightly bent to compensate for the shortness of his left leg.

Then his father turned and looked down at him. "Well, you're fourteen now. Learning the joys of jacking off and feeling guilty as hell, and eavesdropping and feeling guilty as hell about that too. And I ought to feel guilty as hell for bringing a whore in here while your mother's away, but I don't."

His father sipped whisky, took a couple of head-down steps to the right, and stopped. "Time for our father-and-son talk," he said. "Should have had it long ago, I suppose, but you've always been pretty much your mama's boy." He sighed. "I told you you'd understand some day. Maybe you will. Or maybe you'll end up the kind of pansy clod that never understands. So listen. The hardest thing there is to be is a man. It's easy to be a woman. If you've borne children you've been a woman, since that's a woman's job. A woman actually has to work at it not to have children. Being a man is much more difficult, probably it's impossible over a lifetime. You know what a queer is, don't you?"

"Yes, sir."

"There are a hell of a lot of them. In parts of New York and San Francisco you think they are going to take over the world. But they are only the visible part of the iceberg of not-men. The pansies have actively given up trying to be men the way atheists are noisy about having given up being Christian. But all the rest of the iceberg has more or less given up too, only they don't like to think about it much.

"Now, how do you go about being a man? There are certain easy ways. War is an easy way, which is a good reason for so many wars. If you come through combat you can think of yourself as a man. War is also nature's way of controlling the population, as we are beginning to realize now the world is getting to be up to its ass in people. There are a few other simple ways that come to mind, maybe combat sports, maybe climbing Mount Everest or crossing the South Pole, or developing an injection against polio, or getting something big built. That sort of thing." Not limping quite so much, his father went back to the bottle to replenish his glass.

He was trying to listen and to understand, but darkening the edges of his mind was the implication that his father considered him a mama's boy, a pansy, who was never going to be a man.

His father returned to stand before him, slim-hipped and broad-shouldered. "You may have heard about the war between men and women," his father said. "It's always on. Just when you think, well, at least it's not a war with *this* one, you get shot down. The war between men and women is both a joke and the most serious fact you're ever going to run across. Because the main reason it's almost impossible to be a man is women. Now a man is meant to kill bears and fight other men and impregnate women. Not *a* woman, women. But that arrangement's not in women's best interest, women feel, so they invented the family. And society is in the best interests of the family. Okay; society. And money and the need to have it out of society. And manners and morals and alimony and desertion laws and community property. None of these things are in men's best interest, all of them in women's. You look at a lion in the desert and a drafthorse pulling a plow, and you'll see the difference between a natural man and a husband.

"You have to be aware of what society's always trying to do to you. Make a husband out of you, make a kind of family-supporting *thing* out of you. And pansies are what society gets, what women get—mothers, that is—from trying too hard. Maybe you can't win. You have to fight anyway. The most wonderful, beautiful, kind, loyal, self-effacing woman in the world is your deadly enemy in this thing, because she is going to break you in the end. I want you to try understand, be aware of what's happening to you, as you go along just thinking you're having a happy time with the girls, then having a little family, making a living, the whole route. It's all a great big trap to neuter you. Do you know what that means, when they fix a male animal?"

He nodded mutely.

"I don't mean physically fixed like that," his father went on. "It's just an attitude. They have to have you tame, housebroken,

homebroken, worldbroken—I guess I just mean broken. But don't
let them turn you into a pansy, and don't let them break you without a fight."

He said, "I don't—I don't see—"

"Sure," his father said almost tenderly. "I guess you can't. I
should've been working on it before, shouldn't I? Maybe that's
one of the self-defeating things. A man isn't much interested in his
children when they're still young. So the boys get subverted before
they know what it's all about.

"I used to think I was so lucky," his father went on, staring
down at him. "I used to think I'd known it all from the beginning,
laying them and leaving them, fighting and getting to see death up
close without getting dead, knowing that money would always—
thinking I knew it all," he said and laughed shortly. He raised his
voice. "But what I *do* know is that you have to go roaring in—
really hellroaring in, because there are so many things grabbing at
you. You'll never get over the top unless you come roaring in at
ninety miles an hour. Because everything keeps slowing you down,
slowing you down, and all at once you find out that somebody can
take a smack at you and make it stick, and all at once—" He wiped
the back of his hand over his mouth again. "You have to go in at
ninety miles an hour when they try to tell you the speed limit is
only twenty-five. I'm afraid you are going to go in at twenty-five
flat. Do you know what I'm trying to say to you, son?"

He did, almost he did, but some perversity in him made him
say, "No, I guess I don't understand, Dad."

"Never mind then," his father said, turning away. "Maybe later
on. I'd better get back to the office." He limped toward the entry,
his limp very pronounced, and there, before he went out, stopped
and said in a perfectly blank voice, "Thanks for the information."

He thought he must have broken his father's heart, and the
things his father had said to him weren't terrible at all, they were
only sad. He wondered if he could have known even then that
what J.D. had said was all a lie.

15: Captain Easy

STANDING ON THE EAVE of the shed roof, leaning out at approximately a seventy-five-degree angle, supported by a hand braced on the window frame, he felt very foolish as he peered into the lighted room. All was changed. The furniture was anonymous Danish Modern; there were bright rugs on the floor, the woodwork was shiny white, the bedspread pink, red, and orange stripes. Framed prints hunt in decorator clusters on the wall opposite him. Inside the open door were two black-and-blue-plaid bags and a suitcase bound with black straps.

He was cold; snow settled on his shoulders and in his hair, and from time to time he had to change position in order to warm a cold hand inside the waistband of his pants. Snow melted on his cheeks and dripped into the corners of his mouth, but the Don Juan of Dancer remained steadfast at his post, though at intervals he uttered grunts of impatience.

There was not light enough to see his watch. He reminded himself that he disapproved of all that watches signified. He commanded himself to enjoy the waiting, and it was beautiful, with the glowing magic of the swimming pool and the snowflakes drifting down between him and the lights of the lodge, the snow lightly, timelessly falling for tomorrow's pleasure. Maeve had not been able to stop talking about skiing the powder in the Superchute tomorrow, and obviously her obsession was in large part fear of failure. She had looked determined, tired, and frightened.

Without warning she appeared in the doorway with Isobel Macklin. The two women spoke together briefly, briefly pressed their cheeks together, and Maeve backed into the room past her luggage, closing the door behind her. Moving with slow steps, she examined the room, her face expressionless, a hand lifted with fingers extended to comb through her hair. The movement raised her breast under the silk blouse and golden chains. He wondered what she was thinking, what she wanted, how she felt her life had gone thus far. It was a very different Maeve from the Love Derby Maeve, from the Maeve he had been with last in this room. He began to feel ridiculous. The arm that supported his weight trembled with strain.

Standing before the mirror, Maeve began to take the golden chains from around her neck. Her movements were as graceful and seductive as those of a stripteaser, but with a stroke of awe he realized what was missing, what was changed. They had no quality of sex, they were merely graceful. This, he realized, was what he had been finding different about her all evening.

As she removed the last chain her face turned toward the window. She seemed to have heard something, though he had made no sound. She moved quickly toward him, the shape of her knees showing in the heavy material of her skirt; her face came close to the glass, and he tapped the pane in greeting. He had to swing back onto the shed roof so she could open the window.

"I thought you might be here," Maeve whispered.

He leaped onto the window frame, a better entry than last time. He grinned at her. "Consider yourself refenestrated," he said.

Inside the room he stood looking down into her face but not touching her. She had her arms folded over her breasts as though she were cold. Suddenly she closed her eyes, and tears gleamed like beads in the lashes.

Awkwardly, this time, he put his arms around her. Her fingers pressed into his back but with no physical passion. He whispered, "What's the matter, Maeve?"

"I have to ask you something."

"Ask."

"Did you kill Dick?"

The breath was shocked out of him. "What?"

"Did you cut the avalanche?"

When he tried to pull away she gripped him more tightly with her sharp fingertips.

"*Did you?*"

"Christ, *no*, Maeve!"

"Somebody did," she said in a tight, humming whisper. "I saw it. Skied across above where I—above *him*. And stamped. Like stamping on a bug. Just—just there at the corners of my eyes."

His throat swelled with pity. "No, Maeve," he said gently. "No—"

"I tell you I saw it! I have to find out who it was! I have to—"

He pressed her hard against him to stop her hysterical voice. "Maeve, wait."

"It's true," she said, more calmly now. Her breath was hot against his ear. "I'm *not* crazy. It's true. I saw it and I tried not to think about it all those years. But now I've got to know. Easy, was it you?"

"No, Maeve," he said. He tried to speak calmly in the face of his shock, not at her irrationality but at the shameful beginnings of his own revulsion to it, as though it were a physical disease. "No, Maeve," he said calmly. "It wasn't me."

PART TWO *The Deep Powder*

Have, get, before it cloy,
Before it cloud, Christ, Lord, and sour with sinning.

—GERARD MANLEY HOPKINS

Baby, you so beautiful, but you got to die someday.

—BLUES

1: Mariachi Girl

THE FIRST long pink lines and planes of light on the mountain were visible from her window. The distant beard-stubble of trees was powdered with white. She was shivering as she pulled on her tights and her gray matted-wool socks and brought a pair of stretchpants, blue with a darker blue elastic stripe, from her suitcase. This was the morning she had been looking forward to for months, here in Dancer to ski the powder, up with the first salmon-colored morning light, early on the lift and early in the Superchute while the powder was untracked, this one of the few immutable things she knew that gave life meaning, so that it was not just a confused flux of wasted days rushing past.

She had not meant to reveal her mission so soon because she was determined to suspect everyone equally until she had real evidence. But last night she had been so tense and so tired, trying so hard not to show how emotional she was, trying to be rational and reasonable, and then Clary's face at the window. So she had started to pour it all out to him, but obviously he had thought she didn't know what she was saying.

She was here to ski the powder. Yet her restless mind would not stay on this day she had been looking forward to for so long, but instead prowled forward to what was to happen tomorrow, back to what had happened yesterday, and would not pause except by an exhausting act of will in the center of its pacing. But she must be sane, she must not be hysterical, or she could accomplish nothing.

She was here to ski the powder, but there was the one thing that must be done before she could concentrate on the intense, present life she had sworn she was wholly going to live. Solving that mystery was her only chance. She knew this in the depths of her soul.

The sentence upon her could be lifted only by the revelation of the crime and the criminal.

She had seen murder done—she knew this, who had commanded herself so often to be rational that only the command itself had meaning any more. She had seen murder done, and for all these years she had been able to convince herself that she had seen nothing. Then she had realized that she was being punished for trying to conceal murder. On her skis at the edge of the great bowl of the Superchute, she had watched Dick ski down ahead of the rest of them, two or three turns and stop. And, just a shadow in her eyes, a figure had skied out from the trees above her and had stopped with a heavy, stamping motion. A little snowslip had started, rippling and twisting down the fall line. It caught Dick; he slid down with it, still on his feet, not fast; then suddenly the whole bowl was in motion, and the cornice, undermined, slumped down with a shock that knocked her off her feet.

It was as though that breath-evacuating shock had lasted all these years, and perhaps she could claim it had numbed her conscience, because it was only now that she realized what she must have seen; that she had been concealing the knowledge even from herself; that she had, in effect, vengefully stamped with the murderer and exulted to see the avalanche cover Dick Macklin, who had maligned and humiliated her. And it was the enormity of this unresolved crime, and the guilt of her silence, which remorselessly gnawed at her. She knew it was insane, and yet it was more real than anything else she had ever known, super-real; and she knew the punishment could be halted. She had read enough to ask, and had been told that, yes, the deadly progress sometimes unaccountably ceased.

So there was hope. Yet that hope had destroyed what had been a marvelous realization of freedom in which, with Time limited and defined, the means best to employ it were clear. For that brief period she had felt as though she had never been lucid before, only to have that lucidity destroyed by hope, by super-lucidity, and she could not begin that marvelously free Spending of Time until the mystery was solved, the guilt removed. She could concentrate on nothing else until this had been satisfied; then wholly she could expend herself in pleasure and exuberance, in skiing the powder, in skiing with Easy Clary, who had always professed to instruct in

Life as he instructed in skiing. Once, shaking with intensity, he had accused her of wanting pie in the sky by and by instead of the pie set before her. But last night, after she had confided in him, he had had almost nothing to say to her.

It was hope, not hopelessness, that haunted her, that obsessed her always like a shadow seen out of the corners of her eyes, jerking at her attention. Of course it was this that had frozen any passion Easy Clary had brought with him through her window last night, and it was this increasing preoccupation which had turned José, in Acapulco, into a vindictive enemy.

She worked a stockinged foot through one pantleg, pulled the other leg on, tucked undershirt and nylon turtleneck and shirt into the waistband, stretched, snapped, buttoned, and zipped. Panting a little from the effort, she remembered the exertion of putting skis back on after a fall in deep powder snow. She was afraid, not of the cornice, that was irrational—Tim would take care of that— but of the first, so-steep turn at the top of the Superchute; she was afraid she had forgotten how to ski the powder, that special technique; and most of all she was afraid it would not be the thrill she remembered.

She bent herself into a sitting-back skiing position, one knee cupped behind the other, hands raised holding imaginary poles. She came up, unweighting, remembering to jerk up on the outside pole, but her mind bolted again, this time to assure herself that she had already begun her investigation, learned certain things, primed her numb memory about that day in the Superchute nine years ago.

She sat on the bed to take her boots out of their press, force her feet into the stiff leather, lace the inner boots, then the outer. She thought of buying clip-on boots, so much easier; she thought of shopping this afternoon, looking forward to the handsome, new, and always tempting things in the ski shops. The shops in Val d'I-sère. The doctor in Val d'Isère taping her twisted ankle. The Austrian doctor in Acapulco with tinted lenses in his glasses. At first she had spent the nights crying and the days wearing tinted lenses herself, to hide her ravaged eyes. At first she had hated everyone. She had prayed for war, for the bombs to drop and poison all the world, all the world dying together. But when she had finally faced the truth, then the lucidity, the time of freedom, had begun, the relief of nothing more to seek to accomplish, of no more need for guilt, of no more punishment possible now that the ultimate punishment was decreed. She had bravely remembered things Dick Macklin had told her—one, that the only real freedom was to be alone in complete poverty under irrevocable sentence of death. You were free because nothing more could be done to you. She had thought herself very brave; she had made up her mind there would be no surgery to slash away her femininity and raise and dash hope. Her chin had been raised high, and she had thought that the brave could win. But to be brave meant allowing no hope to infiltrate her bravery. First, the possibility that the sentence was not irrevocable occurred to her, and then the possibility that, if she was being punished, there was hope of atonement.

She began to ignore José. Perhaps she thought José must worship her differently now, for her bravery, though of course he knew nothing. There was a quarrel, and he threw her out of his house, figuratively, but her things literally. From then on, wherever she went in Acapulco, they appeared with their din—the mariachis in their dirty, embroidered sombreros, three with guitars, one with a horn, the fifth, who was short and fat with a warty, snouty face, beating a kind of drum. They pursued her until she fled in horror, and briefly there was the strangely powerful urge to return to Dancer to Brad Peabody, as once before she had turned to him in hurt and humiliation. Instead, after the months with her friends in Dallas when she thought her spinning brain must disintegrate from its own momentum, she came back to Dancer, not to Brad's comfort, and not yet to Clary's instruction, but to find the murderer of Dick Macklin in order to save her life.

In the half-crazy time in Dallas the mariachis, whom she thought she had left behind in Acapulco, became symbolic and menacing figures. They crowded into her mind, as in Acapulco they had crowded into bars where she was with their pushing, pursuing racket, their snout-faces, and their indignity. The actual mariachis had been ignorant, dirty, city-peasants who had been hired to shame her because she had neglected José and no longer made the pretense to him that he was the supreme lover. So as the mariachis had turned into Furies in her mind, it came to her that God might be punishing her for ignoring Him, neglecting Him, for no longer making the proper and necessary pretenses to that terrible Lover. God had been the threat and conscience of her Visalia, Companions-of-Jesus girlhood, and though she thought she was free of Him when she had fled Visalia, she knew she could not be altogether free, just as she did not walk under ladders or, unless it caused too much inconvenience, ride in airplanes on Friday. But a God she could believe in could not be so simple, and finally, searching her mind, she found her sin to have been of omission, not commission.

She had loved many men, but she had loved Dick Macklin the most. Many men had hurt her, but Dick Macklin had hurt her the most. And because she had loved him and he had hurt her, she had watched him murdered and pretended she had seen nothing. Because of this she was being punished. There was doubt only on the surface of her mind; beneath there was none.

Leaning over, breathing with difficulty again as she adjusted her laces, she cautioned herself against being overemotional. She must be calm. She stood erect and was pleased by the secure containment of stretch material and stiff boots. All at once skiing the powder loomed close. She had only to put on her sweater, parka, gloves, and earband, wax her skis, which stood in the ski rack in the entry, walk out to the bottom of Big Red One to meet the others, ride up on the lift, ski off at the top terminal and down the piste to the Elevator Shaft, and then—

The weakening reluctance came on her again. Much as she loved skiing the powder, she decided that she loved spring skiing best of all, the warm days in shirt sleeves and straw hats, the pleasant rasping of skis turning in corn snow like coarse grains of glass, the picnics with sandwiches in waxpaper and bread-and-butter pickles and cold wine in *botas*. It would be lovely in the spring when the days were longer and the sun higher and everyone was tan from the sun. She needed the heat of the sun much more now.

She thought with longing of the quality of the heat during the *feria* in Seville. The heat had had weight. She remembered strolling with Rafael in the *parque*, with the heat filtering through the light green leaves on the riding paths that were yellow as the sand in the Maestranza, and the beautiful horses with braided and beribboned tails bearing the handsome young people in fiesta dress and the flat gray or black *sombrero ancho*, the women riding sidesaddle in full rig, and, in pillion behind the men, black-haired girls in flamenco dress, all flounces and bare white backs and shoulders, red flowers in their hair. She remembered the great bay horse halted at the café where a waiter with a tray handed up *copas* of *fino*; and wandering through the *casitas* where many *copas* were offered to Rafael, and to her, who this night shared Rafael's fame; and the *rasciados* on the guitars and the spine-shivering voices of the singers, the electric handclapping of the groups of students, the brown cigars gripped between white teeth, the gypsy children with noble eyes, the laughter and the horses passing and the people looking into the *casita* from the street, wishing they too belonged.

It had been the apotheosis of a particular period of her life, even though she realized that Rafael would be finished with her when the *feria* was over. Because he was Rafael and *Numero Uno* she could accept anything gracefully and gratefully, even to being part of a harem, although this week she was the favorite; and treasure forever the heartbreak faulting of the trumpet on the high notes, the bullring, La Maestranza, with its upper rim of tall gold-and-white Moorish arches and the white canvas sunshades higher still, the golden sand you saw in no other bullring with the two blood-red, concentric circles like the edging of a target, the capes on the railings, the women in mantillas and shawls, the brick seats and flat brown cushions, the popcorn, pop, and beer, and the candy vendors with darting dots of eyes, and all around the dropped esses of Andalusian speech. In the ring Rafael was boyish, quiescent, and slightly bored as he watched someone else's bull in motion, wearing the flat, black, Mickey-Mouse-eared hat on his forehead and holding the collar of the magenta-and-yellow cape in his teeth. People were turning their backs on the ring because the bulls were very bad.

Rafael's first bull, which he dedicated to her, was as cowardly and listless as the rest. She held his hat in her two hands as though not his safety so much as the bull's performance depended on her concentration and her prayers. And slowly, with his magic, he transformed that deadness into charging beauty; Rafael, nearly in the center of the ring, where there could be no quick help for him, turning the bull around and around him as though the red cloth were fastened to its muzzle, standing not a boy now but much a man, slanted and tall, as though his body hung from his tasseled epaulets, his long right arm jerking the *muleta* along in the slow, emotional, ratcheting turning, the bull's black barrel of a body lurching forward, buttocks stained with yellow excrement, great testicles swinging as the delicate hoofs dug in and thrust, stabbing with the great black horned head. Blood stained alike the black flank and the bright gold-and-white pantaloons.

The *oles* were ragged at first, but they gathered power and unison with each circuit of the bull. Then the unbearable tension of the tight grouping was broken as Rafael permitted the bull to tangent off. There was audible relief, cries of, *"Musica! Musica!"* then silence again, the slow accumulation of tension again, as Rafael, fifty feet away, began citing the bull once more, *"Uh-hey, uh-hey, Toro!"* the *muleta* held behind him now and switched from side to side, the bulb of his parts that showed in his left pantaloon leg proffered to the bull (*"Mira, Toro!"*), advancing slowly, one foot carefully placed, with a switch of the hips, before the other (*"Mira, Toro!"*). Rafael halted, confronting the adversary, *muleta* drawn to the right behind him, then to the left, the bull's eyes jerked by reaction to the movement and against its own intelligence. There was unbearable tension each time the great Jovelike eyes returned to the man, and relief when finally the animal gathered its feet together and brushed past Rafael, who spun gracefully away. At last there was the great sigh when he sighted along the sword.

When the beast had fallen the handkerchiefs began to flutter, and Rafael made a circuit of the ring with his affected, long-stretching run, holding up the bull's ears, halting to shake them and grin up at each *tendido* in turn, with the flowers falling at his feet, and the hats, coats, shoes, winesacks, and binocular cases to be thrown back. Completing the circuit, he tossed one of the ears to her.

In the tumult of shouting and movement around Rafael, holding his hat and the hairy ear of the bull he had killed, she had never felt so possessed, and she had realized at last things Dick had tried to tell her about death, things that Rafael understood instinctively, in the bone and blood of himself, that Dick Macklin had tried to understand and to phrase and to pass on to her but had failed, things Easy Clary had chosen to understand brilliantly but only partially. Because Rafael had just faced death, and she could feel his life pulsing like a great electrical current in the emotion and the heat of La Maestranza.

Rafael had retired a year later, a multimillionaire. Now he fought bulls only in the Portuguese style, from horseback. He had gained twenty pounds, she heard. But she knew that he would never be able to stay retired. Always they had to come back again to face death as the ultimate in life.

Isobel was not up yet, and in the kitchen she made a cup of Nescafé and put a slice of bread in the toaster. The kitchen too had been remodeled. Copper-bottomed pots hung in a line; the countertop had been finished with blue-glazed tile. Out the window she could see the Big Red One bullwheel slowly turning, chairs swinging around it. Snow was heaped and rounded on every horizontal surface. The branches of the trees, downslanting with the weight they carried, looked like huge white boxing gloves.

A figure in blue appeared at the bottom of the ramp; it was John Henry. He was talking to someone out of her range of vision. Suddenly he ducked, then straightened. He was packing a snowball between his gloved hands. He wound up and hurled, laughing, enjoying the moment. The person out of sight was, of course, Easy Clary, childishly throwing snowballs. And John Henry childishly threw them back, the two of them enjoying the mock warfare. But how was it possible to be a child when you were past being a child?

Now Clary came into view, skating vigorously on his skis, waving his poles as though trying to catch a train, straining for her attention, or to try to dissolve the strains resulting from last night's unresolved encounter. He was funny, but she was no longer as shallow and easily amused as she had once been. Could the enjoyment of each moment be seized only by someone as simple as a child?

She smiled and waved back at him, but she felt only apprehension. He stopped outside the window, motioning to his wristwatch. A lock of dark hair had escaped from under his cap in his exertions. She nodded, finished the last mouthful of coffee, and left the kitchen.

In the entry a man, his back familiar in a tan sweater, was rubbing wax on a ski bottom. She gasped, but the face that turned to glance over a shoulder at her was Dickie's.

"I thought I'd wax your skis while I was doing mine."

"Oh, thank you."

He indicated the inscription on the black ski leaning against the wall: *Maeve Herron, Dancer Peak.* "I see you've been loyal," he said.

"Dancer Peak is engraved in my heart too," she said brightly and struck a pose. Over her shock, she saw that he resembled his father very little. His hair was darker, longer, and the hairline already hinted at future baldness; his mouth was fuller, chin not so strong. Yet the shape of the back of the head was similar, and so was the line of the jaw. She thought he must be several inches taller than Dick had been, though he did not hold himself as well.

"We'd better hurry," she said. "John Henry and Easy are out there already."

"We can't start up until Tim comes down," Dickie said in a fussy voice. "Have you got enough layers on? It's cold."

"Many, many layers. I only wish I could remember how to ski the powder."

"I'm finally getting on to it," Dickie said. "It's just a matter of thinking you can, everybody says."

"I'm afraid I don't think I can."

"Well, remember the little red train," Dickie said.

At first she didn't know what he was talking about, for she had been struck by his saying he was finally getting on to skiing the powder and the implication that he had not been expert enough to ski in the Superchute nine years ago. Then she remembered the little red train. When she had chauffeured Dickie to and from school, once he had confessed to her that he was afraid he was flunking algebra, and she had told him the children's story of the little red train puffing up the long grade—"I think I can, I think I can, I know I can, I know I can."

" 'Know I can, I know I can,' " she said. "Don't I wish I did!"

Grinning, Dickie zipped himself into his parka and pulled on an ugly brown wool cap with earflaps. There was the distant muffled boom of an avalanche charge.

"There it goes," Dickie said. "We ought to get out there just about the time Tim comes down."

Outside they shouldered skis and poles to walk through the knee-deep powder toward the bottom of Big Red One. Rody and J.D.

Daugherty had appeared, and two men in ski-patrol parkas, packs on backs, were standing on the ramp. She reminded herself she was not here to enjoy this day anyway; first of all she had to identify the figure who had skied across that haunted corner of her memory. That was what had to be done before her engagement with the present could begin; that first.

There were embraces and greetings to exchange with Rody, who looked very tan and sturdy, and with J.D., handsome as ever but with something repellent about him. There were a few minutes of small talk before Tim came schussing straight down the Spoon, throwing up a wake like a hydroplane. Tim gave instructions to the ski patrolmen while the rest of them got on their skis. They began to load; she rode with John Henry.

There had not been time to brush all the snow from their chair, and it was a cold seat. Swaying slightly, the lift began the long climb toward Dancer Peak, which from here looked like a grave white head, with snow heaped up like the folds of a fur collar. The chairhanger creaked past the first tower. Breathing deeply, gripping the safety bar, she gazed through her amber glasses at the sky, where fast-moving squalls were separated by cracks of brilliant blue. The mountain, which was so harsh, bony, and masculine in the summer, was now all feminine curves and folds, sparkling in patches of sun. Beneath the lift the single track of Tim's skis came straight down the fall line. Cold nipped at her chin, her gloved fingertips, her straitly-encased toes, and sharp bits of snow blew against her face as they rose into a snow squall. She was trembling with a combination of sensuous excitements.

"It's so beautiful!" she said to John Henry.

"Man, it's great!" John Henry said, grinning at her, showing his two big front teeth. His face rested like a nested egg on the quilted collar of his parka. Brown hair beetled out around the bottom of his cap. He made motions of trying to tuck his legs up. "*Muy hermoso pero poco frío. Especialmente—cómo se llama?—en el fondo!*"

"*Hablas español muy bien!*"

He made a face. "Terrible! I've been trying to Berlitz-up for some Mexican-type songs I've been working on. It's not my sort of stuff; I mean—do they *mean* it? Yay! Saw your matador in Tijuana —that horseback stuff. I guess he's quite a guy."

"Yes, he was quite a guy." She watched his eyebrows mesh together. It was difficult to realize that John Henry had become a Figure in show business. She remembered so well the amiable semifool he had been, with his tongue-tied manner and affected hip talk. "You've come a long way since you drove me down to Beverly Hills that day, John Henry," she said. "And I guess I didn't even thank you."

"Sure you thanked me!" he said and looked embarrassed. Then he scowled, because Dick was with them now, which was what she had wanted.

"How come you stayed away so long?" he asked. "You don't have to answer that," he said. He lowered his voice, as though it was important that J.D. and Rody, in the chair ahead, and Clary and Dickie, behind them, not hear. "Speaking of quite-a-guys—"

"Yes, he was quite a guy too," she said. The top of the Superchute came into view. The cornice was much smaller than the other time, the last time; there was hardly any cornice at all. Another snow squall swept down on them, peppering their faces with sunlit bits of snow. She said, "Much, much more of a guy than Rafael or anybody else I've ever known."

"Yay!" John Henry said in a restrained tone. "You really liked him, huh? Sure, I knew you did, but—but what'd he do that to you for?"

"I think somebody told him things about me."

The sun broke through the clouds fiercely. John Henry shaded his eyes with a hand. "Too many candlepowers, man!" He produced a pair of dark glasses and put them on. He said, "Well, I always liked him. I never got down on him the way everybody did. I mean, he did what he had to do to get this place built."

"It's been so hard for me to come back," she said.

"I couldn't ski the powder for a year," John Henry said.

She realized that she might have an ally here; also, that she might have disposed of another suspect. But if she disposed of all the suspects on subjective grounds, there would be no one left. In the chair ahead J.D. was swinging his skis, the blue tops and yellow bottoms showing alternately.

"Man!" John Henry said as more of the Superchute could be seen, the long, steeply slanting, perfectly smooth, gleaming bowl of snow, with two white firs high on the north side below the Elevator Shaft. The figure had come out just below the trees and above where she had stopped at the edge of the bowl. She felt suddenly chilled.

She could see Tim's tracks marring the bowl. "What did Tim shoot up here?" she asked.

"He probably just dropped a charge to see if anything would move. You can see the hole sort of over from the trees. See?"

Nearsighted, she could not see the hole; she nodded anyway. Her plan had been to ski out into the Superchute and stop where she had stopped before, hoping that the figure would manifest itself exactly as before, either in actuality or vividly enough in her memory so she could make the identification. But now she knew she was not going to have the courage to ski down out of the Elevator Shaft ahead of the others. She watched J.D.'s skis teetertottering again.

"Where were you?" she asked John Henry suddenly.

"When?"

"When the cornice came down." She didn't look at him, staring at J.D.'s back and remembering that Dick had not liked him, had never considered him one of the faithful.

"We were all kind of bunched up together there, weren't we?" John Henry said. "Right under the trees there. Ease was just starting to take off after Macklin when that first slide broke loose. Wasn't that the way it was?"

"Who?" she demanded. "Who was there all bunched up together?"

"Well, you and me and Rody and J.D. and Clary, wasn't it? Everything happened so fast I can't remember—" He stopped. They were coming into the top terminal, and it was time to raise the safety bar. J.D. and Rody, like a dance team in their precision, rose together, separated from the chair together, and slid down the ramp.

She and John Henry accomplished the same maneuver, stopped below the terminal with the other two. Clary and Dickie were coming in, bar raised. Tim was alone two chairs behind them.

"I see Tim's signature down the middle of the bowl," Clary said, stopping beside her. "Shows us who gets to skim the cream." Leaning on his poles, he grinned at her, his narrow, dark face a little anxious.

"Let's go!" Tim called as he came down the ramp and started along the trail down the shoulder. They followed him, Rody first, then Clary, then she went, with John Henry, J.D., and Dickie behind her. The snow beside the track was dotted with pole marks, like the traces of stitches along scars. Taking deep breaths to open her constricted lungs, she slid behind Clary, who was making sounds like a revving motor.

Ahead of her they began to disappear one by one. Clary dove off into space, and she remembered that too; last time it had been Dick ahead of her. She came to the Elevator Shaft and, without letting herself check, tipped her skis straight down and cut to the right with her downhill leg stiffly straining and her uphill pole dragging a furrow in the snow. She scrambled around in a second stiff-kneed turn, remembering to swing a hand in rotation this time, and she followed Clary in the traverse below the trees to where Rody and Tim had stopped.

Ahead the great bowl gleamed and beckoned in the sun, and there was only the slight curved lip of the cornice, which she knew to be no threat at all. The lift was a spidery line in the distance, chairs hanging motionless.

"All ours!" John Henry cried.

"Who's the leader?" Clary said. "Maeve?"

Last time there had been no question about who was to lead. Dick had exercised his prerogative and had made the first track through the virgin snow, to his death. Tim, bulky in his red parka and nylon overpants, grinned at her and said, "Okay, Maeve, here's your deep powder. Go scratch it."

"Oh, I'm scared to death!" she cried. In skiing instruction one of the most effective devices was for the student to ski behind the instructor, turning where he turned and trying to copy his movements. "Clary, you go first. I want to follow you down."

"Don't have to ask me twice," Clary said. He pushed himself a few yards ahead but didn't start down the bowl right away, as another snow squall drove its shadow past. Then the bowl gleamed again as though it had been freshly cleansed for their use.

Clary yodeled as he started down. He made the first steep turn, with the snow spraying like powdered gold against the sun, and she tried to concentrate on his movements, not on glancing up at the cornice or behind her to see if someone was going to ski be-lately down from the trees, not thinking of anything in this moment except what Clary was doing, the most beautiful skier she had ever seen. With slow and elongated grace he leaned down into the snow and jack-in-the-boxed back up, all in smooth rhythm, with the light snow blowing and drifting around him and the faint, mocking, longing call of his yodeling as he sped in joyous swoops down the white breast. She found herself moving out after him.

Her body remembered. In the fiercely concentrated blotting out of her mind, her body was remembering, sitting back and steering into the first turn by going down, coming up off both feet, turning her skis. She had made the most difficult turn! Confidence came, rhythm came, as she gathered speed. With a powerful beating of her heart she surged up as though pulled by a hook attached to heaven, sinking and rising again in the singing, ecstatic pleasure of the senses, feeling the cold of snow blown into her face mixed with the heat of the sun. Snow sprayed all around her so that she seemed to be speeding inside a rainbow, the cushioned, bottomless trampoline-bouncing and planing of her invisible skis as she surged and sank, swinging in fantastic freedom right and left, half breathlessly squandering the long, so gloriously long, so sweetly, steeply, inclined bowl that must finish—of course it must end, who would want to go down it forever?—feeling delight, feeling exuberance, and at the same time remembering this intimate knowing of pleasure. But already, with the first wild, fearful excitement gone, her mind was beginning to spin in its old self-destroying patterns again—to the figure skiing above and behind her, to the cornice hanging over the top of the bowl. She dared one glance back.

When she fell her skis ran straight down into the snow. She somersaulted over them, freeing them with the momentum of her forward fall, and, as though plunged into some airy liquid, she sprawled and slid gasping under the surface of the snow, not knowing whether she was screaming or only thinking a scream of fear that she was smothering, dying beneath an avalanche. She realized she must be breathing air. Her face was burning, caked with snow. She opened her eyes to gaze up into a fantastically dark blue sky. Panting and sobbing, she began to sort out her legs and skis—a safety binding had released and one ski hung from its strap. *What if she had broken a leg?* She had no time to break a

leg! Floundering in the light snow, she got her other ski downhill
from her body. Thrusting with her poles, she managed to stand.
She beat the burning snow from her face.

Clary was standing a hundred yards down the bowl. He cupped
a hand to his mouth. "Are you okay?"

"All right!" she said, panting. She brushed the snow from her
clothes, trembling, confidence gone. The mariachis of her mind
had returned. She brushed snow from her headband and flipped
her hair from side to side with jerks of her head, trying both to
think and not to think. She must not be hysterical. She must keep
smiling and pretend, at least, that she had not been destroyed by
her fall.

When she glanced up the slope she saw that Dickie had started
down, the flaps of his brown cap bouncing like a spaniel's ears,
lines of sun reflected off the shafts of his steel poles. He sat very
far back through his turns, coming up only a little to unweight, his
turns precise, mechanical—all she could think of, as she balanced
on one ski to scrape the caked snow from the other boot, was that
he was cautious. Dick had never been cautious, and never stylish,
like Clary, but he had always been first.

Rody started down. She skied almost upright, flicking her poles
right and left and making very high-speed, slight variations of line.
Tim, who started immediately after her, was all stately power,
schussing, as though what he enjoyed most was bulling straight
downhill through the deep snow. He caught up to Rody, and they
began making linked turns together, each time missing each other
by a smaller margin—she remembered that they had raced together as youngsters and that Rody had raced in the Olympics so
that they must be very accomplished at this kind of split-second
maneuver—until they almost collided. Tim swung off uphill
while Rody, with a whoop, turned straight down the fall line with
her ponytail bobbing behind her. Rody cut to a stop just below
Clary, throwing up a curtain of slowly settling powder.

John Henry started down last, in his blue parka. He yipped as he
shoved off, as Clary had done, and his skiing was obviously pat-
terned on Clary's style, although more showoff, not so smooth and
controlled. He whooped loudly as he collapsed in the snow, and
she felt a moment's satisfaction that he had also fallen.

But he was up immediately, a snowman, laughing. Slapping

snow off himself, he was already schussing the slope. So in the end, fitting her boot back into her binding and fighting tears, casting one more glance back up at the cornice before she pushed off again, the dying girl was the last one down.

2: Betsy

Hurrying yeah-yeah-yeah through the snow, carrying her powder skis tips forward on her shoulder, stabbing her poles, two in one hand, into the snow, she crossed from the employees' dorm toward the bottom of Big Red One just in time to see Mrs. Macklin, Muthuh, hands in the pockets of her sheepskin coat, come out of the Big House. The lift was running; everybody was up already; she had overslept.

Tom Cline was squatting on the platform, broad-shouldered in his ski-patrol parka, sorting through the contents of a rucksack. He turned his short-bearded face up toward her. "The other hounds're already up."

"Darn!" she said. She dropped her skis and began scraping packed snow from her boot bottoms. Bending to fit boot into binding, she was aware that Tom had stopped whatever he was doing to watch her. "Pretty Buttsy," he said.

She finished latching on her skis, picked up her poles, and slid over to the get-on. The chairs were loaded with snow, and she waited for one that had been partially cleared. "Don't freeze the pretty!" Tom called after her. She grinned back at him as she settled herself with her poles beneath her to protect her from the snow.

She was almost glad to be riding the chair alone this morning, a big, wide-open day with the sky clearing, big-blue above the flying carpet clouds, the snow big-white; the two cleanest colors there were. Snow was heaped like sugar on the branches of the pines, everything was clean. Donna McIntyre said she liked ski resorts because the people and what they wore were so handsome. She had felt that once, but now what grabbed her was that the mountain world itself was so beautiful. No place else was everything you could see beautiful like this, a great big opening-out yes instead of the closing-in no of downbelow. Downbelow people plowed everything up with bulldozers and junked it up with advertising and their own dirtiness. Here people couldn't bother anything much, and anyway they couldn't help being better, exposed to all this. "I love you, you big white—" she started, staring up at the head of Dancer with its chin stuck in its coat and one shoulder hunched higher than the other in a kind of shrug. She didn't know what it was except a mountain. "You big white *pretty!*" she said and laughed a lot.

She was still far down the lift line when she saw them come around the side of the Scarp and boom down toward the Intermediate Station to get back on the chair. Clearly in the crystalline air she could hear them laughing and calling to one another, a couple of them well talcumed from falls, all seeming loose and happy. They probably had the Superchute half skied out already. They clotted for a moment at the top of the ramp, and she was able to identify them as, two by two, they loaded. J.D. was with John Henry, Rody Bliss with Tim, Easy Clary with the woman called Maeve, who had had a fall. The one who got into the last chair alone was Dick, in his stupid hat.

She was surprised to see him out with the powderhounds. On a morning like this she would have expected him to find something he had to do instead of getting up on top to ski the powder. Gazing up the lift line to where his chair was rising, she wondered why she bothered to feel anything about him. He irritated her out of all proportion, the least loose man she had ever met. Loose was the operative word in her code. Donna McIntyre was mostly loose, very loose for being as old as she wouldn't admit she was. She herself was completely loose except in one or two unimportant areas. Hung-up was the opposite of loose, and Richard Everett Macklin, Jr., was hung-up in ways she could never have conceived of before she had met him. Yes, Muthuh; no, Muthuh; all right, Muthuh. She had thought he was hung-up on his father, the original grand old man of Dancer with his picture in Badbody's office like the photographs of stone-faced Gianinnis in Bank of America offices. She had not realized until last night that he was hung-up on his mother. But of course he was hung-up on everything. She didn't feel contempt so much as complete impatience.

Still, that had been a very loose group last night, with dinner and the dancing and John Henry calling up somebody and singing over the phone. After Dick and his muthuh had gone home everything had really begun to swing, with John Henry, who was a big folk-rock type from Hollywood, playing and singing. He and Easy Clary had been having a ball, and she had never seen Badbody so tight, though she hadn't understood why they had all treated the bushed-looking international blonde like queen of the May. After Muthuh had gone she, Betsy, had sat in on the party, and John Henry had made a few fun passes, though Hollywood was not anything that impressed *her*. The only bad part had been Donna hanging on the bar and trying to talk to her whenever she came up with an order. She could tell Donna was getting madder and madder, and finally Donna had gone off with that rotten lift operator, Jack Bacon, their arms around each other's waists—though it looked like more to keep from falling down drunk than sexing it up—and Donna had looked at her meaningfully, like, see-what-you've-made-me-do? and you'll-be-sorry-for-the-way-you've-acted-tonight! She was supposed to crack up with jealousy because Donna was going out to the parking lot to screw that dirty, smelly Jack Bacon in the Mercedes.

Donna was never going to get her to come back that way. The thing she liked about Donna, besides that she was very loose, very rich, and took care of her, was that though in a way Donna was like her mother, in a more important way Donna was *not* like her mother, who, after spending all day working with women in the beauty salon, just had to get away from women at night and so spent every night tanking up with different men at the Bar None and sacking down with them. All these men seemed to her now to have been very much like Jack Bacon.

Another of Donna's attractions was that she was so clean. Donna had so many bottles and jars and boxes and soaked pads and salves and unguents and whole sets of Elizabeth Arden preparations stacked on her dressing table, and she spent so much time with the relaxacisor and vibrators and rubbing and caressing herself with all the various kinds of gunk that at night when she took a tub bath and washed the stuff off she was clean and fresh as a snake out of its old skin, soft and sweet-smelling as a baby, so that being with Donna then was like being with your own mother and with your own baby somehow at the same time, if that made any sense. She did not consider what she did with Donna bad—thank God she was not hung-up in *that* way; she only considered it too rich if indulged in too often, like chocolate candy that might make bumps come on your face or cavities in your teeth. But if Donna thought screwing Jack Bacon in the Mercedes in the parking lot, crudding herself up with that beer-and-sour-sweat-smelling, gold-tooth-grinning old man, would make her, Betsy, come running back, then, *Ha!*

In the end what would make her go back to Donna was that there had to be somebody to help her with her income tax, make sure she made her car and insurance payments, and keep her money straight. It was why she could never live alone. Nor could she stand living in the women's dorm with the waitress-skibums and the housemaid-old-women. She was almost as lonely there as she would have been in an apartment of her own, and besides it was so messy and stinky with cheap cologne and the john sticking, while Donna's house, among the pines that sounded like people whispering when the wind blew, was always so clean and neat, with Mrs. Jacobs, the cleaning woman, coming five mornings a week. There was nothing nice about the women's dorm except that it was a change from living with Donna, which she couldn't take for very long at a time. During the winter when skiing was good, she never felt very sexy, and at first Donna would be under-standing, and then long suffering, and then smaller- and smaller-eyed, irritable and sarcastic, until finally there was a big fight and she moved out.

She knew the name for what she and Donna did, but Donna was no more that way about women than she was about men. She liked everything that felt good, she said. She had endured being married to Ernie McIntyre for sixteen years, until he had coronaried-out, and now Donna had the money for almost what-ever she liked. Mostly she was in agreement with Donna, but she was repelled when Donna, after three martinis, would talk ickly-sweetly about how much nicer women were than men, though she was equally repelled when Donna drunkenly, coarsely, bragged about different men and young boys she had made. As for herself, it was not that she liked women better than men in that way, it was that men were so selfish. On the few occasions with men that hadn't been on, off, and back to the office, she had found male-female sex to have a lot of swing to it. But she knew that even these two or three exceptional men had looked on her, as Mr. Finster put it, as nothing but a pussy with a big, gawky, softball player around it.

She had gone to Hollywood during Easter vacation of her senior year with a group of high-school beauty-contest winners. There had been a thing about what could you *do?* She had been first baseman for three years on an undefeated girls' softball team in Spokane. There had been a good deal of laughter about this, but she hadn't been ashamed of it until later. The trip to Hollywood had been a drag. They had met third-rate movie stars and toured Beverly Hills in a bus, visited three movie studios and attended a banquet, but everything had been shabby. Even the screen test which was supposed to have been the purpose of the trip was a letdown. At the banquet she had danced with Mr. Finster, who was an agent. He said for her to be sure and look him up if she came back to town.

She had gone back after a semester at Whitworth. She got a job working in a service station where girl attendants wore tight overalls. It had taken her some time to get up the nerve to phone Mr. Finster. What seemed to her now to have been most of the next several months was spent on her back beneath Jack Finster and a number of other men all looking very much like him, with hairy bellies they kept inside a kind of girdle so they didn't look sloppy fat when they were dressed, and who stank of cigars and old deodorant and talked a lot about friends having coronaries or strokes or the big C. From working in a service station she felt she had become one. She knew that nothing in the way of a career was going to come of this, but she didn't know what to do. It had been the lowest point of her life, a paralysis of self-disgust and man-disgust and a little fear, and of not-caring-whether-she-got-up-in-the-morning-or-not, though there had been certain material advantages in the way of meals in nice restaurants, drinks in cocktail bars on the Strip, clean motel rooms with tile baths, and one trip to Las Vegas, where she had won two hundred and fifteen dollars on the crap tables. But finally she had a quarrel with Jack Finster, and he told her she was nothing but a pussy with a big, gawky, softball player around it.

She met Mary Koestler at a movie where she had a job as an usherette. Mary quit to take a waitress job in Redondo Beach and urged her to come to work at the same place and room with her. There she would wander along the broad, clean beach that stank faintly of gasoline, from the tankers blowing their tanks off El Segundo, and watch the surfers on their striped boards sliding along the blue-green shoulders of the waves, hot-dogging, hanging-five, getting wiped, the lithe tan boys with pale palms raised, balancing as the boards slipped and sped away from the wave's curl. It was, she realized instantly, all she had ever wanted without ever knowing what it was she wanted: the brown clean bodies with lacy designs of salt on the skin, the cool water, the clean shapes of the boards, the excitement, and the skill. With her strength and her timing she quickly became a fair surfer, and she loved the sweet, guitar-playing, campfire companionship at night beneath the piers on the endless beach, with the lean-bellied, big-shouldered tan boys with their blondined hair, and the whole cool mood of no hop on and off but of long, sweet, many times not-ever-ending playing.

It ended when she went to Aspen with two boys and Mary Koestler, skis instead of boards strapped to the top rack of the Chevvie panel in which the boys lived when they were not living on the beach. As soon as she saw skiers and skiing she knew that this was even closer to what she wanted. There were shabby aspects to surfing, boys who never bothered to scrub the tar off their feet, coarse talk, and belching and farting in mixed company, which was one of the areas she had to admit she was hung-up in; the whole ho-dad bit. There was nothing crummy at Aspen, although she never did get used to the cold. She knew this was where she wanted to be, this was what she wanted to do, and she wangled a job as a cocktail waitress and stayed behind when Mary and the boys returned to L.A.

So she learned to ski. As a cocktail waitress she had an entree anywhere she chose to apply for a job, plenty of free time to ski, and plenty of money to keep herself in clothes and skis and even make payments on a Karmann Ghia, though she had not yet solved the problem of loneliness. She went with a bunch in Aspen who smoked a lot of pot, and after a while she began to be tired of the trip-parties they seemed to think were God. She left Aspen for Sun Valley, and finally, last spring, she came west to Dancer, where the powder was deep and frequent, where she found the most fun people, the easiest hours, the longest ski season, and the security of the relationship with Donna McIntyre—Donna and the relief from Donna, moving into the women's dorm while knowing she could always return. All this made her feel she was home at last. Her life was complete, loose, cyclical, and lovely, and she enjoyed almost every minute of it.

As soon as her chair passed over the Intermediate Station she could see the Superchute with the tracks wiggling down it. They had made only one run without her. Now they were beginning to unload at the top, disappearing in single file around behind the cornice, all but Dick, who must have seen her. He waved, waiting for her at the top in his Charley-Brown hat. Yes, Muthuh; though it was a good sign he had come up today with the powderburners.

She extracted her poles, raised the footrest, rose, and, with the chair nudging her, curved down off the ramp to stop beside him. "Hi," she said.

"Hello!" He was smiling all over his face. She wouldn't have waited for him, she would have been halfway down the bowl by now, but it was hard not to care a little about someone who was obviously glad to see you.

"How's the snow?"

"Wonderful!"

"Saw your muthuh down below."

His smile faded a little, and she wondered why she had to be snotty. She dug her poles in and, knees bent and cupped together, ran down to the observation rock, from which it was possible to see down into the Superchute. A wisp of snowcloud hung in the bowl, blowing away to nothing as she peered over the edge. Far below, the snow was scalloped and torn with tracks; but where it was still untouched it glistened with blue jewels. It had to be good for you to look at something that beautiful. Over on the far side of the bowl tiny skiers began to appear out of the Elevator Shaft, slanting down below the trees.

Dick came up beside her, and it occurred to her that his presence hung her up. She could feel something inside her shifting gears in order to pretend a snottiness and an indifference she did not really feel. At first she had liked him because he was so different from anyone else she had ever known, because he was so serious and they talked seriously about important matters—things she had never thought of discussing with anyone, or perhaps never thought of at all. She had enjoyed shocking him because he was so simple in his college-graduate way, but she had realized he was humble about being hung-up, wanted to change, would like to get loose if only he knew how. In his peculiar way of putting things, he had as much as said he went for her because she was so loose, the greatest compliment he could have given her. But after seeing him last night with his mother, and talking to Badbody about him, she had found herself disliking the fact that he wasn't just some young guy working at the lodge, that he was rich and his mother owned the place. She had decided in a kind of leaning-over-backward reaction that she didn't have any use for him. But now she was very conscious of her own hung-up coldness, and it irritated her the more.

He was looking worried. "Is something the matter, Betsy?"

"What is this, some kind of private party or something?"

"Pardon me?"

"That blonde didn't really want me to come along this morning, did she?"

He looked even more worried, sticking his lips out. "Well, you see—you see, my father was killed up here on a day like this, and Maeve—"

"Oh, sorry," she said and, embarrassed, shrugged as though disinterested. "Let's go, huh?"

But his skis were blocking hers. "Just a minute," he said. "You didn't tell me what was the matter really."

"Nothing's the matter really. Let's go! I want to cut up some powder before it's all gone."

"But why did you say 'muthuh' like that?"

She didn't answer, blowing a steaming, impatient breath. Dickie was standing with his head bent in his weirdo hat. "She doesn't like you any better than you like her," he said.

"She what? She doesn't *what?*"

"Doesn't like you any better than you like her," he said. "Her darling boy infatuated with a bar waitress and all that."

Infatuated. She swore beneath her breath. "*Jesus!* Care *less!*" she said aloud.

"Well, just a minute. This is as good a time as any. It's more than that."

"What's more than what?"

He just looked at her, his eyes serious, white-rimmed. She understood that he was trying to say something tender, and she was ashamed of her antsyness. She thought he might be as lonely as she had once been and was too stupid or proud or just hung-up to admit it to himself or maybe even to understand it. He had said some really good things to her and made her think to say some things she was proud of saying back, although it had irritated her that instead of making a pass at her he had just talked around it, talking himself out of it instead of her into it.

He said, "I'm very fond of you, Betsy."

She stared at him. Are you kidding? she almost jeered. But it was a serious moment. She could think of nothing appropriate to say, though she supposed now, in gratitude for this little gift, she would have to give him the big one. "Okay," she said finally, meaning that.

"I don't expect you to say you feel the same. I just wanted you to know."

"Okay," she said.

"Shall we go?" he said, sidestepping around and freeing her skis.

"Okay," she said.

He led her down the trail to the Elevator Shaft. He skied without much bounce but not badly. *I'm very fond of* was something you said about hamburgers or stewed rhubarb. He was really funny! Still, he tried; she had to give him that. She remembered the time he took her into town for dinner and afterward read the bill carefully and argued with the waitress about some two-bit item; so tight. Why didn't she say to him, "Listen, to get loose, first you've got to loosen up. And while you're at it, for God's sake, get rid of that goddam hat. And change barbers." And so many other little items. Men had said many things to her, but she didn't think anyone had ever said he was fond of her before this. Fond, fondle? She giggled, skiing in Dickie's track. She supposed she had to be his date today, skiing the powder. But when they hit the bowl she couldn't hold herself in and she barrelassed down through the uncut snow, whooping, bounding like a merry-go-round horse, and loving it. She was surprised and not too pleased when she stopped at the bottom to get her breath and found Dick there waiting for her.

The next run they caught up with John Henry, J.D. from the Loup Garou, and Rody Bliss. Maeve had pooped out, Rody said not too kindly when Dick asked, and Easy Clary had gone down with Maeve since he had a private lesson at ten. Tim had gone to work. The five of them made three more runs, but now John Henry, though funny and full of jokes, was beginning to can-up a lot. He admitted he was tired and went down too, and the next run Dick decided he had to quit and go to work. The three of them kept at it like yoyos, but more and more people were showing up, and by eleven the powder in the Superchute was skied out, so she went down herself.

The lower slopes of the Spoon were crowded with skiers. There were long lift lines waiting at Big Red One, the Platter, and Blue Two. Flags fluttered from the slender poles surrounding the sundeck and the lift terminals. She boomed the Spoon from about halfway down, making no friends, and ran out to a stop in front of the sundeck, where leaning skis and poles made a picket fence. She unwound her longthongs, panting from the non-stop run down the mountain, legs aching, sweating, happy about a number of things she didn't pause to examine. She stood her skis upright, slapped the bottoms together to knock the snow off, parked them among the others, and mounted the steps to the sundeck. The tables were filled with people all in dark glasses. She couldn't help swinging a little as she crossed the deck between the tables.

"Hello there!" Donna McIntyre called.

Donna was sitting alone at a table with a Bloody Mary in front of her, wearing her Bloody-Mary-colored Jacques Fath ski suit, her perfectly smooth, perfectly brown Elizabeth-Arden face with satin-red lips smiling. Donna was revolving her gold-rimmed dark glasses by one earpiece. "Powder fun, Betsy-dear?"

"Yay!" she said, realizing that now she was going into her for-Donna pose, as opposed to her for-Dick pose. Maybe no one ever realized just how hung-up he was. But her mood was not affected. "Pooped but happy," she said, sitting down. She took a long drink of Donna's Bloody Mary.

"You're all sweaty!" Donna said.

"I love to sweat," she said, seeing through that one. She grinned at Donna, who put her dark glasses back on.

"Someday you will simply have to teach me to ski deep powder snow, Betsy-dear," Donna said, her red ribbons of lips smiling.

"Nothing to it. Just got to be loose." She shrugged her shoulders in illustration. But Donna was never going to learn to ski deep powder snow. Fresh from the powder herself, she realized just how hung-up Donna really was. Donna said often and forcefully that she liked everything and anything that felt good, which was supposed to mean she was so free and loose, and balls, as she said, for what society thought. But what Donna didn't realize was that she was only loose about that one place and what felt good there. She couldn't understand, being too old, too hung-up and unchangeable, that there were many other things that felt good in many other ways, like skiing the powder, like sliding the shoulders in storm surf, like a really good trip, things that felt good all over, eyes, ears, smell, and all over your skin too, and there was the extra that the other body things were not something just anybody could do, because they were a little tough, a little demanding, a little scary, and if you were going to do them really well you had to go all out and no holding any cool. Donna would never understand that sex, sex the way it meant body-fun and not just coming, could be a whole lot of different things.

The curved dark lenses covered Donna's eyes; the perfect mask of a face was anxious, a little tired.

"Bad night?" she asked, taking another sip of Donna's Bloody Mary.

Donna smiled stiffly. She said in a low voice, "It is very lonely in my little house, Betsy-dear."

Betsy-dear assumed a mock-solemn expression that turned genuine. All at once it seemed to her that she, whose greatest vulnerability was her fear of loneliness, was the one to whom other lonely people looked for help, as though they thought she had it made. She wanted to protest that she certainly didn't have it made. Could they all be so much worse off? She saw that Dick Macklin did not merely want her on her back in bed, that Donna did not merely want her drowsy on the deep-pile rug in front of the hi-fi or in the great, round, silk-sheeted bed to cuddle and play with. It was something more serious than that.

"Surely you won't be staying in that awful dormitory over Christmas," Donna said.

"I don't know," she said, feeling disturbed and, strangely, responsible. Of all the things she didn't want to feel, responsibility headed the list.

"I have some lovely presents for you, Betsy-dear," Donna said.

Irritated and disgusted, she excused herself coldly, rose, and went in toward the bar. Her good mood restored itself as men turned their heads to stare after her. Women did too. She had known for a long time that something funny happened to her behind when she walked, but she didn't mind being stared at. She felt, amiably, that if they liked what they saw, that was fine, and if they didn't, that didn't hurt her, so it was all right too.

3: Elizabeth Steinberg

THE JONES CABIN on Juniper Lane in Dancer Valley overlooked the lodge, the lift terminals, and the valley floor. Already this morning she had been called outside to view the fifteen inches of smooth new snow the cabin wore like a thatched roof, and the snow stacked so attractively on the beam ends. Just a little too cutesy, this; she was sure the Joneses' architect had been very pleased with how prettily the snow was going to stack on those exposed beam ends. Now in the sun the beams were beginning to drip. The whole background music of the cabin this morning was the drip of melting snow.

Mildred and Wayne Jones—Wayne was a professor in the Math Department of the university—loved their cabin and they loved Dancer, though they were outspoken against some of the policies of the ski-area management. They loved coming up to the cabin in the winter. It was semi-coping with nature, Mildred said: stamping a path to the door, pulling supplies up the hill on the toboggan when there was a heavy snowfall and the roads were blocked, shoveling the snow off the roof, bringing logs up from their storage under the house, putting up with the power and telephone failures during blizzards—Wayne loved all that sort of thing. And of course the cabin at Dancer was so wonderful for the Jones children, aged fourteen, twelve, and ten, what with the skiing, the skating and sledding, and the coping. Coping did seem to be one of the important things to do with the magic mountains. She didn't remember Clary mentioning it.

Steinberg packages were mingled with Jones packages under the Christmas tree. She and Chris and Mikey were spending Christmas at Dancer with the Joneses, and today she had promised herself she would look up Chuck Clary, whom she had not seen since Mikey was a year and a half old. Clary and Shelley had had another fight. Shelley had called him a righteous bastard, and that was the last time Clary had come to see them in Berkeley.

Last night all the kids had stayed up late playing Hearts and had rubbed burned cork on the noses, cheeks, and chins of the recipients of the black queen. It had been wonderful fun for all except Mikey, who, two and a half years younger than anyone else, had been accused repeatedly of cheating. She had finally had to be packed off to bed, weeping bitterly.

If she were divorced she would have only Mikey. Shelley would never give up Chris.

Now Chris had gone off to ski school with Mildred, Wayne, and the Jones children, and she was sitting on the floor listening to the eaves drip while she laced Mikey's boots. She had not remembered that lacing boots figured so largely in the skiing life. Perhaps it was part of coping. Perhaps things like coping with bootlaces, snow, tire chains, and toboggans took your mind off your failure to cope with the important things in your life.

Milly, who in Berkeley had always seemed to go with the half-timbered English Department wives, had never been a special friend of hers. But, back from Mexico, living in a sublet studio apartment in the city, having notified no one in her loneliness and defeat that she was back, one day she had met Milly on the street in front of I. Magnin's and Milly had seemed the only friend she had. She had found herself in the St. Francis, telling all to Milly and weeping over her cocktail like a silly schoolgirl. Milly blessedly had given no advice, only sympathy, though they had explored the possibility of her going back to Shelley and Milly had promised to see if she could find out how Shelley felt. Milly had persuaded him to let the children see their mother again at the Jones cabin at Dancer during Christmas vacation. It had been a logical first step; she had to see the children before she could find out how she felt herself. She had had no direct contact with Shelley.

"That one's too tight," Mikey said.

"Too tight," she said and loosened it. "Okay now?"

" 'Kay."

If she tried to take them both away, Shelley could make a brutal fight of it. Lawyers, courts, and judges were the Reality-Principle, the Crock, in full panoply. But maybe, just because she was honest, she was going to have to fight for Chris's and Mikey's honesty, and not let Shelley turn them into the kind of intellectual crook he had become. Christopher and Michelle Steinberg; even the names he had chosen for them were phony. Coming from a poor but intellectual Chicago background, he was so much more bourgeois than she was, sprung from the really solid middle of the Pasadena middle-class.

She had jumped at the chance to come to Dancer for this week because this was a way, without making a project of it, to see Clary again—to find out, she told herself, if he had managed to hang in there. Once she had hoped, dog-in-the-manger, that he would fall on his face, Crock-out. Now she prayed that he hadn't, because one of the few things that had kept its value through the bitterness and unhappiness of her vale of tears was the idea of Clary's Way, as opposed to the Steinberg Variations. She was going to make no plans for the future until she had seen Clary. She had much to talk over with Clary, because she had been to the far corners of the spirit he had never visited, coming almost full circle from WASP Berkeley, and that wasn't even as complete a circuit as she had actually, before this invitation from Milly, been considering. In those last horrible weeks in Ajijic, fed to the bottom of her soul with rum, pot, peyote, and senseless soul talk with beat, fake poets and neurotic, superbourgeois, self-indulgent tricksters pretending to be painters, she had decided she would go all the way back, back to Pasadena, where she would marry some rich, stupid, honestly bourgeois bourgeois, some divorced or widowed old high-school beau, and live it up with colored maids, swimming pools, her own XKE, and the whole bit for the rest of her life, and to hell with the struggle.

The ultimate straw that had caused her to leave Sheldon Steinberg, the Guru, professor of philosophy at the University of California, her lord and master and father of her children, was finally realizing he had become just the kind of intellectual hypocrite he was always so quick to spot among his peers. He had taken Chris and Mikey out of public school and enrolled them in the Mercer School, which was ever so neatly *de facto* segregated by its nine-hundred-dollars-a-year tuition. He didn't want his kids to go to school with colored kids. She had managed to avoid facing the fact that he was That Way for a long time. She had had to face it when a Negro boy had punched precious Chris in the mouth in a schoolyard scrape. That was when the pontificating about the Mercer School's smaller classes, modern methods, intelligent teachers, and enrichment programs had come to a head. She had laid it on the line, finally and no-retreat. If he took Chris and Mikey out of public school and put them in a *de facto* segregated school, he who had been so proud of himself marching in the integration parade down Market Street with the rest of the Berkeley-faculty Dutiful Liberals, then he was a hypocrite and a bourgeois nigger-hater bastard, and she was through. He had called her bluff, or else there had been no way he could back down, so she had moved out and moved in with Abel Ransome in North Beach, not believing this was really happening, sure that something would give. But nothing had given, and finally she and Abel had gone on down to Ajijic. She had not really thought this was going to be the answer to anything, and the Crock had quickly shown up all the more hideous because its appearance was slightly different.

She finished tying Mikey's second bootlace. "There we go. Now go get your parka on, friend." She went into the bathroom to frown critically at herself in the mirror as she combed her hair. Not too bad, skin good, eyes clear, becoming-enough streak of white in her hair, figure still good. Abel had put on a one-man show in Ajijic, consisting of twenty-three nudes, all her and her all.

"Mommy?" Mikey called, knocking.

"I'm tinkling, Mikey. I'll be right out."

Mikey was apt to hang on her. She had provided herself with a fine, sturdy chunk of guilt by going off and leaving her children. Mikey was more possessive than ever, Chris more standoffish than ever. She had always loved Mikey more, the vulnerable, not-very-pretty one, with her insecurities and her clutching for love, who for all her faults had that wonderful, candid honesty that had nothing to do with cheating or not cheating at Hearts. "Just a minute, friend," she called as Mikey knocked again.

Now she and Mikey must get out of the house for a walk down to Dancer Lodge, where she would encounter, quite by chance, her old beau, Charles Clary. When she came out of the bathroom

Mikey was holding her parka and looking troubled. Mikey had done a pretty good job of washing the burned cork off her face.

"I didn't really cheat, Mom," she said. "I just didn't *see* any more of those—what do you call those black things?"

"Spades," she said, helping her daughter on with her parka. She parceled out gloves and caps, she put on her own parka, and they made a dash outside through the drip from the eaves. Juniper Lane was very slippery, the packed, opalescent snow scarred by tire chains.

"I didn't, Mom," Mikey said in an almost-crying voice, endowed with her own guilt by last night's little society of nay-saying guilt-makers practicing at being grownups. She squeezed the small gloved hand holding hers, feeling the whole parental sub-clause of the Reality-Principle like a strait jacket, like stocks; yet there was so much pleasure in it, love in it, life in it, so much value. When the children were difficult she and Shelley used to repeat those words of Babar to Celeste: "Truly it is not easy to bring up a family, but how nice the babies are!" And how would she say it to Clary?

"Listen!" she said to Mikey in her I-mean-it-now voice. "I don't care if you cheated or not. Do you think all those big kids didn't cheat when they were seven? If you really didn't cheat, why, you're wonderful! I think you're wonderful anyway."

Mikey looked solemn and no longer weepy. "Did you cheat when you were seven?"

"Simply all the time."

"Did Daddy?"

He had never stopped. "He was *awful!*" she said. So she would forgive her child her cheating, and not forgive her husband his. Or was it that she had, over the years, become finally an adult of sorts, while Shelley had only learned how to trick himself? Once she had been hypnotized by his self-assurance into thinking his maturity, his self-knowledge, was high as the stars above hers, when so much of his wisdom had been pretense, to himself as much as to her and Clary. She did not want to become a mother to her husband, for-giving his small failings and understanding the great ones, being tolerant as she would be tolerant to a child; impossible! She looked down and smiled her most cheerful smile at Mikey, wishing the child didn't look so comically like her father. Chris, the handsome little bastard, looked like her, but was pompous, humorless, and purse-lipped, with his 162 IQ hung around his neck like an amulet. She had felt a sneaking affection for the colored boy who had bloodied that protuberant lip. Maybe she resented Chris because he had never needed her.

"Where're we going, Mom?"

"Down to watch the funny people skiing."

At the end of the street they stopped to gaze into the valley, which looked in the brilliant sun like a painted-postcard romanticization of itself. Cars were parked along a skein of roads with crisply cut edges, and people in bright-colored clothing, skis on shoulders, were converging on a low, sprawling, snow-roofed building. There were a number of smaller buildings ranged around it, all with snow-rounded roofs. Smoke penciled upward here and there. A car came up the hill past them with a rattling and slipping of chains, spoiling the silence.

"See the chairlifts?" she said to Mikey, pointing. The lifts ran out of a large irregular area beyond the deck of the lodge, and lines of skiers queued from the terminals. Chairs descended, empty, swung around, and sailed up again, bearing two skiers each. How long since she had been to a ski resort? Thirteen years? That winter before Clary had been drafted to Korea she had gone skiing with him a number of times, had even bought boots and skis and a parka with a fur collar that had embarrassed him, taken lessons. Shelley had not been interested in skiing.

"It's pretty, Mom," Mikey said.

It was certainly pretty. Pretty, she thought, rather than beautiful, which this valley must have been before it was infested with machinery and candy-box architecture. The snowy valley had a Grandma Moses–New England Christmas–cum–Sunset Magazine aspect, with the skiers dashing down the slopes, the coniferous bristling of the mountains, and the incredibly dark blue of the sky past the bare white head of the tallest mountain, which must be Dancer Peak.

"It's fun-pretty," Mikey added.

"Exactly," she said. It was a warning to her that she must not put down this place or skiing out of envy for what they meant to Clary. Hand in hand, she and her daughter went down the hill. Along the roads on the valley floor cars were parking, people unloading skis and poles from top racks, sitting on bumpers to lace boots, rubbing colored wax on colored ski bottoms. There were many young men and girls with cute behinds in tight pants. Thirteen years ago there had been no stretch material and "downhill pants" had been very floppy compared to these, though surely all this streamlining was for looks rather than speed. Socks were no longer worn outside pants, she noticed. Equipment was shinier and more multitudinous; in fact, it seemed to her to be a very thinged-up sport, cluttered with expensive-looking gadgets. There were very few fat people though. Shelley had the quality of looking fat even when he was underweight. She felt a flush of vengeful pleasure remembering the little packet deep in the safe-deposit vault of her mind, her secret weapon which she would never bring out to destroy Shelley in actuality, though she employed it often in the savage and relentless infighting in her imagination—the comparison, on several intimate indices, of just how much more of a man Abel Ransome was than he. Don't hate him, she advised herself, commanded herself. Sometimes it would come over her in waves that sickened her. Don't hate; bad for you. But the fact remained that Shelley had cheated her out of twelve years that could have been fun, that could have been memorable, that could have been so many things, but, except for childbearing, had been nothing. The worst thing about being separated from your spouse, she knew from experience not merely her own, was the sickening hate that came and went like fevers, and must be akin to the ferocity that infected all civil wars, as though you could hate the most savagely what you had once loved.

Under the lodge's porte-cochere was the stainless steel figure of a dancer on skis splayed out against a wall like a Tarot Hanged Man, very cutesy. Inside the lobby was a long counter with arches dividing it into a number of windows. Through one was visible a man seated at a desk. Looking up to meet her eyes, he smiled aloofly; he wore Madison Avenue black-rimmed glasses and had country-squire, well-bred good looks, though this must be the management Wayne and Milly disapproved of. Skiers clumped through the lobby in boots, looking, she thought, rather self-conscious in their tight-behind pants, though she had to admit ski clothes were more becoming than they used to be. She was feeling a little inadequate in her own plaid slacks. Further along the coun-

ter people were lined up under a hanging sign that said: SKI
SCHOOL.

Her recollections of skiing at the Sugar Bowl were of getting
very cold and then coming inside to hot toddys around a roaring
fire and a good deal of hearty singing. Here there was a country-
club atmosphere that was not folksy at all. She lined up and
waited while people ahead of her arranged for ski lessons or presented problems. "What are we waiting here for, Mom?" Mikey
asked.

She didn't answer, coming just then to the head of the line and
facing through the arched window a tanned, blond Brunhilde
whose Germanic accents she had already heard.

"I'm looking for a ski instructor named Charles Clary."

"I'm afraid Easy Clary for all this week is booked." The German girl opened a blue notebook. "Maybe—"

She explained that she didn't want a lesson, she was a friend,
and was told to look for Easy Clary on the deck at noon, which
was soon, or if she would leave her name— She said to tell Easy
Clary that Mrs. Steinberg had been looking for him, and was reminded of Shelley's demeanor whenever confronted with a German accent. It was as though he must try to turn into a lovable
funny man so he would not be persecuted, and then must react
against that, so he was alternately clownish and at his bombastic
worst. It was very easy to be Jewish in name only, wasn't it?

She and Mikey went out on the dark, soggy planks of the sundeck and sat down at a table. The sun was so warm she had to take
off her parka. She sipped a beer and Mikey spooned at a dish of
vanilla ice cream while they watched the skiers coming down a
long slope that was cut into fat humps of snow like an overstuffed
comforter. At the bottom some rejoined the lines waiting to ride
back up on the lifts, while others slid over to the sundeck to remove their skis and come up the steps, brown-faced and happy,
flop down in chairs, remove sweaters, and order cold drinks. There
were many remarks such as: "Great up in the bowl!" and, "Terrific
powder on the Big Top!" She noted a number of cutesy names like
"Big Top," "the Chute," "the Superchute," "Cape Horn," and
"the Spoon."

She enjoyed vignettes and exchanges she glimpsed or overheard.

Directly behind her was a very beautiful woman, perhaps a little younger than she was, with a tanned, frail, curiously tragic face half hidden behind amber glasses, and long blond hair held back by a violet earband. She was sitting alone at a table with a beer before her, staring up at the mountain as though there were something, high on that great white head, she was trying to read.

And to her right was an encounter she found interesting. A big-boned girl who was handsome in a way that suggested she was not aware of it, with her hair tied into two pale brown puffs with rubberbands and a broad forehead shining with sweat, came across the deck with a kind of caricature Marilyn-Monroe sway, to plump down opposite an older woman whose makeup was applied so thickly it resembled stucco and who was wearing an obviously expensive skiing suit of dull, rich red. The big girl rudely sampled the older woman's drink, words were exchanged, and tension crackled—mother and daughter in some traditional argument, no doubt.

"Mom! Mom! There goes Christy!" Mikey cried, rising, pointing. Sure enough, Chris was passing, leading a long line of children in the wake of an instructor in a black sweater. Chris was sliding confidently on his skis. He would master this intelligently, earnestly, and joylessly, as he mastered everything he set out to do. "Looks pretty good, Mom," Mikey said. She was the most loyal of siblings and received the shortest of shrifts in return. "Can I go tomorrow, Mom?"

"We'll see," she said, recognizing in herself the dim hope that Clary would find Mikey as enchanting as she did, and special lessons or assistance would be offered so that Mikey would be able to one-up Chris; that through this, somehow, she and Clary—whoops! careful! Popular Romances, she jeered at herself.

Then she saw him. Miraculously she saw him among the skiers in their hundreds descending the long, bumpy snow hill, though he had always had that star quality that made him stand out in any crowd. While the other skiers on the hill made stiff, jumpy turns, jolted stiff-legged around, or showoffed back and forth, he turned continuously, slowly, very beautifully, each turn linked to the last, skis so close together they looked like one ski, knees, ankles, and hips all flexing and extending together with a lightness suggesting that he had mastered levitation; almost breathlessly she absorbed his curving progress down the hill; it was as though her body was remembering, after thirteen years, how to ski.

He looked frequently over his shoulder at a tall man in green pants and parka—like something flushed from the greenwood—who must be a pupil. Clary was calling back instructions or encouragement while he swung from one lovely, cool turn into the next, and Robin Hood lurched and wavered along behind him.

They ran out to a stop on the flat below the sundeck, removed their skis, and chattered for a moment, Clary illustrating something with planing gestures of his free hand. Then Clary set his skis upright in the snow and came on toward the sundeck, his face as brown as Abel Ransome's face but with more life in the color, teeth very white as he smiled a greeting, waved a gloved hand, laughed at something called to him, and came at last up the steps, sweeping off his cap from thick, dark, stylishly disheveled hair. And she knew he had hung in there. The almost twenty, the thirteen, nine, seven years had passed and he was just the same, not soured nor cheapened nor Crocked-out nor changed in any way, still full of joy and creating joy for others, still making each day memorable. She knew he must be exactly as she remembered him, who had known him since the eighth grade. What grade were they in now?

Then he was coming toward her. She didn't start up or wave, frozen into an impossible, bursting happiness because he had seen her too! He was coming to her, smiling in a different, private, almost shy, almost troubled way for her, and his smile washed away all those mistaken, foolish, cheating-at-Hearts years. My God! she thought, talk about Popular Romances! My God, it's like the end of a corny Hollywood movie! My God, he is going to come right over here and grab me in his arms and kiss me the way they do, all soft focus, and he'll put an arm around Mikey too, and it will all fade into endless happiness in the sunset, and it's true, it's true! It's true after all the sneering jazz, truth is beauty and beauty truth, God's in his heaven and all's right with the best of all possible worlds!

She had started to rise when he went on past. Turning, she watched him sit down with the beautiful girl with the long, blond hair. She watched him put a hand on top of the girl's hand, and the girl's other hand moved to rest on top of his while they smiled into each other's faces. *Don't the moon look lonesome shinin' through the trees?*

She couldn't just sneak away, as she felt like doing. Mikey's spoon tinkled greedily in her ice-cream dish. She pushed her chair back with a harsh scraping and turned to face the table behind her.

"Hello, Chuck Clary."

Recognition. Pleasure. He jumped to his feet. He embraced her, like a brother. "Elizabeth!" The blond girl smiled up at them; *she* didn't have anything to worry about. But it was a sad little smile, in the curiously familiar face of some minor luminary.

Disengaging but still holding her hand, Clary said, "Elizabeth, this is Maeve. Maeve—Elizabeth." She called Mikey to come meet the people, but Mikey turned shy. Asked to join them, she brought her beer over, and Mikey leaned against her, gazing suspiciously at the other two.

"You finally came up where the air is clear!" Clary said. "Where's the Guru?"

"He's not with me," she said meaningfully, and Clary got it and nodded once, frowning. The girl made an affected hitching motion with her head, showing off the long, shining hair.

"The snow must be turning bad in this sun," the blonde said to Clary.

"It's still good skiing," Clary said.

Was this what you talked about up here where the air was clear? she wondered. Just how the snow was, and the skiing? It didn't seem enough. Don't be sour, she told herself.

"Going skiing, Elizabeth?" Clary asked, showing her his good teeth.

"I've forgotten how. Too many years."

"It'll come back." He raised his eyes as another man came to the table, tall, well built, all in royal blue with a smooth, long face and wavy hair that grew close in at the sides of his forehead.

"Private party, Ease?"

Introductions were made. The newcomer's name was John Henry—there seemed to be no last names up here. He was as full of hipsterisms as a jazz musician.

Sitting, chatting, she realized that she was part of a very handsome group that others looked at admiringly. A foursome of idle and fun-loving young people depicted in a full-color ad on glossy paper; at first she was bitterly amused at her fraudulent credentials; then she found herself responding physically to John Henry's admiring and complimentary eye, as frankly appraising and how-about-it-honey as Abel Ransome's had once been. She felt all at once sleek, feline, and confident. The chemistry of sex and the physics of casual attraction came back to her as easily as Clary seemed to think skiing would come back.

Her daughter seemed very heavy, leaning against her shoulder, but she noticed, only a little ashamed, that it did not slow her down much.

4: *Captain Easy*

IT WAS a too-much coincidence that both Golden Girls would show up at Dancer at the same time, but obviously Elizabeth and the Guru were having trouble. Her little girl stayed with them the whole time on the sundeck, and her boy joined them for lunch. John Henry and Elizabeth took to each other enthusiastically; he supposed that she had to punish him a little because of Maeve.

He had made up his mind that today was going to be great because last night had been such a flop. He had tried to convince himself that Maeve had merely been very tired, tense, and sentimental about coming back to Dancer. He knew it was more than that, but almost as an act of will he had determined that he and Maeve were going to enjoy today, to see if they could pick up on what they had started once—to see if he wanted to, if she wanted to, and ignore whatever it was that was hanging over Maeve. It seemed almost a test, and so to hell with what was wrong, and all-out on what was right.

He announced a party at his house that evening, Christmas Eve, left John Henry with Elizabeth and the little girl, Mikey, on the sundeck, and walked Maeve to the Big House, where she was going to rest. Then he went up the mountain to give a private lesson at one o'clock.

He spent an hour getting an Oakland TV executive to ski with his knees bent. It didn't make his determination to happy-it-up today exactly downhill work, but finally, shouting, "Great! Great! Great! Keep going! Keep *going!*" he exhorted three competent turns out of Stiff-Knees, and so the lesson ended gratifyingly for them both.

When he had put away his skis he went into the lobby to ask

Badbody to his party. Badbody sat framed in his arch, before a cluttered desk, and paid no attention when he rapped on the glass. Another, sharper rap caused Badbody to glance up and frown. Beating on the window with raised fists, he assumed a desperate expression; he began choking himself with his two hands. Badbody beckoned him inside.

"I feel the need to talk to someone sane," Badbody said, leading him into the inner office, which had been Dick Macklin's and now was used for private conferences or by Isobel when she was in residence. "Though I realize I am using the term loosely," Badbody said. "All we have here is sherry, I'm afraid. Can you put up with sherry?"

"Fine."

Badbody brought out a bottle of Dry Fly. He stood tall, spare, and broad-hipped in his sport jacket and gray flannels, frowning at the level in the bottle. "I think I'm going out of my mind," he remarked.

"Going out of your mind why?"

"I'm having one of my days when I don't think I can stomach people any more."

"Stop eating them then," he said and hooted with laughter.

Badbody didn't even smile. There were slashes of dark flesh like paint beneath his eyes, and he moved heavily as he produced glasses and filled them. Badbody handed him one and indicated the couch, seating himself in the desk chair with little automatic tugs at the knees of his slacks.

"I had that arch glazed so the yahoos wouldn't be at me all the time," Badbody said. "Now I can't stand to look at them either—a difficulty for someone in my position."

"Jesus!" he said, because Badbody sounded as though he meant it.

"They are so miserably cheerful."

"They're trying to have a good time. If they didn't want to have a good time they wouldn't come up here."

"I wish they'd stay at home."

"You're bringing me down. It's a great day! Sunshine! Powder snow! Everybody's happy!"

"You haven't been near the clinic," Badbody said. "The doctors are happiest of all. I detest the happiness of doctors."

It was Badbody's usual solemnly ironic style, but there was no humor in it, only bitterness, and he felt uncomfortable.

"I came to ask you to a party at my place tonight," he said. "But you're going to have to get this hump off your back."

For the first time Badbody smiled a little. "I'll come gratefully. At what time? I'll have to attend the Christmas Eve traditional here first."

"*After* that. Cheer up! Where's the old acid wit?"

Badbody shook his head. "Tell me something," he said. "Tell me what's wrong when a person turns completely negative. It's been hinted by various sources, and I've just begun to realize it myself. All I want to say is no to everything."

"Start saying yes!" he said, not knowing whether to be serious or not. "You'd better get out skiing, Brad. It's only raining *in*side."

Lips pursed, Badbody shook his head again. "I'd be certain to break a hip on my first run, and at my age I simply don't want to." He managed another bleak smile. "Besides, as I've often told you, I suspect skiing is not really fun at all, but only a gigantic hoax perpetrated by the ski instructors and the United Orthopedic Surgeons. Tell me something frankly," he said. "I can't believe you still enjoy this as you once did, but I can't believe you're a fraud either. Aren't you fooling yourself a little, Captain Easy?"

"Little bit of a fraud actually," he said, grinning.

With great concentration Badbody packed, tamped, and lit his pipe. Badbody, he thought, had been asking for help, and he hadn't been able to help.

"How's Maeve?" Badbody asked. "Did she ski the Superchute with you this morning?"

"She didn't make it too well. She got pretty tired. She's taking a nap now."

Badbody blew a smoke screen. "I gathered it was to be a kind of Dick Macklin Memorial."

"Something like that," he said. He disliked thinking about Maeve's wild idea of last night, that someone had cut the avalanche down on Macklin.

The pupils of Badbody's eyes, magnified by his glasses, seemed to be flickering as though spelling out a message in code. Then Badbody swung around in the swivel chair to confront the glass-covered topographical map of Dancer, which showed the present installations and the proposed new lifts. "I have a theory," he said, sounding as though he'd just come down with a cold. "My mother was a violent Christian Scientist at one time, and this is a revision of Mary Baker Eddy, the Peabody Theory of Disease.

"All disease is error, of course," he continued, swinging back. "Imaginary. I'll take the illustration of a Little Leaguer who misses a pop fly. What does he do? Immediately, to excuse himself, he begins to limp. He may or may not realize he is feigning this. It may be very real to him. His ankle may actually ache. Or, if he needs it enough, actually swell." Abruptly he said, "I suppose you never missed any pop flies."

"Ha! And limped."

Badbody nodded. "Now, the limp is necessary to excuse failure. We know, don't we, that as we imperceptibly grow older, life becomes imperceptibly more complex, more real, more earnest, more conducive to failure. My theory holds that all disease is only the Little League limp become more complex, real, earnest, and deadly. An excuse for failure to cope with the impossible complexity of life."

"Or just failure to cope with life."

"Or failure to cope with guilt," Badbody said. "I haven't as yet explored the possibilities of guilt."

"All the same thing, isn't it?"

"I don't understand you."

"You were talking about disease as an excuse for not living. Guilt works just as well, doesn't it? Guilt—disease." He flipped a hand.

"I'm talking about a disease like cancer," Badbody said, turning with a show of casualness to pick up the sherry bottle. "Another?"

"Badbody—" He cleared his throat, shamed by his inner curling and shrinking, which was strangely akin to what he had felt last night in the face of Maeve's hysteria. He hated his fear of this, like a soldier trained to bravery who feels his legs shaking at the first sight of the enemy. "Badbody, are you talking about yourself?"

Badbody poured sherry into the two glasses, corked the bottle, and placed it on the center of the desk. They sipped in silence. "No," Badbody said. "I've just been thinking about everything—and nothing. Everything negative and nothing positive. I suppose you wouldn't understand that."

He didn't understand, but he felt a prickling at the base of his spine as he watched Badbody take off his glasses and polish them with his handkerchief.

"Actually, I'm talking about Maeve," Badbody said.

"What?"

"Maeve has cancer."

"Ah, Jesus!"

"Hopeless cancer," Badbody said.

"Ah, Jesus, no!" he whispered. "How do you know?"

"Isobel heard of it through mutual friends in Dallas." When Badbody replaced his glasses, his eyes were blurred and damp behind the lenses. There were painted-looking spots of color on his cheeks now, beneath the dark slashes. "I *hate* it!" Badbody said raggedly.

He thought about Maeve trying to ski the powder and failing, about Maeve last night. He took a deep, shaky breath. "Did Isobel hear how long she's got?"

"Apparently not very long," Badbody said and began to polish his glasses again.

"So she's come back to ski the powder all the way out," he said.

"I don't know if they can ever say exactly how much time there is," Badbody began. "It depends—"

"Fuck time! Did you know that one of the first things the peasants did in the French Revolution was smash the clocks?"

Badbody looked at him uncomprehendingly, applied a match to his gone-out pipe, and said, "I didn't know whether to tell you or not."

He nodded, closed his eyes, tried to think. Maeve had come back to Dancer not to die but to try to live, which was courage, but any failures became terrible defeats. He had noticed early last evening that she did not smile much. He had noticed that a fire had gone out in her, and he had thought in his male pride that he could rekindle it. He wondered if she was afraid or unafraid, and found in himself a growing mixture of empathy and apprehension.

She was resting in her room in the Big House with death growing in her while he and Badbody sat here drinking sherry. All at once there burst in him the revelation of what he had to do. Hadn't he always known? Badbody had said he thought *he* was going out of his mind, but wasn't it he, Captain Easy, who, like

Lucretius before him, like Don Juan even, must ultimately go mad with desperation, searching for those scarcer and scarcer flowers among the coarse weeds of life? Badbody had asked if he still enjoyed his life, and he had answered truthfully, but not completely truthfully. Already he had been tempted to give up that life for Martha Schroeder. The time had come, and Maeve had come, who needed him, for his own salvation.

Through the open door and the arches over the counter he watched the tired, wet, mostly happy skiers passing in the lobby. He made excited, revving-engine sounds in his throat. "I guess I've been fooling myself more than a little," he said.

"Pardon me?"

"Time to shift," he said, turning back to Badbody. "When you're not enough for yourself any more. When you need someone to—do things for. A better thing to do," he said. He knew he was making no sense.

"What are you going to do?" Badbody asked.

He didn't answer because he didn't specifically know yet.

"We are talking about Maeve?" Badbody said.

"Of course," he said. "What I'm going to do for Maeve."

Looking at him through glasses that had misted again, Badbody said in a quiet voice, "But why *you?*"

He didn't understand what Badbody meant. Rising, he felt a tremendous relief, as though his god, watching him, had almost despaired, and perhaps in the end had cheated a little with a last-minute warning prod under the table to remind him of the proper means to salvation. Because, of course, it was the end of the First Personal Principle, and he was ashamed that he should be so relieved that he was finally finished with it.

The miracle was that what he and the Guru had worked out so long ago as their Second Personal Principle, out of a grudging and abstract admiration for the selfless missionaries, social workers, and teachers—the Schweitzers with their Lambarénés—had been projected correctly: the means by which the incomplete person, incapable of the First Personal, could fulfill himself by service to humanity in large or small section, by serving a cause judged worthy, just, good, and sufficient, or by serving even one other person—that possibility recognized too—thus the self might be given a larger and more intense reality than through a failing dedication to First Principle alone. So he could cheerfully admit his own defeat and soberly turn to the next thing, which was serving Maeve. It was something for which he was so well equipped, as though it was for this that he had been preparing himself all along, and the fact that there was so little time was merely the greater challenge.

"What are you going to do?" Badbody asked again.

"Going to go wake her up," he said. "Get the party started." His voice seemed unfamiliar. He took his dark glasses from his parka pocket and put them on. He thanked Badbody for the drink and left to get Maeve up, to get the party started.

5: Miss Bliss

SHE NEVER MISSED a Christmas Eve at Dancer Lodge because of Tim on exhibition in his Santa Claus rig. Tim had been drafted as Santa Claus the very first Christmas and had never been replaced: M.C. and gift-giver each Christmas Eve to the children of guests and employees and, by extension over the years, to any children resident in the valley or connected with Dancer's present or past who was registered with Badbody's secretary, Annie Sprague.

Badbody would buy presents in the Cope five-and-dime, multiples of four different items chosen according to age-group and sex. The selection in Cope was limited, and the feeling among the children was that the needle was stuck. Stevie now had two plastic model helicopter kits. Stevie disliked Christmas Eve at Dancer Lodge but wouldn't consider missing it. He was deeply pained at the spectacle of Timbal Khan the Mountain Man dressed in a Santa suit, laughing ho-ho-ho and passing out cheap plastic gifts, but loyalty demanded his presence.

Loyalty did not enter into her own feelings. At first there had been some kind of revenge in seeing Tim, embarrassed and inept in his fake-fur-lined red robe, cap, and beard. But over the years he had lost his shyness, and last Christmas she had realized with a shock that he was good.

Now as she watched him, down at the other end of the lounge, bent over to adjust his pack preparatory to making the grand entry, she wondered if his personality actually changed when he donned his white beard. The room was full of children and their parents, and already a Christmas mood was being born, with Helen Fraley playing carols on the piano beneath the soft lights on the silvered tree. Candlelit children's faces were clustered around

the piano, and heads were frequently turned, looking for Santa
Claus. She made her way through the children to stand smiling in
the curve of the piano, because, over the years, she had come to
occupy the position of Santa's assistant, matching name on the list
with present from the bag and handing the package to Tim for
presentation.

"Ho-ho-ho!" He was coming. There was a hush. It was a magic
moment, and the ridiculous intensity of it made her realize how
few genuinely magic moments there were. "HO-HO-HO!" Tim
roared, coming slowly along the aisle the grownups made for him,
massively fat with pillows, his broad face tanned almost black
above the curly white beard, his blue half-rounds of eyes exactly as
Santa Claus's eyes should be, the great pack hefted on his shoulder. "Merry Christmas! Ho-ho-ho!" And the children, turning,
ceasing their dovecote giggling, were all expectancy even though
most knew they would receive nothing more than a model helicopter kit or a nursing-doll set. "Merry Christmas!" Tim said,
putting his pack down beside the piano. John Henry had appeared
behind Helen Fraley, his big guitar hung around his neck on a
strap. "Ho-ho-ho!" Tim said in exactly the tone Santa Claus
should have, beginning to fumble in his pack.

Now Tim became an M.C. of some proficiency, making heavy-
handed topical jokes that laid his juvenile audience in the aisles.
He remembered children's names. She had to admit, as she helped
him with self-effacing know-how, that he was very good with children, better than Cope School's Miss Bliss, though of course it was
easy to be good with children if you didn't have to deal intimately
with the little beasts five days out of seven and nine months out of
twelve.

She tried to think about herself as Mrs. Santa instead of merely
Santa's assistant as she handed Tim the packages and whispered
the names of the recipients. He called the names in his booming
Christmas voice, and children came up shyly, some giggling and
some solemn, but each one (even Stevie!) with a little wonder in
him, and to each one Tim said something personal, which was the
real gift accompanying the cheap formal one. It was here, once a
year, that Tim had his finest hour. Perhaps he was more spectacular coming full-bore down the mountain with a toboggan, or acting
as the fine lay diagnostician Dr. Cannella had once told her he

was, or blowing avalanches with hand charges, but she suspected he had come to these Mountain-Man skills out of an inner insufficiency and just plain muscular ability, while here he gave happiness and more than a little excitement fashioned out of an awesome will power that was one of the surprising incongruities of his character.

Finally there were no more presents, and Santa made an expansive gesture to Helen Fraley, who immediately thumped into "Jingle Bells." Tim led the singing in his big, tuneless voice, she and Helen joined in, then the children's shrill voices, then everyone. During the song Tim, all showman, took up his empty pack and, with another series of Ho-ho-ho's and Merry Christmas's, strode out to applause.

Guitar chords sounded. John Henry was sitting on the end of the grand piano, hunched over his guitar, which gleamed richly in the candlelight. Suddenly tears ached at the back of her eyes. In this traditionless place, in this traditionless state, at an age where she found herself needing tradition like nutriment, she realized that of course Tim as Santa Claus was a tradition, and that John Henry, before he had gone to Hollywood, had always played the guitar for the kids on Christmas Eve. It was even traditional that she hand Tim the presents in this little intimacy of being Santa's assistant, or Mrs. Santa, in what was perhaps more of a relationship than she had ever had with Stevie's father. Unashamed of the tears in her eyes, she listened to John Henry chording, knowing from the chords what his first, traditional song would be, and in her mind now she was ready to say, "All right, Tim. If you want to. All right, Tim." All it took to disrupt a rational mind was a little sentiment.

John Henry's voice was exactly the same as it had always been, but controlled and professional, as it had never been before:

> "Santa Claus is comin', it's almost day!
> Oh, Santa Claus is comin' and it's almost day!
> Peekin' round the corner and it's almost day!
> *Yay*, peekin' round the corner, it's almost *day!*"

He sang through it once and then, waving a hand and calling encouragement, got kids and their parents singing with him. She went over to the bar for a drink, feeling very sentimental indeed.

Stevie caught her eye, grinning fiendishly. He held up a helicopter kit in one hand and three fingers of the other. Damn Badbody for a cheapskate anyway.

The opening of the gifts reminded her of a passage in a mystery novel she had recently read. The tough detective, making love to a girl in a negligee, had "undressed her as though she were a Christmas package." It seemed to her now a very good image, what with the blue ribbons on the negligee and the busty body inside. Once she too had been such a package. If only the right man had come along and pulled the right ribbon, he would have opened not so bad a gift. But in her case what mattered was not so much the quality inside as the problem of undoing the wrappings. No one any more could undo her with a little pull on a blue ribbon. There were so many knots, knots on knots tied over the years. Tim would never know how, and no one else would ever bother, to untie all those knots to get at the real and trembling gift inside. A sort of outer come-on of a gift was easily available; Tim could have it now for the asking—bed, hot meals, a son.

Now John Henry was singing:

> "Hush, li'l baby, don't say a word,
> Daddy's goin' to buy you a mockin' bird . . ."

She asked the bartender for a bourbon on the rocks. The man beside her turned and said, "Well, Merry Christmas, Rody." He was Herbie Allen, chairman of tomorrow's giant slalom, who would have brought his daughter Amy to the lodge for the Christmas gift-giving. Now there was no more sentimental foolishness; she was all racing-mother.

"Merry Christmas, Herbie. Bring Amy over?"

"Never miss it. Say, I've been meaning to phone you, Rody. How's she doing this year?"

Amy was not doing well in the third grade, and Herbie knew it. He watched her worriedly as, without answering, she signed the chit for her drink and sipped it, frowning.

"Not too good, huh?" Herbie said.

"What if I did a little work with her this vacation, maybe an hour every night? Could you or Ellie run her over?"

"Sure!" Herbie said. He had a delicately handsome, pink-tinted face, a small mustache, and he sold insurance. "Say, that's wonderful of you, Rody. I mean, that's a real break for Amy. We'd really appreciate that."

"Forget it," she said. She looked at him. "Who's forerunning the race tomorrow?"

"Ben Gleeson said he would. We ought to have two—somebody else'll show up."

"How about letting Stevie forerun?"

Herbie twisted up a corner of his mouth to nibble his mustache. "You're kidding," he said. She wasn't kidding, and he knew she wasn't. "That's too tough a course for a kid that age," Herbie said. "Even if he's—I mean, listen, Rody, I don't think you ought to—"

"He skis that mountain fifty times a weekend, Herbie."

"Well, I mean, I know he can ski the course," Herbie protested, a real nitpicker. "But I mean, how are Class A racers going to feel about an eight-year-old kid forerunning the course?"

"You tell me one of them that would bitch about Stevie forerunning."

Herbie threw up his hands in the constricted space. "All right, Rody! If you want to take the responsibility. I mean, it's all right with *me.*"

"Thanks a lot, Herbie," she said. When he left, after admonishing her to come out early in the morning and help the ski club pack the course, she whispered, "And a *ho*-ho-ho!" As though it were a cue, Tim appeared, changed out of his Santa Claus suit. He squeezed up to the bar in Herbie's place and ordered a beer, not seeming to notice her although he must have gone to some trouble to join her.

"You're really good, you know," she said to him. "Do you know you're really good?"

He grunted and looked embarrassed.

"You're terrific, Santa Claus," she said.

But there was no flattering him. "I don't mind doing it," he said. "I just get tired of everybody kidding me about it."

Unreasonably irritated, she swung around on her bar stool. Isobel Macklin was standing close by, with Badbody. "He's a terrific Santa Claus, isn't he?" she called to Mrs. Macklin.

Mrs. Macklin peered at her as though she'd never seen her before. "Oh, it's little Janet Bliss," she said as Tim, his face flaming, slid off the bar stool to stand in the presence of the woman who

owned Dancer. "Yes, I think he's a perfectly marvelous Santa
Claus," Mrs. Macklin said. "Thank you very much for doing this
for us, Tim. You give a great many people a great deal of pleasure."

When she and Tim had turned back to the bar again, she said,
"You see? Everybody thinks you're terrific."

"What did you make all that fuss for?" Tim grumbled.

"You have to make a fuss once in a while or nobody knows if
you're still alive or not." She studied the side of his face through
half-shut eyes as she sipped bourbon. "Have you ever thought
about growing a beard?" she asked.

"No," he said curtly, gazing off across the lounge.

She saw where he was looking; Clary and Maeve were sitting at
a table with another woman and John Henry. Grinning thinly, she
watched Clary too. She had seen him with many women, squire,
stud, and gigolo, but she had never seen him so attentive as this,
almost too attentive, she thought, as he lit Maeve's cigarette, arranged Maeve's glass, smiled at Maeve, talked to Maeve. Their
faces were golden by candlelight, black voids of shadow appearing
and changing in them as they moved. They were handsome people.

"Look at Easy," she said.

Tim grunted.

"Captain Easy at work and play," she said. But she realized that
Clary was at work untying ribbons. It was exactly what he was
doing. She wondered what he would find in the package. Something truly awesome, some fantastic, male-delighting essence that
made men flock around Maeve as they had always done, or only an
empty box? Because in the end the men all rejected Maeve, didn't
they? Called her a whore, as Macklin had done; sent a bunch of
mariachis to hound her out of town like the Mexican in Acapulco.

Now the four at the table were rising. The woman with John
Henry was small, with a lush figure and a stylish stripe of white in
her hair. Clary was looking over toward Tim at the bar, an arm
raised in a questioning signal, his gull-wing eyebrows raised.

"We're supposed to go to a party at Easy's," Tim said. "Do you
want to go?"

"Love to go," she said. She did not get to parties much, and she
would like to watch Clary in action, and Maeve too. Now the two

of them had stopped to talk to people at another table. Clary had his arm casually around her waist, his brown face laughing but curiously strained, hers practicedly gay. As they leaned over the candlelit table the impression was that they generated their own candlelight.

With how many women, she wondered, had Easy Clary generated such warmth and light, and with how many men had Maeve? Maybe, she thought, bitterly envious, it was only practice, like learning to ski or to come down through slalom gates, this ability to generate heat and light, lust and love. What right had Clary and Maeve after all these years to find each other, as she herself and Tim had never been able to do? Was it that being what they were, skibum and sexbox, they had far fewer knots to untie?

Though in the end, she reminded herself, they would come apart. Clary would lightweight on his way while Maeve gracefully continued her descent from producer to bullfighter to Mexican playboy to ski instructor and on down. But wouldn't it have been worth it, each affair? Even if it ended badly, even humiliatingly, still worth it?

I'm so jealous, she said to herself, full of tears and savagery, self-pity and hatred. And now she must go over and ask Jeanne Betz if Stevie could spend the night with Billy so his mother could go to an Easy Clary party. Whee! She knew she should not be going to the party, that she should take Stevie home for a good night's sleep so he would do well forerunning the GS tomorrow. But it was Christmas Eve, after all, and surely this one time she could forget duty for pleasure and go with Tim to Easy Clary's party—because it looked as though they were going to get together at last, she and Tim.

6: John Henry

THIS CHICK WAS too much—she was the maraschino cherry on top of skiing the deep powder today. She was giving him back to himself after a shaky night last night, as though she knew just what he needed. Party at Easy Clary's with everyone there: Maeve in a long dress with her brown arms bare, looking great but like something so far off that maybe it was just as good to see postcards of it as the real thing; J.D. bull-chested in his red-and-white-striped sweater; Rody with the ponytail she was maybe a little too old for, but still cute with a high, round behind in stretch slacks; Tim talking away at Isobel Macklin, and Dickie and Badbody in jackets and ties, and Clary putting records on the phono; all of them in Clary's cabin with a stack of magazines falling over on an end table, and the leather couch and leather chair with dark wooden arms that looked as though they'd had a lot of drinks spilled on them, and the paperback books slices of color on the shelves, and the disks and hi-fi components stacked, and the polar-bear skin in front of the fireplace, burned in many spots by sparks, with a snarling fake red mouth and yellow teeth. On the wall adjoining the fireplace was the enormous blown-up photograph, three-by-three at least, of Clary in the powder at the top of the Superchute with a hint of the cornice swelling top left, and top right one of the trees, the slanted one, showing straight. It was one of the photos the crazy photographer had printed tilted so that the Superchute looked like a sheer cliff.

The changer dropped the first disk, the arm swung and began to track; big sound from the speakers.

And there was this great girl, extra girl to his extra man, though she wasn't exactly a girl—he thought she was Easy's age probably

—very small with a vestpocket-Venus shape, so although she probably wasn't five feet tall she was built like a real boat, fine cans in a gray wool dress, very lovely hips, and all her seams a little curved to fit her. She had brown hair with a stripe of white in it, olive-shaped face, and olive-shaped eyes with silvered lids. There was no doubt they were going to make it tonight, and he felt lazy and like stretching every time he met her eyes, but he knew too that she was going to give him just the right amount of hard time before they did make it, and that was great too. She spoke right up. The best part now was that he kept wanting to touch her, to see how the texture was and check the temperature, and he kept stopping himself. It got to be a game with him, standing beside her by the fireplace where the fire was hot on their calves, very close but not quite touching, leaning down a little so he could hear her in the beat from the hi-fi, nodding as she spoke, but not particularly paying attention to what she was saying because he was enjoying *her* so much.

"You've just got the two kids, honey?" he said when it seemed time for him to say something.

"Honey!" she said.

Now he didn't look at her, and that was a nice game too. "I keep thinking about honey because you are honey-colored, honey."

"Oh, that's nice," she said in her ironic way but seriously thanking him for the compliment. "Just the two kids. Boy and girl."

"That's a cute boy."

"He's got an IQ of 162 and I don't think he's so cute. Maybe I'm just sick of IQs."

He glanced at her quickly, allowing himself that. Very nice!

She said, "My husband goes around with a bunch of people who all have IQs. What they are thinking of doing now, they are thinking of putting the IQ next to the Ph.D. Then no one will have to associate with anyone more than ten points away."

He thought she was really funny, brainy too. She was older than he was; she had such a great bod and that color that was just too much, almost he let his hip touch hers where they stood pleasantly cooking in front of the fire, but he stopped himself. Everything was good, wasn't it? He had called down to Teddy again just now and the situation had sounded a lot better. Clary and Maeve were making it big together and that was just fine.

"Don't like IQs, huh?" he said.

"Nope."

"Well, you are talking to the right guy then."

She chuckled. He leaned down close to her face, closing his eyes because it would be so nice to open them again. When he opened them he was looking at her mouth with its pale lipstick and little bite-you teeth showing in a smile. Her mouth said, "Oh, now, we have our little arrangement, haven't we? Do we have to keep pursuing it?"

"Yay, why not?" he protested. "I like to pursue it." He was going to get a hard-on just talking to her. "I think you're *great!*" he said.

She sighed. "Oh, well, go ahead and pursue it if you have to. You won't mind if I get a little shaky sometimes?"

Speechless, he shook his head; so sexy talking like this inside the general conversation of the room with the hi-fi jumping and the fire so hot on his legs he almost, but not quite yet, had to move away from it. His glass of cheap red was empty, but he would have died rather than leave this for a minute.

"I mean—your name's Elizabeth?" he asked.

She nodded. "You're an old friend of Chuck's?" she asked. "You remind me of him a long time ago, a little."

"Who's Chuck?" he asked, mind not on it.

"The host."

"Oh, *Easy*. Captain Easy. You must be an older friend than I am, honey. We've all got names Dick Macklin gave us. He was king up here till he died—that's Mrs. Macklin over there, she owns the place. Easy"—his hip touched hers accidentally—"Timbal Khan, the big guy; Badbody, with the glasses—he's Brad Peabody, the manager. I'm John Henry Collins."

Her red-brown eyes met his with just as intense a touch as her hip's touch had been. "I'd been wondering about the 'Easy.' You mean your name's not really John Henry?"

"Well, it's Ralph Collins, but my agent thought John Henry'd be a lot better to work with."

Her silver-shaded lids came half down over the red-brown eyes

as she frowned. Her color reminded him of the color of his cheroots, and he took out the case and offered her one first as a matter
of politeness, saying, "Sorry I don't have a cigarette." She took one
and lipped it very naturally. He made pleased sounds as he held up
the flame of his gold Zippo.

She round-mouthed-out smoke and said, "I've got your first
record."

"Well, that's not really my first record, honey," he started to explain. "There was one—"

"That's the one I mean, Ralph Collins."

Whenever he found anyone who'd heard and remembered that
old Ralph Collins' "B & O Lines" he felt so grateful his eyes would
mist. He thought he would have to kiss Elizabeth right now right
at the point where her honey-colored shoulder faired into her
honey-colored throat right in front of everybody. Instead he said,
"No kiddin'!"

"No kiddin'," Elizabeth said.

Touched again! Careful! Easy came by with the jug of red so
blessedly he didn't have to move except half a step forward away
from the fire. He watched Elizabeth watching Clary, thin-legged
and buttless in his black skipants, going on around the room filling
the glasses. She said, "We've—I've got another one too. Are there
more coming?"

"One just getting pressed."

"I liked the first one." She pulled on her cheroot. "My babysitter liked the John Henry one better. She buys more records than I
do too."

"Big with the babysitters."

"What's the new record?"

"One side's Mexican stuff. Very big now. Second side's different
things, more what I like to do. One side bread and one side what
I've got to say. A folk-rock I wrote myself and I've got my fingers
crossed on, and a 'John Hardy' I'm real happy with."

"I've got Leadbelly's 'John Hardy' on a funny little offbrand
record. It has a fantastic guitar passage in it."

"I love you! I can't handle twelve strings like Leadbelly or I'd've
done it even more like that one," he said, laughing. Elizabeth
looked at him with her steady eyes and the cheroot oddly not out

of place between her lips. She removed it and turned to tap the ash into the fireplace.

"You sound as though you don't always get to do the songs you want to do," she said.

"Maybe half and half." He made a long face. "There's been some give and—you know—*take*. There's a thing they say, square records don't fit too many machines. You've got to round the corners off. It's a kind of three-way thing. My agent's in it—he's supposed to be looking out for my image. This image bit is very powerful right now."

Elizabeth nodded, still looking at him, but all at once he knew she wasn't thinking about any of that; he could read written right on her frowning, serious face that she was thinking about the Liberty Singers, and his fine mental hard-on faded away, gone.

"What was all that singing on the phone tonight when we first came over here?" she asked.

He laughed, not too bad a laugh either; he could be phony full throttle. He said, "My agent says I give away twice what I make. I mean, I like to help out with these kids—they call them shut-ins; they're crippled with polio or muscular dystrophy or something, and some of these kids aren't going to get out of their rooms till they die. I go to see them, and this one I call up every night to talk to him, sing him a song. It's important to them."

"I think that's wonderful," Elizabeth said, sounding as though she meant it, *but*. Maybe she did mean it; just because she had "B & O Lines" and that old ten-inch Leadbelly didn't have to mean she was thinking Frisco Daley and the Liberty Singers.

They stood there with nothing to do but flick ashes into the fireplace and sip wine. Elizabeth looked over at Maeve, who had come out of the kitchen. "That's an old friend of Chuck's too?" she said.

"Maeve? Yay."

"He seems to be in love with her with quite a lot of abandon. I would have thought he'd be more of a butterfly, flitting from flower to flower."

"Oh, everybody was always in love with Maeve."

"She looks familiar," Elizabeth said.

He didn't feel like telling her Maeve was the Mariachi Girl. Of course he had known this Elizabeth was an old chick of Easy's, he just hadn't *realized* it. When you got to thinking you were pretty great stuff on the guitar it was a good idea to listen to something like that break of Leadbelly's in "John Hardy," and when you got to thinking you were the great lover it was a good idea to realize Easy Clary had probably been there first. He was surprised to find it didn't seem to matter much; he was beginning to feel horny again. He grinned at Elizabeth; as she had said, they had their little arrangement. Nothing had fazed that yet.

Clary came back with the jug. He solved the problem of Elizabeth's height by squatting on the floor before her with the jug between his knees. "You left the Guru?" he said.

"Yep."

Looking up at him, Clary said, "They were my best friends in college. We worked out the principles of living together."

"Now we're working out the principles of living apart," Elizabeth said.

"You're getting a divorce, huh?" he said. "Tough on kids."

"Maybe," Elizabeth said curtly.

She and Clary were looking at each other in a communicating way, Elizabeth leaking smoke out of the corners of her mouth and her little bitey teeth showing in not quite a smile. He said uncomfortably, "Well, I'll move along and talk to—"

She put a hand on his arm. "No, don't go." She said to Easy, "Did you really kill Goliath? I came up here to have my faith rebuilt, and all I find is you rather sickeningly in love."

What was queer was that after she'd said it Easy actually did look a little sick, something happening in his eyes, a tightening at the corners of his mouth. Easy rubbed a hand nervously over the back of his head.

Elizabeth said, "Actually I wanted to see if you were still hanging in there."

"Still hanging in there."

"Sticking to principles?"

"Second Principles," Easy said.

Elizabeth glanced over toward Maeve, standing very straight-backed with brown smooth arms hanging at her sides as she talked to Badbody and Isobel. "Well, the trouble is that Shelley didn't stick to *any* principle," she said. "Ours or his or anybody's."

It came to him finally what principles they were talking about. "What's this, First Personal Principles?" he said.

Elizabeth looked surprised.

"He's one of us," Clary told her. "Southern California branch."

"I knew you reminded me of something," she said, but she looked irritated. "But you had your corners rounded off, you said. That's what happened to my husband—he let them round the corners off until there wasn't anything left but the hole in the middle. What do *you* say, Miss Lonelyhearts?" she said to Easy.

Easy stood up. Elizabeth looked small but very tough with the cheroot between her lips, like an old pol, her arms folded over her big-girl's cans. "I guess what I want is to be told I've done the right thing," she said when Easy didn't answer.

"I guess I have to tell you you've done the right thing then," Easy said. He didn't sound as though he really thought so.

"Well, of course we made a mess of ourselves," she said. "I mean we did so very badly *compared*. You're so goddam lucky!"

She said it loudly, and in a sudden silence as a record quit and another dropped, everyone looked over at them. "Whoops!" Elizabeth said.

" It wasn't luck," Easy Clary said. "I go out to slingshot practice every day."

Elizabeth snorted, then she broke up, laughing. When she had sobered she said, "Anyway, as we know, Shelley was never much good on First Personal. So we did the Schweitzer Second—I mean, all out for liberal causes, anyway—Ban the Bomb, Fair Play for Cuba, marching with the coloreds, the whole route. And I'll tell you First Principlers it is a really tiresome route." She took the cheroot from her mouth and frowned at the glowing tip before she said, "Though I do believe in it all still. But he never did. He was just going through the motions. And do you know why he was? Because he was looking for something to fill up that hole-in-the-middle so he could pretend it's not there."

She was talking in that can't-stop way he had found women getting divorces often talked. Easy was looking worried.

"Are you hollow, Clary?" she asked suddenly.

"Maybe I was getting that way."

"And you have your shut-ins, don't you?" she said to him.

"Sure," he said, seeing what she meant.

"Maybe shifting into second's a thing that comes with getting older," Easy said.

She looked from one to the other of them fiercely. She said through her teeth, "You're kidding yourselves. *That's* all that comes with getting older. It takes a *man* to really know how to kid himself," she said. "I *know*. I know what Second Personal is too. Give up on yourself so you can busybody on somebody else. I may be the Guru myself now, and I tell you the Second Personal is Giveupsville. I mean, even *he* couldn't kid himself he loved unfortunate people. If they're unfortunate they're just that much harder to love. But the *hell* you can love humanity if you don't love people, and the hell you can love anybody at all if you don't love yourself, which is right back to the good old, solid old First Personal again. Hell, I suppose he couldn't help it," she said with a gesture as though she were throwing something over her shoulder. "I suppose it just wasn't in him. But beware!" she said, this time only to Easy Clary. She said it as though she meant it.

"Maybe you're being a little tough on the Guru," Easy said.

"Maybe," Elizabeth said. "But he fooled me so. And you too— you were just as big a sucker. Do you know why I'm so mad? Just *furious*. It's not the twelve years. But he made me a bad person. Second Personal cuts two ways, and revenge is just as Second Personal as self-sacrifice or whatever it is. He made me feel guilty for him. I mean, if you Second Personal for the whole goddam colored race because you feel guilty because of what your own race or anyway your goddam husband did to them, then that's really bad." She stopped and with a quick motion flung the butt of her cheroot into the fireplace.

She was a lot of girl, but she was talking too much.

"Anyway, *I'm* the Guru now," she finished.

There was a moment of silence under the beat of the music. Looking very troubled, Easy said, "I don't know what you did that was wrong."

"Ha!" Elizabeth said. "Just believe me and beware the Second Personal, lover. You're wanted," she said, and Easy turned.

Maeve was standing in the kitchen doorway, slim as a boy, her shining hair falling slickly inside one shoulder. She was pointing at Easy; catching his eye, she beckoned.

"The spaghetti king is needed in the kitchen," Easy said and departed with the wine jug.

"Ha!" Elizabeth said again, but sounding as though she was winding down. She smiled at him. "What a bore for you, John Henry."

Leaning down so that his face was close to hers, he said, "What'd you do you thought was so bad?" He thought she probably wasn't going to answer, and probably he shouldn't pursue it and endanger their arrangement, but for some reason it had grabbed him as very important that he know. He said, "I mean, what'd you mean you Second Personaled for the colored race?"

"I ran off to Mexico with a nigger painter," Elizabeth said. "It seemed important at the time."

7: J.D. Daugherty

PROBABLY HE shouldn't have come. He was worried about that fat barman the union had sent out stealing him blind. Anyway, these people were nothing to him any more. Maeve was nothing to him. He had come because Clary's parties were almost always talked about for a long time afterward. There was the time somebody pissed on his wife on Clary's porch, the time somebody got bitten and stitches had to be taken, the time three cars piled up together on the ice at the bottom of the road; and there had been so many philosophical discussions about Life and Sex and Principles and all the other skibum crap that he thought if he had to listen to any more of it he would bite an arm being waved at him, or piss on some fuckoff on the porch, too, probably Clary.

Probably he should have brought Peggy. He had told Clary she had to stay home with the baby, though he knew she would have loved to come. She was always whining that they never went anywhere. But he didn't trust her since he had been shook to realize she wouldn't mind smoking marijuana if somebody would produce some, and Clary had the kind of friends who would be able to produce it. He didn't want Peggy to fall for Clary's skibum jazz either, as he himself had once stupidly fallen for it. If Peggy got hooked on Clary's Principles she would crab about the way he was even more than she already did.

He was standing with a cheap glass of cheap red in his hand next to the couch where Isobel Macklin was talking to Badbody and Rody Bliss. Tim Soderburg stood at the other end of the couch with a cheap glass of cheap red in his hand, like the other book-end. Maeve and Clary were in the kitchen making spaghetti, or just making it, and Hollywood Boy was over in front of the fireplace with the stacked Jew-girl. Dickie Macklin was bent over, his hands in his hip pockets, examining the titles of the records in the case. Clary went for rock-and-roll big; the music, at least, made him feel at home.

Finally Dickie wandered over toward him. He felt close to panic; everything today had been dripping with Macklin. But he and Dickie couldn't just stand there pretending each one was alone.

"So how's the ski-resort business?" he asked, not quite looking at Dickie, and Dickie, not quite looking at him, said it was as good as could be expected. They talked about Dancer. He fed Dickie the questions to keep Dickie running on about everything, and from Dickie's answers he got the impression that Dickie wasn't too happy with the way Badbody ran things, as a lot of people weren't, but didn't want to say so straight out.

Dickie said, "Tim's been talking to Mother about opening the other side of Dancer with an aerial tramway."

He whistled. "Big money!" Badbody would be against that one; Badbody had been think-small since there had been a little recession that had scared some area operators. He glanced at Badbody, sitting between Rody and Isobel Macklin, smoking his pipe. Badbody kept his job by servicing his boss, he was sure of that; immediately he snarled at himself for thinking the same sort of crap about Dickie's mother he had loud-mouthed about Dickie's father. He was the world's greatest contortionist, his foot in his mouth and ass on his brain. "I guess aerial trams are all the thing now," he said.

"Yes, I think so," Dickie said in the stiff, far-off way he had, and the conversation gave up. How could Dickie even stand to talk to him? But it had been a long time ago.

John Henry's girl friend said, in a silence when a record quit, ". . . so goddam lucky!"

When everybody looked at her she clapped a hand to her mouth and said, "Whoops!" Clary was standing with her and Hollywood, holding the jug of wine.

"Lucky!" Rody Bliss said with a laugh, as though it fitted right into the conversation she and Isobel were having across Badbody. "Lucky I had a chance to work for him," she was saying, "though it wasn't for very long." So they were talking about Dick Macklin.

He and Dickie, both aware of it, gazed at each other woodenly as the music began to beat again.

He turned toward the conversation on the couch as being better than standing there strung-up with Dickie. Isobel had her hands folded together in her lap, Rody a bright, tight expression on her round face. "Everybody said he'd changed so much toward the end," Rody said.

He watched the flesh beneath Isobel's eyes turn pink. She looked offended and at the same time as though she was going to cry. Instead she laughed, maybe needing to prove she could. "Oh, I don't think so," she said. She stared at the kitchen door for a moment before she went on, "Dick was the most complete man—he went at life head on. He was never afraid, and he never had to boast about his triumphs the way most men do. It was only that toward the end he was so worried about money, you see."

He hated to see people come unzipped from too much liquor. He didn't want to listen to Isobel talking about Dick Macklin in this compulsive voice, and he was afraid she was going to start crying. To make even more of a strain, Maeve came out of the kitchen just then and joined them. She stood, brushing a hand up and down her bare arm, looking at Isobel.

"Of course he was very distressed by the lack of capital," Isobel said as though she'd been addressing Maeve all along. "I remember he said that money was—was filth from the past that strangled the present."

No one said anything to that.

"There was a dream he used to have," Isobel went on. "He was riding a bicycle along a road that got steeper and steeper until it actually"—she illustrated with a tilt of her white hand—"leaned over backward. He had to pedal faster and faster. He said it wasn't actually a nightmare because he always made it, but he was never *sure* he was going to make it."

Staring down at her, he felt his breath burn in his nostrils. It was as though she were telling him his own dream. His dream was so like that, not a hill and not a bicycle, but running heavy and slow, and people—though he wasn't sure they even were people —snatching at him and pounding after him. They never seemed to catch him before he jerked awake, but he was sure he was never

going to get away. He wondered suddenly if Dick Macklin had
been having Internal Revenue trouble.

Maeve said in her light voice, "Once he told me you didn't
know how to live until you almost died."

There was another silence. Badbody said, "Of course he'd
changed, Belle, but maybe not from lack of capital. I remember an
account of a political prison in Hungary. When the prisoners realized there was a revolution going on outside, many of them
wanted to break out immediately. There was terrible fighting between those who wanted to escape and those who wanted to wait
and see. Afterward it was found that no one who fought to break
out was over forty, and no one fighting on the side of caution was
under forty."

The corners of Isobel's mouth turned contemptuous. It looked
for a moment as though she were going to cut Badbody down. He
was aware of tunes being whistled behind the phony fronts here.

Rody stepped into a bad moment and said, "Well, Dick Macklin certainly made things happen."

Maeve stood like a statue, listening, her arms hanging at her
sides, her face stiff and pinched-looking.

Isobel said, "Yes. Yes, he did. So much so that it really did
occur to me—because he could always make things happen—that
he actually might have made that avalanche come down—" She
stopped on a harsh hiss of breath from Maeve.

"Oh, no, he didn't," Maeve said. "I can assure you of that."

He felt the hairs at the back of his neck prickle. And Maeve's
eyes turned slowly toward him. In them was some kind of triumphant accusation or knowledge he didn't understand. Without another word she turned and disappeared into the kitchen again,
leaving a sick silence behind her in the powerful beating of music
from Clary's hi-fi.

8: Captain Easy

RHYTHM AND BLUES were jumping on the hi-fi as he came back into the kitchen with the half-empty gallon of wine. Crouching, swinging, and finger-snapping, he grinned at Maeve, who stood holding the pan of spaghetti sauce. He felt foolish and desperate.

She tossed her hank of fair hair and smiled back at him, somewhat preoccupied, or maybe it was embarrassment. "Shall I put this on now?"

Nodding, he put down the wine bottle and turned on a burner for her. He continued to sway and snap his fingers at her, as though the music had turned him on. Why didn't he cut his losses and stop?

"But how can we seat ten?" Maeve asked.

"No problem. Do you want to dance before I set up the tables? It's now or never."

"I'm just too—" She made tight motions with her hands and shoulders, indicating something.

He extended a finger to part her blond bangs, revealing the small scar on her forehead. "Just the one flaw," he said.

"I'm afraid not, but thank you. I like your house, Easy."

"Take it, it's yours," he said. Just the one flaw! The full freight of what he had said hit him, almost sank him. "*Mi casa es suyos,*" he said.

"*Tuyos,*" Maeve said, in her voice the disheartening preoccupation.

There was an unpleasant rush of blood to his head as he bent to get out the big spaghetti pot. He put the pot in the sink and turned on the tap.

"Can't I do something?" Maeve asked.

"There's salad."

"I'm very good at salad."

He got two heads of romaine from the refrigerator, viewing with despair his hesitation to remark that two heads were better than one, the corny joke produced out of his self-consciousness and in turn censored by it. The self-consciousness was the shameful thing; he hadn't been able to see Maeve yet for looking at himself looking at her.

He brought out the oil, vinegar, and condiments, lit the oven, and then took the card tables into the living room to set them up. When he returned to the kitchen Maeve was breaking lettuce into the salad bowl. The ticking of the alarm clock on the shelf over the sink was audible.

The motion with which Maeve swung her hair as a preliminary to turning her head pleased him. As she started to speak he bent to kiss her mouth, his fingers gripping her bare arms, tense with the effort of keeping his thoughts from affecting his senses. Her lips responded to his, but her eyes were open while they kissed; Maeve was watching him too.

"Tomorrow we're going up to find some powder," he said when he released her. "Even if it doesn't snow tonight. I know places nobody else but Tim knows. We'll get your confidence back."

"It's just that I don't want to break a leg," Maeve said.

"Did you know that skiers heal the fastest? They're usually back skiing in ten months, but it takes industrial fractures twice that long to—" He had thought to reassure her, but listening to what he was saying he felt a cool film of sweat on his forehead, cool trickles down his sides. "It's because skiers want to get back skiing," he finished hurriedly.

Maeve measured oil into the salad bowl and began turning the leaves with the wooden spoon. Water ran into the pot in a thin, noisy stream.

"What have you been doing summers, Easy?" she asked.

"I usually carpenter in June and July to get a stake together. Then whatever—but all that's going to change."

Her eyes turned toward him questioningly.

"Now you're back," he continued. "I thought this summer I might do whatever you wanted to do."

"That sounds like a proposition," Maeve said, smiling.

"I was thinking of the compromise we talked about some years back."

She uncapped the bottle of vinegar but put it down without measuring any into the bowl. She raised a hand to comb her hair with her fingers. He told himself he must think only about her, what she was feeling, what she needed, concern himself only with her and not continue to examine and re-examine himself.

He grinned maniacally at her. "I thought it might be time for our careers to run along together for a while," he said. "I could take the manager's job over at Bojangle, if that sounds good. They've been after me."

"Oh?" Maeve said faintly, and he realized how minor a position was the administration of the Bojangle Peak Ski Area, how little and how late. He wished he had not mentioned it. He wished he could stop talking about time. How many more gaffes was he going to perpetrate? Courage was grace under pressure.

He lifted the pot of water onto the stove while Maeve silently tossed the salad. Out in the living room a record finished, and in the silence before another began he could hear the voices of his guests. Maeve went to stand in the doorway. Then she went out. When she had gone he leaned heavily against the sink, breathing as though he'd been running.

He stared in hatred at the clock ticking on the shelf above the sink, reminding him of his rule never to make love with a watch on, and reminding him how late it was. Maybe it was too late. Maybe by now the First-Personal-Principle curse of all that polyunsaturated self-concern had hardened the tender arteries of the heart, corroded tiny vital circuits, so it was impossible now to shift his attention outward instead of inward.

When Maeve came back in he put his arm around her, and they stood before the stove gazing down at the pot in which the water did not boil. She felt very tense under his arm.

"I just heard a funny thing," she said.

"What was that?"

"Isobel saying Dick had cut the avalanche himself. She said she actually thought that!"

He blew his breath out in a sigh. She was back on the subject of Macklin's death; momentarily it relieved some of the weight of his own failure. Leaning against him suddenly, she whispered, "Did J.D. and Isobel have an affair? Were they having an affair?"

"*What?*"

"It would explain—"

"*J.D.?*"

"He's the only one I can't account for," Maeve said. "And he did schuss the Spoon and try to kill Dick just the day before."

He felt helpless in the face of her tenacity. He released her to make sure the gas was turned up all the way under the pot of water. "Maeve, you've got to stop this."

She raised her hands to lay them over her temples, fingers burrowing in her hair. "I know it," she said calmly, reasonably.

As though humorously protesting, he said, "You're making me jealous of Macklin!"

"So was José."

"José?"

"Though he didn't know it," Maeve said and added, "José hired the mariachis."

"Oh."

She shook her pale hair, and he thought she laughed. It was as though this came over her from time to time like a fever, and broke like a fever; as though now she could detach herself from her delirium long enough to laugh at it, while knowing it would return.

"Think about me," he said. "Think about skiing the powder."

She smiled at him with what seemed real affection for the first time this evening. He said, "Think about—" He said, "Love," instead of what he had started to say, the coarse expression censored like the corny joke.

"I was thinking about Dick when I fell today," Maeve said. "I crossed my tips when I looked back over my shoulder—"

"Serves you right!" he broke in. "Think about *now! I'm* now! All that about Macklin is past and doesn't matter. Only now matters!" When he stopped she was smiling at him, but her eyes had become shallow and inattentive. Angrily he said, "Or you might think about the possibility that Isobel's right."

She stepped back, her eyes widening, and at least he had her attention. "I don't mean he committed suicide," he said. "Just that when he saw the cornice coming down he said okay."

"I don't understand."

"You're ready to die when you've used up living," he said, sweating, shaky-voiced. "The only tragedy about dying is when you've left chunks of your life lying around you never got to use. I think Macklin might've thought he'd used up all the best parts of his."

She was shaking her head again. "No, not—"

"You have to stop pretending Macklin's ghost is haunting you, Maeve!"

Her cheeks flushed in hectic stripes, she looked angry and embarrassed, or maybe only frightened.

"Your business is *your* life and you'd better tend to business. Listen!" he said, speaking rapidly so she would not be able to break in. "People spend their lives beavering away at something so at age sixty-five they can stop beavering and start living. But it's too late then and they can't, and it's so damned wrong, putting off starting living till tomorrow and tomorrow and tomorrow. It never comes!" How easily the words rolled off his tongue, how practiced, how facile; for the first time they seemed to him merely facile. For the first time he felt not merely a monument but a fraud, and more of a fraud than he had admitted to Badbody. What he was losing here was the only meaningful battle of his life.

But he had to keep talking, didn't he? "It's wrong putting off living till some tomorrow that never comes. For any reason. It's just an excuse to get out of living, Maeve. Living instead of dying is what we have to do."

"But that kind of living is what I've been doing all this time, Easy," she said, her face normal again.

Unable to meet her eyes, he watched the heavy rise and fall of her breast, thinking that now she would compare her own living of all this time with his, as once Dick Macklin had made such a comparison. Instead she said, "Yes, I believe you though. I must believe that."

"*Have* to!"

"But you don't know! You say the past doesn't matter, what happened to Dick doesn't matter. But it does! It's infecting me, you see. You see, there has to be some hope, and it's the only way I can"—her voice faded, became small and dry—"I don't know how to say it," she said, her hand to her breast and the knuckles of her tan hand turned white with pressure.

"I don't know how you know about being haunted," she went on in the faded voice. "It's that I saw what was done and tried to bury it. Repress it. And it's the way psychiatrists say, when you try to repress something like that it infects you. So it's been infecting me deep down inside where I— And you see, the only way to stop it is to find out who—" She stopped.

He was suffering with the sense and nonsense of what she was saying. She stared at him with her dark eyes that weren't really looking at him at all, and with a wisp of a sigh she said, "Oh, of course I know you can't undo anything. It's just that it's the only hope, and there has to be hope, doesn't there? I just have to do this first before I can—enjoy anything."

He saw that the fever was back. Her eyes glittered with it. "We are always arguing some goddam hopeless thing," he said, but he didn't think she even heard him.

She made a humming sound in her throat, as though she had tried to laugh and failed, terribly. "Oh, Easy, maybe I've had it," she whispered. "Maybe it's the way you said with Dick and I've lived all the good parts there are."

"Not you!" he said. He knew how false he sounded; the fraud. Why couldn't he give himself to her? Even to cause his arm to move, his hand to grip the cool flesh of her shoulder, had to be willed.

"There's something else," Maeve said, glancing quickly toward the doorway behind her. "The things Dick said to me the night we were paid—he must have known you'd come in the window. Did *you* tell him, Easy?"

"Christ, no! But if you have to feel guilty about something, that's a lot more reasonable than thinking you saw somebody cut the avalanche down on him. That's just crazy!" He caught her other shoulder with his other hand and held her facing him. "Maeve, what about *you* and *me?*"

She closed her eyes. Slowly she shook her head, her body heavy between his hands as though he were holding her up. The tips of her teeth appeared to dent her lower lip. "No," she whispered. "No, I try so hard to be rational, but— No," she said, shaking her head again. "You have to love me, you see; you only think I'm crazy."

"I think you're crazy but I love you!" He tried to clown it through, but he knew he had lost and he couldn't even measure the extent of his defeat. He shook her in his agony, but she didn't open her eyes.

"No, I can tell you're pretending," she said. "God knows, I can tell. It's all in your mind," she said and managed to smile.

"Let's not talk—talking's the bad part!" he caught her to him, pressing his mouth fiercely to hers, straining his body against hers, as though by rough contact to prove it was not all in his mind, that there was something still. But he had to realize at last that she was right, there was nothing at all here for him, and there was nothing for her either.

9: *Badbody*

HE SAT with Isobel Macklin on the leather couch, like an attend-ant lord, half listening to her while he watched Tim and Dickie in conversation, Dickie with his hands in his hip pockets, Tim punc-tuating a statement with jabs of a forefinger. He knew they were not conspiring against him, but he knew too that in the end Tim, who wanted new lifts, and Dickie, who wanted a more efficiently run resort, in combination with Isobel married to Bart Weaver, would mean the end of him at Dancer. It was not that they were conspiring against him as much as it was that all things, now, con-spired against him.

Once he had congratulated himself that his position as manager of Dancer Peak Ski Area was the ideal coign of vantage from which to contemplate life and the world. But the contemplation had become increasingly diseased, increasingly frightened, increas-ingly desperate, and now he had to face the fact that what he had considered his contemplative height was instead a hole in which he hid in fear and trembling. He had realized this once before, the last time he had seen Maeve, the night of the dead dog.

In the years between he had been able to convince himself that he ruled this little kingdom. Now, with Maeve returned con-demned, he must realize that he was only suffocating in his chosen prison. Yet the prospect of being freed, evicted, was so terrifying that his mind now was continually filled with fantastic images of himself cast out naked upon the blasted heath of the downbelow world with which he no longer had the slightest acquaintance; of himself bent with defeat and age clerking in a haberdashery, filling gas tanks, cringing before cigar-smoking employers, slinking along skid row among filthy winos, incarcerated in a veterans' hospital where there were high cribs instead of beds and crazed paupers screaming. That he had saved a good deal of money eased nothing, as though the money vanished with the means that had accumulated it.

Though the Observer had lost his irony, his objectivity, had, indeed, lost any claim to the name he had given himself, still he was fascinated by his own mental process, whereby, terrified of losing his position, the only solution seemed to be to resign it. He knew this was the reflection of an even more morbid paradox in which the suicide feared not life but death.

Since last night when Isobel had told him about Maeve's cancer, he had been unable either to look at Maeve directly or to keep his eyes away from her, as though he must search always for the signature of death upon her but could not bear to confront the mark of the beast. Her disease proved almost too perfectly the theory he had outlined to Clary. Become the Mariachi Girl, or even before that, she must have seen she was on the downward path, seen life as he himself had come to see life, as tilting always more steeply down. Her great affairs were past, the present did not hold much, the future nothing. Left were only small encounters with men, each less satisfying, shabbier, more humiliating, and uglier than the last. So, within her womb, death had been conceived.

By the same theory he himself was condemned. Sitting beside Isobel Macklin, he felt the realization like pain filling his chest, filling his body, as though his heart were bursting. He held his breath and the pain receded. For the first time he was brought face to face with the monster at the bottom of the path, and he did not flinch and turn away. Confronted inescapably by death, he began to breathe deeply, very conscious of the sensation of breathing, of the opening and closing of his lungs, of the raw rush of air through his nostrils, of life.

He found himself closely watching the obliquely narrow kitchen doorway. Maeve and Clary were in there; once or twice he had caught glimpses of them, although for all he knew they had retired to the bedroom and would reappear with nature smiling on the lineaments of gratified desire. The easy rider's talents were at last turned to a great cause. He was surprised at the extent of his own jealousy. "Why you?" he had asked Clary, who had not even considered an answer necessary.

At that moment Maeve appeared in the doorway, bringing a red-and-white-checked cloth to spread on the card tables Clary had unfolded earlier. This time he watched her in motion, spreading the cloth, smoothing it, the toss of her head to flick the lock of hair back; a beautiful woman misting in his glasses. He remembered when he had been unable to take his eyes off her because she had been bursting with youth and health and good looks, all that juice and all that joy. She had said she could marry someone and stay at Dancer, and perhaps she had meant him. But they had gone their separate ways, and now she was back condemned, as all of life was condemned by its own mortality.

Beside him Isobel said in a quiet voice, "Do you remember when we sat in the mango tree and watched Roosevelt drive up to the Pali?"

"His face was so red."

"Such a little while ago," Isobel said as together they watched Maeve Herron return to the kitchen; and he knew that what Isobel meant was that they had been young such a short time ago, and now were middle-aged, and soon must be old.

"Do you remember how long the years were when we were that age?" he said. "That was before inflation—in those days a year was a year, not a month."

"I think there really is supposed to be something about time moving faster because of the body consuming itself faster," Isobel said, who had always been braver than he.

He took off his glasses to polish the dampness from them, and she said, "My years have been fuller than yours, Brad."

"I suppose they have been, Belle." He was not offended. He looked from the kitchen doorway to the plump girl, Mrs. Steinberg, who was standing with John Henry, smoking a cheroot. She had a becoming streak of white in her hair; was it the Mark? Rody, Dickie, Tim, and J.D. stood in a circle of conversation, J.D. resting a buttock on the back of a folding chair; all those athletic bodies consuming themselves a little faster every year?

Isobel sighed. "So many memories here. Perhaps he really loved her, Brad. Should I have let him go?"

It was a question that did not signify, nor did she wait for an answer. "I think he just loved what she represented," she went on. "He said a man had to be free or he wasn't a man. My God! I didn't consider that I was buying him! He said he could have been a bankrupt *man*. But he would have hated that. I couldn't let him lose Dancer, could I?"

"Of course not, Belle."

"I never thought I'd done anything to *him*," she said. "I only thought he had done things to me."

He nodded inattentively.

"Poor Maeve," Isobel said. "Perhaps I should have let him go away with her and be free—pretend to be free. I think he would have come back if—"

She stopped as the record on the machine finished, and the changer turned itself off with a snap. In the silence the wind sounded like a siren running down.

"Another storm coming in," Tim said in a cheerful voice.

Clary appeared with the wine bottle to fill the glasses on the table, and the guests began to gather expectantly. Maeve came out of the kitchen bearing plates. He watched her face in profile as she spoke to Rody, smiling, warm brown, thin, but not visibly haunted by the terrible consciousness.

Pointing to the enlarged blurred photograph of Easy Clary in the powder, one of a series that had been taken that first winter, Mrs. Steinberg said, "Is that you, Clary?"

"That's me at the top of the Superchute."

"So steep!"

"They're trick photographs," John Henry said, laughing. "Illusions!"

"I'd love to do that," Mrs. Steinberg said. "Could I do that, Clary? I used to ski at Sugar Bowl, didn't I?"

"You did."

"You can do it!" John Henry said. "And I'm just the old-time ski instructor that can show you how. Right, Ease?"

"Right," Easy said. He disappeared into the kitchen and brought back a steaming dish of spaghetti. Sauce, salad, and garlic bread were produced—the regular Clary-party repast. Maeve dealt with the seating arrangements, assigning Dickie, Rody, and J.D. to one side of the table, and Isobel, Tim, and Mrs. Steinberg to the other. He found himself seated next to Maeve at the foot of the table. John Henry and Easy sat at the other end.

At dinner Easy was not the evangelist of the Pleasure-Principle he had been last night, and Maeve was very quiet, but John Henry kept the table amused. Mrs. Steinberg helped, and Isobel seemed in a good mood. Dinner was over and the plates cleared away when he was moved to propose a toast to the Great Past Time. "And to Maeve, it's spirit."

"Hear, hear!" Dickie said. There were murmurs, glasses were raised. Next to him Maeve tossed back her hair with the hitching motion and smiled at him.

"No, here's to *now*," Clary said almost rudely, leaning forward in a kind of downhill position, wrist extended, glass tilted in his lax hand.

"Now?" J.D. said.

"Now."

"Yes, I think I would like to drink to now, too," Isobel said.

Smiling at him, Maeve said, "Thank you for your toast." He saw something happen in her eyes, which, while still looking at him, were not focused on him any more. She said in a bright, artificial voice, "Those great old times." She turned away. "Remember the time you schussed the Spoon, J.D.?"

J.D. grinned a little.

"And almost hit Dick," Maeve said.

Everyone seemed to flinch at the same moment. He was struck by how completely miserable Easy Clary looked.

"You almost did hit him, J.D.," Maeve said. "It really did look as though you were trying to kill him."

J.D. attentively watched his fingers turning his half-full wine glass. Lips pursed, an eyebrow raised, he turned to glance at Easy.

Easy leaned back in his chair and said, "Maeve thinks somebody cut the avalanche down on Macklin."

John Henry's laugh was immediate and natural. No one else laughed.

He could feel the exact shape of his heart as it pumped. He pushed his chair back a foot, from which position he could watch Maeve's intense face as she sat with her back very straight, gazing down the table at J.D. All at once, miraculously, he could detach himself—must detach himself—and become the Observer again, watching the embarrassed, amazed, and pained faces around the table.

"What the hell, Maeve?" J.D. said.

"Well, you did, didn't you?" Maeve said in her clear voice. "You really did try to kill Dick the day before he—"

"Maeve!" Isobel said, and Maeve stopped.

J.D. leaned his chair back on its rear legs, squinting. Elizabeth Steinberg looked as though she thought this all must be part of some elaborate joke. Dickie opened and closed his mouth without speaking. Clary sat looking miserably down the table at Maeve.

"You're kidding," J.D. said. Outside the sound of the wind rose to a dull climax, wound down again. "You're kidding, Maeve," J.D. said.

In a whisper Rody said, "Tim, could somebody do that?" He didn't hear Tim's reply, making his own answer. Of course it was impossible; no one by any conceivable intricacy of premeditation could hope to start an avalanche, in a bowl where there were six other skiers, designed to kill only the hated one; no spur-of-the-moment way either; no way, by stopping perhaps just a little more strongly than necessary out of a murderous opportunism, so selectively to start the slip of snow. He could dismiss it from his mind, staring at Maeve in fascination.

She looked almost sexually excited, her tan cheeks slashed with pink. "I saw someone," she said as though now she was confiding in J.D. "Easy won't believe it, but I saw someone skiing across above me. And he *stamped* to—"

"Well, for Christ sake, *I* wasn't above you," J.D. said. "I was—" He turned to John Henry as though for support, his neat blond brows knitting together. "There wasn't anybody up above you," he said in a rough voice. "You were up by the trees, for Christ sake!"

"You hated him," Maeve said. "Everybody knows that." As though she had practiced this for dramatic effect, she leaned forward and said, "You can't deny you skied down the Spoon and tried to kill him." But her voice was shaking, and the pink was fading from her cheeks. "You—"

"Yeah, well, what about Easy almost killing him under the lodge?" J.D. said, balancing his chair on its back legs.

The Observer looked at Easy, sitting now with his chin resting on his hand, eyes rolling toward J.D.

Maeve whispered, "What?"

J.D.'s fury showed through his taut control as he turned, stiffly casual, toward Easy. "Beat hell out of him in the basement that day, didn't you, Ease?"

"We had a little policy disagreement," Easy Clary said.

Maeve's eyes had a white-rimmed, scared look. The Observer realized that she was very near the edge.

Rody banged a hand on the table and said, "You mean you saw somebody *do* it, Maeve?"

"I saw him! He skied across and stopped and—"

"You didn't see *me*," J.D. said in the rough voice. He lost his balance and, as his chair fell backward, stood erect, reaching one hand back to catch the chair. He held his napkin balled in the other fist.

"You hated him!" Maeve cried despairingly. "He knew you hated him!"

"Every goddam one of us hated him! I'm sorry, Mrs. Macklin."

"I didn't," John Henry broke in firmly. "Not me, J.D. I mean, include me out, man."

"All right, you didn't hate him," J.D. said. He tossed the balled napkin up and caught it. Cords worked in his throat; his eyes suddenly appeared to be of different sizes. "You didn't have the guts to hate him, is all. You just include yourself all the way out of hating him, though. Go call up your cripple boys or something." J.D. looked around the table with his head lowered, eyes peering out from beneath blond eyebrows. "Bartenders get to know things just by keeping their goddam mouth shut," he said. "I know Easy clobbered Macklin because John Henry told me, and everybody knows about Tim plowing that Caddy of Macklin's. And how come you let everybody up on the mountain that morning, Tim?"

"Shut your mouth!" Tim said deep in his throat.

Maeve's face jerked toward Tim, and in his pity for her in her hysteria, the Observer could feel his detachment slipping. He tried to hold on to it as to his own sanity, but he was thinking that any toast to the Great Past Time at Dancer must, by protocol, be made first of all to Dick Macklin, furnishing forever the necessary acknowledgments to Dick's existence, paying him that tribute and that penance, who filled the past and occupied the present, and lay across the future like a barrier. But all at once, as Tim's chair scraped back and he saw the frantic hopelessness that filled

Maeve's face, his detachment was gone forever as he realized that she was almost insane with the knowledge of death. He caught her hand, and her hand, like straining strands of wire, clutched back at his.

Tim said in his deep voice, "What do you think you mean, why'd I let them up there?"

"How many times do you think you've been lushed to the eyeballs in the Loup Garou, moaning about it?" J.D. said.

"J.D., please!" Isobel said in a shocked voice. "Please, Tim. Maeve, this has to stop!"

"I guess I'd better be going," J.D. said. He made his way around the table, put on his loden coat, drew the gloves from the pockets and donned them. Easy was lighting a cigarette. J.D. looked pleased with himself as he opened the door. Falling snow was visible, drifting brightly in the porchlight, before the door was pulled shut.

Still holding Maeve's hand, he rose. "I'm going to take you home."

"Yes," Maeve said. "Please," she said, rising quickly to stand beside him, her fair head close to his shoulder.

Others began to get up; all, finally, except for John Henry, Mrs. Steinberg, and Easy Clary, who sat puffing on his cigarette and nodding to the thanks and good nights of his guests.

10: Timbal Khan

As HE CLOSED the door behind them the snow fell in cold feathery flakes on his burning face. He could hear the wind coming through the trees further up the mountainside, louder and louder, like a train coming, like a punishment; the wind hit in a harsh gust that stung his face. Rody stood beside him with her collar turned up around her ears, hands in pockets, the snow decorating her hair under the porchlight.

Flashes of embarrassment, of fury, of fear like falling came over him, intensified until he could hardly breathe, and then receded. He turned to look up at where the mountain was invisible in the dark and the storm. "I'm just as glad to get home early," he said. "I'll have to get up early tomorrow."

"Me too," Rody said.

There were two inches of snow on the railing already, blown into inward-leaning scallops like miniature cornices. With this wind from this quarter the cornices on top would be building fast.

J.D.'s tracks were already erased. He and Rody bent to the wind as they moved out to the Scout. Inside he pulled out the choke and turned the key; the engine spun and caught. The windshield-wipers brushed the snow from the glass in long, gangling strokes. Another burst of wind rocked the Scout on its springs. Rody sat two feet away from him with her arms hugged to her chest. Between them was the carton filled with his Santa Claus outfit. He turned on the heater. The fury and the fear came down on him again, like the wind, mixed with a suffocating anxiety, as though he must placate something that had been offended.

"You want to go somewhere for a drink?" he asked.

"Not to the Loup Garou."

"That son-of-a-bitch," he said, out of what seemed a need to show his rage. Rody's head turned toward him, but he couldn't see her features in the darkness.

"I guess I don't need a drink, Tim," she said.

"Okay."

"She wasn't joking, was she?" she said. "She thought he really did kill Dick Macklin. First I thought she was sick and then I thought *he* was."

He could take some comfort that probably everyone else had been similarly confused. He shifted into four-wheel drive but didn't put the Scout into motion, though he didn't know what he was waiting for. Many things from the past seemed to be hanging inside the metal cab in naked revelation of themselves. The heater was still blowing cold air.

"It doesn't make any sense though," Rody said.

"No."

"You couldn't just skin up to the Superchute and stamp to make the cornice come down and kill the one person out of a whole bunch you wanted to kill."

"No," he said. He had been stunned, first by Maeve's accusation and then by J.D.'s; now his mind began to function a little, and the feeling that the mountain was falling on him to fade. "No," he said firmly. Maeve, if she saw anything at all, saw someone make a sudden stop, which was a stamping motion to set ski edges anyway.

The evening had started so well. He had had a good talk with Isobel Macklin about an aerial tram; he had even mentioned to her his plan for a whole circus of lifts and trails on the northwest side of Dancer, to be served by the tram or a gondola, which would make Dancer the number-one ski resort in the Far West. Mrs. Macklin had been so flattering, so approving, so favorable, that he had begun to dream again of those great days of lift-building.

But sitting in the Scout with Rody, listening to the idling of the engine, the click of the wipers, and the whir of the heater, he could hear the groaning, creaking, turning of the Big Red One bullwheel above him. It didn't matter what those who had heard J.D. thought now; what mattered was that he could never again pretend to himself that he had not known what was going to happen. Somewhere in him had been the realization that they were going up the mountain to ski the powder in the Superchute, and he had not stopped them. So he had betrayed the mountain and, though he had not killed Macklin, he had let him die.

He let the Scout into gear. It rolled forward as he released the clutch, wiper blades clacking back and forth excitedly. Through the windshield, in the headlights, everything was cushioned, soft and white. Another flurry of wind sprayed a confusion of snow against the windshield, and in his mind's eye he could see the cornices building, the Superchute cornice swelling hugely. With the wind in this quarter they could build in moments, the snow swirling over the ridge and sucked down, the snow-thickened turbulence solidifying into a great stationary wave of snow before your eyes.

Warm air began to stream out around his ankles. "That's better," Rody said.

Silent and preoccupied, he drove slowly down to the main road, where the plow had cleared a lane. He was thinking of the charges he must make up before morning, of going up as soon as it was light to knock the slides down so that the mountain would be safe and clear when the lifts opened at ten o'clock. The eccentrically flashing orange light on top of the snowplow came in sight, and he followed the plow into the parking lot, where he halted beside Rody's VW.

"You'll be all right without chains if you start right home," he said.

"I'll make a deal with you, Saint Nick," Rody said. "You tell me your secret and I'll tell you mine."

"Huh?"

"Trade you guilty secrets."

"I don't know what you mean."

"Yes you do. J.D. hit you pretty hard in there. You're still— Come on, let's get together, huh?" Her voice was rough, teasing, yet serious.

His hands were sweating inside his gloves. He took off his gloves and laid them on top of the Santa Claus box. In his mind doors opened, slammed shut. He said, "You've been reading too many detective stories."

"I don't care what you did or didn't do," Rody said. "I just think it might be a good idea if we could tell each other something. Like trading hostages."

"But there isn't anything," he said. He was getting hold of himself again.

On the mountain now, invisible in the night, long, frail scarves were blowing out from the ridges, falling as the wind died, billowing out with a new gust. During the night, as the temperature fell, the lighter snow would blow into longer veils, float longer when the wind died. He counted over again the charges he must put together, where two blocks would be required, where three, where a face could be cut with skis. Only one stick of powder was needed for the Superchute cornice, if you knew just where to toss it. The cornice formed in a lateral concave shape, and, as it built up, a section of snow was squeezed down to form a kind of bracket holding up the shelf of the cornice. If a charge was set off just above or just below the bracket, the whole cornice fell almost in one piece.

Rody was sitting with her chin inside the collar of her coat. She said, "Well, I guess it's up to me to get us off dead center. I'll show first. I didn't go to bed with Dick Macklin."

His face burned again. "You don't have to say that."

"Yes I do," Rody said.

"It doesn't matter any more."

"It matters to me," Rody said. Her tough voice shook a little. "I've been hung on that lie as long as I'm going to be. He never even made a pass at me, Tim. Though I can't say I didn't want him to, the way things stood."

"What do you mean, the way things stood?"

"The way *you* stood, I mean."

He didn't understand, stunned once more. He could only shake his head.

Rody made an impatient sound. "I mean because I was so damn jealous of Maeve. You'd always been my fella, Tim."

He tried to remember how he had felt that night when she had told him she had been ravished by Macklin, going out into his old Jeep where he had taken her wildly on the cold seat, hitting top and bottom. So it had not been true, and it should matter to him that it was not true. But it was too long ago, and there was too much else that mattered.

Rody said, "It was all a stupid lie. I guess I just wanted you to think she wasn't the only hot stuff around. Then afterward there was no way I could get off the hook."

"Well, I'm glad you told me, Rody," he said.

"It was easy. Because I'm not jealous of her any more. I was looking at her tonight during all that hysterical business, and I realized—my God!—I was pitying her!"

"Pitying her?" he said stupidly.

"What goes up must come down. I came down early—Olympic athlete and all that—and got it over with. Now she's coming down and I'm sorry for her. Okay, your turn."

"There isn't anything," he said. Something caught in his throat and hurt there; he waited until it had gone. "There isn't anything, Rody," he said.

"No communication," she said. "Well, I tried." She opened the door and piled out.

"It's true, Rody!" he cried after her.

"Okay," she said, a formless shadow between him and the night behind her. "Well, Merry Christmas, Tim." She slammed the door. He could see her more clearly as she leaned over the VW's hood to brush off the snow. Then she disappeared into the little car.

In the all-wheel-drive Scout, he followed her out of the parking lot to make sure she got started home all right in the blizzard.

11: Elizabeth Steinberg

ISADORA DUNCAN, Constance Chatterley, and Fanny Hill were right and it was the only thing that was worth the candle. Waves crashed on the beach, the flames licked higher, planets wheeled and changed, stars fell, the earth moved. She lay with her eyes tightly closed, trying to keep the rockets from going off. So lovely. The wonder wasn't that the rockets were beginning to stir, it was that she was so happy and free and full of a kind of cool-headed appreciation, because there was nothing involved and so nothing was tied up; there was no guilt (well, not yet,) no pressure, anxiety, impatience. Oh, God, she really should take this up with truck drivers, casual men in bars, gamekeepers, guitar players. Why weren't guitar players more celebrated? Oh. No, wait. But it was only a minor soaring with a few thousand colored lights, only a go-on-forever, hold-your-breath little one. Oh, God, it would be all right just to go on like this, right—like—this, never stopping or going further either, never even bothering with stepping up the pace into the big-league, profound, all the way, washing-up-on-the-beach finishers with the full orchestra coming in and the drums hitting harder, and the rockets.

"Oh, God," she said aloud, partly to inform him she was loving it, and partly because the sound had come up in her throat to be shaped into words. "Ah, God!" Thank you, God, for this. Thank you, John Henry Collins. Oh, so lovely. The rockets were trying to break loose again. Ah, God, so happy. No afterward lying tense and arguing, fighting, hating, so that all the good was gone; just to go to sleep like babies and wake up and start all over again from the very beginning, God's Greatest Gift, with no revenges or punishments or martyrdoms necessary, just good, clean, never-stop-doing-that sex, first things first and no second things at all. "Ah, God!" she said, fingers in his hair, trying to keep her savage, straining fingers from hurting him, from smothering him. But enough of this shallow water-color pleasure now; well, all right, maybe not quite enough, just a little more; she was a born nymphomaniac, there was no doubt about it and how nice to know it. Oh! Lovely! But that was just about enough now, just about time—

She didn't know if she signaled or if he was perfectly timed and tuned to her, or just to women. When she got her breath back she said, "That was perfectly lovely."

He sat braced up on one arm, grinning down at her happily. He had a sallow-brown, taut-skinned torso with sprays of black hairs on his chest, which was rising and falling in the little light from the lamp on the bedside table. She smiled back into his smooth, oval, beardless-appearing face. Long, wavy hair grew close around his forehead in a pleasant scalloping. He looked pleased with himself, as he should be.

She wondered if he were as simple as he seemed, with his hipster talk and his muscular dystrophy shut-in boys. Don't try to find out! she warned herself. It was so much better if it could remain a casual, uncomplicated, uninvolved delight. She had never really looked closely at him before, and now she watched him rise and pull on black-and-white polka-dot pajama pants, pleased with his muscles and his taut skin. He padded barefoot over to the glass-topped table on which stood a bottle of scotch, a bucket of ice, a bottle of soda.

Hair tousled, he stood over the table, frowning and scratching his sides, "On the rocks, honey?"

"Just on the beach," she said. He grinned, dropping ice into the two glasses. He poured scotch, gauging the amount with one eye closed and the tip of his tongue appearing. He brought her her drink, lit two cheroots and gave her one. She lay naked, flattened and shameless, on the bed, taking a long drag on the cheroot. She blew smoke and propped herself on an elbow to sip her scotch.

"When'd you get back from Mexico, honey?"

"About three weeks ago."

"You and the colored guy broke up, huh?"

She nodded reluctantly, wary. She lay back with the cheroot gripped in her teeth.

"How was it?" John Henry Collins asked.

"Not as good as with you," she said, hoping it was what he wanted and they could get this little formality over with.

"I was wondering why you left your husband for a colored guy," he said, just asking, just wanting to know.

She supposed it was the male after-sex bonjour tristesse, the old cliché of questioning the prostitute; maybe, as far as men were concerned, afterward was the time for the letdown, for fighting, for questioning, for resolutions. But a clever woman ought to be able to steer past the depressed area without trouble, especially with John Henry Collins, yay! Though she suspected his simplicity was, at least in part, assumed, a pose, a defense. His simplicity was such as to make Chuck Clary seem complex by comparison, and yet at the same time she realized how much Clary shared that simplicity. And so she had chosen Shelley Steinberg as the more mature, the more complicated, the wiser, and had found he was only the better dissembler.

"I guess it was just some kind of social protest," she said.

He nodded, scowling. "You take it very big about deseg and all that, huh?"

Did they have to talk about race relations with their scotch, cheroots, naked bodies, and the smell of sex still powerful in the room? She remembered telling John Henry and Clary earlier in the evening that she was the Guru now. She pulled the sheet up to her waist.

"Sometimes," she said.

He sat there entangled with his whisky glass and his cheroot, looking as though he had wilted. He turned to present his bare back to her, as though he were addressing the bathroom door. "I guess you've been wondering about me," he said in a somber voice. "You probably wondered why I'm not down there with the Liberty Singers."

She was beginning to feel anxieties about getting home to the Jones' cabin, and the first frettings of guilt. She hadn't wondered why he wasn't with the Liberty Singers, a band of militant desegregationists and earnest young folk devotees who were getting a lot of publicity lately, organizing folk-singing workshops and giving concerts for Negroes in the Deep South.

"Do you think you ought to be?" she asked. Maybe there was no non-involvement possible except in rape.

He uttered a hollow laugh. "You dug my shut-ins were a cop-out right away, didn't you? And J.D. did. You know? I didn't even know it myself until tonight."

She wasn't sure what he was talking about, but she reproved herself for her impatience with the imprecision of his words. She must be serious with his seriousness. He was a human being, after all, not all joy and joy-making, but pain too. She remembered a definition of the sin against the Holy Ghost as the turning of human beings into things. So had she sinned trying to think of John Henry Collins as merely a happy stud. Was she going to find all men not merely boys, but frightened, guilty boys? Was this the wages of sin, the price paid for attempting to keep pleasure uninvolved, the punishment for her hubris in considering herself the Guru now? Had Adam put on his fig leaf in shame after sexual success with Eve, and Eve hers when the subject had turned out to be desegregation?

John Henry was gazing unhappily at the window. Dimly visible through the steamed glass snow was falling. A faint white band was snow piled on the balcony railing. She watched John Henry brush hair back from his forehead. It was so like a gesture of Christy's that something soft turned over inside her. All the world of men was human and in trouble, and the only sin was not to realize it in your selfishness, in your own fear.

She raised herself to sip scotch, which she didn't want. She leaned forward to put the glass down on the floor, leaned further forward to rest her cheek against his warm back.

"Tell me about it," she said.

His voice had an echo-chamber sound. "Oh, well—hell, it's so stupid."

"Tell me about it."

"Coward," he said. "Always been. Am. Always will be. Yay!"

"Because you don't want to go down to Mississippi and be beaten up by people much more cowardly than you are, who are insane with fear?"

"You dig. But—no, not just that. Of everything. Everybody. It was like what J.D. said with Macklin. Like a goddam puppy wagging its tail and licking around, hoping nobody will get mad at it. I mean, I've never been able to stand it to have anybody mad at me. Chicken! Well, sure, I'm afraid of those cats too. I mean, you see pictures of them. They're fat and they've got freckles and—" He stopped.

Her ear against his back, she could hear his heart beating. She had an awed sense of revelation, as though she had been chosen to hear the frightened heartbeat of the world of men. What was being asked of her, who was only a silly Pasadena girl, Stanford coed, married to a Jew, mother of two, who had just quit in utter defeat as mistress and status symbol to a phony, and frightened, Negro painter? Something was being demanded of her, and John Henry Collins was only the voice.

He made motions with his arms, like a Fancy-Dan boxer. "I have these daydreams, yay!" he said almost gaily. "I mean, here's all these fat, freckled peckernecks coming for me. I'm standing there like John Wayne. Bam! straight left. Zap! right hook. I mean! Last month I started going down to the Judo parlor. You ought to see me throw those nigger-haters! Then I have these night dreams. Then they're always kicking *me*. That's the way the dream always comes out. They're kicking me in the—you know— and in the face. They keep kicking me. It doesn't hurt, it's just so goddam awful. Well, I know it's just that some people can't take the physical stuff. You know—pain. But why does it have to be me?"

Tears came for Man who went down to the Judo parlor not so much to defeat injustice as his own cowardice in the face of injustice. She put both her arms around him. He was trembling as he had not trembled in passion.

He said, "I mean, the bad thing is—deseg and all that is big with me too."

"So you think you ought to be down there?"

"Yay."

She thought he might have inquired a little more about her own experience in the field. Beyond a certain curiosity about Abel Ransome's prowess, he seemed to have no interest in the other color except his own response to it, his own attitudes toward it, his own cowardice, and his own guilt. Maybe that had been the real tragedy all along. Yet she thought she had the power to grant him his wish, to send him to Mississippi if that was what he wanted. She didn't see that being kicked by frightened men in Mississippi was going to do anything for him. It would not pay for anything, correct or change anything, though certainly if enough John Henry Collinses went to Mississippi despite their fear, the kickers would eventually vanish from sheer moral exhaustion. Although they were human beings too; she was to remember that now.

"Did you hear me tell Clary I was the Guru now?"

He didn't answer. Perhaps he had nodded and she hadn't felt the motion. She said, "I'm the Guru, and I can tell you things to change your life."

"What?" he said hoarsely. He cleared his throat. "What?"

"If you'll listen."

"Sure."

"Are you sure you know why you want to go to Mississippi?"

"Well, I—"

"Justice and wrongs and all that?"

"Sure. That."

"And playing your guitar and singing for shut-ins is just a cop-out?"

He didn't answer. She remembered how she detested Shelley when he forced her into a dialectic like this. She said, "Well, if the shut-ins are a cop-out, maybe going to Mississippi is a cop-out too."

"What?"

"Maybe worrying about civil rights is a cop-out."

"A cop-out from what?"

"From the most important thing—you."

She felt the tightness of his muscles. She grinned, her cheek resting against his back still, watching the snow falling against the dark, damp glass of the window. Beside the TV set his white skis with the black stars on their tips leaned, perfectly parallel, against the wall, poles beside them. Across the room was his guitar in its black case. He hadn't offered to play for her.

"I *know*," she said. She knew everything, including just how superior to be with the boys in her life. "It's so much easier to go down to Mississippi and be kicked by hoodlums than it is to face a lot of other things. That's so clean-cut. This is right, that's wrong. Right and wrong are so easy. There's no doubt. You don't even have to think. It's so much harder, maybe it's impossible, to face the things where right and wrong are all mixed up. Nobody's going to solve anything in Mississippi, or Africa, or South America, or the Caribbean, or Vietnam—anywhere else the boils start breaking out—till each one of us"—she felt herself beginning to run out of conviction—"until each one of us faces the really hard things right inside ourselves." She made a face at herself, still with her arms around the waist of her last lover.

"I don't know if I dig you, honey."

"Well, get out your pick and shovel."

"It's just that all my life, it seems to me, I've always tried to cop-out of everything that was—*you* know."

"Yes, I know."

"I've been scared for so long," he said. "I'm so sick of being scared."

"Well, don't change," she said gently. "Be one of us."

When she released him he swung around to face her. It had only made her feel impatient and disgusted to see Shelley cry. This Christmas Eve she felt infinitely tender.

"I wish I could do something for you," he said. "You're so goddam great."

"You already have."

"Let's go again."

"I'm afraid I'd better start for home before the snow gets any deeper."

"Quick one?"

"I'm feeling mental," she said. "Do you know how that is? If you want to do something for me, though, you can take me skiing in the powder snow tomorrow morning. That's what I want to know how to do."

"Maybe it's a cop-out," John Henry said and managed to grin at her.

"It's not a cop-out if you know it's one."

"I think you're great," John Henry said. "Sure, I'll show you how to ski the powder tomorrow. I'll be your snow Guru."

He had to put chains on his Porsche to drive her up the hill. She made him stop at the bottom of Juniper Lane, afraid he would get stuck if he tried to go further. He kissed her good night and said good things to her, and she was very happy. Although the wind was cold as she trudged on up the hill through ankle-deep snow, with her head bowed against the blowing snow and her fists balled in the pockets of her coat, she was warm enough, physically and mentally.

12: Badbody

Suggesting that they go to his room had seemed indelicate, so he and Maeve were settled in the inner office with two bottles of Mumm's in an icebucket.

"I'm all right now," she said, smiling at him, reclining on the couch as regally as a Roman matron, sipping champagne. Sitting opposite her in the desk chair, he saw her coiled brown fist lying in her lap.

"Of course you're all right."

He watched her eyes wandering restlessly around the room, fixing on the glass-covered topographical map over the desk, which showed Dancer Valley and Dancer Peak, the roads, lifts, and ski slopes, including the Superchute.

"Why did Dick call you Badbody?" she asked. "To put you down?"

He shook his head. "Once when we were undergraduates we took out a pair of nightclub dancers. We made up false names—he was McDickens and I was Lee P. Bradbody, which turned into Badbody."

She laughed, preoccupied, as though listening to something inside herself. He thought he knew for what she was listening.

"I was his best friend," he said. It was not a non-sequitur, it was only a beginning, because now was the moment to reach for the last possible gold ring the merry-go-round would ever swing him past. His heart was beating hard, high in his chest. He waited until her eyes moved again, this time to gaze up at the huge, enlarged-past-recognition photograph of the skier in the powder at the top of the Superchute.

"That's not Clary, you know," he said. He was proud of the steadiness of his voice.

She gazed at the photograph a moment longer before she frowned at him. "It isn't?"

"Clary has his. Don't you remember a fast-talking photographer from Los Angeles taking pictures of us all up in the powder? Later in the winter he came back to sell us these blowups."

"Of course you used to ski," Maeve whispered.

"Not since that day."

Nothing moved in her face; only her eyes, staring into his, grew enormous. The slashes of pink flowered in her cheeks. She didn't flinch when the wind flung snow against the windowpane, harsh as blown sand. Her dark eyes glittered with what at first was fear and then was not fear. She opened her lips slightly to frame an inaudible word. "You."

"Perhaps we've been obsessed by the same thing," he said. "Perhaps if we shared this we'd both be—relieved. I'm the one you saw above you. I skied out into the bowl, and when I stopped a little snowslip started and ran down toward Dick. It was just enough to start the whole bowl moving, and the cornice came down. That's all there was to it, Maeve."

"Yes," Maeve whispered. "Of course," she said, eyes fixed on his, smiling a little, stiffly, dazedly. "Yes," she said, nodding.

It was strange but right that he could keep himself from shaking by watching the steadiness of the champagne glass held in her hand. He sighed. "That was all. Sometimes I can even forget the —forget it. You see, he really was my friend, but of course I realize that I hated him too. And of course I was forced to despise myself sometimes, because of him—very much on that particular day. After the night before, when you and I—"

Maeve nodded—he thought to stop him, and he stopped. She looked into his eyes and nodded.

He said, "I wonder if a psychiatrist would say that snowslide was started willfully. Wishfully. I think I might think so if I were— deranged. But I'm sane enough not to believe it. I just didn't hate enough to—"

She made a sibilant sound to stop him again. "Do you know?" she said intensely. "It mattered so much, but now it doesn't matter." She let her head lie back on the couch. Her face was full of color, and when she closed her eyes tears gleamed on the lashes. He watched her hand slowly droop until her glass rested on the floor. The empty hand rose and was extended to him. He took it awkwardly. He knelt beside her. His cheek against hers, he smelled the perfume in her hair, felt the cool of her tears, heard her make a swollen sound in her throat. "You!" she said.

When she released him he straightened to polish his glasses. Maeve looked like a tired child resting. "While I'm on my knees," he said and cleared his throat. Her face became instantly strained; it was as though he could hear her holding her breath. With a twinge of irony he thought of the proposals she must have heard, modest and immodest. He had chosen his words very carefully, and he said, "I want to spend the rest of your life with you."

He didn't think she understood. She started to speak, once, twice, finally she said, "Then I guess I will have to tell you something."

"I already know."

He felt ridiculous on his knees beside her. It was pleasant to feel ridiculous and know it did not matter, but he rose and sat in his chair again. Maeve's face was pink with embarrassment—because he knew her most intimate and pitiful secret. "Oh," she said, shaking her head inconsequentially. "Oh, I'm afraid it won't be— very nice."

"I want to share everything with you, Maeve."

A flustered hand rose to comb at her hair, tears leaked from her eyes. "Oh—oh, I don't—you mean, you *know?* And you *want*— How do you know?" she said suddenly.

He told her. Now he thought she must think, knowing him, that he was not in love with her but with old easeful death. Instead he loved her because he knew he must, for his salvation, love life entire. But maybe she could understand.

"Do you think I'm pretty, Brad?" she said childishly.

"Yes, very pretty."

"I don't know how long I'll be pretty." Her voice took on an edge. "I don't know how long I have."

"Does anyone?"

Incongruously she giggled. She touched her lips with a shaky hand. "No, of course not. I *do* know that. But you're not just— not just doing this because—just because?"

"Not just because."

She raised her glass to her lips, the liquid in the little bowl agitated now, her eyes watching him over the rim, nostrils turning bone-white with her breathing.

He said, "Do you remember before when I wanted to take you away? What I really wanted was for you to take me away. You're the only person who can rescue me."

"Yes. All right," Maeve said. Then she turned pink with embarrassment again. "But I haven't got money, Brad. Nothing. Zero."

"I have money."

"Your job?"

"You're my job."

"Position," she said, smiling over her glass, long knife-cuts of lines forming at the corners of her mouth when she smiled. "I insist on being a position." She laughed, a delighted laugh. "It's so funny," she said. "We couldn't talk about a dead dog but we can talk about a dying bitch. I think that's very, very funny."

Suddenly she turned away from him, her face hidden by a curtain of hair, and he heard her sob.

"Maeve," he said, but she said impatiently, "No, I'm all right. I'm all right now." But she didn't turn back, and after a time she said, "You see, I was so crazy because there was this terrible—this superstitious, powerful *thing*. That if I could just find out who'd started the slide, then I'd be—it sounds terribly silly to say it, but it was so strong. That then I'd be reprieved. You see, it's stupid, silly hope that makes you a coward. And crazy. But it was so strong, it kept coming on, and on, and *on*."

Her voice rose with excitement. "But I *have* found out! I really have! And maybe in a way I am reprieved. I mean, not in the silly springs-eternal way I'd thought. But because—it was *you*! And you want to be with *me*! And because there really isn't any hope, but there doesn't have to be. Do you understand?"

Yes, he could understand all of that.

"I can be brave again now!" Maeve said. "I can be proud of myself again! I'm all right now!" Her voice broke, and she wept.

So as not to intrude, he rose to open the second bottle of champagne. The cork cracked against the ceiling with vigor. He tipped the foam into his glass, savoring emotion as though unaccustomed lungs were accommodating deep breaths of sweet air. His mind danced from prospect to prospect; he was in a fever of anticipation to begin what could begin now, what he had been putting off for almost half a century. Some classical corner of his mind was exalted by the rightness, the proper shape of the design, this success after his previous defeat, both in the face of death. He had no fear now, no lack of certainty in his ability to carry this through, and he realized that he had found the courage in himself that Dick Macklin, at the end, had not been able to find, that he had won a victory that Easy Clary had not found it in himself to win; as Maeve's final lover, he would share the rest of her life, face death and so face life at last.

"I know a house in Hawaii where we can start," he said. "It's on the island of Kauai, on a long beach with palm trees and hibiscus, and the sun shines even when it's raining."

"That sounds lovely, Brad—Bradley Peabody," she said.

When he turned, holding the bottle, she was lying back on the couch again. Her long-lashed eyes were closed, her soft, pale mouth faintly up-curved. "I'm so relaxed!" she whispered. "It's as though—I'm just going to close my eyes for a little while." She fell asleep as she spoke, and he sat down on the couch beside her, sipping champagne and gazing at her lovely face through his misting glasses. He was thinking of going home to the endless beaches, the pale blue water, the delicate rain with the sun shining through it, the long beautiful days, the years without seasons, of Hawaii— with Maeve. He was startled from his vision when the door was flung open.

Easy Clary leaned in the opening. His hair was drenched with melted snow. "There you are!" Clary said in a thick voice.

He put his fingers to his lips, indicating Maeve asleep.

"What the hell are you doing in here?" Clary said with no effort to lower his voice. He came on in and slumped into the desk chair, stinking of wine. He looked like a rained-out Bacchus with his hair clinging to his scalp in damp tendrils and his determinedly drunken face.

"Brad and I are going to Hawaii, Easy," Maeve said in a sleepy voice. "Isn't that lovely?"

Clary's white-rimmed eyes beneath dark, wild eyebrows flashed toward him. "You didn't give me a chance, Maeve!" he said. The chair squeaked as he swung it to reach into the liquor cabinet for a tumbler.

Clary held the glass out to him like a beggar, and he took up the bottle and poured champagne. "Thank you kindly," Clary said. "This can't be serious," Clary said contemptuously, anxiously. He rubbed a hand hard across his mouth. "*Hawaii!*"

"Very serious," he said.

"Feathers falling from the great chicken, Maeve," Clary said, ignoring him now. "Really good, really cold powder. I ought to know, I've been standing in it outside your window for a goddam hour." Clary threw back his head to drain his glass at one swallow. He put the glass down and propped his fists, at the ends of long arms, on his knees. "Going to be the greatest skiing of the year tomorrow, Maeve. Snow's so light you can't even make a snowball. Throw it up in the air, it won't even come down. Got to come skiing the deep powder tomorrow, Maeve. You can't quit just because you had one bad day!"

Maeve murmured something, smiling, eyes closed. He wondered if she were hiding in sleep as Clary was hiding behind his drunkenness.

"What's she say?" Clary asked without looking at him.

He shook his head. "I didn't hear."

"How can I be such a goddam failure?" Clary said, leaning forward to pluck the champagne bottle from the bucket. He squinted at the level, filled his glass, plopped the bottle back into the melting ice, and drank deep. "What the hell do you think *you're* doing, Castorp?" Clary said. "You're quitting here?"

"Don't you think it's time?"

Clary shrugged elaborately.

"Let me tell you a story."

"Sure, tell me a story. Tell me something."

"This was back in Honolulu after I'd got out of college. I worked downtown in the Honolulu Paper Products office, and I had an apartment in Waikiki, not very far from Fort de Russy. There were coastal guns at the fort and sometimes they fired them for practice. On this Sunday morning I thought they were having gunnery practice. I remember there were some cups and plates drying on the sink, and one of the explosions jarred a plate, which slid down and broke. I was going to the beach, in my swimming trunks and go-aheads, and a towel over my shoulder. I went down to Kalakaua Avenue, and just as I got there I saw an airplane coming low over the tops of the trees at the back of the Royal Hawaiian, where the lei-makers always were."

He took a deep breath, watching the steady rise and fall of Maeve's breast with her brown hand lying relaxed upon it. Her hand moved slowly from her breast to fumble for, and limply hold, his hand.

"The plane had a red circle on the fuselage," he went on. "I suppose I realized right away what was happening, though I can't remember. Anyway, you understand that the airplane—I suppose it was a Zero—was very close, just down the street, coming low and not at all fast. Then it was right across the street from me. I was the only person out and—I don't know how to explain this—my relationship with the pilot was very close for that fraction of a moment while we looked at each other. I could see him clearly. I think I'd still know him anywhere. I remember how he raised a hand to his goggles. He had western features and he was quite pale. What I'm trying to say is that he represented death there facing me. I gave him the finger. It was a salutation used a lot among boys in Hawaii. I stood there and gave him the finger, and he looked back at me and flew on down Kalakaua just above the tops of the palms and disappeared. So I gave death the finger that day. But it was the last time."

He did not know if Clary had understood or not, though he knew Easy Clary would understand if he wanted to. Once he and Easy had understood each other very well. Clary sat staring at him fiercely with his slightly-too-close-together eyes.

"I can't make out if you're talking about Maeve or not," Clary said.

"About myself."

"You want to get that finger up again, huh?" Clary illustrated. He shrugged and nodded.

"You and Maeve," Clary said as though he couldn't believe it.

He said carefully, "I think Maeve will be able to face what she has to face. I want to face it with her. Partly for my own sake, you see." He could feel the sweat on his forehead like cool lace. Partly for his own sake, who must stop thinking of death as the monster at the end of the road, and instead as a companion to become familiar with, and to trust. He glanced at the window as the wind exhaled hugely again.

"There really isn't much in a person's life absolutely his own," he continued. "Everything we have is common to everyone else. Except the one thing. I am finding it absolutely necessary at this particular moment in my life to grasp this. Not merely the idea, the thing itself, the real nettle. I think I can do this with Maeve. Somehow a long time ago I lost myself, and this is the way I can get myself back again. You must have observed how we become more and more encumbered with things, petty cares and worries and the like—piled on and on as we go along until we become so enormously fat there is no finding the individual under all the fat. But I know that by going through this with Maeve—for Maeve—I can find myself again, and be free to—"

"Free to *exist* all to hell," Clary broke in. He sounded as though he had intended to say it contemptuously but had failed or changed his mind in the enunciation. "Okay," Clary said. "You're going to take care of her, huh?"

"Yes."

Easy nodded. He tipped his glass to his lips again, rubbed a hand over the back of his head. They both looked down at Maeve. "She's so hooked on Macklin getting killed," Clary said.

"Maybe not any more."

"Bully for you!"

"Did you ever realize why Dick had to humiliate her the way he did, Easy?"

Clary nodded.

"Out of his own humiliation. The lion retreating back into the cage, realizing he was afraid to be free."

Clary cocked an eyebrow and touched the back of his head again.

"He'd boasted so much about his posture in life, but when the chips were down he was afraid of losing his *position.* I'm not saying he wasn't a brave man—" He stopped, startled at an unfamiliar pride in his voice; he had had no practice boasting.

"But you, you just got brave," Clary said roughly. "Congratulations!"

"More champagne?"

Easy shook his head. "Hope you make it," he said. "I'd been thinking I ought to put you out of your misery," he said contemptuously.

He wondered if Easy's pride begrudged any other's triumph or understanding in the field he considered his own, the evangelist resentful of his own converts. But of course Easy Clary was afraid too. They looked at each other, and he could feel Clary's hostility. "Use your phone, Badbody?"

He nodded, and with a creak Clary swung around in the chair, picked up the phone, punched the outside button, and dialed. Clary leaned back in the chair, waiting. It was a long time before he said, "Hello, Pussy—no, never mind that hurt crap. I'm coming over—yes, right now—listen, tell you how I want you waiting. Pajama top—those white ones. No pants. Maybe a little cologne between the tits. Ready? Set? Go!"

Clary hung up, swung out of the chair away from him, muttered, "Bless you, my children," and hurried out the door. In the dark outer office there was a crash and foul cursing, then the slap of running feet, and Clary was gone.

He sat smiling down at Maeve asleep. There was not much to do—write a note to Isobel, pack a few essentials, put chains on the car. It was time to go, and he was anxious to start. He pressed Maeve's hand until she smiled, but she didn't open her eyes. "Maeve," he said, "let's start. Let's begin." It was time for the sleeping beauty to awaken, her prince having come not to slay but to help her meet the dragon.

PART THREE *The Cornice*

. . . Just once,
Everything, only for once. Once and no more. And we, too,
Once. And never again.

—RAINER MARIA RILKE

There are no truths outside the gates of Eden.

—BOB DYLAN

1: Timbal Khan

HE LAY COMPOSED on his bed, hands crossed over his heart, waiting for morning and trying to keep his mind on the snow buildup, the cornices growing and falling, the steeper faces sluffing, the whole process of the mountain, beset by storm, maintaining its equilibrium. When he had last looked at the Min-Max it had indicated twenty-five degrees, and it would be six to ten degrees colder on top. Snow was falling at the rate of an inch an hour down here, which meant three or four times that on the upper slopes, where the anemometer count had shown the wind velocity to be over fifty miles an hour.

He tried to think only of the mountain and the problems that were developing, but his mind kept turning in upon himself, and finally he gave into it and lay staring at darkness, regarding his own loneliness in its easy and undemanding familiarity, in its old dull aching. Once he had had Maeve to conceal it from himself; the make-believe Maeve invented and maintained so he would not have to face his loneliness or the fact that he had retired defeated into it without a struggle.

Coming back, Maeve had destroyed that old excuse, that old illusion that he needed no one, destroyed the Maeve-of-his-memory who had never existed even in the strumming-guitar, confidence-whispering, tumescent fantasies of those nights in the T & O Social. The screen that had protected him from the void of himself was gone forever, and he did not think he could bear the loneliness of the rest of his life.

His face burned and he was sickened with shame whenever he thought about Rody.

When Maeve's return destroyed the illusion of herself he had turned immediately, automatically, comfortably, to Rody, almost tricking himself into thinking he was doing her a favor instead of fleeing to her in panic. Now for the first time he was able to see her side. She had taken him seriously when he had asked her to think about their getting together, she had confided in him as she never had before, but in his own monstrous, panicky selfishness, he had hardly heard her. She had asked him for a very little thing, only a kind of token, and he had been unable to give it to her. He could not bear the naked emptiness that suddenly confronted him, but he was unwilling to surrender any of his own intactness to the only person who could save him. He groaned with pain for his failure, and for Rody's hurt.

When an hour had passed he got up to look at his weather gauges again. The wind was still from the storm quarter but the barometer was up. He counted the flashes of the center bulb of the anemometer, one eye on the minute hand of the clock. Twenty-one flashes in thirty seconds times two gave forty-two mph. It was six o'clock. Switching on the outside light, he squinted at his snow stake through the window glass; less than an inch this last hour.

Slowly, carefully, as though it were still a part of resting, he began to dress; fishnet longjohns, two-ply underwear, silk undersocks, boiled-wool socks, black turtleneck shirt, worn soft blue levis, clip boots, red sweater, light nylon storm pants, ski-patrol parka, storm jacket, gloves, black watchcap.

In the darkness he plodded through the deep snow to the bottom of Big Red One. There was no wind here, but he could hear its heavy roar far above him, the sound fading away as though the barometer reading had just this moment been received by the elements. He had to shovel out the door to the concrete cell beneath the bullwheel. Inside, he switched on the light and the electric heater. He went outside again to stuff the teapot full of snow, and he set it on the hotplate.

In the pallid glare of the bare lightbulb he lay down on the sour-smelling cot and, shivering, stared up at the rusted steel plate in the exact center of the ceiling, remembering the sound of the bullwheel turning that morning nine years ago. How could he drunkenly, stupidly, have spoken of it in the Loup Garou? He felt no more anger at J.D.; he was surprised to find he felt no more guilt

for what had happened that day, for his failure to the mountain
and to his job. The guilt he felt was for his failure with Rody last
night. He would find her today and tell her what she had asked to
know.

The teakettle began to sing on the hotplate; the room was
warming from the glowing electric heater. He sat up, feeling suddenly cheerful. She would be at the race to watch Stevie forerun,
and he would see her there after he had finished his snow-safety
work.

He made himself a cup of sweet tea and began to tape together
the brown blocks of explosive, fused them, stowed them in rucksacks. When he went outside in the first gray light there was no
longer any sound of wind on the mountain. The colored flags on
the giant slalom course on the Spoon hung snowy and bedraggled.

It was after eight when Tom Cline and Frank Dow appeared,
wading through the knee-deep snow. They were the only two who
would make any effort to get here.

"Merry Christmas!" Frank said.

"It's sure a white one," Tom said.

"Where you been?"

"The road's blocked. We had to come in on the plow."

"Big pine next to Boland's blew down," Tom said. "They're
cutting it up now. There's a bunch of ski-club people coming in to
pack the course. I thought I'd give them a hand with the Snocat
when we finish up on top. You run Big Red yet?"

"We'd better go up and shovel the chairs out at the Intermediate Station first."

Tom cursed long, blasphemously, and repetitively. "And this'll
be one of the mornings Keck can't get his pickup started, I'll bet."

"Maybe Barrett'll show," Frank said, shaking his head as he
said it.

Frank worried and always showed up, Tom cursed and showed,
but Keckley and Peter Barrett were not apt to appear this morning
for a while. It was against all regulations to go out on avalanche
patrol without a companion, but what else was there to do when
there were only three of you and the mountain had to open at ten
o'clock?

"We'd better not wait," he said. "We'll all go up on the Big
Top, and you two go on down and dig out the chairs at the Inter-

mediate Station. I'll go on up the ridge and knock off Cape Horn and on up to the Superchute from there."

"Well, you shouldn't," Frank said, scowling. "But I don't know what else we can do."

Combing snow out of his beard with gloved fingers, Tom said, "One recoilless rifle and aiming stakes, and we could clear the whole fucking mountain from the top of Blue Two."

"Well, let's get going," Frank said.

With their heavy rucksacks they trudged on skis to the bottom terminal of Blue Two. Above the Big Top towering cliffs of cloud opened for a moment to reveal a patch of brilliant blue sky. The lift hummed into operation as soon as he pressed the Start button, and the snow-laden chairs began their powerful ascent. Blue Two was a modern, smooth-running, expensive lift that gave a tenth of the trouble Big Red One did—and had no personality. He stopped the lift so they could brush the snow from three chairs. Tom and Frank loaded in the first and second; he pressed the Start button again, caught the third, and sat with his rucksack beside him and skis propped on the rest. He sailed up over the GS gates on the Spoon. Just past Tower Five he took out the first charge, fitted fuse-lighter over fuse, and pulled the toggle. There was the pop of a struck match, tar-smelling smoke. He tossed the packet as far out to the left as he could.

A dimple appeared where it struck the snow; after a long moment there was a muffled *whroooomp* and a high, fanning flurry of snow, which slowly settled to reveal a dark-rimmed saucer. The Spoon was all right. Frank held up a circled thumb and forefinger.

Nothing more needed to be shaken up until just below the Midway, a complicated succession of slanted towers and shining-turning sheaves. He tossed his second charge a hundred feet below the platform.

Again the dull thump, the slowly rising, slowly settling flower of snow. This time an acreage of smoothly slanting snowfield came to life, buckled, began to move, still holding its shape by some kind of surface tension. As it slid faster and faster it humped, tore apart, fled wildly out of his range of vision. His breath came fast, as it always did when a big one went down. Tom turned with a hand cupped to his mouth and shouted, "That fucker *went!*"

One more charge, and the Big Top was checked out. At the top they sidestepped out of their chairs and swung packs onto their backs again; they made slow headway down the ramp through deep, wind-packed snow. In the lighter snow in the shelter of the terminal he dug his way through many layers of cloth and urinated into the snow, sighing with satisfaction. As though it were a cere-mony, Tom and Frank joined him, making yellow, steaming holes.

"Well, take care," Tom said.

"I'm kind of spooked about Cape Horn," Frank said in his wor-ried voice. "Don't you try to ski it out, Tim. You shouldn't do that without somebody along."

He grunted.

"About an hour and a half?" Frank asked.

"About that." He wanted to ask if they had seen Rody and Stevie with the ski-club people waiting to come in and pack the course, but it seemed a silly question.

"Let's go, Frankie!" Tom said, and the two of them started down toward the top of the Spoon on their route across to the In-termediate Station of Big Red One, Tom making tight, linked turns and yodeling, Frank skiing more cautiously, both of them humpbacked with their gray rucksacks on. They disappeared among the trees.

Timbal Khan the Mountain Man schussed straight downhill into the saddle and began sidestepping up the other side to the ridge above Cape Horn. This was a long, hard climb in the deep snow, and a cloud slowly settled down on him until there was no visibility. He climbed fifteen or twenty steps up to the right, kick-turned, and climbed fifteen or twenty to the left, the heavy mus-cles in his legs knotting and flexing pleasantly. He was panting deeply when he reached the top of the ridge, and he rested there with his lungs heaving, leaning on his poles. The cloud slipped away, blue sky showed again, like a promise; then high clouds sealed the sky again. Trees below him were shedding their loads. From here he could make out the tiny, stationary chairs of Big Red One. A distant, echoing thump meant that Tom and Frank had reached the Intermediate Station and shot the Scarp.

The snow was deeper than he had calculated, the going more difficult. He didn't look at his watch because he didn't want to feel rushed. Below him pines stood in clusters on the long, smoothly runneled face of Cape Horn. Traversing now, stepping uphill from time to time to maintain his high line, he reached the point he wanted. Cautiously he started forward; immediately the snow began to fall away behind and below him, like thick cloth parting behind the shearing of his skis. The snow sluffed downward a hundred feet or so but started nothing big. He heard distant yodeling.

As though it were a reproach he slid uphill to a stop. He was already breaking the rule that no avalanche work be done singly, and now he was making dangerous the only route to the top safe enough to be tackled alone, risking not only his own life, but the lives of those who would have to come looking for him if he got into trouble. But tossing charges here would take longer, and he would run out of explosive before he got to the Superchute cornice.

He threw the first charge from the top of the ridge: nothing. He skied on and tossed another: nothing. Finally he exploded a three-pounder just below the outcrop, and with a huge sucking rush like water going down a drain the whole of Cape Horn climaxed, shaking the trees as though they were twigs as it rushed down the slope to pile into the gulley at the bottom and splash in one great suddenly halted wave up the other side. He stood panting, gazing down the rough, ugly mountainside after it.

He began to climb the ridge again toward the near shoulder of Dancer Peak, trying to make time, tired legs lifting skis in deep snow, his muscles feeling like ropes wetted and pulled tight. In his pack only one three-pound charge was left. He couldn't see the face of Dancer; a cloud hung just above the shoulder line, trailing streamers of fog. He stopped to rest, wiping his sweating face. He had climbed about five hundred feet.

The Tasket had already sluffed, but he lit and tossed his last charge anyway, and a long narrow slide, like a rough tongue, rushed down. He began the last long traverse over to the top of Big Red One, which was running now. He was late.

When he reached the top terminal Whitey, the attendant, was whistling as he shoveled snow off the ramp.

"Hi, Tim! Frank just called up worrying about you, but I told him I could see you coming across."

"Get on the phone and tell him to send up some more charges or come up and help me knock down the Superchute cornice, will you?"

He dropped his rucksack and skied down to the big rock that hung like an observation platform over the Superchute at this end of the cornice. The cornice was very big for this time of year, swollen, streamlined, convex on top, concave where it hung out over the bowl beneath it, fifty yards long and shaped like a perfectly symmetrical boomerang, a beautifully poised wave of snow. It was the biggest of the cornices, and, because of its structure, the easiest to knock down. A three-pound charge a little to the east of the middle would drop it. The other possibility was to walk out on it, anchored to a helper with nylon climbing rope, and stamp it down. It looked as though it wouldn't take much stamping.

"Hey, Tim!" Whitey was leaning over the ramp railing. "Hey, Tim, Frank had to go over on the Spoon because they're starting the race. Tom says he'll be up or send Pete Barrett if he can find him."

He nodded impatiently. It was almost ten-fifteen by his watch, past time for Big Red One to open to the paying skiers, although there probably weren't many on hand yet this morning. If the race was starting this early Tom must have packed out the course with the Snocat.

He took a Baby Ruth from his parka pocket and ate it as he sidestepped slowly back up toward the ski-patrol shack invisible beneath a huge mound of snow. Inside he heard the muffled ringing of the telephone, two long, two short. Whitey's phone jangled, and, grousing, Whitey planted his shovel and hurried up the ramp in his green-and-yellow rubber bootpacks.

A moment later he reappeared. "Hey, Tim! Frank says that little kid of Rody Bliss's got hurt and he won't let anybody but you—"

He spat out the last bite of candy bar. "Where is he?"

"Frank said he hit that big tree on the Spoon. He—"

He was already in motion down the shoulder, past the Elevator Shaft that dove into the Superchute, heading for the Chute and the long schuss down to the Spoon and the big pine there.

2: Miss Bliss

She knew he must be dead. Not dead because he still moved, made tentative stroking motions with his hand as though brushing at cobwebs, with the ski-patrol blankets covering him and a trickle of blood dried already on his cheek where it had leaked from under his white racing helmet which was smashed down to his eyes—not dead but dying.

Numbly, helplessly, in an arid agony, she knelt in the snow beside her son, afraid to touch him lest he come apart under her hands like a fractured bowl, a bowl that had been meant to hold so much. From her childhood during the war she remembered hearing of an airplane pilot having to be "scraped out of his helmet," and she could not keep this from her mind in the awful helplessness of the waiting. Frank Dow was standing beside her, one boot braced on the wire basket on the toboggan. When she glanced up at him he said quickly, "They're trying to find Dr. Cannella, Rody. I mean, we'd better not try to move him till Cannella shows up. Or Tim."

Stevie had already screamed at them that no one could move him but Tim, although he had allowed Frank to splint his spiraled leg. She hadn't seen it happen. She had stationed herself above the Beak where there was an S curve she had thought would give him trouble. He had sailed through it like a pro and disappeared over the brink of the Beak. When he had not reappeared on the lower half of the course she had assumed he had fallen but would be up and running again as soon as he got himself together. Instead Frank had come snowplowing down from the top, towing the toboggan.

She could hear people whispering around her but she didn't listen to what they were saying. Several people had been sent for Dr. Cannella but he hadn't been found yet, and so everything hung suspended in time, in heavy, slow-breathing, surely slowly dying stasis, while Stevie with the blood on his face and the smashed helmet pushed down to his eyes made the pathetic little motions with his gloved hand and didn't speak.

And then Tim's voice said, "Let me in there," like sound from a deep cave, confident and confidence-inspiring. She felt an irrational elation, as though now that Tim were here there was a chance.

"I wasn't going to let anybody but you take me down, Tim," Stevie said suddenly, clearly.

"That's right," Tim said. "You would've hurt my feelings." His brown slab of a face struck a careful balance between solemnity and cheerfulness; he looked at her once, with unforgiving eyes. "Just as well you had your helmet on, Stevie," he said, but what he meant was, "At least she got a helmet on you before she sent you down."

"They can't find the doc," Frank said as Tim knelt beside the splinted leg.

"I'd just as soon go down now if you guys want to take me down," Stevie said. "I'm getting kind of cold."

Casually Tim said, "Where do you hurt most, Stevie?"

"Well, Frank splinted my leg okay," Stevie said, and his voice caught for an instant. "It kind of hurts a little here too." His fingers stroked at the inside of his shoulder.

Tim took off his gloves and felt with big, square, gentle hands. A fine lay orthopedic diagnostician, Dr. Cannella had said.

"My head hurts, Tim," Stevie whispered.

"Back doesn't hurt though, huh?"

"Nope."

"Okay, now we're going to skid you into the basket," Tim said. "If it hurts any at all in your back, you say so and we'll stop, okay?"

Back—he was thinking broken back. She rose and stepped out of the way as Tim and Frank maneuvered to get their arms under the blanket-swaddled little body. Stevie made no sound. Fascinated, she watched not Stevie but the drops of sweat on Tim's forehead. With what seemed to her miraculous efficiency they had Stevie in the too-large basket.

"Hi, Mom," he said softly to her. "I guess I didn't make any dollars that run."

Tim started down the hill, holding the handles of the toboggan like a wheelbarrow behind him. He didn't snowplow down, as the other ski patrolman did, but schussed in a steep traverse. She watched him go, with Frank trailing behind, carrying Tim's poles and Stevie's skis and poles. Just drop those in the trash, will you? When she put on her own skis to follow them, she found herself scrambling stiff-legged on her edges like a beginner.

When she got down to the clinic Tim and Frank had already taken Stevie inside, and he lay, still in his helmet, on a wheeled table in the long, yellow-stucco corridor. As though he had been waiting in the wings, Dr. Cannella entered the far door, taking off his sheepskin coat. His shoes rapped on the tiles as he approached. When he and the nurse had wheeled Stevie on the gurney through a door she was certain that now Stevie was going to be all right. All this equipment and all this knowledge and technique could not fail.

"You'd better get up and blow down the Superchute cornice," Tim said to Frank. "I didn't get it done yet."

Frank said, "Okay," gave her what was meant to be a reassuring smile, and left. "Thanks, Frank," she said, not loudly enough for him to hear.

A phone began to ring, and the nurse came squeegeeing on rubber-soled shoes to quiet it.

"Do you think his back's broken?" she asked Tim.

He shook his head curtly. He wouldn't look at her. "I'd better get back up the mountain," he said.

"Okay," she said. Down the corridor was an alcove in which there was a plastic-covered couch, a matching easy chair, and magazines nurse-arranged on a low table. She stumped along the hall in her ski boots to sit on the couch, surprised to find that Tim had followed her.

"Listen, Rody. You've got to get off his back."

Anger beat in her temples so that she thought for a moment she would lose control of herself. "Why?" she said.

He didn't answer, having lost his nerve, or else pitying her her broken-up son. She said, "You mean because I've almost killed him?"

"He shouldn't've even been on that course. What were you giving him dollars for he didn't make?"

"For every A racer's time he beat, if you have to know." Her anger flooded back at the thought that she still had to face Herbie Allen. "I'm not supposed to let him do anything dangerous?" she said. "What am I supposed to do, keep him in bed all his life?"

"Maybe you'll have to," Tim said, red-faced, and immediately looked as though he wished he hadn't said it.

It shook her to terror again that he might know something about Stevie's condition he had not wanted to tell her. "Look who's talking!" she said through her teeth. "All-Out Soderburg. Wasn't that you I remember coming down Exhibition like a damned idiot?"

"That's not the point," Tim rumbled. "It's *you* making him. Not him. Trying to make an Olympic competitor out of an eight-year-old kid."

With a quirk of humor, inside the steel-cage strain of the waiting, it came to her that he was talking to her and she was talking to him; at last, in their disagreement, they were communicating. Yet she felt pure and sure and right. What better thing in life could you give your own child than the possibility of this victory over everyone else in a particular world, for even just one so-brief, so-bright moment to know that he had triumphed? She had never realized till now what she had accomplished with her second in the Hahnenkamm—second in the *world!* To rise out of the crawling, teeming, crummy mass of people beaten down by the world and pulling one another down and beating and trampling one another trying to get a leg up; for that one unforgettable-ever moment to soar in glory and sunlight where all the rest could look up at you in envy out of their crumminess! And this establishment of yourself, your specialness, your *quality*, was something that could never be taken away because it was a fact and so it did not die.

Even if you could never pull it off, just the faintest of chances justified the effort. She knew it was true. She knew it was right. But she also knew that in the world of competition, tougher and tougher as it had become, no longer could a person do it alone. There was simply not enough will. The will, like the muscles, craft, equipment, everything, must be guided and aided by specialists. It was what she could do for Stevie, who had a will but not will enough for the awesome competition he must face, and if she looked a pushy-mother helping him that was just a price you paid. She could see clearly, in this moment of vision, that her own faults and failures were wrapped up in her determination to furnish Stevie with the essential will, but it just did not matter very much because she did not matter as she existed separately from Stevie. It was right, all of it was right, she should never have questioned it.

"I want him to be a winner, Tim," she said. "Not just a loser drudging through life for nothing."

"You ought to let him make the decision for himself."

"He's too young to know what he's deciding. Later on it's what he'll decide."

"You don't like people that are the way you're talking," Tim said in his deep voice. "I know because you've said so."

She stared back into his blue half-circles of eyes, wordless for a moment. He had hit a larger target than the one he had aimed for. Because although she knew now unalterably that she was right preparing Stevie for the Olympics eight years away, there was terrible danger in building her own life around Stevie racing, Stevie in the Junior Nationals, Stevie on the FIS team, Stevie on the U.S. Olympic Squad, Stevie in the Winter Games—her life shaped to this one cause and meaning because there were no others. There was still the responsibility of her own life, and so she must construct some alternate for herself, something besides Stevie to dedicate her otherwise-emptiness to, because when Stevie finished his Olympic competition, if he got there, from that apogee onward he must in his turn build his life for himself, and then she must wither and die unless she had an alternate plan, interest, dedication, preoccupation, to turn to. She felt a wistful envy of Tim, who had his mountain and thus did not really need a son, or a wife, even if he thought now that he did.

So the danger was not that of which Tim disapproved—parents of young athletes pushing their kids too hard. Instead the danger was that the parent became a zombie, unable to live for himself, trying pitifully and ruthlessly to live through his child. She must never do that, yet it was what she was risking; not Stevie's death, but her own. This is your life, Miss Bliss. She had better learn to live it instead of clinging to Stevie's, before it was too late to learn. It struck her that it was getting perilously late.

Dr. Cannella appeared in a long white gown and cap, like some kind of minister, to sit down beside her. Her heart swelled up to choke her, for perhaps all her reasoning and resolutions had been only tragic irony. She nodded to his words: "Your son is going to be all right, Rody."

"Thanks," she said. Tim stood there with his fists clenched.

"Now Stevie's got a little skull fracture," Dr. Cannella said in his rapid voice. "It's a definite fracture, you understand, and he will have to go into the hospital for a few days. A friend of mine is up from the Bay Area skiing this weekend, and I'd like to have him look at it. He's had a great deal of experience with this sort of thing. There would be a consultation fee for this, Rody. I assume you have insurance?"

"Yes."

"Yes. Now, in addition—I assume he broke his leg before he hit the tree. He did hit a tree?"

"He hit that big pine up on the Spoon," Tim said.

"Yes. Well, there is a spiral fracture of the right tibia. Now, Rody, we may have to pin this together. I'm not sure yet. It's a pretty bad one. I've been more concerned about his skull. That could have been very dangerous. The helmet saved his life, there's no question about it. Now, the left collarbone, what we call a green twig fracture—more bent than broken actually." Dan Cannella laughed and said, "He's going to be carrying a good deal of plaster, Rody!"

"His back's all right?" Tim asked.

"Yes. Luckily."

"He really clobbered," she said raggedly. "I guess he was skiing all-out." She didn't look up at Tim.

"He really clobbered," Dr. Cannella said, displaying his even lower teeth like so many white grains of corn.

She said, "When can he ski again?"

"Well, I'd rather you didn't pin me down on that yet."

"Race?"

"Oh, yes. No problem that I can foresee."

"Can I see him?"

"A little later." Dan Cannella said. "Why don't you go have a cup of coffee and check back in about an hour? By that time I hope Dr. Peters will have seen him. You can ride along to the hospital with him."

They got to their feet at the same moment. The doctor patted her arm and strode off. With Tim, she walked slowly back along the corridor and outside, squinting her eyes against the sudden sun. She stopped to watch the stiff-legged skiers coming down the Bunny Hill. She said to Tim, "Buy you a cup of coffee?"

"I've got to get back up and see if they knocked that cornice down."

"Well, thanks for everything."

But he didn't leave her. His face had turned a dark and painful red beneath his burn. She realized that he was going to propose, here in this unlikely place. But it was not an unlikely time; it was the great American movie-ending, the two of them brought together because of the badly hurt little boy. Now each, presumably, lost his bad traits and selfishness, felt love and the vast harmony of the world singing across the final clinch. And it was all bullshit.

"Maybe we ought to get married," Tim muttered.

"Pardon?" she said loudly.

"I said maybe we ought to get married, Rody."

"I thought everything was off last night," she said. "I thought maybe we didn't have too much to offer each other, Tim."

He looked as though he were hurting, but angry too. "I'm sorry about last night," he said. "I was—I want to—" He stopped and chewed at the corner of his lip. "I really like that kid, Rody."

At least he was honest. She would never have been able to believe he wanted to marry her because he loved her, but she would have appreciated an effort to make her think so. For the first time this disastrous morning she was afraid she was going to cry.

"Rody," Tim said, "that kid needs a father."

She nodded. It was true, but if she was going to begin to have her own life, an alternate life, instead of getting more and more absorbed in Stevie's, she had better begin now. The way to begin was not by marrying someone who did not realize she was a living, breathing, thinking, sentient person, who thought of her only as a mother in need of a father for her son.

"And you need a man, Rody," he said, clearing his throat with embarrassment.

At least he was trying. But you didn't marry because you needed a man; at least she didn't. She remembered telling Stevie that you could not marry someone unless you loved him. Tears began leaking down her face.

"How about it, Rody?" Tim said.

"I guess not, Tim. Thanks."

He opened his mouth to protest. His face darkened with anger. He turned away, then swung back. "I need you too, Rody," he said.

But she only shook her head. "You don't really, Tim," she said as gently as she could.

Without another word he strode away, a big, complete man in the armor of his job, who didn't, shouldn't, need anything except his mountain; though she was grateful to him for that final effort. She saw him accosted by one of the overall-clad lift attendants, who spoke to him excitedly, pointing. Tim hurried through the skiers on the run-out below the Spoon, heading for Big Red One, and she wondered what had gone wrong on his mountain.

Starting for the lodge for a cup of coffee, she encountered Herbie Allen with his RACE CHAIRMAN band on his arm and a worried, high-chinned, aggressive expression. He asked in a tight voice about Stevie.

"He's all right," she said and fixed him with such a cold glance that he said in an appeasing voice, "Oh, that's great, Rody. I'm sure glad to hear that."

She marched on past him, not caring whether anybody saw the tears that were leaking out of her eyes again, gritting teeth and stumping.

3: *Richard E. Macklin, Jr.*

THE FIRST SHOCK was seeing his mother with her bifocals on, sitting at Brad's desk.

When he leaned on the counter in front of Annie to wish her a merry Christmas, she looked at him with scared eyes and whispered, "Mr. Peabody's gone!"

His mother glanced up, saw him, and beckoned him inside with an imperative gesture. The little top-of-the-iceberg worried frown pulled his mother's eyebrows together behind her glasses. He seated himself, saying, "What—" She passed him a note written on a sheet of lined, yellow, legal-sized paper in Brad's clear, round hand.

Christmas

Dearest Isobel,

Maeve and I are going downbelow together. I hope you will understand that we must go without delay, and that you will forgive any inconvenience this sudden departure causes. I will, of course, communicate with you when our future becomes clearer. I think I will be taking her home.

Love,
Brad

"My God!" he said. "On Christmas Day! Of all the irresponsible—" He halted himself, unable to make out whether his mother's expression was one of warning or not. "Of all the inappropriate times to leave," he said. "What does he mean, home?"

"I suppose he means Hawaii," his mother said. He noticed that she had turned the brass prism so that Brad's name was face down.

"Some inconveniences have come up already, of course," his mother went on. "I can't make head or tail of what's going on over on Big Red One. An illiterate keeps calling to ask when he can open the lift, and a cleft palate phoned to say Mr. Peabody must be told *not* to open the lift. I can't get in touch with Tim or any of the ski patrol. I really don't know what I'm to do."

"There's an accident at the race. Tim may be over there."

"Surely *all* the ski patrolmen can't be over there."

"There aren't very many of them, you know."

"These races will have to be held so they don't interfere with routines," his mother said in a taking-hold voice. "Anyway, I'm in a muddle. Dick always said that lifts must be kept running. There would be dozens of reasons why they couldn't be, but they must be kept running. So I told the one man he was to run, and then I told the other man he was to see that the lift was shut down if the ski patrol really did insist on it. And I can't get hold of Tim. I'm feeling just a bit hysterical. I want you to rush over to Big Red One and find out what the problem is. Surely you can find Tim." She gave him a tight smile, a plump, graying woman who looked a little frightened. "Solve this for me, dear," she said as he rose to go.

Outside, he saw a long queue at the Big Red One ramp. The lift was moving, but none of the ascending chairs was loaded. Though Blue Two and the Platterlift were both operating, the more expert skiers were waiting to ride up on Dancer Peak.

He hurried up the ramp past the grumbling skiers leaning on their poles in exaggerated positions of patience. Jack Bacon stood in the doorway of the attendant's shack, his face pale and serious.

Bacon drew him inside the shack, saying, "Christ, Dickie, I'm glad to see you! Christ, Dickie, it's not *my* fault! Your mother said open, so we opened, and Frank calls down yelling like a crazy man that we've got to shut down and stay shut down. But what the—"

"What's the matter with the lift?"

"It's not the lift. Nobody got around to shooting the Super-chute cornice yet."

"Can't they close that side of the mountain and let people ski over on the Tasket?"

Jack Bacon licked his lips and said, "Christ, Dickie, the way I get it, there's some skiers sitting up there *under* the cornice, and Frank's scared silly the slightest thing's going to drop it on them."

"Oh, my God!" he said. Clearly this was Brad's fault, and Tim's, and his mother's; he felt an ashamed relief that he himself could in no way be blamed. "Where's Tim?"

"Christ if *I* know. Listen, Dickie, nobody can blame me. I mean, your mother said go ahead and run, and I thought just the same way you did—what's the problem? If the Superchute's not shot yet they can ski the Tasket and the Chute, can't they? But Frank's screaming he doesn't want anybody up there even breathing until Tim gets there."

"I'm going up," he said and hurried over to catch the next chair. It felt odd to be riding the lift without skis on. As he was borne up above the trees and the lower slopes he could see a racer with a number on his chest twisting down through the red- and blue-flagged poles on the Spoon. A good-sized slide had been knocked down below the Blue Two Midway, and a huge one had come off Cape Horn, leaving a deep, wavy fracture line. A cloud hung over the face of Dancer Peak. As his chair rose he strained forward with impatience to see past the Scarp to the Superchute, where his father had been killed, to see the cornice that had killed him—beneath which, because of the collapse of the snow-safety routine caused by Brad's irresponsible departure, a group of overeager early-bird skiers must be huddled, afraid to move. The cloud that veiled the face of Dancer was descending to meet him, and, before the Intermediate Station, he was encased in it, blind and shivering.

The cloud broke up in time to give him one glance, like an illustration of the problem, into the diamond-gleaming sweep of the Superchute. The smooth, outswept mass of the cornice hung over the bowl, and beneath the cornice was a traverse line in the snow, punctuated by the dot of a single skier. At the far, safe end of the line, below the two trees and tracks down from the Elevator Shaft, was a cluster of skiers. A larger group watched from the observation rock at the near end of the cornice. He pushed his footrest up out of the way, preparatory to debarking. Whitey McCrae appeared to help him out of his chair.

He didn't stop to speak to Whitey but ran down the ramp. Immediately, without skis, he was laboring in deep snow. He was panting when he reached the group of skiers on the observation rock. The skier below the cornice was now a tiny seated figure, a girl in a red cap and white parka, one of her skis sticking obliquely out of the snow. From the marks in the snow it was clear that she

had taken a long traverse in the deep powder from the bottom of
the Elevator Shaft and had fallen when she tried to turn, losing at
least one of her skis.

It was absolutely infuriating that this girl should have got herself
into this dangerous predicament, tying up the whole mountain,
and now was calmly sitting beneath the cornice waiting for someone to endanger his life to get her out. "Why doesn't she put her
skis back on and ski back the way she came?"

"*Shhhhhhh!* For Christ's sake!"

"She's hurt. She can't stand up."

"They were yelling at her for a while just to sit tight."

"Yeah, they finally had the sense to shut up."

As he stared down at the girl he felt the backs of his legs prickling. The cornice was a lovely, streamlined, feminine shape; he had
seen clouds that looked denser. He found himself holding his
breath, and he blew it out in a long sigh. He didn't see what Tim
could possibly do. Go out to the girl with a toboggan, as to any
hurt skier, and take her out of there?

A skinny man in a blue golf cap said knowledgeably, "They'll
have to send for a helicopter to get her out of there."

"Are you kidding? A chopper in there would knock that thing
down in a second."

He started on down the wind-packed trail behind the cornice,
which turned first into the Elevator Shaft and the Superchute, and
further on led to the Chute. No danger signs, no avalanche signs,
had been posted. He thought of the lawsuit that could come out
of this if the girl died. A skier came past him moving fast, a heavy
fireplug of a man in a red ski-patrol parka, with an enormous hank
of brown rope hung over his shoulder.

"Tim!" he called, but Timbal Khan paid no attention to him,
turning with a spray of powder to disappear down the narrow cleft
of the Elevator Shaft.

There was no warning sign at the Elevator Shaft. This was
Tim's fault; today was the final exposure of the carelessness of the
skibums. They could never be trusted. Panting and cursing, he fell
heavily in the snowdrifts as he followed the ski tracks leading
down the Elevator Shaft.

Finally he came out to where he could see, first, the group
standing on the observation rock; then, fighting his way on

through the snow, he could see the skiers below him and quite near now. Tim and another patrolman stood with their heads together beside a toboggan. He was surprised to see John Henry with them, in his blue parka and pants. The girl beneath the cornice had not changed her position. Clouds drifted past, dipping down over the bowl in an enormous silence.

"What are you going to do?" he said, panting, when he came up to Tim and Frank Dow. He did not know the two other skiers with them, one young and pale and the other older with graying hair above his earband. John Henry stood ten feet away, staring out at the woman beneath the cornice.

"We're going to get her out," Tim said, hoisting the hank of rope off over his head and dropping it on the toboggan.

"Tom's gone to get the lightweight toboggan," Frank said. "But Tim doesn't think we ought to wait."

"We can't wait," Tim said. He began to tie the end of the nylon rope to the toboggan; he seemed very awkward about it. He said to Frank, "If we get a rope out there and the cornice comes down, you can find us."

"If the cornice comes down on you it won't matter if you're found or not," the older man said.

Tim tested his knot, then pulled it apart and began retying it, muttering something to himself.

He almost had his breath back. "How did she get out there?" he demanded of Tim.

"She and John Henry came down the Shaft and she just kept going. He yelled at her to stop but she kept going," Tim said. "She thinks she's broken her ankle."

With a blank face John Henry leaned on his poles, gazing out at the girl. Once his eyes glanced up at the cornice above her.

The backs of his legs kept prickling. "No avalanche warning sign," he said to Tim.

"That's right," Tim said.

He felt he wasn't being taken seriously. "Why—"

"Why don't you stop fussing and let me think?" Tim said.

"How do you think you're going to get her out?" asked the younger man standing with them.

In an irritated voice Tim said, "I'm going to ski out there with the toboggan with a rope on it and put her in it. Then you'll all haul it back here. Or else I'll run her over to the far side of the bowl." He sounded uncertain.

The older man said, "If I were doing it I'd—"

"You're not doing it," Tim said.

He watched Tim rub a gloved hand over his face, pushing his goggles up on his forehead. He had never seen Tim unsure on the mountain before.

As though apologizing for his rudeness, Tim said, "There's just no time. It can come down any time. It can come down if the sun gets to it for five minutes."

"How about if I went out with the toboggan, man?" John Henry said in a shaky voice. "I'm a lot lighter than you are."

"No, it's my job," Tim said and turned to Frank. "How about paying out some of that rope? You'll have to make sure you don't hang me up going out there."

"Right," Frank said and hefted the rope with an effort. He began backing up, paying out coils into the snow.

Out under the cornice the girl sat perfectly motionless, gazing down the bowl as though she had chosen that spot from which to admire the view. She held her hands in her lap; her legs were invisible in the deep snow. Just beyond her the tip of her ski stuck up higher than her red cap. Her face was in profile, and she had a quality of serenity that made him ashamed of his own irritation and his own panic. Once she glanced toward them, and John Henry raised a hand to her. Carefully she raised a hand in reply. He realized that it was the woman who had been with John Henry at Easy's party last night.

"Is she hurt?" a new voice asked. Easy had arrived, lean in his black pants and black ski-school sweater with the red stripe around the chest.

"Thinks she's busted her ankle," John Henry said.

"How're you going to bring her out?" Clary asked Tim.

Tim explained; this time he didn't sound irritated. He glanced back over his shoulder at Frank.

Easy stood gazing out at John Henry's girl, very tall, thin, and somehow elegant in black, with his wild eyebrows and his black hair carefully, casually rumpled. He looked very much Captain Easy today.

"That ought to do it, Tim," Frank called.

"*Hey!*" Tim said as Easy Clary shoved off with a thrust of his poles. Tim took a wild step uphill to try to grab him, but Easy was away, sliding along the track the woman had made across the top of the bowl.

"Ease," John Henry said, but not as though he were trying to stop him.

"*Christ!*" one of the others said.

Easy glided out along the track. He looked as though he were trying to ski with no weight on his skis, as though he were almost, magically, achieving levitation. The woman's face turned toward him; she raised a hand to her cheek. She did not look further around, at the overhanging cliff of snow behind her, smooth and white as cotton candy, but Clary glanced up at it continually as he traversed across beneath it.

No one spoke. Tim's hand was held out, palm down, as though warning against speaking. They watched Easy sliding across the great bowl toward the woman sitting in the snow. He was dragging his uphill pole as a brake. As if it occurred to him that even that could be dangerous, he flicked the basket free of the snow.

Clary slowed and came to a stop just below the woman. The two of them remained motionless for an aching moment, in whispered conversation, then Clary bent to peer at something in the snow. He put down his poles and worked with the woman's boot or binding, glancing up at the cornice frequently. Then he straightened, and, taking the woman's two hands, pulled her to her feet.

As he stood with Tim and the others, watching, there was no sound but the whispering of his own breath. He did not see how it could be taking Clary so long.

Clary crouched down and maneuvered the woman onto his back. Slowly he managed to hitch her up with her legs around his waist; she looked small as a child sitting on his back.

"Okay, straight on across the bowl," Tim whispered.

But first Clary raised an arm straight up toward the cornice, a finger protruding from his gloved fist, arm and finger shaken in a gesture of obscene defiance that he, Dickie, found shocking. Now Clary was in motion, slowly slanting off downhill with the woman's boots sticking out on either side of him. He wasn't going to traverse on across the bowl and out of danger.

"You god-damn sponsible showoff son-of-a-bitch!" Tim said in a terrible whisper as Clary peeled off more and more steeply, picking up speed as he swung down the bowl.

Tim's face was black and strained with rage as he turned to peer up at the cornice; and maybe mixed with that rage were the jealousy and chagrin he himself felt—at the injustice that Easy Clary could get away with this. Still he held his breath as Clary, with his burden, schussed the Superchute, not traveling dangerously fast because of the slowing depth of snow, sliding straight down the great bowl, leaving a single broad track, still in danger but closer and closer to the bottom, to the turn into the Chute, to safety and to legend. The figure, which looked a single squat figure now, became smaller and smaller, slowing as it bore left into the Chute, then finally vanished.

It was as though the sigh could be heard all over the Superchute at the same moment, from the group around him, from those standing on the observation rock. His mother was there watching, he noticed for the first time.

Tim said in a casual voice, "Well, I guess we'd better get up and knock that cornice down before anybody else gets in trouble."

Frank plumped the hank of rope down on the toboggan, and the two ski patrolmen began to sidestep up toward the Elevator Shaft; the other two men sidestepped after them. John Henry followed listlessly. He himself, on foot, went last of all.

4: Isobel Bradley Macklin

WHEN, DIMINISHED by distance into a single speeding figure, they had finally vanished, like a spectator with the show over she hurried back through the leg-fatiguing snow to get on the lift. The frightened-of-her lift attendant, whom she recognized as the cleft-palate voice on the telephone, slowed the lift and helped her to down-load. In the chair, with her fur collar turned up around her ears, her hands in her pockets, and her snowboots placed on the footrest, she dropped slowly through space, over the upper snowfields of Dancer toward the lodge and the Big House, her domain at the bottom. But wasn't all of it her domain?

Over to her left was the Superchute, where Dick had died. The cornice that had killed him hung poised in massive restraint. She saw that the few spectators who had been standing over on the east side of the bowl were now hiking back up to the cleft in the ridge. She gazed, consciously shivering, upon the great curved and slanting expanse of snow that gleamed now in the sun.

Swinging slightly in her chair as she dropped into space, clutching the safety bar, she knew that she had paid a long overdue visit to the Castle of the Lord of Death, where she had been exposed to a Lesson. It had been what Dick had once tried to explain to her, the Lesson he had learned when he had been hit by a mortar shell in the Guadalcanal jungle. She had thought he was only bragging.

She had witnessed the Lord of Death's decision that Clary and the woman Clary had rescued should not die, just as nine years ago He had decided that Dick should die. He was not terrible. He was only capricious. It was what Dick had tried to tell her when he had been talking about contingency.

And it was as though, now that she had the message, she could realize in her bloodstream instead of merely in her head that Dick was really dead, truly gone. Her grief had been over long ago, but now it seemed that an almost physical servitude was completed. She had spent nine years as Dick's widow. The fourteen years before that had been spent as Dick's wife. If she had married again she would have continued to be merely the remarried widow of Dick Macklin.

Swinging downward in the chair, she realized that she had never been herself and that she must become herself. And she realized how much of her life there was still to be lived—lived, not eked out. She thought that she might be able to live it here, where the living had always been more highly flavored, no longer the absentee owner of herself or of the pleasure garden, swimming with Time rather than standing beside the stream looking back while Time flowed past.

It was Eurydice, she remembered, who had preferred looking backward to avidly and perhaps ungracefully looking ahead, and so had remained in the gloomy and sunless halls of Death. But Life was where the sun shone so brightly you had to wear dark glasses against the glare and lotions and creams against burns and skin cancer. Cancer . . . poor Maeve.

In her journey into clarity she thought that Brad must have gone downbelow to play Orpheus to Maeve's Eurydice. She almost laughed aloud at the fancy; but perhaps it was not so fantastic. She had felt no rancor toward Brad when she had read his note that meant another man-in-her-life had been swept up by Maeve. But perhaps she could understand, as Brad had said he hoped she would understand. She thought he had taken Maeve away, taken her home, because Maeve was hysterical with the knowledge that she was dying; sometimes, like last night, quite mad with fear. She blessed the two of them, even as she wondered at Brad's qualifications to be a healer of fear.

Yet she did not feel much concerned with the lives of others. She was fascinated by her own. She sailed down past the Scarp where a single ski track slanted across the white precipice. At the Intermediate Station she saw a worried face peering at her through the window of the attendant's booth. News of her descent had probably been phoned ahead. She was, after all, the Boss.

The attendant at the bottom, a man about her own age with an unhealthy, whipped-by-life face and manner, whom she had curtly silenced on her way up, again began to babble that it had not been his fault, he had only done what she had told him to do.

"It was my error," she said to him. "Now I don't think we need hear any more about it." She gave him a cold smile and started back to the lodge.

In Brad's office, at Brad's desk, with Dick's photograph looking over her shoulder, she had just finished telling Annie Sprague what had happened when Dickie appeared. Her son wore his tan lift-coat, its hood rolled into a thick collar, which made him look as though he had no neck. His taste in clothing was as poor as his taste in hair style. She had hoped he would marry Evaline Hamilton, and that Evvy would take him in hand and make a more aesthetically pleasing object of him. Perhaps Evvy hadn't a strong enough personality anyway.

Dickie came into the office, scuffling his feet, his face like a stormcloud. She did not want to talk to him sitting at Brad's desk under the scrutiny of Dick's photograph and the passers-by in the lobby, so she went into the inner office. Dickie followed her, slapping his gloves against his leg with a disagreeable hollow sound. She sat down in the swivel chair, watching him as he made a business of peering at something on the area map.

"What did Tim do about the cornice?" she asked.

"He kicked it down."

"Kicked it down?"

"He roped himself to Frank Dow and walked out on it a little way and kicked it down. It all came down at once." He went over and sat down on the couch.

"I find the irresponsibility almost unbelievable," he said in an outraged voice. "Brad walking out of here without a word to anyone. Tim leaving the Superchute unpatrolled, no warning signs. John Henry letting that woman ski out under the cornice without *doing* anything. And Easy Clary—well, you saw that."

"Yes," she said, nodding.

"Of all the fantastic, stupid, grandstand—"

"Yes, but it worked, dear."

He looked at her as though she had betrayed him.

She tried to understand his envy and frustration, understanding

that her own impatience with him came from love. She realized
that, as she had spent the last nine years not as herself but only as
Dick Macklin's widow, so must Dickie's character have been
formed not only by that potent and enduring presence, but also by
her own obsession with the dead husband rather than the living
son. No doubt Dick had left him with some guilt, burdened his
son as he had tried to burden her. She thought she herself had at
last climbed out of the hole Dick had dug for her, and she was
sure Dickie could climb out of his own hole. Loving her son, with
optimism, very nearly with serenity, she watched him glowering at
the blown-up photograph of the skier in the powder on the Superchute as though it represented the whole spirit of irresponsibility
he objected to.

He burst out, "I don't know where I stand! Am I the manager
of Dancer now or not?"

This was another matter. In this she was the mistress of Dancer,
not a mother. She said in a crisp voice, "Maybe you'd better tell
me what your program would be if you were."

"I've already told you."

"That was hypothetical. For instance, I suspect you would like
to dismiss everyone who had a hand in what you consider today's
fiasco."

"Brad told me once everybody who worked here was a sick
bum," Dickie said sulkily. "I think he was right." Then he took a
deep breath and said, "No, I think Tim should be given another
chance. And I suppose Easy Clary's a good enough ski instructor.
It's just—"

"Tell me what it is you want here," she interrupted.

"I want a ski resort that's run in a businesslike, efficient manner."

"Just a business proposition?"

"That's what I mean."

"The machinery turns, and a certain amount of profit, prefera-
bly a good deal, comes out the other end. Part of this is reinvested
in capital expansion in a businesslike manner, and the rest is dis-
tributed as dividends?"

"That's exactly what I mean," Dickie said.

Her chair squeaked as she leaned toward him. "Tell me something, please. Is this *you* deciding on this program, or you thinking the way you think you are supposed to think as a business-school graduate?"

He licked his lips. "I don't know what you mean."

"What I mean is that your program doesn't appeal to me."

He looked mulish.

She said, "I have already told you my feelings about that program. Either you didn't listen to me or you didn't believe I was serious. I was very serious. I've been thinking of asking Easy Clary to take the position as manager. If he's not interested I'll do it myself, since I intend to make my home here from now on."

"Good God!" Dickie almost shouted at her. "Easy Clary!"

"Yes."

"Because of today? Because—"

"I'd already been thinking about him."

"You must be out of your mind! Everyone's out of his mind!"

"Everyone but you," she said. "But you're very young yet, dear," she said affectionately.

He got to his feet, sallow with anger. He said in a shaky voice, "You must see that I can't remain here if you are going to—if you insist—"

"I hope you'll stay," she said. "Because I need you here. And because you need the experience. This will be your resort to run in your own way someday, but just now it's mine."

He gave her another wild glance, started to speak, turned and stamped out of the office instead. She thought he would come around, in time, to her way of thinking.

She sat in the inner office contemplating without much emotion, as she could do now, the revelation of how she had been tricked. For nine years she had felt that she had tried to hold Dick, that vaunted free spirit, by buying him; that she had tried to bind him to her with her money. He had died as though to prove to her his statement that she had bought nothing.

It was simply not true, as his accusations about her friendship with Maeve were lies. She had not known he was having an affair with Maeve, that he had been in love with Maeve and had been considering running off to a new life with Maeve. She had not gone to Honolulu to get money in order to hold him. She had gone to get the money to save Dancer Peak—and to save Dick from defeat. She had not bought him. He had only sold himself. He had been more in love with financial ease and the things money could buy, the power and position it could buy, than he had been in love with Maeve and freedom.

Now she would take down Dick's photograph so it would not stare over her shoulder at her business, though no doubt this would scandalize Annie Sprague and others. Dickie could put it back up again when he came to occupy this office. It was time for him to begin to honor his father, but it was time for her to stop.

She sat contentedly, thinking no longer of the past, which was dead and gone, and not particularly of the future, but of the pleasure garden of the present, which gleamed with excitement all around her like a dare.

5: Captain Easy

HE HAD BEEN a star before, when, as a pass-catching end, he had won his last football game, the Stanford-Cal Freshman Big Game, literally singlehanded, with a circus catch in the final thirty seconds of play. Now he was more an actual hero than a star, called by the name of hero as he made his way through the crowds in the lodge and on the deck. "Hey, Hero!" and, "Easy, you fucking hero!" and, "So heroic, Easy!" He enjoyed it thoroughly. It was only too bad that no one knew from what depths of non-heroism he had come back.

Passing inside from the sundeck, he encountered the Austrian Admiral. Grinning, red-cheeked, jowly, the Admiral gripped his elbow with one hand, with the other slapped his shoulder with metronome blows. "Easy Clary! You are great hero! I am very proud!"

"Thanks, Hansy," he said, detaching himself. Everyone within earshot was grinning at him. For the first time he felt a little resentment that they should all think it such an easy, downhill kind of feat, of coordination, flash, and luck. He had not been at all certain the cornice would not come down. He had been prepared to embrace Elizabeth in such a way as to create an airspace between them on which they could survive until Tim dug them out.

He did not know, now, how far he had thought out what he was doing, though it had not been merely reaction at seeing Elizabeth sitting stiff-backed and scared-to-death under the cornice. He had not gone out there to die, but maybe he had gone out to face death just to show himself that he could face it.

As he made his way through the lodge accompanied by the hero tune, he noticed his tendency to swagger, stand tall, grin a lot. His step was light. He felt young and full of hell, contemptuous of words, disgusted with the sentimentalities and rationalizations of philosophy, an advocate of natural action. Requiring recognition was only the First Principle, which was a way in which you should live, not talk. Never again would he consider a Second Personal surrender of himself to a Martha Schroeder, even to a Maeve. He admitted readily Badbody's right to that particular rescue, or salvage, and he was very grateful for the chance which his luck had presented him with today.

He started for the men's room, hero-stardom having affected his bladder like a quantity of beer. He felt as though, without even realizing it, he had been catching age like a cold. He had thrown it off with the antihistamine of public approbation, and his own. No more easy and comfortable love affairs with older women. Tonight he might track down some tough young girl, like Betsy-the-barmaid.

When he passed the arches over the counter in the lobby Isobel Macklin, sitting at Badbody's desk, beckoned to him. She wore pearl-rimmed harlequin glasses, wisps of pale hair had come loose from her clubwoman's coiffure, and she looked harried. He went around behind the counter, moving as though suspended from his shoulders.

"Hello, Big-Deal," Annie said.

"Care to touch me?"

She touched his arm, gasping. "Too *much!*" She indicated Isobel with informative workings of her eyebrows that he could not interpret. He went on into Badbody's office, and Isobel nodded for him to sit down across the desk from her.

"That was a very spectacular rescue, Captain Easy," she said, regarding him with her slight but potent frown.

"Nothing."

"Though it may have been Tim's prerogative," Isobel said. "If the cornice had—"

"If the cornice had come down Tim would've known where to dig. Nobody else would have known where to dig for him."

Isobel said, "Would you rather I complimented your judgment or your courage?"

He grinned and slid down in his chair until he was supported by the back of his neck. He noticed that the brass prism with Badbody's name had been turned name down. "Did Brad clear out?"

Isobel picked up a yellow pencil and held it between her two hands. "He and Maeve have gone away together." She drew a long breath and said, "He left me a note saying he was taking her home."

"To Hawaii. They told me," he said.

Isobel leaned back in her chair while he faced her slanting in his. She did not seem interested in learning what he knew about Badbody and Maeve that she did not know. It was Isobel, he remembered, who had told Badbody that Maeve was dying.

"I'm afraid the trouble this morning was due to the system Brad set up," she said, frowning again. "He made his own presence essential."

"I guess Dickie will be taking over now."

He thought she shook her head slightly. Suddenly she looked emotional, the flesh beneath her eyes turning pink as though tears were pressing there. She said in a flat voice, "I want Dancer run as Dick wanted it run. As a pleasure garden."

"I'm not so sure he would have run it that way," he surprised himself by saying. "I think he might have just gone on building lifts."

She nodded once, though more in recognition of his statement, he thought, than in agreement. "You're not in favor of building more lifts?"

"I think more lifts are fine—more terrain open, shorter lift lines, more skiers. But I suspect these lift-building types of wanting memorials, not pleasure gardens."

Isobel looked down at the pencil she held. This time when she nodded it was in agreement. Musingly she said, "But Dick wasn't always like that."

Almost beneath where they were sitting now, Dick Macklin had spoken of sitting down running a successful operation, fat-assed, uxorious, and grateful, as though admitting that he had sold out to the Crock. Maybe he had not always been like that, but that wasn't what mattered. But he nodded in his turn, to be agreeable.

"I'm afraid Brad was a bad manager in many ways," Isobel said.

"He wasn't always like that," he said. He was feeling a pressure

he didn't want to recognize yet, and his mood had slipped a little.
Out the window he could see the skiers coming down the Bunny
Hill and the bottom of the Spoon, from which the slalom gates
had been cleared. For the most part the bunnies skied very badly,
but they were having a great time. At least they were trying. He
urged them on with silent cries of "Go! Go!"

Waiting for whatever was forthcoming from Isobel Macklin, he
tried to recapture the sensation of Elizabeth perched on his back
with tight knees like a jockey. When he had stopped beneath
where she sat in the snow, she had looked at him with enormous
eyes and said, "Oh, you glorious *fool!*" When they had started
down the bowl she had said in his ear, "Will you always bail me
out when I'm in real trouble?" Now he was trying to get all the
sensations, things said, done, and felt, realized and permanent in
the scrapbook of his memory. Because, of course, it had been the
Greatest Day.

Isobel Macklin said, "I want you to take Brad's position."

Though he had known, trying not to know, what was coming,
he affected a classic doubletake with a whooping sound of awe.
"Me?"

"I want you to manage Dancer."

"Out of your mind."

Isobel shook her head and looked irritated.

"You mean sit inside here watching other people ski?"

"I want you to run a pleasure garden here."

"No! Good God, *no!*"

She said severely, "You talk about the pleasure garden. You make
judgments and pronouncements. But you won't help me to
achieve one. If you believe in a principle you must be prepared to
do something to achieve it. I can't believe you are just a bum."
She pursed her lips tightly.

"That's me."

"No, I don't believe you are," Isobel said as though sure she
was getting to him.

He had talked too much, hadn't he? And he had talked too
much just now about the failure of the Second Principle, claiming
he had forsworn it forever. Was the laugh going to be finally on
him, the hero? Was it for this the cornice had held off? Was he

going to be doomed by his own principle and big mouth to sitting down fat-assed running a successful operation, insuring that all the bunnies, and not himself any more, had the great times?

Leaning toward him as though with the clincher, Isobel said, "No one is going to insist that you sit inside all day, Easy."

He managed to grin back at her. Didn't she know he was a monument? What would his disciples say, his students and his friends? They wouldn't even know all there was to laugh at. Reluctantly he began to examine what he would be getting into. It was all very well for Isobel to claim she wanted a pleasure garden here, but the existence of the pleasure garden, and of his job, would depend on the pleasure garden's earning an acceptable profit. And it wasn't a job, it was a position. In a job you worked for someone, as he worked for the Admiral, and quit when you had had enough, but in a position you indentured yourself to the establishment, the power structure, the whole Life Force-Judeo-Christian-Platonic-Finance Capital-Madison Avenue Hammerlock, the Crock of shit.

He was shaking his head but at the same time his mind was racing through lists of improvements, changes, policies and the repeal of policies that would make a greater pleasure garden of Dancer. Mocking silent laughter tickled at the back of his throat.

"If you want to make this a pleasure garden for Dick's sake," he said, "I'd think you'd want to have his son running it."

"He doesn't believe in the principle," Isobel said.

"Oh, well, it'll come."

"I hoped you would help to insure that it does," Isobel said. She continued to watch him, a clever woman used to getting her own way.

He struggled to sit upright, and she leaned back in her chair with her hands on the leather-covered arms. She swung away to face the arched window on the lobby. "I must tell you that I intend to spend most of my time here now," she said. "It's only fair to warn you that you will not be untroubled by my presence as Brad was."

When he said nothing she swung her chair back. "I would like you to begin immediately," she said.

"It's only fair to warn you I wouldn't sit in here a minute when there was fresh powder snow."

"I wouldn't expect you to."

"It's only fair to warn you that I get drunk sometimes and I get in fights at the Loup Garou. And I sleep with whoever I want to."

"I would only expect you to conduct yourself so as not to damage the pleasure garden," Isobel said. She was smiling, sure she had won. "Will you start in the morning then?"

"I'll think about it," he said, rising. He felt heavy and uncertain. "Thanks for having me in mind," he said, to keep her off balance.

Isobel Macklin nodded to him, and he left, no longer swaggering, filled with apprehension that had little quicksilver trickles of elation running through it. He needed advice. Suddenly he knew he must see Elizabeth, and not merely for advice. Maeve's old dream, which for a reluctant, too-little and too-late moment he had embraced, came back to him; now it was bright and tantalizing and Elizabeth was in it instead of Maeve. He was managing Dancer, and Elizabeth, whom he had saved from the avalanche, was helping him. They would live happily ever after, working hand in hand as missionaries of the pleasure garden. He made excited, mocking, warning sounds as he bounded down the stairs in search of Elizabeth.

He found her sitting on the deck in a patch of pale sunlight, her white parka zipped to the throat, one seam of her pantleg undone, and a pristine white cast on her foot and ankle. MICHELLE STEIN-BERG had been inked on the cast in childish print, and Michelle herself, wearing a red parka a size too large, sat with her mother.

Elizabeth gave him a thin smile as he sat down opposite her. "Somebody said they'd shot it down," she said. "It was very beautiful in its way."

"They should've knocked it down by now." He didn't know how he was going to say what he had come to say in front of the little girl.

"You met Mr. Clary yesterday, remember, Mikey?" Elizabeth said.

The child stared at him with candid eyes in her monkey face. She had an almost comical resemblance to Shelley Steinberg, once the Guru. "Did you save my mother's life?" she whispered in a slightly accusatory tone.

"I did. I did."

"You ought to sign my mother's cast," Mikey said. A pen was

produced, and he inscribed his name: CHARLES CLARY. Elizabeth, the new Guru, maybe his conscience now, watched him not quite fondly.

"Quite a Christmas morning," she said. "Lots of excitement up here in the mountains where the air is clear. Too much for me, I'm afraid."

"Ankle hurt?"

"Hurts."

"Mommy, when're we going to phone Daddy?"

"I don't know, dear," Elizabeth said. "I told you I was only thinking about it." Squinting into the sun at the skiers descending the mountain, she repeated, "Thinking about it."

He could not protest in front of the small facsimile of Shelley. He looked long at Elizabeth, who might be the guru now but would always be the original Golden Girl. When she looked back at him with blank eyes, smiling the thin smile, his rosy but fragile vision burst with only a whimper.

"I've just been offered the job as manager of Dancer, Guru," he said. "Now. Immediately."

Elizabeth raised an eyebrow and nodded as though she was not surprised. Her face was golden-brown in the sunlight, drawn a little around the corners of her mouth with pain. Shiny yellow crutches lay against the chair beside her. She labored to raise her cast to the seat of the chair in front of her, and he helped her lift the smooth, hard plaster.

"Thanks," she said. "Going to take it?"

"Tell me."

Mikey looked suspiciously from face to face. Elizabeth said, "What happened to the other man?"

"He quit." He didn't elaborate.

"Does the other woman enter the equation?"

He shook his head.

Elizabeth managed to give the impression of a computer having data fed into it. Her full lips were turned down judiciously.

He said, "It was put to me that I was to make a real pleasure garden here."

"I see."

"What're you guys talking about?" Mikey demanded.

"Life, baby," Elizabeth said. She sat considering him in silence for a long time; finally she said, "I think you ought to take the job if you want to take it."

"Position," he said, feeling disappointed. He had thought she would tell him to watch out, danger! hang in there! and he had been prepared to argue about the changes he would make so that skiing at Dancer would be so much more pleasurable. "Just like that?" he said.

"After pain a formal feeling comes," Elizabeth said. "I had detected symptoms of the feeling of failure, and though all is changed by the recent Hairbreadth Harry-ness, still it is a thing to beware of. Forestall."

"You don't think I ought to go for the record? World's oldest skibum?"

"Records are attempts at immortality, which implies dissatisfaction with the life one has. If you will remember," Elizabeth said in doctrinaire style. "The Guru's advice to you is to do what in best conscience you want to do, not what you think you ought to do."

"What's a Guru?" Mickey asked.

"It's a kind of teacher, honey," Elizabeth said. "It's a joke your daddy and I and Mr. Clary had a long time ago, when we went to college together."

He said, "I wish I knew if you were telling me what you think I want to hear or what I ought to hear."

Some of the composure left Elizabeth's face, and she looked tired, worried, and in pain. "That's too complicated," she said. "I've got problems of my own."

"Sorry."

"I need some advice myself. Regarding Mr. Bell's nationwide system of communications."

He said in a suddenly thick voice, "I don't know, Elizabeth. I'm feeling very emotional." He blinked his sun-dazzled eyes.

"Oh, I too. Oh, absolutely," Elizabeth said, smiling fixedly at the skiers weaving and dancing down the hill. She said, "But I've been sitting here making discoveries about myself. And about the First Personal Principle. Clary—I think the center begins to wear out. Its importance does anyway. And all those funny little lumps along the periphery grow and grow and get—more and more precious. And I guess the sum of the parts gets to be the whole thing." She darted one glance sideways at him. "And maybe there's a satisfaction in the center getting less important and the peripheries more. Sort of the process of everything going *on*. Do you read me?"

"I read you," he said.

"I suppose it's only our old friend the Life Force," Elizabeth said.

"It's the Crock," he said. The sun faded behind a cottony cloud, and immediately he was shivering without his parka. He looked down at his name, with Michelle Steinberg's, on the white cast. "What one wants to do, not just what one *ought* to do," he said.

"Maybe they are the same sometimes, Clary," Elizabeth said, and they sat without speaking for a long time.

"Anyway," Elizabeth said in a different voice, "you can see that one is sitting here in a kind of Bell Hell."

"What's a Bell Hell, Mommy?"

Elizabeth said seriously, "Honey, it's a funny name for a situation where you know what has to be done but you don't quite have guts enough to do it."

"What if one did the tough part for one?" he said.

"One would appreciate that," Elizabeth said, "very much."

She sat staring with bright eyes up the mountain while he rose, tried to give Mikey a friendly smile, and took his leave. He went inside to get some change from the bar and occupy a phone booth.

In the stuffy, reinforced-glass box he listened to the phone ring in Berkeley. "Hello?" Shelley's remote voice answered. He deposited coins on demand.

"It's Clary," he said.

"Oh, hello, Chuck."

"You'd better come up here and collect your wife and kids."

There was silence on the echoing wire.

"Better come and get her, Shel," he said.

"I don't know what she's told you. I just don't think I can do it, Chuck."

"If you don't come and get her I'm going to move in. You wouldn't like that."

"I'm not sure I'd really care very much by now, Chuck," Shelley

said in a reasonable, professorial tone. "She's fairly used goods, you
know," he added, no longer so reasonably.

"Come off it, you sell-out son-of-a-bitch!" he snarled. "Do you
think I like seeing her go back to you?"

There was another, shocked silence. In Berkeley, Shelley cleared
his throat, a mechanical, grating sound.

He said, "She's got a broken ankle. That'll make it easier for
you."

"Skiing, I suppose," Shelley said coldly.

"Skiing. Yeah."

"Perhaps I will drive up this afternoon."

"Go, boy."

"Yes, well, all right then, I'll start right up," Shelley said. "Is—"

That was enough, and he hung up. Sitting slumped in the dusty
cubicle, looking at the phone book hanging from its chain, he had
never felt so lonely—the first strong, cold breath of the Future-
Imperfect, he supposed. He sat in the glass-walled box and
watched the skiers passing, who came and went without seeing
him.

Finally he returned to the bar. He wrote a note with Betsy's
pencil on a paper napkin, notifying Elizabeth that her husband
was coming up to Dancer to get her. He sent Betsy out on the
deck with the note and a Bloody Mary for Elizabeth, a Shirley
Temple for her daughter. He patted Betsy on the left buttock as
she departed. It was something he had never got around to before
now.

He sat at the bar to drink a beer and think about himself, to try
to separate the grain of what he wanted to be from the chaff of
what he thought he ought to want. Was he called to be a philosopher or philanthropist, First or Second Principler, skibum or ad-
ministrator? He did not really know what he wanted or what he
was; he knew only that he had not yet solved his life. His spirits
surged upward as he found himself engaged in man's proper study.
How, after all, could the equation of a man's life be considered
solved until its end, when all the returns were in? Solved meant
completed, didn't it? He laughed silently in his throat, drank beer,
and wiped away the mustache of foam.

It wasn't what you thought you *ought* to do, but what, in your good conscience, you *wanted* to do. That was the only self-evident truth, wasn't it? That was the true principle, wasn't it? At least it was his own principle, and although he knew that there were many principles, perhaps as many as there were people who had them, he knew that the only principle valid for your own life was *your own.*

6: John Henry

HE FELT so good and quiet now, he felt really good now, when this morning, watching Elizabeth under the cornice, he had felt so awful. When Easy Clary had gone out after her it had been that much worse. He'd known Easy would make it. But now he felt very good and as though he had finally shaken hands with himself on everything, because Elizabeth in the Superchute under the cornice and Easy going out to get her had torn it.

Now he sat in the maple easy chair in his room, watching a bunch of clods on TV with the sound turned down so it was only a mutter, sipping whisky but not to get drunk, and a cheroot forked between his fingers. He was waiting for the telephone to ring.

He picked it up on the first squawk, and Frisco Daley in Pine Flat, Mississippi, was saying, "Is that you, man? What's up, man?"

"How's it go, Frisc?"

"It's going. I mean, like not too bad. Few dents in the bus from some rocks got kind of flung at us. What a dump this is. But we had a hell of a hootenanny at the workshop last night—I mean, you ought to hear some of these cats when they get goin'. This chick got *moved* last night. I mean, she was singing up off the bottoms of her big flat feet. Goin' on down to Jackson tomorrow."

"Nobody got, you know, hurt yet?"

"Not yet, man. I mean, you get so nervous. We all laugh at Charley Feathers—he spends half his time restringing his box to keep his hands from, you know, shaking. But we tread pretty light and get by. Nobody's trying to rub anybody's face in it. I mean, it *goes*—you know? What's up, man?"

"Well, you know what they said when they got the colored astronaut up in orbit?"

"Huh?" Frisco said.

"The *jig* is up!" he said, laughing shakily. "I mean, I'm on my way, man."

There was a silence. "You're kidding?" Frisco said.

"I'm on my way! I'm going to drive it, Porsche-it. What'll it take me from here, a couple of days?"

"Don't drive, man! *Fly.* I mean, you don't want to be here in any heap with out-of-state plates, like especially New York or California. Fly. Pick you up in Jackson tomorrow. I mean, no kidding, man, you're *coming?*"

"I'm coming, Frisco."

"Can we get out a press release on it?"

" 'John Henry Collins joins Liberty Singers!' Yay!"

"Man," Frisco said, "how come?"

"Couldn't have you go on thinking I was chicken, could I, man?"

"Hell, I didn't! Everybody bugs different, man."

"Anyway, I'm coming," he said, watching past the receiver the meaningless motions of the shadows on the TV tube. He had talked too long; now a kind of euphoria was wearing off like a pep pill, and he saw he was only, drearily, going to go on being afraid. He resented Frisco Daley, who was an authentic, who thought he was the new Woody Guthrie or maybe even Joe Hill; there was no question about whether *he* did this kind of thing or not, he *had* to do it. But of course he, John Henry Collins, had to too; the bill that was due was as simple as that.

"Okay, see you, then, man," Frisco said in his distant voice. "I'll get a press release out right away. We got reporters around all the time, waiting to get shots of the action. See you in Jackson. That'll be us in the red, white, and blue bus with all the rednecks around it chunking rocks."

"See you, man," he said and hung up. While he still had steam up he put in a call to his agent. "Hi, Sid."

"How's skiing, John Henry?" Sid-the-agent said in his nasal, patronizing voice.

"I'm taking off for Mississippi, Sid, so don't put together that tour we were talking about. I don't know how long I'll—"

"What the hell are you talking about?" Sid shouted at him. "I'm not letting you go down there and get your nuts kicked off, you hear!"

"Well, I'm going," he said.

"Goddamit!" Sid said. "I've worked my ass off trying to make something of you, kiddo! You stay out of that race shit, you hear me? I've already got you signed at the University of Washington for the tenth, and pretty close to signed in Portland. Now you—"

"I'm going to Jackson tomorrow," he said. "So long, Sid."

"John Henry!" Sid yelled at him, but he hung up.

He stood up, taking deep breaths to get his breathing back to normal. One of these days he had to take a long look in on himself to see why he was more afraid of Sid getting mad at him than of being kicked in the crotch by freckled fat rednecks in Jackson. "Yay!" he said aloud, trying to cheer himself up once more.

He picked up the phone. "Honey, this is room twelve, Mister Collins, again. Anybody phones for me, anybody at all, I've just checked out. Hear?"

"Yes, Mr. Collins. Are you leaving, Mr. Collins?"

"Yay. Tell the desk to add it up, will you?"

He finished his whisky, put his parka back on, and walked through the crowded lodge lobby, looking for a familiar face. He found Elizabeth sitting on the chilly sundeck with a Bloody Mary in front of her, her foot in a cast propped up on a chair, and the yesterday little girl sitting beside her. He had never liked a woman so much, but he supposed there weren't even any pieces to pick up now.

He managed to grin and say, "I guess you won't be so anxious to ski the powder with me next time."

Elizabeth said, "Mikey, this man we met yesterday is Mr. *John Henry* Collins."

The little girl looked at him, very impressed, with eyes like life-savers. She didn't resemble Elizabeth much, not too cute. "Will you sign my mother's cast?" she said.

"Love to sign your mother's cast," he said. He saw that Charles Clary had been here and gone. He took the pen handed to him and put his name down below Captain Easy's. "Goin' to Jackson, Elizabeth," he said.

"Are you?"

"Guess I better. Have to," he said, nodding to her anxiously, wanting her approval. She looked at him hard; something wrong with her eyes, worried for him. "It's all right," he said. "I know why I'm going and all. Just because that's the way you pay the bill for all the bread and honey and stuff. Not anything, you know— *else*. I *want* to go," he said, feeling himself making a face trying to grin.

"Then you're brave," Elizabeth said.

"No," he said and laughed a little. He felt the sun on the side of his face, and he squinted up at it.

The little girl said, "We play your record all the time at my house."

"Yay! That's what I like to hear!" He said to Elizabeth as casually as he could, "Sorry this morning turned out the way it did."

"Don't ever be," Elizabeth said.

"Look, there's Christy!" the little girl said. They looked where she pointed, on the crowded Bunny Hill; Christy was her brother that he'd met yesterday. "He's getting good," Mikey said.

"He'll never break *his* ankle," Elizabeth said.

Mikey got up and stood leaning against her mother. She said to him, "My daddy's coming to get us this afternoon."

"All of us," Elizabeth said, to his raised eyebrows.

"No kidding?"

"No kidding."

He said to the little girl, "Well, you tell your daddy he's the luckiest daddy in the whole world, will you?"

"Do you love my mommy?" the little girl said, with lifesaver eyes again.

"Everybody does," he said. "Because your mommy is the *greatest*, and the *smartest*, and the *most*." He got to his feet. "See you, Elizabeth."

She looked at him with her olive-shaped, red-brown, dry eyes, and said, "Take care of yourself, John Henry Collins."

"Oh, sure," he said. " 'By." He didn't touch her, remembering how it had been touching her and not touching her last night, and of course there was no way now with the little loyal-to-daddy girl watching like the warden. " 'By, Chick," he said to Mikey. He left.

He packed, checked out, and started in the Porsche for San Francisco, where he would hop a plane to Jackson, Mississippi, to pay his bill or find out about himself or whatever it was he thought he was doing. On the way up the summit the "Chains Required" signs were out, but he ignored them. He had all the traction he needed.

7: J.D. Daugherty

SOMETIMES HATE CAME on him like the flu. Then he would just have to sweat it out, sick with it. The crap they told about in *American Opinion*, what he read in the newspapers, the past indignities and future injustices planned for him by Internal Revenue, great armies of nameless resentments and fears, all came crowding down to bug him all at once, until he would begin to think he was cracking up.

He had faced the fact that maybe he had hated Macklin not for anything Macklin had done, but for what he himself had done. He was just starting to face the fact that maybe that was what the whole hate thing was.

He had stayed on at the Loup Garou this Christmas night to help out his new bartender, Eddie Bricker, because, although the evening hadn't started out busy, you never could tell about Christmas night. It was blowing some outside, which might tend to keep people home, but the weather report called for clear and cold tomorrow. Clear and cold meant another great ski day, and he would be up there hitting it. He wasn't going to let that crazy bitch's accusing him of killing Macklin spoil the powder for him.

He didn't know why he had lost his cool like that except that all at once he had had the cornered feeling of everybody at Clary's against him, the hate thing crashing down on him with the comsymp big-government Democrats making law on top of law, and the bartenders who wouldn't show up for work, and the ski-bums odd-jobbing around the lodge all winter and going on unemployment all summer and laughing at the responsible citizens who paid Internal Revenue and county taxes so the government could support the fuckoffs. Now he was ashamed of blowing because obviously Maeve was sick, and ashamed and afraid of hating like that because the possibility had come on him that maybe he was sick, too.

What with Maeve running off with Badbody, which made so little sense there wasn't any point even thinking about it, and Rody's boy getting almost totaled forerunning the race, and the Jew-girl from Clary's party hung up under the Superchute cornice with a broken ankle, Christmas Day at Dancer had had a lot of swing to it. What didn't swing was Timbal Khan Soderburg back in his old spot, sitting hunchbacked at the bar, silent and black-faced like some big animal. He had thought Tim might be down on him because of last night, maybe even looking for trouble, but obviously Tim was only hurting.

After ignoring Tim for a while, he began to feel sorry for him. "That kid of Rody's is going to be all right, huh?"

Grunt.

"What do you make of Badbody and Maeve going off like that?"

Grunt.

A voice began heavy-breathing out of the music on the juke-box—"*Baby, baby, can't you hear my heart beat?*"

"All I know is Maeve better get to a fucking doctor," he said to Tim.

Tim worked up a snarling sort of grin as though trying to be agreeable. Poor bastard, hurting because Easy Clary had stolen his thunder on the mountain, making a circus out of snow safety, which Tim took pretty seriously. Lonely old Tim Soderburg with his snarl of a grin and one poached eye looking anxiously at him, the other hidden by a big hand. He took Tim's glass and refilled it, on the house.

Grunt, thanks.

"*Baby, baby, can't you hear my heart beat?*"

" Seen John Henry, Tim?" he asked.

Grunt, no.

Finally he left Tim alone to wait on other customers, and so Tim was sitting alone, hunched in his corner, putting down brews too fast, when Easy Clary came in with a bunch of the kind of people he was apt to accumulate on a wild night, instructors and skibums and the rich kid staying at the lodge who drove a Ferrari and three or four babes. Martha Schroeder was with them. They were all tight from somewhere they'd already been, calling Easy, "Hero," and "Big Leader," and Clary was swaggering, full of king-studdery, as bad as he'd ever seen him, all loud talk and the big laugh and sound effects. Easy danced with one of the babes who had on low-rise white pants and a blouse tied up under her tits to show her bare belly. Martha sat on the bar with a pain-in-the-ass expression, and he didn't want to talk to her. Everybody had to make his own Christmas.

Big Leader came over to the bar with his dark hair mussed to cover his bald spot and blotches of excitement on his cheeks. "Hear about our friend John Henry?"

"What about him?"

"On his way to Mississippi to join the Liberty Singers."

"The crazy son-of-a-bitch," he said, and at first he was shook. Then he congratulated himself that he had seen it coming.

"Ain't got nothin' but love, babe!"

He was drawing Easy a beer so he didn't see the action when it started. There was cursing, a scraping and banging as Tim's bar stool fell over backward, and he jerked around to see Clary with his hands up in front of his face and Tim swinging on him. Clary ducked, and people went scrambling out of the way.

He almost gave a cheer for Tim, and then he almost gave one for Easy Clary, who had finally let himself mix it with somebody who could put him on his ass.

Tim swung and missed again, and Clary lefted him twice in the face, very quick, and then swung a big loop right as though he had a weight in it. He hit Tim so hard in the gut the sound was like a big book dropped flat. Tim almost canned up over the bar stool. When Tim came on again, Clary hit him fancy and fast with the same combination of two lefts and a right. This time Tim didn't stagger back. Black-faced, blood at the corner of his mouth, he just pushed a fist into Easy's face where Easy's hands were up blocking, and Easy fell the whole length of the open space in front of the bar, knocking down a woman and another bar stool, and a lot of people catching him at the end, like acrobats on TV.

He stood behind the bar making calming motions to Eddie Bricker and taking nervous sips from his highball, very excited but feeling better already. Maybe it was just what everybody needed.

"Well struck, old man," Easy said in a blurred voice. Tim stumped down toward Clary, and Clary came right back and started smacking Tim with lefts from three feet away, as if Tim were a punching bag, but not so frisky and not going in with the right again.

He watched, grinning, sipping his drink and savoring this fight as much as the heavyweight championship held in his living room, appreciating those lefts but appreciating even more what Easy was knowing now, that he wasn't going to be able to keep Tim off balance with them all night. And finally Tim hit Easy with one of the overhand pushes again.

"Knocked him cold," he said to Peggy, telling her about the fight when he got home. "You really don't see a guy get knocked cold too often. He was really out." He laughed to remember Martha Schroeder and Barebelly pretending they weren't fighting over who was going to hold Easy's head in her lap.

Peggy sat straight-backed on the bed with Honey-boy over her shoulder and one tit hanging out of her nightgown, used nipple like a red rubber eraser. Over next to the window was the six-hundred-dollar color TV he'd bought her because he hadn't thought of anything for her for Christmas until it was too late to buy anything else. The set wouldn't take up here without about two hundred dollars more for an antenna probably. What a rotten Christmas present it was anyway.

Honey-boy burped and spat up. Peggy said, "Oh, dear!" wiping at the mess with a diaper. "Goodness, Jimmy," she said, "was Easy hurt? I would've thought Tim would've just killed him."

"He's all right. I wish Tim'd kicked the shit out of him a little more than he did. Easy's laying there with half the women in the place hanging their bulbs in his face and pulling his hair to get his head over in *their* lap, but nobody's wiping any blood off poor old Tim's fucking face."

"I wish you wouldn't curse so terribly, Jimmy. What if the baby—"

"Oh, for Christ sake, how would he know what all the noise is?"

"Well, they do know," Peggy said. She didn't look too bad tonight, with her red-gold hair hanging sexily over one eye. "I mean, you'd feel pretty terrible if when he starts talking he starts saying those terrible words."

"Be proud of him," he said, watching her try Honey-boy on the tit again. Honey-boy had had enough.

"I don't think you ought to let people fight like that in the Loup Garou," Peggy said.

"Why not?" It had been good for Tim to get this morning out of his system, good for Clary to take on somebody who could wipe him, good for everybody. All it had cost was a broken bar stool and maybe half-a-dozen glasses; cheap. "It was a great fight," he said.

Peggy shrugged the big slack breast back inside her nightgown, coloring as she saw him looking at it. "Here," she said, suddenly handing him Honey-boy. "You hold him for a minute, Jimmy."

"He'll piss all over me!"

"Oh, he won't either. Come *on!*"

He felt the tiny, very warm body inside its wrappings. He looked down at the thin dark hair, the insignificant nose, like a monkey's. He chuckled to feel the legs kicking. "He's got gas, he's farting all over the place."

"Oh, Jimmy!"

Honey-boy kicked, waved his arms, made sucking noises. It was the first time he'd ever held him that Honey-boy hadn't screamed. "Hey, boy, you'd better get those eyes uncrossed," he said.

As though Honey-boy had heard and understood, the eyes got themselves sorted out, and the dark brown dots of the eyes of his son, Allen Daugherty, stared up at him. Reflected in the pupils, he saw himself.

"He's really an awfully good baby," Peggy said as though she were trying to sell him.

He gazed down at the tiny, perfect images of himself. He held the still, warm little body against his chest. *Baby, baby, can't you hear my heart beat?*

"What do you see, kid?" he whispered.

The tiny, barely human eyes held on his for just a moment before they got screwed-up and crossed again, and the petulant arm and leg movements began again. But those eyes had seen him, and he had seen himself in them. He handed Honey-boy back to Peggy.

"Oh, Jimmy," she said, "don't you love him at all?"

He was having a little trouble because what-it-was-all-about had just caught him by the throat, but finally he said, "Sure I love him, hon. He's the greatest baby. He's the real bull tyke."

8: *Richard E. Macklin, Jr.*

THE ONE THING that seemed certain in this angry and discouraging time was that it was silly not to write his friend Christopher Brooks. So after dinner he wrote a long, frank letter asking Topher what he had been doing and giving his own history, managing not to complain about his mother and the situation at Dancer. He sealed and stamped the letter and took it to the lodge to drop it in the mail slot in the lobby. He also took in his pocket his Christmas gift for Betsy, a pair of pale gold-and-pearl earrings.

Passing the arch through which he could see Brad's desk—now, he supposed, Easy Clary's desk—he was sardonically amused that his mother would never know that he had not resigned and left Dancer only because he was afraid that, if he did, he would never see Betsy Kimball again.

Alone at a table in the lounge this Christmas night, he found that he was sharing Betsy with her Lesbian friend, Donna McIntyre, who must also be lonely. He had a couple of highballs without much effect on his spirits. Hoping to amuse Betsy, he told her that his mother had offered Brad's job to Easy Clary. Betsy said it was a good idea, Clary was a real swinger. It was one of a number of words she used that he did not like.

At eight o'clock the combo began to play. He listened with distaste. The members of the combo were all, in their way, skibums who, whether they skied or not, nevertheless drank too much, slept through the morning, and led irregular lives that reminded him of Easy Clary's life. Over his third highball he decided that he had been completely justified in the stand he had made to his mother. What Clary had done in the Superchute had been shockingly irresponsible, and Clary should be reprimanded for it.

Betsy was taking orders and delivering drinks in her tightest blue stretchpants, a waitress's apron, and a white lace-trimmed blouse that was very fresh and attractive. She had never seemed so unobtainable, and he was worried about giving her the earrings. What if she laughed at them?

Couples were moving out to dance on the square of polished floor, sedately at first but little by little wilder, more abandoned, and full of fun. It was the kind of dancing he had never been able even to try, and he watched them with mixed disapproval and envy as they postured lewdly in what were clearly parodies of sexual intercourse.

"Come on, chum," Betsy said. She stood beside his table making movements with her hips indicating that she wanted to dance.

He started to push his chair back, but instantly he was sweating with embarrassment. He looked up at her through the sweat that stung in his eyes. "Well, you can't, can you? I mean, you're on duty, aren't you?"

"Who's going to crab on me? You?" She kept making the motions with her hips, and with her hands too now. "C'mon!"

"I can't."

"What do you mean, you can't?"

"I don't know how."

"You don't have to know how. Come on, I'll show you how. I thought you wanted me to show you how to get loose."

"I can't," he said. She looked at him so coldly he knew he had lost her forever. How could it be better to lose Betsy forever than to make a fool of himself on the dancefloor? He would lose her that way too, and it was better to lose by abstaining than by failing.

"Come on, hung-up," she said. He could only mutely shake his head. Piercing the crust of his self-consciousness was the realization that he was failing her in some conflict she was having with the third member of the triangle, who was watching from the bar. Betsy wandered away. More and more couples were taking to the floor; soon there would be no room for dancing anyway.

He noticed that a number of new people had arrived in the lounge. One of them was Easy Clary. He went out to dance with a girl in white pants and white shirt tails tied together below her breasts so that an expanse of belly, including her navel, was exposed. Once, when Clary was turned toward him, he gasped at the ski instructor's grinning face. There was a band-aid across a corner of his mouth and one eye was hideously swollen. He had been in a fight, the man his mother had chosen to be manager in Brad's place, in his place. The band-aid and the swollen eye made Easy Clary look like a leering pirate, and now he was dancing with a finger stuck into the girl's navel, the girl wiggling as though the finger were controlling her movements; disgusting.

Jack Bacon wandered over with a drink in his hand. "You should've been down to the Loup Garou just now, Dickie. Easy and Tim Soderburg had it out."

"I can see he's been in a fight," he said.

"He was in a fight, you know it," Jack Bacon said and wandered back to talk to Betsy and Donna McIntyre at the bar.

The rock-and-roll beat was monotonous and untidy, the horn squalling. Now he watched Easy Clary with a certain satisfaction, knowing that Timbal Khan had inflicted those wounds. Easy left the bare-midriff girl at a table and came across toward the bar, but not to get a drink. He said something to Betsy, his hips and hands moving as hers had moved when she had made her invitation to dance. She followed Clary back to the floor.

In a muddle of pain and fury he watched them. At first she danced in a restrained, almost childlike manner, making unsure movements with her hands, while Clary, leering, grinning, and crouching, obscenely emphasized hips and thighs, his and hers, gradually moving faster. Her movements, too, became more unrestrained; courted, she responded. Her hands were no longer unsure; her first smile was gone, and now she was expressionless and seemingly hypnotized by her partner. He had never seen anything so graphic or so savage. He remembered his father saying that men were supposed to kill bears, fight each other, and impregnate women. "Go, Hero-Leader!" he heard someone call to Clary. It came to him suddenly and breathlessly that Clary was seducing her, and more, that Clary, without seeming to notice him, knew very well he was here and was also a candidate for the position his mother had conferred, and was showing him in this cruel way who was the master.

The music stopped, and the dancers were transformed from

wildly antic maenads and satyrs into sweating skiers leaving the floor. As though Clary had only been warning him, he let Betsy go.

Red-faced, pushing tendrils of hair back into her topknot, she wandered with the other dancers back toward the bar. She took up her tray and moved between the tables, soliciting orders. She paid no attention to him as she served drinks and made change. Donna McIntyre had disappeared.

Then Betsy came over and sat down with him, and in a sudden, loosening burst of gratitude he said, "You were marvelous."

She looked surprised. "Well, thanks! You're still fond of me, huh?"

"Yes, I am."

Her face was still pink and damp from her exertions. The lobes of her ears were delicately pink. She smelled cleanly of sweat.

"Well, when're you going to get loose?"

"You have to teach me."

"You want me, huh?" she said, but not quite in a teasing way. Of course she must have been stimulated by the dancing—and by Easy Clary.

"Yes, I do," he said. He reached into the pocket of his jacket to touch the little box containing the earrings. He could not imagine the proper, refined pearl-and-gold appendages on those pink ears.

She tossed her head as though flattered, smiling, her dramatically painted eyes not meeting his. She brought a leather cigarette case from her apron pocket, a cigarette and a folder of matches from the case. He took the matches and applied flame to the white tube pursed in her lips.

"What else do you want?" she asked, still avoiding his eyes. She waved the hand with the cigarette. "You know, what else?"

"Well, someday I hope to run Dancer as it ought to be run," he said.

She looked disinterested.

"And I want to get married and have children."

Her lips curled. "Well, *I* don't want to get married and have children," she said. "Just in case you thought that was going to shoot down my cool."

It was an expression he didn't understand. "You don't want to have children, Betsy?"

She shrugged disdainfully. "You just like the idea of kids because you like to get your gun off," she said coarsely. "Men, I mean. And we—women, I mean—throw up for a couple of months and wheelbarrow around for the last two. And your bust falls down to your middle and you get varicose veins, and then your man takes off to find somebody else that's not a wreck to get his gun off with."

He was laughing before she finished, and she flushed. He felt a power coming from his father. It did not matter that Clary had excited her with the dancing; when the dancing was over she had come to *him*. Women, his father had said, not just a woman; but he only wanted this one.

"What do *you* want?" he said.

"Ski the powder and dancing and a whole lot of fun. You don't get to ski the powder when you have to stay home and babysit. When do you think Peggy Daugherty gets to ski any more?"

"I can afford a babysitter."

Betsy sipped from his glass. "You probably can," she said. "But I think you're too tight to. Your muthuh brought you up hung-up and you're too damn tight."

"I'm not tight any more!" he protested. "You're going to help me be loose now, aren't you?"

"Hah!" she said and rose and left him.

He saw that Donna McIntyre had reappeared. She was looking at Betsy out of the anxious eyeholes in the smoothly painted mask, but Betsy avoided her as she made her round. In his new strength he could allow himself to pity the woman.

When the combo began to play again and the tables emptied couples out onto the dancefloor, Betsy returned to him. Her face had turned pink again, not from dancing this time but from some emotion or embarrassment.

"You want me a lot, huh?" she said.

"Yes."

"And you're not tight any more, huh?"

"No."

"Well, I'm a girl that works for tips. Make me an offer." Her face turned red as she said it. She lit another cigarette and exhaled copious smoke.

He said recklessly, "Five hundred dollars."

He was pleased that she looked shocked. Her tongue flicked out to remove a fleck of tobacco from her lower lip. "Oh, well, okay, that's all right," she said. "Let's see your money."

"I can give you a check."

She tapped her cigarette needlessly in the ashtray. "Oh, I'll take an IOU from *you*." She brought a pencil stub from her apron pocket, turned the paper coaster over, and pushed pencil and paper toward him. "You write it."

"What'll I write?"

"You know what! I owe Betsy Kimball five hundred dollars for—uh—services—uh—delivered Christmas night. And sign it."

He wrote it and signed it. She took the coaster from him and, without reading it, folded and slipped it into her breast pocket. Her face was flaming. "I just wanted to see if you'd really write it, you crazy bastard."

"Don't back out, Betsy." He loved the color in her face. He loved it that she was flustered now by this taunting game she had begun. "Come on over to my apartment," he said.

"What if your muthuh catches me?"

"She won't."

"Okay, you go on home and I'll come as soon as I can." She rose and left him. From the rear the rims of her ears looked like rosy petals.

When he started home she was talking to Donna McIntyre, and Easy Clary was dancing with the girl with the bare midriff.

In his apartment he put Miles Davis on the record player and tried different combinations of lights before he took off his clothes and donned his bathrobe, wishing he had some brandy to offer Betsy when she came and wondering if he could risk a trip into the Big House to get a bottle. He suspected Betsy might scoff at too extensive preparations, and he sat tensely on the edge of the bed, trying to concentrate on the music.

Opening the door without knocking, she came in and tossed a roll of clear plastic onto the bed beside him. She hadn't even put on a parka for the walk over from the lodge. "I got some Saran wrap from the bar," she said.

"What's that for?"

"So I won't get knocked up! You haven't got anything else, have you?"

"No."

"I knew you didn't," she said. She looked around the room, bending over to examine the book titles, raising her eyebrows at the bright record jacket propped beside the record player. "You like cool jazz, huh?"

"Yes."

"It doesn't do a thing for me," Betsy said. She looked up at the display of weapons on the wall. "Where'd you get those?"

"In Fez. In Morocco."

She sat down on the edge of the bed to take off her boots. The lamp cast a slant of light across the lower part of her face. Her eyes were in shadow.

"Here, pull off my pants," she commanded, raising her legs.

He grasped the instep straps of her stretchpants and pulled. With her pants off she was fat-legged in pink longjohns. She rose to step out of these and was naked from the waist down. Her plump thighs were yellow as butter in the lamplight. He stared at her with his breath hurting in his chest. He was reminded of a Toulouse-Lautrec whore, though there were no sad blue and green tones here.

"You think it's going to be worth five hundred dollars?" she asked.

He managed to say, in her hardboiled style, "I don't know yet."

Betsy reached in her breast pocket for her leather cigarette case and slid a cigarette from it. As though this were a test, he lit it for her with steady fingers. He thought she was more embarrassed than he was.

Blowing smoke at him, she said, "Well, come on and find out." She tore a piece of plastic from the roll, handed it to him, and gave the belt of his robe a jerk.

When she lay back on the bed the light gleamed on her belly. Her hand holding the cigarette concealed her face. "C'mon," she said. "I haven't got all night."

He stripped off the plastic abomination as he came down to her. He was quickly done.

"Well, you are the *fastest*—" Betsy started, then with an exclamation she rolled out from under him and sat up. "I felt that!" she cried. "I really did! Did you lose that—"

"I took it off," he said. Sitting up, he leaned forward to kiss her pale mouth, feeling very pleased with himself.

She pushed him away. "Damn you!" she said. "Have you got a bottle of coke to squirt with, or anything? I've got to—"

He kissed her again, on the corner of her mouth. She pushed at him again, but not so hard this time. He kissed her pink ear. She sat on the edge of the bed with her pale round legs sagging apart, examining him with her shadowed eyes.

"Oh, well, to hell with it then," she said.

He kissed the small pink ear lobe that he loved. What was there in him, he wondered, that, loving her ears, he would want to change them by giving her the kind of earrings Evvy Hamilton would wear?

"To hell with it then," she said. "If that's what you really want."

"I'll take care of you always," he said.

"Ha!" she said. "I'll take care of *you*, you mean!"

He clasped her tenderly in his arms, which was what his dream had been, and was in turn clasped by her.

9: Timbal Khan

IN THE SHARP SILENCE as the chair mounted in crystal gray light toward the face of Dancer Peak, the only sound was the periodic rattle of the chairhanger passing over a sheave. He swung up and out over the dulled landscape with the sudden black of the pines and the myriad ski tracks converging to become one great track where the trails were. It was very cold. He could not separate the ache of the bruised flesh of his face from the cold's ache. He bent his head before the icy wind flowing like fluid disapproval from the Dancer face.

At the top terminal he slid obliquely out of his chair and leaned against the attendant's shack to press the Stop button. The lift came to a halt, each chair with a curtsy. Forcing his gloves through the loops of his poles, he skied down the ramp, under the lift, and began the long traverse through skied-out snow beneath the face of Dancer toward the southeast shoulder. He reached it just in time.

In the east the first scarlet rim of the sun showed. With motion perceptible to the eye it rose, both light and ponderous, huge over the white eastern peaks, and in the magic, breathless moment of the sun coming up, all the black-and-white world was bathed in pink, the color of the world refreshing itself each day, more sign of hope than a rainbow could ever be. The pink spread, intensified, caressed with warmth his battered face. As the red-orange disk broke loose from the peaks he turned to gaze around him at the mountain world: the Patmore range to the south, with three peaks higher than Dancer, though it was difficult to believe from here, where Dancer dominated the Sierra; to the west, peak on jagged peak diminishing toward the Central Valley; to the north, Mount

Blasingame, Mount Forrest, and Mount Galleon with its stone sail clearly identifiable in the pink light. He turned back to feel the vital warmth on his face once more and looked down the valley. Here and there plumes of smoke rose from chimneys; the road was snow-covered still, though patches of black showed where it snaked through the lower valley toward Erskine. When he had seen it all he shoved back hard with his poles, and started on his journey around Dancer Peak.

As soon as he had made four turns down the back of the shoulder he was in fantastic terrain, as frozen and sunless as the dark side of the moon. This was the windy side of the mountain, with blown hoarfrost coating the trees into dully gleaming caricatures of speed, a streamlined forest amid glazed, wild, red and brown rock outcrops that fell steeply to the south fork of the Maiden River. He wove his way slowly down into the goblin forest on changeable snow, wind-packed one moment and the next shallow powder with the crunch and scrape of ice beneath it. Traversing through the trees, he passed beneath a jagged hogback of volcanic rock pointing straight down the slope. Beyond this ridge, in deep powder snow once more, he began to climb toward the top of the first of the back-of-Dancer bowls. As he gained altitude a fragment of sun became visible over the shoulder, diamonds glistened in the snow, crystal caught fire in the trees. Climbing steadily, panting, scrambling for a hold with his uphill pole, finally he was high enough and he stopped to survey the concave, treeless expanse of the Big Bowl, which could easily be served by a lift to the top of the peak. He pushed off and, holding a high line, started across the bowl in a muffled, ticking silence of suspense. The snow held. From time to time he stepped uphill to maintain his line. Slowly, keeping high, he crossed the top of the bowl.

Then he was falling. Falling through air, he felt at first very calm, sprawling and twisting to try to keep his skis beneath him, knowing that he had started a big one but that there was nothing up above to come down on him. His skis cracked against a hard surface; he fell heavily on his side, bounded up onto his feet but spun on, the momentum of his fall carrying him over and out in an elongated eggbeater. His skis struck straight down like lances into the snow; he screamed once with pain as he fell over again, not so violently this time. He dropped at last heavily on his back, the tails of his skis impaled and crossed beneath him, his arms flung out.

Gasping for breath, staring up at this unfamiliar, sun-edged, cruel aspect of Dancer, he was conscious of a frightened whimpering. It was himself. He was terrified that he had torn an Achilles tendon. He groaned as he sat up to unfasten his skis and slip his boots sideways out of the bindings. He got to his hands and knees. Then he stood up. It was a long time before he could summon the courage to raise and flex his foot. It worked. He cursed in gratitude and looked up once more at the snowy head outlined against the dark blue sky. Dazzling glints of sunlight knit and moved along the right side of the peak. He worked his foot to find out how sore his ankle was and breathed sweet air into his lungs.

Calmly he put his skis back on. He had lost both his poles, but he could see them back up the bowl a way. He climbed up to get them and continued to climb, favoring his aching ankle. He had fallen a long way behind the climax slide. He didn't stop until he reached the fracture line. The break was exactly as tall as he was. When he had rested he started north along the ragged, wavy wall until he found a place where he could kick steps in the snow and get on top.

Next was the Northwest Bowl, the North Bowl, and what he called the Double-Barrel, two bowls smaller and steeper than the big ones and filled with light powder. Past them he came into the Badlands, masses of black igneous rock with twisted junipers squatting on top of outcroppings like octopuses. Wincing with pain and weary, he started up the long wind-packed slope of the ridge behind the Chute, on past the Elevator Shaft, and along the north shoulder to the top terminal of Big Red One, his starting point. The climb out of the Badlands took him more than an hour; he was sweating with the healing sun on his face, and his legs were trembling with fatigue. He knew his ankle was sprained, but he had made his circuit, been punished and forgiven. The lift was running. Whitey was shoveling snow. He thought he was probably happy.

The door of the ski-patrol hut above the lift terminal had been shoveled out, and he stuck his skis in the snow and went inside. The cold was intense; his breath fogged in front of his face. He built a fire in the oil-drum stove, doused it with kerosene and lit it, opening the damper until the stack roared with draft. He sank into the canvas chair in front of the stove with a huge sigh, took off his right boot, and squeezed his ankle hard between his two hands. He looked at his watch; very close to ten o'clock. He was glad to be alive.

He limped to the door to cram a pan full of snow and put it on top of the stove to boil for tea, moving slowly, aching and tired, and at peace as he had not been for many days. He went over to the phone and pressed the office button.

"Hello?" a woman's voice said; Mrs. Macklin, not Annie Sprague.

"It's Tim checking in. They can go ahead and start loading on Big Red any time now."

"Thank you, Tim," Isobel Macklin said.

He held the buzzing mechanism to his ear for a moment before he hung up. Then he stood beside the cherry-glow of the stove-pipe, watching the snow melt to pearly water in the pan, the water begin to bubble around the edges and roll into a boil. He made his tea and saturated it with sugar and plumped himself down in his chair again, savoring this rest for his body, the good sharpness of the heat on his propped-up stockinged foot, the taste of the sweet tea.

When he had finished his tea he taped his ankle, put his boot on, and began buckling, snapping, and zipping himself back into uniform. He was starting out the door when the phone rang, two long and two short. It was Tom Cline.

"Tim, there's some fucker piled up on the Chute with a compound, and Pete's afraid to touch him."

"I'll be right down," he said.

He buckled on his first-aid belt. Outside, he latched on his skis and strapped his poles to the side of the toboggan. Dragging the long toboggan with the Stokes Litter on top of it, he started straight down the north shoulder. He checked only once, before he made the first, tight turn into the Elevator Shaft, and then he schussed the Superchute through deep snow as Easy Clary had schussed it just twenty-four hours ago, the handles of the toboggan bucking in his grip. He swung over into the Chute still in his full-bore schuss, faster and faster now on the packed snow, heading for two people standing by crossed skis.

As he sped down toward the accident, the compound fracture everybody else was afraid to touch, with the speed and the snatching of the wind at his goggles and the damped pitching of the toboggan handles in his grip, his heart came to a kind of singing like the pan of snow coming to a boil on the stove, or as close to singing as it was ever going to come.

10: Elizabeth Steinberg

SHE KNEW the war was over as soon as she saw that Shelley was wearing his Jomo Kenyatta sweatshirt. It was the gem of his collection, a dark, fierce head of Kenyatta on light gray material, THIS IS THE MAN printed in jagged Japanese-style letters above the head, BURNING SPEAR in smaller lettering below. The sweatshirt showed Shelley still had his sense of humor, or perhaps that he hoped to get back in touch with hers. It was necessary to have humor when you had capitulated to reality.

They were walking from the parking lot to the lodge to say good-by to Chuck Clary, the new management, before starting home for Berkeley. They might have been, she decided, any jerk family up for skiing, two kids in ski clothes, Dad round-shouldered in his war-surplus parka and baggy gray faculty flannels, and Mom hunching along on crutches with a much-inscribed plaster cast. Chris, who was ashamed of the funny old folks, was walking ahead pretending not to be with them. Mikey walked between them, a kind of buffer state.

She had had no chance to talk to Shelley alone. That pleasure was still ahead of them. He had skidded into a ditch last night and had not been able to get a tow truck to pull the car out until eight this morning, and he had only just arrived. He had spent the night in an improbable-sounding hotel in an old-time gold-mining town, and she could see that he was going to work up a number of entertaining stories out of the experience. Extending this line of thought, she realized that he had chosen to assume a clown's role in the face of his cuckoldry.

"I think Chuck's taken the job as manager here," she said.

"Ah?" Shelley said.

"Yesterday he said he was going to."

"He held out for quite an honorable length of time, actually."

"It's his job to make Dancer a pleasure garden, he says."

"Ah!"

They made their way through the skiers converging on the lodge, and she saw that Shelley was not much interested in the ski-resort sights. Perhaps he was preoccupied.

"Your washing machine has broken down," he said.

"Did you try reversing the plug?"

"The trouble seems to be of a more profound nature. There were melodramatic thumpings and a considerable amount of smoke."

"Christy says the motor burned right up," Mikey put in.

Shelley paused before the cutesy steel skier under the porte-cochere. "This is the system of skiing taught here?" he asked mildly, a balding, blue-chinned, bent-nosed, careful-eyed college professor complete with studied indifference to dress. She hoped he would not need to overwork his sense of humor on this day.

"That's what Mom looked like when she fell down, I bet," Mikey said.

They both smiled upon their younger child. The older had already preceded them into the lodge.

As they mingled with the holiday crowd in the lobby, her heart was beating faster. She looked for Chuck Clary through the arched window, but he was not at the manager's desk. Seated there was Mrs. Macklin, whom she had met night before last. Mrs. Macklin was reading a paper on the desk before her, frowning, a yellow pencil held between two fingers like a cigarette.

"Who is the lady?" Shelley asked.

"The boss."

"Ah!" he said. "I see Chuck's new career will be studded with success."

A feeling of hate turned over within her, moved and stretched as though to warn her. She managed to smile at her husband. She crutched over to the ski-school window to ask the big blonde where Easy Clary could be found today.

"Today he has the beginner class. I think you will find him just —here." The girl made gestures with a manicured hand, indicating the area before the sundeck.

Shelley and Mikey joined her as she moved toward the stairs, where Chris was waiting for them, looking bored. Nervously careful, she descended the stairs; she would have to learn how to do this better. Behind her Shelley said, "The ladies' library committee has called you each week, faithfully."

She didn't answer, saving her breath; it was almost as though she were holding her breath. She had thought the last survivor was gone, shot down, surrendered. She had told Clary what she had thought he wanted to hear, and all last night she had lain awake trying to communicate with him by thought wave or ESP or whatever the extrasensory machinery was, to tell him that she should not have pretended to be the Guru. There was no Guru.

Stumping as fast as she could go on her crutches, she passed out onto the sundeck into a world of brilliant sun, gleaming snow, and brightly clad skiers on the slopes, and, just—here, miraculously— but not miraculously at all because he had always had that star quality—she saw him. He was leading a class half walking, half sliding on skis across the flat area, waving his poles at them in illustration of something and calling encouragement. It was a mixed bag of students, two children, a man in a war-surplus parka longer, more faded, and even shabbier than Shelley's, two cute girls in tight-behind pants, and a fat woman in a black sealskin parka. They followed their leader in his narrow-legged black pants and black sweater with the red stripe, moving slowly and very awkwardly across the snow. There was a mixup as the fat woman fell down, blocking traffic, which Clary solved by lifting the woman bodily to her skis.

She leaned against the deck railing and watched, both laughing and crying. He had not taken the position as manager after all. He was still holding out. He had hung in there. She felt like Francis Scott Key, and she wished she could sing it to heaven: Look, he has hung in there!

Instead she cried his name, her voice sounding shrill and emotional to her ears. His head jerked toward her; a patch of white tape showed at the corner of his mouth. Balanced on one foot, she raised her two hands and clasped them over her head like a prizefighter.

White teeth flashed in his brown face. Stretching himself tall, he raised his arms with his poles extended to form a giant, glorious

V-for-Victory sign. When he waggled one of the poles she knew he had recognized Shelley. She turned away so that Clary would not feel he must come over to greet them. Christy's cool, handsome, self-contained face swam in her eyes, and she saw his coolness ruffled.

"Why—why're you crying, Mother?"

"For joy, bud," she said. He had never seen her cry before, had he? She had not forgotten her realization of her responsibility to humanity, and she smiled at him through her tears and put out a hand to rumple his hair. He was tall for nine, almost as tall as she was. One of her crutches fell, and he bent to retrieve it for her. "Thanks, Christy," she said.

Then Shelley's face confronted her, nakedly hurt but nakedly anxious too, and she squeezed her features into a smile. "I'm all right," she said. "I'm just so goddam happy to be going home, that's all." She crutched on back across the sundeck with her husband, her son, and her daughter moving in an awkward cluster around her. Clary had hung in there and she was happy for him, but just as happy for her own capitulation, her own accepted responsibility, her own consenting-adult, considered opting for her husband, who was what he was and was not what he was not in his Jomo Kenyatta sweatshirt worn for her, and for her children whom she loved, who were hers, were her own self extended, and for whose future, whatever in life it held, she felt a fantastically powerful curiosity. Her family forever in its own makeshift, patched-up pleasure garden.

She was surprised at the sudden confidence with which she began to swing herself up the stairs. She was coordinated, wasn't she? She was competent, wasn't she? And wise now, wasn't she? Gritting her teeth as she labored up the long staircase, she confronted the rest of her life and saw that it could be good, depending upon her, and determined now and for all future time that it would be good, memorable, lived as well, day by day, as she could live it. Because she could make what she wanted of it, couldn't she, with her knowledge and her power, her wisdom and determination? Couldn't she hang in there in her own way? Of course she could, anyone could, if only he knew the way.

11: Captain Easy

Now IN THE middle of the afternoon he led his beginners' class in a shallow traverse across the Bunny Hill, calling back over his shoulder, "Shootdown position! Hands above your gunbutts, spring in the knees, chin up, ready for anything!" He was talking more, and more loudly, than his usual form, but he was feeling a little hysterical with a number of emotions that included a reluctance to taste of his new loneliness, and an ironic realization of the godhood of a ski instructor to a class of beginners, and love. He had identified the love when Elizabeth and the Guru and their two kids had appeared on the sundeck this morning. Waving back at them, he had realized that he loved them, and, in a spreading of realization, that he loved Maeve and Badbody, and John Henry-gone-to-Mississippi, loved them all. But now they were all gone, and although there was as yet no pain or even sensation of loneliness, he was nervous and talking more and more loudly than usual in this new and shaky time that must be the beginning of the Future-Imperfect.

He touched the band-aid at the corner of his mouth and looked back over his shoulder at his class faltering along behind its leader. Walter was first in line, serious and intense in his war-surplus parka; Walter was here to learn how to ski, and no one had better get in his way. Then came the two boys, Robert and Jamey, eleven and nine, giggling as they engaged in continuous guerrilla skirmishes; then the two Young Ladies, Jackie in her violet outfit and Helen in rose, very much together; finally there was Plump Jean in her sealskin parka. Jean had been full of fun and laughter all morning, calling him "Le Moniteur," but now she was tiring and her sweet-natured, soft face was congealing with worry.

"Ready for anything that comes at you!" he called back to them. "You bend your knees so you can ride it out if it gets bad. And you lean forward so you can grab anything good."

"Ooooops!" he said, for Plump Jean had gone down again. He kickturned to go back to her.

Walter said, "Christ, she slows us up!"

"Chacun à son gait," he said. He did not much like Walter, one of those who insisted on his rights. He liked Jean, who when she fell down couldn't get up without help, who was hot in her seal-skin parka and red-faced with exertion, but who knew what was important. He grinned in passing at the Young Ladies in their bright, tight-in-the-crotch pants. They still blanked their faces and drew a little together when he turned on the charm for them. He was full of love, but he was full of First Personal resolve too, and he was going to enjoy the challenge of separating Jackie and Helen. The way to do this, as he knew, was not to push but to let them compete for him. Since they were at Dancer for a learn-to-ski week, he had plenty of time.

Plump Jean lay in the snow with her legs and skis tangled, and in her now vulnerable face he saw something sad and a little frightened beneath the jolly plumpness. Her eyes were as violet as Jackie's pants. Smiling wanly, she said, "I guess I'm getting tired, Moniteur. I'm sorry to hold up the class like this."

"Good for them. Makes them feel confident. Remember that confidence is all."

"Mine's going," she said. She was still trying to smile, but it was coming hard. She looked down at her disarrayed skis. "What do I do now?"

"Get your skis across the hill," he said, pointing with his pole. She struggled valiantly. For a moment he thought she was going to make it, but in the end he had to help her up again.

"I guess I just can't do this," she said.

"Sure you can! Let's see your shootdown position now." He coaxed her into traversing posture and slid back to the head of the line again. He would give the class a little extra time at the end of the day to make up for the waiting.

He started on across the hill, glancing back from time to time at Walter's determined face, at the boys engaged in aggression and retaliation, at the blankly wary and pale-lipsticked faces of the

Young Ladies, and at tail-end Jean who looked discouraged. He called, "Enjoy what you're doing, class! Spring knees and tiptoes and enjoy! Your knees bent so nothing can trip you, and leaning forward so you can grab the lollipops!"

He laughed at his expressions and at his attention to his own knees, the distribution of his own weight. Did he think he was always going to be able to keep from tripping? What lollipops did he think he was going to grab? One or both of the Young Ladies, not because their faces or the fit of their pants so inspired him, but out of First Personal duty to keep his hand in, to maintain himself as ruthless, confident, and loose in his traverse of the slope of life?

Bending his thoughts to two-girl procedures, he found himself wishing Jackie and Helen were a little more exciting in themselves. What was exciting to him at this moment was not so much the forward lean to grab at lollipops as his concern with the knee-spring necessary to absorb the shocks. Proud laughter ached at the back of his throat when he considered his escape from the latest plot of the Crock—from Martha Schroeder and the Future-Perfect; from Isobel Macklin and the Second Personal dedication; even from Maeve; even from Elizabeth. He raised his poles in a V-for-Victory sign to encourage his class and to congratulate himself. He had squeaked through again, and although he knew now that he could not hope to hold out forever, still he was enormously proud that as he faced the Future he was still in command of his life and his principles.

He made a tight loop of a turn and stopped below the beginners' class. Far up the Big Top pines spired against the sky, and the viciously curved, shining, swift-shape of a bomber appeared, seeming to climb straight toward heaven with its con trail fattening behind it. He laughed with pleasure at the slowly mounting suspense of the airplane's climb and the beauty of the vapor trail against the dark beauty of the sky. Skiers in formation came at speed over the horizon of the Big Top, golden with the afternoon sun behind them, and trailing their own golden and iridescent clouds-of-passage. He became intensely conscious of the patterns of the trees against the snow and the lifts rising upward and outward with their burdens and the concentrated benevolence of the head of Dancer inclined over the valley. All his life he had sought for meanings, but now it came to him powerfully that meaning must not be imposed upon the beauty of the skiers sweetly curving down the upper slopes, or on the great countermotion of the plane mounting in its slow ejaculation against the sky like the veritable shape of the joy of sex, that there need be no grand design to the huge, slow immanence of time moving from birth and youth to age and death.

His class had stopped too and were waiting for his next move with various expressions of expectancy on their faces. Only Plump Jean had taken the moment to look up the mountain at the trees and the golden speed of the skiers against the sky. "Now we're going to kickturn and traverse back the other way, class," he said a little shakily. "Poles behind you and lean on them. You first, Walter."

Walter kickturned creditably. Robert fell down in shock at facing straight down the shallow slope, and Jamey joined him, weakened by giggles. Both of them recovered while Jackie leaned on her poles, raised a ski straight up and flopped it over. She grinned happily at him, flushed with her triumph.

"That's a good kickturn, Jackie!" he said. Helen, in her rose-colored pants, didn't do as well, and he paid her no attention, sowing seeds of disunion. He saw that Jean looked frozen.

"I can't do it," she said.

"It's easier up here than it was down on the flat."

Her soft chin quivered. She had a small, rounded, appealing blade of a nose, nostrils flaring with emotion. She braced her poles behind her and leaned back as she had been taught. She kicked with her right leg but not high enough to bring the ski upright. Chin quivering, nostrils flaring, she kicked again. This time her arms bracing her poles collapsed and she sank back against the slope in cruciform, her arms outstretched and poles trapped beneath her body, her skis opposed like those of Dick Macklin's dancing skier.

"Oh, for Christ sake!" Walter said.

He gave Walter a warning glance and stepped uphill to bend over the fallen woman. Her eyes were full of tears. "I can't do it, Moniteur."

"You almost had it that time."

She shook her head. "I'm so afraid," she whispered.

The situation seemed to hold more intensity than was warranted. He leaned closer to offer her his hands and pull her up, but she didn't take them, rubbing her glove across her eyes. A lock of hair had escaped her black knit cap.

"I can help you do all this if you really want to do it," he said. "Don't be afraid."

"It's not just this," she whispered in a voice so low he could hardly hear her. "I guess I'm just afraid of everything."

Emotion thickened his throat. Staring down into her damp, hot, violet eyes, he felt a great relief that he did not, after all, have to go dutifully goating after the Young Ladies with their pretty bodies and minds as blank as their faces. He did what he wanted to, didn't he? He did what, in all good conscience, he wanted to do rather than what he thought he ought to do, didn't he? He glanced up to see if the fuzzy chalk line still climbed the sky. He had come to realize that his search was not for the meaning of life, only for its beauty; perhaps he must further realize that his life was to be governed by his own awareness of that beauty and not by rigid principle merely. He scowled up at the faces of the rest of the beginners' class, as though they might not understand that a consenting and partial submission was not a defeat.

And then, saying, "Come on, I can help you with everything," the Moniteur grasped the fat, important woman's hands and with a strong heave brought her to her feet.

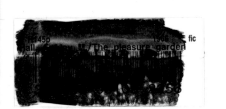